Second Edition

No Justice No Peace

Algernon McNeil

A Historical Fictional Novel Of Suspense

ISBN 978-0-615-99100-9

Printed in the United States of America

Cover Art by: Louis Thomas
Cover Design by: Anita's Marketing Concepts, Inc.
Edited by: Annie Robinson-Harding

Dedication

To the African American generation of today:

A few years ago, I spoke at my class reunion on the subject, "History can and sometimes does repeat." Even with a system in place to stop it, it can happen.

During the Civil Rights Era, Americans, black and white lost their lives in the struggle for civil and voting rights; as a result, the old Jim Crow laws that restricted voting and basic rights were overturned in 1965. Now, history is threatening to repeat itself, and it could happen. Laws have been passed in several states to again suppress the African American vote, and subject young, African American men to racist, vigilante justice. There are 25 states with *"Stand your ground laws,"* that has made it dangerous for young, African American men to simply walk the streets. These laws were introduced by elected officials, the new Jim Crow, and the social network has made it easier for them and their sympathizers to spread their racist, hate propaganda throughout America.

Civil and voting rights afforded African Americans the opportunity to pursue their dreams and go as far in life as their abilities and work ethic would allow, even as far as the presidency of the United States. However, since the election of the first African American President, the political climate has changed to the point that African Americans must recommit to avoid the injustices that plagued our community before the Civil Rights bills were passed.

Today's, right-wing, radical agenda is proof positive that the new Jim Crow's society of discrimination is alive and gaining strength. Any laws, introduced to improve conditions in the African Americans community, and would afford African Americans equal justice are promptly rejected. Their goal is to turn back the clock, to a time when African Americans had little or no voice in the political arena, local or national. This is the beginning of a new chapter in Jim Crow's historic and persistent fight for race supremacy. Their success or failure will depend on your commitment to education, family and a faith-based community, the vehicle of the civil rights movement; with the same courage and determination that turned pre-civil rights liabilities into assets of today.

Stand up and be a positive role-model for your children. The choices you make in life, in many instances, will be the choices they make.

I realize that there are many problems in our community that need to be addressed. The facts are; African Americans are given longer jail sentences than whites for basically the same crimes. African Americans are subjected to false arrest and convictions even with proof of innocence. African Americans are targeted for stop and frisk, and police brutality against African Americans is still a major problem.

You should take personal responsibility for yourself, but in the present environment, as an African American, sometimes that is still not enough. But, you must hold your head up and speak out; do the very best you can. Let nothing or no one stand in your way to achieve your goals. Your course of action will determine your future and that of generations to come. The ballot box can be a weapon, use it.

You are the offsprings of a strong and determine people. I hope you develop an optimism that will strengthen you, and transform your frustrations into a vehicle to success.

Sincerely,
Algernon McNeil

P.S. Most of the incidents in this book are true. Come together as a faith-based community and make a commitment to your future or the racist environment that you read about in this book will be your future. The fight is not over.

From the Author's Desk

Let me first thank you for purchasing the Second Edition of, "No Justice No Peace," a Historical, Fictional Novel of Suspense, about Wilson, N.C... But before you began reading the book, I want to give you a brief history of the proud and determined African American Community of Wilson, North Carolina, per-capita, one of, if not the most productive African American community in America.

In the early 1900s, the African American community of Wilson, like other African American communities in the south, was burdened with the ugly, darkness of racial discrimination, which inflicted a sense of inferiority.

An incident at Wilson's only public school for African Americans brought the community together and stood firm with courage and determination, a potentially dangerous position for African Americans during that time period.

Mrs. Nowell, a bright, young lady from Washington D.C. was teaching at Wilson's Graded School, also known as Sally Barbour School. She was physically assaulted by Wilson's school superintendent Charles L. Coon for refusing to change her teaching methods; new methods that accelerated her students ahead of the white students in the Wilson School System. There was immediate outrage in the African American community. The failure of the school system and the assault on Mrs. Nowell spurred the community to assess and think, and the educators and community leaders to ponder how to improve the chances of success for African American students.

The community began developing an informal system, but within that informal system, there was organization. They simply used what they had to achieve their goals; which included a quality education for African American children.

African Americans took their children out of the public school, after the assault on Mrs. Nowell and built the Independent School on Vance Street. Their source of strength was the family, and community unity that was faith-based, which created an atmosphere of courage and determination that would last for generations.

During the 40s, 50s and 60s, Wilson's African American community totaled less than five thousand residents, but produced an unbelievable number of top level professionals; doctors, lawyers, judges, congressmen, PhD's, actors, military generals, Silver and Bronze star recipients, Oxford Scholars, NASA engineers, Authors, NFL Players, and the list goes on. The community was laced with dedicated people from all walks of life; beauticians, barbers, maids, truck drivers, small business owners, butlers, janitors, factory workers, taxi drivers and a long list of others. There is no doubt that, they were the backbone of Wilson's proud African American community.

In spite of limited resources and overcrowding, our schools excelled, academically and athletically. This was a direct result of the community's faith and unity, and the dedication of the educators in Wilson's African American schools; the ghost of Sally Barbour.

My goals in writing this book were to feature Wilson's African American community during the 40s, 50s and 60s, our struggles and individual accomplishments; and to integrate true events into an exciting, fictional novel of suspense.

I sincerely hope African Americans throughout America will read about the proud African American community of Wilson, N.C.; our struggles, and more importantly our strength and success; and what can be accomplished through the family and a faith-based, unified community. Our road was long and hard, but we never gave up. (See, Courage, Determination, Success, pages 319-341).

This is a work of historical fiction. But most of the incidents in this book, mirror incidents described to me by residents of Wilson during the 40s, 50s and 60s. Some of the names, characters, places, and incidents are the product of the author's imagination and are used fictitiously.

Acknowledgement

I have to first give praise to God, I am truly blessed.

My literary journey has come a long way, but I know I couldn't have done it without the love, encouragement and support of my beautiful wife, Bonita and daughter, Tina.

To: Annie "Tunk" Robinson-Harding. A friend and role-model, to me and thousands of others whose lives she has touched. Thanks for your help.

To: Coach Sam Gray. Without the discipline, the will to win and a die-hard attitude you stilled in me at a young age; this book would have not been possible. Thank you.

To: the Farris, and Thomas Law Firms and families of Wilson, North Carolina; Robert Farris Jr., Allen Thomas, Billy Farris, Albert Thomas, and Charlie Farris. Thank you for continuing the fight for justice, for African Americans, that was started before the civil rights bills were passed, and now is a part of the legacy of the late Robert Farris Sr. He stood up for justice, regardless of color. Hard to the core, but fair, and tried to do what was right. From the African American community of Wilson, we thank you.

To: Paul Capps. Again, you were there when I needed you, and always willing to help. Thank you.

1952

Wilson, North Carolina was the richest county on the east coast and one of the richest counties in America, per-capita. Tobacco money was as plentiful in Wilson as oil money was in Texas. Tobacco fields, warehouses and processing factories dominated the landscape in the city and county; giving the tobacco industry the power to dictate the agenda in Wilson; and Wilson adhered to its simple agenda; tobacco, money and more tobacco.

The walls of several banks were adorned with life-size photographs of African Americans working in tobacco fields; a simple reminder of the African American role, and Wilson's life-line, tobacco.

Wilson was a small, city of 24,000, located 45 miles east of Raleigh, the state's capital. West Nash Street was a testimony to the millions of dollars that flowed through Wilson annually from tobacco sales. Large, two and three-story mansions lined both sides of the streets for as far as the eyes could see. West Nash was recognized nationally as one of the most beautiful streets in America.

East Wilson, the African American community was light years away from the paved, tree-lined streets in West Wilson. There were outdoor toilets, dilapidated houses, and dirt streets that flooded after heavy rain, which were common place in most of the east side. The reported drowning of an African American man in a large pothole on a city street was the result of the city's insensitivity toward the African American community.

Several African American men were reportedly forced to admit to crimes of which they knew nothing about, after brutal beatings by white police officers; many of them were ranking Klan members. Rogue officers made weekly visits to pick up their share of profits for allowing black bootleggers to operate. Black prostitutes were forced to service and pay some of the officers. There were no legal consequences for their "Dodge City" style of policing the East Side, so the officers made it their money-making playground.

The Cherry and Briggs Hotels were flooded with tobacco buyers from all over the world, by late summer. During business hours, they spent millions of dollars on tobacco; at night, they patronize the city's sub-culture which included; gambling, alcohol and transplanted prostitutes, black and white.

Rich whites, white prostitutes and tobacco buyers were immune from arrest and prosecution; law enforcement was instructed to turn their heads.

Homicides in Wilson were infrequent, with only five to eight per year; and most of those were black on black. There was little or no investigation unless a white was the victim. The case was usually closed when the victim was black, unless there was an eyewitness. The general consensus in the 50s, when an African American was killed was, *"Just another dead nigger."* That was the attitude in Wilson and the south in general.

The Civil War had been over for almost one-hundred years, but some southern white's were still trying to re-establish the routine of life that the war interrupted.

Introduction

Ronnie and Butch Grant-Howard were adopted, after Rose Grant, their mother, was brutally raped and murdered. Ronnie, age 8 and Butch, age 6 at the time of the murder, remembered little or nothing about the incident.

Ronnie graduated from college and served in Viet Nam as a First Lieutenant in the U.S. Army's 1st Infantry Division.

Butch was an All America football player at Indiana and was drafted to play professional football.

They were both well educated, outstanding young men, but after the perpetrators and subsequent cover-up of their mother's murder were revealed, they were determined to get justice. Law enforcement and the court system was not an option, so they devised a plan and executed it to perfection.

Chief Buck Watson was a confidante of Wilson's great money and handpicked to protect their interest, which included the tobacco industry. He was smart and cunning and knew enough about psychology to strike before he was struck. Devoid of empathy; whatever was asked he did, cover-ups and murder if necessary; his loyalty to the industry was never questioned. He was once a rogue cop who extorted money from black bootleggers and prostitutes; now, a corrupt chief who took payoffs from the tobacco industry.

Sergeant Billy Price was the infamous, lead investigator assigned to the East Side. His violent, brass-knuckle methods of investigation enabled him to climb the ranks. He was a Mississippi native who strongly believed in race separation.

White Americans, stood shoulder-to-shoulder with African Americans, and even lost their lives in the long, struggle for justice and equality; let us never forget their sacrifice and contribution.

-Algernon McNeil

Chapter 1

January 6, 1952
8:15 A.M.

There had been a light, ice storm two days before and low clouds still hung over the city. A rare, 28 degrees and murder jump-started the early January morning. A young, black woman was found strangled to death in her home on South Carroll Street, on Wilson's east side, the African American community.

Detective/Sergeant Billy Price and Detective David Batts stepped out of the side door of the Wilson Police Department; they were on their way to start the murder investigation, Wilson's first of the year.

Sgt. Price, the lead investigator on Wilson's East Side, was breaking in a new partner; he was assigned as Batts training officer.

Batts was five-nine, one-forty and looked more like an Eagle Scout than a street cop. His father's, big tobacco money influenced his promotion. Price knew his small, physical stature, soft demeanor and lack of experience could be problematic; making him an easy target for the hard-core criminals on the East Side.

Price gazed at the low, gray clouds, turned his top coat collar up and briskly walked across the cracking, slick, concrete toward his police car. Batts was a few strides ahead, walking toward the driver's side.

"You know where Carroll Street is?" Price snared in a hostile tone. Batts didn't respond, glanced back, or break his stride; he simply walked around the frost covered car to the passenger side.

After they were seated, Price rolled his eyes as his eyebrows tugged together in irritation, then quickly switched the heat on defrost, full blast. For a long moment, he simply stared at Batts, cataloging every aspect of him, from his sky-blue eyes, to his brown, cap-toe shoes. The features of Price's face began to show emotion. "You're not ready to be a detective; you know it, and I know it." Price held tightly to his opinions; in most cases, whatever he said or did was without apology.

A terrible despair settled on Batts. What little confidence he had shattered like broken glass. He flicked a glance at Price and looked straight ahead avoiding eye contact.

"The first thing you'll learn about me is that, I don't bite my tongue; I'll say what I believe. So if it was left up to me, you wouldn't be on the force at all. I know how you got this promotion, it was bought for you." All the muscles in his face seemed to drop. Price suddenly reined in his burst of emotion and abruptly turned away from Batts, mumbling something under his breath.

After the windshield defrosted, Price headed out of the parking lot and turned left onto Goldsboro Street, then left at Nash Street, heading east. Early-morning, business district traffic was dense, east and west on Nash Street, slowing his progress. Four blocks east on Nash Street was the Atlantic Coastline railroad tracks that separated the African American and White business districts and communities. The gate came down as they approached Lodge Street and moments before they arrived at the tracks; halting traffic for a long, slow freight train heading south. Price pulled to a stop, put his cold hands over the heating vent and began to slowly rub them together. He looked like the kind of man that wouldn't have sympathy for his own mother. "You ever worked the East Side before?"

"Not much, I was never assigned that area, but I backed-up other officers a few times on some week-end calls." Batts felt intimidated by Price's tone of voice.

"That ain't worth a rat's ass. You can get killed if you don't know what you're doing. Some of them coloreds will smile in your face and cut your damn head off. It's dangerous as hell down there, especially for a white face. They don't care if you're a policeman. Some of them bad niggers will kill you if they get a chance."

Price's statements got Batts' full attention. He nodded like he understood, and the first sign of that demon of fear creased his face. "I'll remember that, Sir."

"I don't want to have to say this again, but I'm responsible for you, so you follow my orders. Don't do nothing or say nothing unless I tell you too. I ain't gonna get hurt or killed trying to save your ass. Is that understood?"

"Yes Sir, I understand."

"Now, in a crowd of coloreds you don't ever know what might happen and the potential for a problem is higher. It's cold, but I'm damn near sure that there will be a crowd when we get on Carroll Street. So you need to keep your eyes open and be ready for anything." Price lit up and took a long drag. Moments later, the gate went up. He cracked the window, threw the cigarette out and flicked the switch to activate the siren. Cars pulled to the side, enabling him to pick up speed. He carefully drove several blocks east on Nash before making a right turn onto South Carroll Street. A large crowd had gathered in front of 107, the reported address of the homicide. The well-kept, brick house stood in the middle of the block.

South Carroll was a one block dirt street with three-room shotgun houses and well-kept, single family homes. The street was littered with large pot-holes that were frozen over from the ice storm two days before.

The crowd moved back as the white, unmarked Ford pulled up. Batts' head was moving like a searchlight; his emotion was showing signs of fear. Price killed the engine, but didn't say anything for a long moment. He stared at Batts, then turned away and blew out a long, frustrating breath before facing Batts again. "Look at me," said Price. Batts slowly faced Price. Price continued. "Now you have two choices. You can pull yourself together and do your job, or sit in this car like a coward and I'll call the station to have a patrol car pick you up." Price was angered beyond words.

Batts responded in a low, unsteady voice. "I'll be alright." He then looked away. "I'm alright." He desperately tried to steady himself against the onslaught of fear.

Price stared at him, barely controlling the urge to grab him and shake him. He gradually calmed himself, and said, "Ok, listen up. The first order of business is, you can't show fear, not down here. Somebody in that crowd will remember and challenge you later, if not today. You hold your head up like you can, and will kick any ass in the crowd, and kill one of them niggers if you need to. It ain't what you can do; it's what they think you can, and will do. But you can bet on one thing; sooner or later, somebody will try you. The second thing is, forget that protect-and-serve bullshit; you protect yourself. Now, I can't watch you every second, so you pull yourself together." Batts nodded, and with a great effort he looked more composed, but signs of fright were still visible in his eyes. Price continued. "We'll go in there, look around and get enough information to fill out the report. We'll need the coroner and the ID unit. I'll talk with the victim's family and I'll make it quick, then we'll get the hell from down here." He clipped his badge on the lapel of his top coat, as did Batts. "Let's go, I don't like this crowd any more than you." Batts nodded and glanced at the crowd. He took several deep breaths, forcing himself to calm before getting out. Price stepped close to him as they walked toward the house. "Relax and keep your eyes open. Just remember what I said about showing fear."

"The dead woman is over there," yelled an old-timer from the crowd trying to get the detective's attention. He was pointing toward a room attached to a one car garage near the back of the house. Price nodded, then headed toward the room, scanning the crowd as he walked; Batts was on his heels. The garage and room had a fresh coat of paint and signs of renovation. There was a breezeway between the room and the house with a clear view of Wainwright Street.

Price walked toward the room through the ice covered, winter dead grass. He cautiously stepped up the wooden-steps onto the porch. The ground was visible through the cracks in the wood that had rotted from the elements. He pulled the screen door towards him and pushed the door open. His motion was frozen by the sight of a nude woman on a blue, sofa-bed, and the strong odor of death. Trauma was evident on her beautiful body; her blue eyes were blood-shot and half-open. Bruises and teeth marks littered her smooth skin around her face, neck and breasts. He walked toward the bed, Batts was close behind. A ball of emotion had knotted in Batts' chest; this was his introduction to homicide. He cleared his throat in a desperate attempt to calm himself.

Price noticed the door leading to the garage from the room was cracked open. Three sofa pillows were stacked in the corner near the door. There was a six-chair, kitchen table a few feet from the foot of the sofa-bed. He motioned to Batts. "Look in the garage, but don't touch the door-knob; make sure you look around good." Batts slowly walked through the door. Price's eyes swung slowly around the room. Several beer bottles were on a table beside the bed; there were used condoms in and around the bed "There was more than one person here," he said, talking softly to himself. "This was done by a pack of nigger dogs. They'll do any damn thing, even kill, for a piece of ass."

Batts walked in from the garage. "I didn't see anything in there but a car; it looks almost new. It was unlocked, so I looked inside and searched the whole area, that's it."

Price didn't respond his eyes were focused on the bruises around her neck. "Somebody beat and strangled her to death." He paused and looked at Batts. "Call the station and have them send the ID boys down here to get prints and pictures. I want to get from down here as soon as possible. Use the car radio, and while you're out there, see if you can find the person who found the body. They gave their name when they called, but I don't remember it. Make sure you don't touch the doorknob."

Batts took a handkerchief from his coat pocket and slowly opened the door. The potential for bodily harm from the crowd temporarily paralyzed his motion. After a moment or two, he walked out onto the porch. An old woman and two young boys were standing on the ground near the bottom step. The old woman had the collar of her long, black coat pulled up over her ears, and a green scarf neatly tied around her snow-white hair. The oldest boy had dried tear marks under his bluish-gray eyes.

Batts was glancing aimlessly around the crowd. It was cold enough that his breath hung in the air around him. "Can I help you?" He asked, never taking his eyes away from the crowd.

The old woman spat out a wad of snuff and wiped her mouth with the handkerchief she pulled from her coat pocket. "Yessir, I was the one who found the body and called the police."

"What's your name?"

"Maggie Wade, I live next door."

Batts eyes were still focused on the crowd. He pulled his .38 from his belt hoister and put it in his trench coat pocket, his finger was on the trigger. "You wait right here. I'm going to the car. I'll be right back." He took a deep breath and exhaled slowly, then walked toward the police car. His heart was beating like a bass drum.

It was Saturday morning, and after word spread of Rose's murder, a surge of grief gripped the black community and Wilson's rumor mill began to turn. The parking lot behind Kirby Sutton's store at the corner of Nash and South Carroll was full of people, shivering from the cold, morning air. Batts called the police department and swiftly walked back toward the room, looking to his rear every other step. He cautiously walked up the steps. "Sergeant Price, the woman that found the body is out here now."

"I'll be right out," Price said, the door was slightly cracked. Moments later he walked out, closing the door behind him. "What's her name?"

"Maggie Wade," said Batts.

"Do you live around here Maggie?" Price asked.

"Next door; these here is her children."

Price looked up at the dark, overcast sky, and then swung his attention back to Maggie. She was old and frail. "I need to talk with you and them boys. Can we go to your house? It's too damn cold to stand out here."

"Yessir. Come on Boys." Maggie walked toward her house with her arms around them.

A cold, damp breeze had kicked up. Price pulled the collar of his trench coat over his ears, and cautiously walked down the steps. "Batts, you can wait in the car for the fingerprint men and let me know when they come."

Maggie and the boys were already in the house when Price walked on the porch. She opened the door before he could knock. The boys were standing beside her. The youngest boy was holding her apron. "Come in." Price nodded once and walked inside the small, brick house at 109 South Carroll Street. Maggie smiled, pointing her open hand toward a chair in her living room. "Have a seat, Sir."

He sat down in a chair near the large picture window as he glanced around the room. Maggie and the boys sat on the couch facing Price. The hardwood floors were shining like glass and the furniture was old, but well polished in her small, but well-kept house.

A look of hollowness had invaded the boys small faces as they sat close to Maggie. Maggie looked from one to the other for a moment and put her arms around them; pulling them even closer to her as she said, "Bless your heart. Everything will be all right. We got to put our trust in God to help us, I know He will."

Price cleared his throat to get Maggie's attention, then pulled a note pad and pencil from his coat pocket. "I'll need her full name and age, if you know it."

"Rose Ann Grant. I think she was about twenty-six or twenty-seven. I ain't really sure about her age."

"Now, tell me what happened over there?'

"I don't know. The boys knocked on my door a little before eight. Ronnie said that Rose was in the room and he couldn't wake her up. I told them to stay here; I got my coat and keys and went over there. I was thinking she had too much to drink, until I saw her on the bed."

Price crossed his arms and leaned back in his chair. "Did you see anyone over there last night?"

"Nosir, but Ronnie did." She looked at the boy on her left.

"Come over here Boy." Price signaled with his hand. Ronnie hesitated. His eyes were red and desolate. "Come on." This time Price extended his hand. Ronnie got up and reluctantly walked across the room. He stopped directly in front of Price, brushing the tears from his eyes with the heel of his hand. He looked back at Maggie, then turned to Price. Price spoke soft and friendly, with a smile. "You don't have to be afraid, just tell me what you saw. Okay?" Ronnie nodded; his head was lowered, looking down at the floor. "Hold your head up and talk," Price suggested.

Ronnie hesitated, then slowly raised his head. "After me and Butch looked at T.V., I went to the room to ask mama to pop some popcorn for us. Some men were in the room with her, they were white men."

A short pause followed; there was an immediate change of expression on Price's face; any thought of race mixing was toxic to him. His voice deepened. "Are you sure they were white men?"

"Yes, Sir."

Price cleared his throat and narrowed his eyes. "Now, they could have been light skinned colored men, right?"

"No Sir, they were white. "

Price looked at Ronnie, trying to decide if he was telling the truth, when there was a knock on the door.

"Come in," said Maggie.

Batts walked in, his cheeks were rose-pink from the cold. "Sergeant Price, the ID boys are here."

"Ok, tell them to make sure they get prints and pictures from the garage too. You knock on every door on this street. See if anyone saw or heard anything last night." Batts nodded and turned to walk out. "Batts, after you talk to the neighbors, look around on the outside."

"Yes Sir."

Price turned his attention back to Ronnie. "Ronnie, do you remember anything else about the men in the room with your mama?"

"One of them had a picture of two guns, right here." He pointed to his shoulder. "He didn't have no shirt on, and he was real tall."

"Is that all you remember?" Price asked. Ronnie nodded. "You're a big Boy, and you helped me a lot. How old are you?"

"Eight and a half years old."

Price playfully rubbed the top of Ronnie's head. "All right, that's good enough, but I might want to talk to you again later. Okay?"

"Yes Sir." He walked back and sat beside Maggie. A smile creased her face; she put her arms around him. "He's a big boy; that's my big boy."

Price nodded his approval and smiled. "Maggie, I need to talk with you. Can the boys go in the back?"

"Yessir. Come on Boys; you can look at T.V., and after I talk with Sergeant Price, we gonna eat some pancakes." Maggie got up slowly and walked toward the back; years of hard labor in the tobacco factories were evident in her movement. Ronnie waved at Price, Price nodded and smiled. Moments later, Maggie slowly walked back in the room.

"Was she married, or did anyone live with her?"

"Nosir, she won't married. She moved here from New Orleans to work in the factory."

"I knew it! I knew damn well she won't all colored, but them blue eyes and that straight hair had me going for a minute; she was Creole."

"What's that?"

"The best I can tell you is they're mixed with French, Spanish and Colored. I'm from Mississippi, and you see a lot of Creoles in that part of the south, especially in Louisiana. Maggie nodded like she understood.

"If I can use your telephone, I need to call the station," said Price.

"Yessir."

Price called the station to have the coroner sent to check, and release the body to a funeral home, then he turned his attention back to Maggie. She pulled her apron down over her knees after shifting to a better position.

"The factory is closed now, so where does she work?"

"She did work at the Stop Light Grill on Pender Street, but she quit. I kept the baby boy when she had to work. Ronnie goes to school."

Price sat straight up and looked directly at Maggie. "I need for you to be honest with me, because I know she can't afford that new car with other bills, working in the factory and at the Stop Light Grill part-time?" He leaned over, trying to make eye contact. "Come on, be honest. If I'm going to find the killers, I need all the information I can get. Anything you can tell me will help."

Maggie hesitated for a moment. "Rose was a beautiful woman and white men came to take her out. She said, they was rich, tobacco men and they gave her a lot of money, but she never called any names. If she did, I'm too old to remember. She said, that they was old men, who just wanted to be seen with a beautiful, young woman."

A silence developed after Maggie's statement; emotions swept over Price. "So, she was a whore, a prostitute."

"I don't know, but whatever she was, ain't nobody had no right to kill her. She ain't never hurt nobody."

Price shook his head in disgust, then reached in his pocket and pulled out a pack of cigarettes. He lit up and reached to his left to get an ashtray. After standing, he glanced at Maggie, and then stared out the window. The whole scenario caught him off guard. "I can take anything but race mixing," he said, in a deep southern drawl. "In Mississippi, if a white man was caught with a colored woman, the Klan would hang his ass the same as they would a colored for raping a white woman. I'll find them and make sure they hang." He sat down; his face was blood-red. He put the half-smoked cigarette out.

A strange look had spread across Maggie's face. She closed her eyes and lowered her head. They remained silent for a while. He lit another cigarette, desperately trying to compose himself; tension filled the air like a heavy fog. After a long moment, he calmed.

"After I finish in the room, I want you to go with me inside her house. There might be something in there that could help; names or addresses of family members we can contact in New Orleans. We'll go over there after lunch. Did she talk about her family back home?"

"Nosir." She hesitated and looked at Price bewilderedly. "I'll go with you to the house, but I can't read or write," her voice was soft and low as she lowered her head.

"That's all right. Just answer a few more questions and I'll be finished. Who was her best friend?"

"I know her first name is Carol, but I ain't sure about her last name, but I think it was Spells."

Price responded with a smile. "I know her, she lives across 301. I can find her; I arrested her a few times."

Maggie mumbled softly to herself in a thinking mode. "What did you say? Who are you talking about?" Price said.

"There is a white man who lives in Wilson that took her out a lot. I never saw him, because she didn't let men go in her house, in the room, but not in her house. She said he gave her a lot of money."

"Did she call his name?"

"Nosir, she just called him her baby. She said he was younger than she was." A knock on the door broke Maggie's concentration. "Come in."

Batts walked in shivering from the early morning cold. An early, January, arctic blast had swooped down on Wilson. He was rubbing his hands together trying to restore circulation. "Sergeant Price, the fingerprint men just left. Doctor Pitt is in the room, he wants to see you." Batts was still rubbing his hands together. "I knocked on every door on this street and I didn't get any answers. I also looked around outside, but I didn't find anything."

"All right, I'll be right over."

"Yes Sir."

Price turned his attention back to Maggie. "Do you have a key to the house?"

"Yessir. Do you want it?"

"I'll get it when I come back, we're going to lunch, just wanted to know if you had one."

The parking lot behind Kirby Sutton's store was empty, and only a few people were standing in the street, when Price left Maggie's house. The cold morning air had taken its toll. He turned his coat collar up and swiftly walked toward the room. Doctor Pitt was examining the body when Price walked in. Batts was standing near the foot of the bed. "How are you doing Doc?"

Doctor Pitt was focused on marks around her neck. "I'm all right," he answered without looking up. He was a short, white-haired, well-dressed man in his mid-sixties. He was one of only a few white doctors in Wilson who would treat black patients. He was a Detroit native.

"What did you find?" Price said, just before he lit a cigarette.

Doctor Pitt didn't answer right away. His focus was still on the bruises around her neck. He fanned the cigarette smoke then said, "She died from strangulation; her windpipe was crushed, and there are signs of a sexual assault." He looked up at Price, and then turned his focus back to the body. "She was also physically assaulted, someone beat her really bad." He slowly shook his head.

Price's tone immediately changed. "She might have died from strangulation, and was probably physically assaulted, but I don't think she was sexually assaulted; she was a prostitute, a whore."

"Prostitutes have the right to say no, and they can be sexually assaulted," said Dr. Pitt, in an aggravated voice. He paused and stared at Price. "I need her full name and age; I have the address."

Price got the notepad from his coat pocket, wrote the information down and gave it to the Doctor. Doctor Pitt got his hat and bag off of the table and walked toward the door. He turned and faced Price, gazing at him a second before speaking. "I'll sign the death certificate, Sergeant. You can have the body removed whenever you like." He was visibly disgusted as he walked out, closing the door with a degree of force.

"Go to hell, nigger lover," said Price in a low voice. He dropped the cigarette and stepped on it. "Go and tell Maggie to call a funeral home of her choice." He looked at his watch. "It's almost eleven o'clock now; we'll come back after lunch. I'll meet you at the car, you can drive. That's the only way you'll going to learn the streets on this side of town. Let's get out of here. We need to see the chief first, and then we'll go to lunch."

History can and sometimes does repeat. Voting rights, civil rights and even freedom are not guaranteed. Take them for granted and watch history repeat. The world can change again, my friend.

-Algernon McNeil

Chapter 2

January 6, 1952
10:10 A.M.

The clouds were starting to lift, when the detectives headed south on South Carroll Street, toward Wainwright Street. They made a round-right at Wainwright onto Roberson Street, heading west. Roberson Street had wood-framed shot-gun houses on both sides. A ditch ran the length of the dirt street from Wainwright to South Pender Street. Rainwater and raw sewage filled the ditches and spilled over into the street after heavy rains.

They drove another five blocks on Roberson Street before running into South Pender Street. There was a coal yard across South Pender Street where trucks were being loaded for deliveries on the East Side. People were in line with toy wagons, wheel-barrows or anything that would hold enough coal to stay warm over night.

"Headquarters to car 5"

"Car 5, go head, answered Price."

"Car 5, check on a shooting and possible homicide at the Sinclair Service Station on Highway 301, over."

"10-4, over and out." Price glanced at Batts, "What in the hell is going on? This is the second homicide today and it ain't even eleven o'clock yet. Turn left, that will take us to 301 south. The Sinclair Station is about a half-mile or so on the right." Batts put the magnet-based, red light on top of the car and turned the siren on. He turned left onto South Pender Street, heading south toward 301. Price shot Batts a quick glance. "Slow down, these streets are still slick, and we want the shooting to be over when we get there. If there is a homicide, dead people don't walk; they'll be there, when we get there." Batts nodded, immediately cutting his speed. "And watch that traffic when you merge onto 301; them damn Yankees will run right over you, especially them coloreds and Jews out of New York."

The traffic was heavy as usual in the south-bound lane on 301, but yielded to the red light and siren as Batts entered the intersection at South Pender. He made a careful turn onto 301 and proceeded at the speed-limit. A half-mile south of the intersection, he turned right into the service station yard. A large green dinosaur, the Sinclair Gas logo was featured on top of the service station facing 301. The service station was constructed of white-painted brick, and it appeared to have been there for at least fifty years.

Price got Batts attention, "Whoa! Hold up." Batts came to a complete stop. "That's a good way to get your ass killed. When you answer a call, shots fired, don't ever drive up to the building. You don't know what's going on, or who fired the shots." Batts nodded.

Moments later, a short, barrel-bellied, white man came out of the building. His gut was protruding in rolls beneath his dirty, oil-stained shirt, and the sleeves were rolled up above his elbows. Motor oil nearly covered the legs of a nude woman tattooed on the inside of his right forearm; his fingers and hands were callused from years of hard labor. He waved both arms, and pointed to a black car parked near the garage section of the service station; the hood was propped up by an iron pipe. He walked toward the police car as Price and Batts were getting out. "He's on the other side of that black car. I don't know if he's dead or not. I kicked his foot, but he didn't move."

Price put a cigarette in his mouth, struck a match and lit it. "I'm Sergeant Price, and this is Detective Batts." They walked toward the black car. There was a blood-trail that started at the office door and ended at the feet of a black man lying motionless on his back in a pool of blood. Price looked down at the body a second or two. It appeared that a large caliber bullet had left a gaping hole in the left side of his upper chest. The hole looked big enough for Price to stick his fist into. "He's dead. Did you shoot him?" He looked up at the man. "You got a name?"

"Yes Sir, I shot him, Billy Roy Bass is my name."

Price smiled and looked down again. "What in the hell did you shoot him with, a cannon?"

Billy Roy smiled, but didn't respond. "There was two of them nigger. I shot at the other one too, but he ran in the woods back yonder." He pointed to a section of woods that stretched from 301 around the back of the building. "That's him, that's that other nigger."

A young man was walking out of the woods, waving his hands in surrender. "Don't shoot," he said, now holding his hands above his head.

"Put your hands down Boy; the shooting is over," said Price. The man dropped his hands and began to brush the ice covered, dead leaves from the pants and coat of his gray, pin-striped suit. He stopped at a distance, still showing signs of fear. Price motioned with his hands. "Come on in, ain't nobody gonna bother you, come on in Boy." The man walked toward Price, never taking his eyes away from Billy Roy. "Do you know that dead boy over there?"

The man looked toward the body with a degree of sadness. "He's my cousin, Earl Cooper. My name is Jimmy Cooper." He struggled to maintain his composure. He pointed at Billy Roy. "That man killed him for nothing."

"I'm in charge here and I didn't ask you nothing but your name." He stared at Jimmy, scanning him from his shiny, black processed hair, to his mud-caked, wing-tip shoes. "You must be from up north, dressed up like a cheap, New York pimp." Price studied him quietly for a moment. "Where are you from, Boy?"

Jimmy took a deep breath and looked away for a moment. "I'm from right here in Wilson, but I live in New York now."

Price smiled, nodding his head; Batts laughed out loud. "Just like I thought, "said Price. His smile died abruptly. "You speak when you're told to speak. You understand?" He gazed at Jimmy, waiting for a response.

"Yes Sir, I understand."

Price turned his attention to Billy Roy. "What in the hell happened here?"

Billy Roy stared coldly at Jimmy, and spat a wad of tobacco juice near his feet. He looked physically strong, but weak in the smarts department. In fact, his IQ might range in the single digits. Batts took a notepad from his inside coat pocket and began to take Billy Roy's statements. "Them coloreds came in my station and bought a can of brake fluid. They went outside and opened it, then came back in and told me to put it in their car. He didn't ask me, he told me. Ain't no nigger gonna talk to me like that; so I told him I won't gonna put shit in his car, and to get his black-ass off my property."

Jimmy clenched his jaw, trying to compose himself as he said, "That ain't what happen and you know it." He shook his head and narrowed his eyes. "You killed him for nothing, just because he wanted his money back."

"Shut up Boy, you'll have your chance to talk," said Price. "All right, what happened after that?"

"When I asked him to leave again, he backed up and put his hand in his pocket. I got my gun from under the cash- register and shot him; both of them coloreds ran out. When I got outside, that Boy right there was almost in the woods; I shot at him too. The other one was on the ground. I ain't gonna take no chance, cause I know that all of them niggers keep a gun or a knife in their pocket." He spat again and wiped his mouth with the back of his hand.

"Is that it?" Price said.

"That's it, that's the damn truth."

"Batts, go over there and see what that dead boy got on him. Look in and around the car good," said Price. He turned his attention to Jimmy. "You got a knife or a gun on you?"

Jimmy immediately threw his hands up. "No sir, you can search me."

"All right, put your hands down."

Jimmy stood there in silence, while Batts searched in and around the car. "I don't see nothing," he said, walking around the front of the car, still looking as he talked. He looked around another minute or so, and headed back to Price. "The only thing in his pockets was this money. I didn't see a gun or a knife."

Price put the money in his pocket without counting it, then looked at Jimmy mischievously. "I'll make sure his family gets it. Now tell me what you saw, and if I catch you in a lie, I'll kick your black-ass all the way back to New York. Go on and talk." He stuck a cigarette in his mouth and lit it. Jimmy stared at Billy Roy. Price took a long drag on his cigarette and exhaled strings of smoke through his mouth and nostrils. "I ain't got all day, Boy. You gonna talk or what?"

"After Earl bought the fluid, he asked him to put it in his car; we never went outside. He refused, so Earl asked for his money back. Earl didn't have a gun or a knife, he ain't never been that kind of person. Most of the fingers are missing from his right hand; he was holding the fluid in his left hand. He couldn't have pulled a gun out if he had one."

"That's a damn lie, Nigger." Saliva was spraying from Billy Roy's mouth as he talked. He took an aggressive step toward Jimmy, Batts stepped in between them.

Jimmy stood his ground and responded quickly. "You got mad when he asked you for his money back, and you never asked us to leave. You just pulled your gun out and shot him."

Billy Roy was fuming, his face turned redder. "I should have killed you too. If I ever see you again, Nigger, I will." He stepped toward Jimmy again.

Price stepped in, "All right, that's enough. Batts, take him inside and call Dr. Pitt, and one of them colored funeral homes. Oh yeah, call the station for the ID boys. I'll get the rest of this Boy's statement."

Batts nodded, Billy Roy was still fuming. He stared at Jimmy and gritted what was left of his tobacco-stained grill. He was half-way to the office before he took his eyes off of him. A small crowd had gathered on the yard between the gas pumps and 301.

Price had been writing on a notepad a minute or so when Batts came out of the office. "I need to talk to you a minute." He signaled with his hand for Price to meet him.

Price stepped a few steps away from Jimmy. Batts began whispering furiously in his ear. "All right, thank you," said Price. He stood there for a minute, debating his next move. He walked back to Jimmy and asked, "Where did Earl live, was he married?"

Jimmy blew out a frustrated breath. "Yes sir. He and his family lived at 318 Hadley Street; he had four children. His wife has been sick a few years and unable to work. I don't know what they gonna do now." He shook his head. "This ain't nothing but cold blooded murder."

Price stared at Jimmy, and then wrote the information down. "What's his wife name?"

"Miss Eula Mae Cooper."

"When are you going back to New York?" Price eyes were focused on the notepad.

"I probably need to stay for the funeral to help Miss Eula Mae out; she ain't able to do much. But I'll come back for court."

Price's expression changed in a flash. He had an evil glint in his eyes. "It ain't gonna be no damn court." Jimmy looked stunned, trying to digest what Price had just said. Price continued. "How many white men have you ever known to be convicted for killing a colored? Anyway, Billy Roy killed him in self-defense for trying to rob him with a gun."

Anger burned threw Jimmy's body, but he held himself still. "The other officer said Earl didn't have a gun."

Price responded quick and cold, "The officer said he didn't find a gun, but I found it." He turned his back to the small crowd, then he dug into the inside pocket of his trench coat and pulled a .22 pistol out. He smiled, then said, "This is what I call my throw-down pistol. If I ever have a reason to kill one of you niggers, I'll throw it down near the body. Right now, this pistol belongs to Earl, but if you tell me again that Earl didn't have a gun, it belongs to you, and I'll throw it down on your dead body. It's your choice; and I'm only going to ask you once. Have you ever seen this gun before?" He cocked the hammer back.

Jimmy's eyes swelled, his legs felt like rubber, but he stood perfectly still, except for the thumping of his heart. "Yes Sir."

"Whose gun is this?"

"It's Earl's gun." Jimmy lowered his head and shifted his weight from one foot to the other.

"Speak up Boy, I can't hear you!"

"It's Earl's gun."

Price nodded. "That's better. Now, my advice to you is, get your ass back to New York and stay there for awhile. Your family don't need two deaths so close together. And those people at the court house wouldn't take kindly to you calling that white man a lie. You need to leave Wilson as soon as possible, today. If I see you after today, I'll shoot you on sight, and I'll have a good reason. You did try to help Earl rob Billy Roy, am I right?" Price started to raise his gun again.

Jimmy spoke quickly. "Yes Sir, I did."

"Now get your ass away from here, out of Wilson." Jimmy nodded and looked toward Earl's body through tear-filled eyes, and then walked toward 301. He never looked back.

Billy Roy and Batts were sitting on the ledge of a large glass window with their backs to 301, when Price walked in. "I didn't know Bud Bass was your brother. How long has he been a judge?"

Billy Roy smiled. "I don't know my damn self; I know it's been a long time. He put me in business here."

Price walked around the counter and opened the drink box. He pulled out a Top Cola, opened it and sat down in the squeaky, dingy, desk chair. There was a large confederate flag hanging from the ceiling that covered most of the window. "You need to call Bud and let him know what happened here. Tell him to call me." He sipped his drink and lit a cigarette.

Billy Roy got his spit-cup from under the counter, spat in it and smiled. "He's in Rocky Mount with that young gal, but I'll tell him when he gets back."

"Bud's getting a little old for that. Them young gals will take his old ass away from here," said Price smiling.

Billy Roy spat in his cup again and smiled broadly. "I told him that, but he asked me if I knew of a better way to go."

Price sipped his drink again. "That nigger is on his way out of town, so you shouldn't have any problems. I'll talk to the chief about it when I get to the station."

Billy Roy looked relieved as he smiled. "I preshate that."

"That's alright, but don't talk to nobody but Bud about this. Just so we're on the same page; I'll write this up as an attempted armed robbery." He pulled his .22 pistol out again.

"This was that dead nigger's gun, the other one got away. All you'll have to do is keep your mouth closed and I'll take care of the rest." Billy Roy nodded his appreciation.

The struggle for civil and voting rights was a sprint; keeping them will be a marathon. Quit the race and surrender your freedom.

-Algernon McNeil

Chapter 3

January 6, 1952
11:14 A, M.

The detectives headed north on 301, turned left at South Pender, then turned left at the first light onto Nash Street, into the African American business district. A number of small, successful business-es lined both sides of the street, from South Pender to the Railroad tracks; doctors, lawyers, drugstores, beauty shops, barber shops, and even a movie theater to name a few. In the forties and early fifties, people dressed in high fashion to patronize Downtown's night spots where top, African American entertainers appeared. Downtown was the heart of the African American community.

They drove another four blocks west on Nash Street, passing the Cherry and Briggs Hotels before making a right onto Goldsboro Street. The police department was on the right, on the ground floor of a three-story building. The Utilities Department and City Hall oc-cupied the top two floors.

There were two, young black men standing at the front desk with their hands cuffed behind them, when the detectives walked in. One of the men was bleeding from his mouth; the other had a two inch cut over his left eye. A muscular, white officer was standing behind them with a long, black nightstick he was lightly tapping in the palm of his hand. The officer behind the desk got a large key from a desk drawer and gave it to the officer guarding the black men. His eyes looked huge through the thick glass in his wire-frame glasses. "Lock them Spooks up," he said, trying to sound tough.

The man bleeding from the mouth looked shock. "We don't know nothing, and you know we ain't done nothing. Why are you locking us up?"

The desk officer looked at the man and smiled. "You'll know something before you leave here. I'll have a few officers talk with you later. I'll bet, you'll know something before they leave your cell. Lock them up." The officer took the key and started pushing the men in their backs with his stick, toward the holding cell down the hall. The officer behind the desk turned his attention to Price; his tone of voice immediately changed. "Sergeant Price, the chief is waiting to see you." He had a half-smoked cigar cramped in the corner of his mouth and a thick fog of cigar smoke filled the air.

"Thank you," said Price. "Batts, you gas the car up, while I talk with the chief. We'll go to lunch after that."

Batts nodded. "Will do; I'll be in the office when you finish." Price walked down the long hall towards the chief's office. The Detective and Uniform Divisions were located at the end of the hall next to a holding cell. The officer had just locked the men up when Price walked down the hall.

"Sergeant Price, can I speak to you for a minute, Sir?" A voice said from inside the cell.

Price slowed down and looked before walking in that direction. When he was close enough to see into the dimly-lit cell, a big smile creased his face. "Damn, Charlie Jr., you're up here again."

"Yes Sir, but I need a favor."

Price's expression changed. He paused and stared before speaking. "If you want me to tell your wife to get you out, I ain't doing that again. That woman gets tired of you getting drunk and wanting to fight her. One day she's going to blow your ass away." Price smiled. "You'll be alright, you got two cellmates now." Price didn't give him time to respond; he turned and headed toward the chief's office.

The holding cell was a seventy-two hour lock-up for black, petty criminals, drunks and ass-kicking with a rubber hose. It was also used for, "being black in the wrong place."

The door was cracked open when Price got to the chief's office. Chief Watson was standing at the coffee pot. A large window behind Watson's desk gave a clear view of the Wilson County Courthouse and jail. There was a quarter-size grease stain on the red tie that hung from his fat neck, and his blue suit looked like he had slept in it the night before. "Chief Watson," said Price.

"Come in, want some coffee?"

"I need some, its cold." He turned his top-coat collar down.

"How do you want it?"

"Give me two sugars and cream."

"That colored gal ain't even cold yet and there are all kinds of rumors going around in the colored section." Watson handed the hot coffee to Price.

"Thanks Chief."

Watson then flopped down in the chair behind his desk. His weight was over three-hundred pounds, and the chair cracked when he sat down. "Tell me about the Sinclair Station first. Budd Bass owns that place."

"Yeah, Billy Roy told me he was the Judge's brother."

Watson forced a half-smile. "I know Billy Roy; he don't know his ass from his head; not bright at all. What was going on, what happened out there?"

Price smiled. "I thought something was wrong when I first saw him, but anyway, two coloreds tried to rob him at gun point. He shot and killed one of them, the other one got away."

Watson shook his head. "They didn't know that they were dealing with a crazy man. I'll read the report later, now tell me about Carroll Street."

After sipping his coffee Price answered, "We don't have a lot now, but Doctor Pitt said she died from strangulation and she had been sexually assaulted; I don't believe that. She was a hooker. It looks like it was three or more men in the room. There were several beer bottles and three of four used rubbers."

Watson leaned back in his chair. "Did anyone see anything or know anything?"

"I talked to the old lady that lived next door, and the dead woman's son. Her son said he saw some white men in the room with her last night. The old lady said that white men came to pick her up regularly; she said they were tobacco buyers. She also said, there was a young white man that lived in Wilson who came to take her out a lot. Some white men could have been there last night and she probably went out with some white men before, but I think some niggers killed her. I got a snitch that lives in that area, I'll ask him about it. If some niggers did it, he'll know something and some names."

Watson was nodding his understanding. "All the buyers are gone, so if there were white men in the room, they were probably poor white trash. Some of them are worst than niggers."

"I don't know about that, Chief." The old lady said the young white man gave her a lot of money. Poor white trash doesn't have a lot of money. She also said, he bought her a new car. They're white trash, if they were in the room with her, but not poor white trash."

"You know C.L. Washington, don't you?"

"I don't know him personally, but I've seen him in court several times."

"He called me a little while ago; he said rumors were going around that she was killed by some white man. There must be something to it, so I don't want this thing to blow up. Check around, and if some white men names do come up, I need to know before you question anyone. After you write the report you check with me…. The Newspaper people would blow this thing up just to sell papers." Watson lit a cigarette and sat up in his chair. He narrowed his eyes in a thinking mode before speaking. "My personal feelings tell me that if they were white men, I hope we burn them for just being down there with that nigger whore, but I need to be perfectly honest with you." He paused and pulled on his cigarette. "Some white people in this town, you don't question, especially about killing a nigger. That's why I told you if any white men names came up to check with me first. Do I have to say more?"

Price nodded understandingly. "No Sir, I understand."

"One more thing; C. L. Washington is a leader in the colored community. He has a law degree and his family has plenty of money. We need to work with him, and at the same time work around him. Something might come up that only you and I need to know. He's colored, but he's a hell-of-a-lawyer, smart as hell. You need to stay as far away from him as you can, and never have a conversation with him about this case, unless I'm present. That's an order."

"Ok Chief."

"Now get some lunch, and get back down there. Oh, tell Batts to keep his mouth closed about this case. The less the public knows, the better; especially about the white men being down there."

"Yes Sir."

The conversation with Watson had a negative impact on Price, but he knew he couldn't respond.

Africans were enslaved by a white master who was himself enslaved by greed and hate; so much so that he was willing to reduce the life of a human being to that of a wild animal.

-Algernon McNeil

Chapter 4

January 6, 1952
11:52 P.M.

The overcast day had turned into blue skies and the temperature was now a tolerable 45 degrees. Price and Batts left the Police Department on Goldsboro Street and turned right at the light, heading west on Nash Street; Batts was driving.

Price lit a Camel, tossed the match out the window, and was blowing smoke as he talked. "Since you headed this way, let's go to McClallens for lunch. We need to get back on Carroll Street so we can look inside her house."

"Do you really think white men killed her? That old woman could have told that boy to say that," said Batts.

Price was looking straight ahead and didn't respond at first, but moments later said, "I didn't think so at first, but I do now." He hesitated. "I don't give a damn about that whore, but I want to find that white, nigger loving trash no matter what the chief said." He was fuming now.

"What did he say?"

Price frowned and glanced at Batts. "To me, it's not worth repeating."

Batts turned left onto Pine Street and parked near the corner. A deep frown still creased Price's face as they walked toward McClallens. They walked in and took a seat on the red stools that lined the counter. A wide aisle separated the restaurant from the toy section, which stretched from the front of the store to the "white only" restrooms in the back. An aisle, mid-way the toy section ran the width of the store.

"Are we the only ones in Wilson having lunch today?" Batts said, as he looked down the empty counter. Every day a group of old men would meet for lunch.

A bottle blonde waitress with a hint of facial hair walked toward the detectives. "It's still early. What can I get for you?"

"Ham and cheese on rye, and ice tea," answered Batts.

She then turned her attention to Price. "What about you, Sergeant Price?"

"I'll have the same."

The waitress wrote down the order, and then looked at a black woman and her child standing behind the stool next to Batts. "What do you want Girl?" She asked, in a not so friendly voice.

The well dressed, attractive black woman looked at her for a moment. "Not a damn thing Girl." She said in a friendly voice, and then smiled. The short smile died as she shifted her shopping bags from her left hand to her right hand, took her child by the hand and walked out.

The waitress found herself at a loss for words. She stood there for a moment looking at the woman as she walked out. Her face turned beet-red with anger. "You can't be nice to them coloreds." She turned to fix the order.

"You ever thought about joining the Klan?" Price asked. "Most of the officers on the force and Sheriff's Department are members. I know a few Judges that are members too."

"I never thought about it, but I know a lot of boys that are members," said Batts, glancing at Price.

"You need to think about it, especially with this job. You never know what might come up, or when you might need them. They carry a lot of weight around here. They can do things in the colored section that we can't do, and get away with it."

"I'll think about it," said Batts. But he wasn't buying one word of that bullshit Price was trying to sell. He glanced at Price and smiled.

The detectives ate their lunch like it was their last meal, and headed back to South Carroll Street. They drove south on Pine Street and took the first left, another left, then a right and they were heading east on Nash. A parade of Lincolns, Cadillacs, and Roadmaster Buicks were also heading east. The back seats were occupied by maids and butlers being driven home from a Saturday, half-day's work. The uptown and downtown shopping districts were crowded with shoppers buying sale items from Christmas.

There was a car wreck in front of the Ritz Theatre, blocking traffic on East Nash, in the downtown shopping district. Lee "Hank" Williams, a black officer was directing traffic at the corner of Nash and Pettigrew; Officer Rudolph Best, Wilson's other black officer was writing the wreck report. "Turn right, and then left at Barnes Street," said Price, as they approached the intersection of Pettigrew and Nash. "When we get to Pender Street, turn right. We'll go to Carroll Street off of Wainright." Just as they passed the coal yard heading south on Pender Street, Price spotted several men gambling behind the store at the corner of Gay and South Pender. Price grabbed Batts arm to get his full attention, "Batts, turn right at the corner and park beside the store near the front." Price jumped out before the car came to a complete stop. With Batts walking close on his heels, he steals up on them. "Everybody stay where you are," said Price in a loud voice, totally surprising the gamblers; his .38 was in his hand. "If you run, I'll shoot you in your ass."

Four men were on their knees around an old army blanket they were using as a smooth surface to roll dice. A fifth man was standing watching the game. They all knew Price's reputation and made no attempt to flee. "You Boys know gambling can get you thirty days," said Price. "Now stand up against the wall." The four gamblers stood up and backed against the wall. The other man gazed at Price, but didn't move. "You too Boy," said Price, directing the man with the barrel of his gun. The man's gaze sharpened and his jaw tightened as he slowly backed up against the wall. "Empty your pockets on the blanket and I might let you Boys go." The four gambles quickly threw their money on the blanket. "That means you too, Boy, unless you want to get locked up." Price then stared at the man for a moment. "Don't I know you?"

The man didn't answer, but glared at Price, "I ain't been gambling and I ain't no damn Boy," he said in a low, firm voice. He then turned toward Price. Price backed up, lifting his gun shoulder high, pointing at the man's face. Batts then pulled his gun. "I ain't been gambling and you ain't taking my money, unless you kill me first."

Price's anger was swelling. "You other Boys can go." The men walked away at a fast pace that quickly turned into a full run. Price looked toward the street where a small crowd had gathered just a few yards away. "Batts, fold the blanket up." Price then stared at the man again. "What's your name, Nigger? Now tell me you ain't no nigger," he said in a low voice with his back to the crowd. The man didn't respond, showing no fear of the gun pointed at his face. "Today is your lucky day," said Price smiling. "If we didn't have any people standing around, I was going to do just that, take your money off your dead body. But I'll see you again; I'll remember this. Now get away from me before I change my mind and kill your ass anyway." The man stared a hole through Price before walking away. Price and Batts walked toward their car through the now, mumbling crowd; their guns were still in their hands. "Let's get the hell out of here; these crowds are dangerous, I told you that." Price said just above a whisper.

Batts made a U-turn in the coal yard and stopped at the stop sign at the corner of Gay and South Pender. "Turn right, then left at Wainwright Street, that will take us to Carroll Street," Price said.

Batts looked at Price like he wanted to speak, but didn't. Moments later he asked, "Have you ever seen him before?"

There was still a hint of anger in Price's voice when he answered, "Yeah, I know that nigger and he knows me. I can't think of his name, but I know they call him Smokey. He just got out of prison for killing a man across town."

Batts looked at Price and smiled. "He looks hard, and that scar on his face made him look even harder."

Price quickly responded in anger. "That's one of them niggers that I was telling you about that don't give a damn about the police. If you ever have a problem with him, you'll probably have to shoot him, so make sure you kill him, cause he'll be back if you don't." Price hesitated. "All I can say is he's lucky. If we didn't have a crowd around, I would have shot him dead." He lit a cigarette, and said, "In Mississippi, if a white officer tells a colored to move, he moves, but not in this damn town. Some of them, you have to kill, or they will kill you. Smokey is one of them niggers."

They turned onto South Carroll Street off of Wainwright and parked behind a black Cadillac in front of Maggie's house. Batts glanced at Price, then said, "Do you think that car belongs to one of those tobacco men?"

Price looked directly at Batts as if he was asking a stupid question. "Hell no, they wouldn't be caught dead, down here in the day time. They don't give a damn about her being dead. The buyers are gone anyway."

They walked on Maggie's porch and Price knocked. "Come in," Maggie yelled.

"How are you?" Price said, to the couple on the couch. The new car and the couple's professional appearance temporarily neutralized his racist attitude.

The tall, well dressed man stood up and smiles as he said, "Fine, thank you. I'm Sam Howard and this is Virginia, my wife." He looked like an educated man of high principles.

Price extended his hand. "I'm Detective, Sergeant, Price and this is Detective Batts," Batts nodded.

"Pleased to meet you." Virginia smiled warmly. Her long, black hair, light brown eyes and slender frame drew Batts' attention. Refined and charming; her gray suit, black sweater and soft make-up enhanced her professional appearance.

"We're investigating the homicide. I'm sure you know about it by now."

"Yes," said Virginia. "Ronnie is in my second grade class at Sam Vick. He's a good young man and a bright student. I felt really bad for him when we got the news. My husband and I had to come to see if we could be of any service."

Sam smiled, walked over to Maggie and took her hand. "I know you need to talk, so we'll get out of your way. But if you need anything, please feel free to call us."

Virginia opened her handbag, took out a notepad and pen, and began to write their phone number down. "You can call day or night if you need us," handing the number to Maggie.

Maggie nodded. "Thank you, bless your heart. All I can think about is them boys. I don't know what to do."

"You're welcome. When we come back, we'll talk about it and hopefully find some solutions. Maybe by that time, some family might be located," said Virginia.

"Can we say goodbye to the boys?" Sam asked.

Maggie pointed to the back room. "Sure you can, just go in the back; you know they got them eyes on that T.V."

Sam and Virginia walked to the back and seconds later were back out. "They're both asleep; we'll see them when we come back," said Sam, in his deep clear voice. "They've been through a lot in the past six or seven hours, and they're so young."

"We'll be back, Mrs. Wade," said Virginia. She hugged Maggie and joined Sam at the door. He put his arm around her; tears were running down her face as they walked out.

Maggie felt her eyes watering as she turned her attention to Price and Batts. "Have a seat." She was trying to hold back the tears.

The detectives sat on the chair the Howard's vacated. Price waited for Maggie to compose herself. Moments later he asked, "Did someone move the body?"

"C. L. Washington's Funeral Home. I called them because there could be a problem paying for the funeral. Lawyer Washington is good about helping people."

Price slowly nodded. "We need to look inside the house. Maybe we can find something that could help."

Maggie considered the idea before speaking. "I hope we find out where some of her family is. I love them boys, but I'm too old to keep them." The detectives stood and walked toward the door. "Let me get the key." Maggie got up slowly and walked toward the back. "The boys will be all right until I get back." She got her coat and keys, then joined Price and Batts, who were waiting on the front porch. "Sergeant Price, this is the key to the front door. It will take me a while to walk over there. These eighty-one year old legs have seen their best days," she said smiling. She gave Price the keys and tied a green scarf around her head and ears.

Price and Batts walked over and entered the house. They were walking in and out of rooms when Maggie walked in.

"Have a seat Maggie," said Price, walking up the hallway from the back of the house. "This house is laid out," shaking his head in disbelief.

Maggie sat on a red velvet chair beside the telephone table; obviously tired from her walk to the house. She barely had enough breath to speak. "After that walk up them high steps, it will take me the rest of the day to catch my breath," she said smiling. "I remember when I could jump up them steps, but them days is long gone."

"Officer Batts, you start in that bedroom," said Price, directing Batts with his head. "Any papers you find with names, addresses or phone numbers, put them on the bed so we can look through them later."

Batts walked in the bedroom looking around at the elegant furniture. A large, expensively framed picture hung over the head of the round bed. Pictures of Ronnie and Butch sat on the mantel of the fireplace that occupied the entire wall. A thick, red carpet complimented the bedspread and drapes. Batts was still looking around in amazement. "This looks more like Hollywood than it does Wilson."

"Sergeant Price," said Maggie, "I forgot to tell you something. Rose told me if anything happened to her, for me to look under the bed and get the strong box."

Price walked in the hall from the dining room. "Did you hear that Batts?"

"Yes Sir," said Batts; instantly falling to his knees. He looked under the bed and pulled out an iron-framed box.

Maggie leaned over in her chair to see what Batts had found. "That's it, and the key is on the keychain with the house key."

Batts put the box on the bed, and Price walked over to open it. Insurance papers, and an envelope addressed to Maggie were on top of a large amount of cash. Price looked at the cash again as if he wasn't sure what to do with it. "Maggie, there is something in here for you."

Maggie got up from her chair that was directly in front of the door and slowly walked across the hall into the bedroom.

"Will you read it to me, Sir?"

Price opened the envelope and began to read.

"Miss Maggie, I did the best I could for my children, so they could have a better life than I did. I know you didn't approve of everything I did, but I tried to be a good person and a good mother. I just got tired of working like a dog, in the Tobacco Factor; six and sometimes seven days a week and still could not pay my bills. I was saving this money for my children's education, but use it as you see fit. I have no family responsible enough to take care of them. Their father is dead, so you're all they have left and I know you love them very much. Tell my boys to be good and I love them. Thank you, Rose."

Price took the money from the box to count it; his eyes lit up like a Christmas tree. "Seven thousand dollars in here and I don't make that much in two years." He exchanged glances with Batts, shaking his head, and then reluctantly gave the money and box to Maggie.

"This is yours.

"Thank you." The memory of Rose brought tears to her eyes, which she brushed away with the back of her hand as she walked toward the door. She stopped just short of the door and slowly turned around. She stared at Batts, then at Price. "I worked in that same tobacco factory for almost 30 years. Twelve hours a day, six days a week, for eighteen cents an hour and they didn't even want you to go to the bathroom, if you needed to go. You got a half-hour break for lunch." She hesitated and took a deep breath; tears were slowly making their way down her face. "Being colored, sometimes you're forced to do things you don't really want to do. Y'all ain't never been colored, or had to raise a family on eighteen cents an hour, so y'all don't understand. I'm God fearing, but I can understand." She turned around and walked slowly through the door, holding the doorframe to support her aging, weak legs. Price and Batts stood silent as she walked out.

The detectives looked through the house, after Maggie left, but found nothing relating to the case. They left Carroll Street heading to Carolina Street.

"I wonder how long it took her to make all of that money," said Batts. Price shook his head slowly, but didn't respond. He lit a cigarette.

All men are made in the image of God; God, as everyone knows is not a Negro, therefore, the Negro is not a man.   *-Author unknown*

Nothing in all the world is more dangerous than sincere ignorance and conscientious stupidity.   *-Shakespeare*

Chapter 5

January 6, 1952
2:03 P.M.

The detectives turned onto Carolina Street Extension, off of Highway 301. They were going to interview Carol Spells, Rose Grant's best friend. Carol was a part–time prostitute, and a full-time alcoholic. Her years of alcohol abuse had taken a toll on her eye-catching figure, and added years to her once beautiful face. Her expensive tricks in hotel rooms were now reduced to alcohol and cigarette money in the back seats of cars.

Price frowned and shook his head. "Damn, I forgot to look up her address, but I know she lives in this block. I'll ask that drunk walking toward us".

Batts gave Price a quick glance and smiled, as he said, "The way he's walking, he probably doesn't know where he lives, or even worst, who he is."

Carolina Street Ext. was a short, two-block street with duplex and single family houses on both sides. Junk cars and car parts occupied most of the landscape at the end of the second block. Price pulled beside the red-eyed, wino walking toward 301. The odor coming off him, even in the cold air, was a mixture of wine, urine and unwashed flesh. "Hey Boy, what house does Carol Spells live in? I know she lives in this block."

The man stared at Price for a moment, then pointed to a gray house down the street. "Down yonder, that gray house," he said, before catching his balance on the hood of the car, holding his wine bottle close to his chest.

"All right, Boy. You can go." said Price, smiling.

The wino nodded, and staggered toward 301 holding his wine bottle.

They drove in front of the gray house and parked. Price opened the door, got out, then tight-roped his steps between the car and a ditch, filled with icy, stagnant, water. The house had suffered years of neglect. Cardboard was taped over broken window-glass to block the cold, winter air. Price and Batts walked on the porch. Price knocked on the gray door through a screen-less, screen-door and moments later Carol Spells opened it, holding a bottle of beer. She smiled and stepped back, extending her hand in a welcome gesture; dressed in a dingy, white bra and panties of unknown color that revealed her pubic hair. "Sergeant Price, come in. I ain't seen you in a long time."

Price looked at her in disgust, and turned his head before speaking. "First of all, go in the back and put some clothes on your ass," he said, in a moment of intense fury. "I ain't no damn trick, and if I was, I wouldn't pay for your nasty ass." Carol quickly disappeared in the back room. When she reappeared, Price and Batts were standing in the living room where the floor was littered with alcohol bottles and trash. A foul odor was coming from the kitchen that was across the hall from the living room. The space between the wood-stove and the wall was occupied by a large, pregnant, black dog.

"Why don't you clean this pig-pen up?" Price said, looking around in disgust. "It stinks in here, and so do you." He held the back of his hand over his nose.

Carol smiled, looked directly at Price, and took a sip from her beer before answering. "Do you want to move in, or do you want to talk?"

Price's face instantly reddened; he walked toward her in an attack mode and knocked the beer bottle out of her hand. Carol's eyes lit up with fear. She backed up quickly, holding her hands up in front of her face. "Who do you think you're talking too, you nasty whore!" Price shouted as adrenaline shot through him. "You watch what you say to me; I'll kick you in your stinking ass." He was loud and pointing his finger in her face. But in spite of his anger, he knew he had to keep his cool.

Carol sat down in the chair on top of soiled clothes. "Yes Sir." Her voice was barely audible.

Price paused for a moment. He knew Carol might provide information that could lead him to the killer. He didn't want to compromise the investigation because of his personal feelings. He changed expressions in a desperate attempt to calm himself. "Look Carol, I know you and Rose were friends, and you want the killer caught as much as I do. Is that right?"

Carol was still frightened, but managed a response. "Yes Sir."

"Look at me," he said softly, forcing a smile. Carol lifted her head and looked at Price; her eyes were glassy with tears. "I need to ask you some questions, and I want you to think hard to remember all you can. Right now, you're my best hope in finding the killers."

Carol wiped her tears away before answering, "Yes Sir."

Price hesitated for a moment, giving Carol time to collect herself. "How long did you know Rose?"

"I met her about two years ago, when we worked in the tobacco factory on Mercer Street."

"I know about the tobacco buyers; I want to know if there was any one else she went out with on regular basis?"

"Rose told me, she went to a party in Raleigh and met a white man from Wilson."

"Do you remember his name?"

"No I don't. She called him baby face because he looked so young. He was a few years younger than she was."

"Did you ever see him?"

"No, but she told me he was tall, with blonde hair, really good looking. She also said they got together several times and he always gave her a lot of money. She said he took her to Raleigh one night and they stayed in a hotel. The next day, he gave her money to buy a new car."

"So that's the car in the garage?"

"Yes Sir. But after he bought the car, he wanted her to stop seeing other men. He wanted to marry her and leave the south. She tried to explain to him that, the other men were friends who liked her and gave her money to help her with her children, but he didn't want to listen."

"Did she say where he worked?"

"She never said, but someone in his family died and left him a lot of money." Carol hesitated and wiped her eyes. "When she kept going out with other men, he hit her one night. After that, she wouldn't go out with him again, he kept asking, but she didn't." Carol got a half-smoked cigarette off of the table next to her and lit it. "I was at her house Thursday night. She told me, he wanted to talk with her about something real important," Carol said, blowing smoke from her nostrils. "She was afraid to go out with him, so she agreed to let him come to her house; not in the house, but the room. She never let any man go in her house around her children. He was in love with her, but he couldn't control her." She paused and pulled on the cigarette. "That's probably why he killed her." Carol shook her head.

"Is there anything else you can think of?" Carol's eyes narrowed. She took a long pull from her cigarette, appearing nervous and reluctant. Price eyed Carol suspiciously. "Come on, you know anything you tell me will never leave this room. I'll check on it, but your name will never come up. I need all the help I can get, so you need to tell me everything you know."

Carol took a deep breath. "I can't remember who told me because I was drinking at the time, but I heard Dan Williams; at the Bluenote saw the white men that killed Rose. Either that, or he knows who saw them. They said that it was three or four white men in her room. I was drunk and there was a lot of noise in the room."

"Did you hear another name?"

"No Sir."

Dan Williams was the owner of The Bluenote, a popular jazz club on North East Street; patronized by pimps, prostitutes, gamblers and tricks. In the late 40s, he was charged with the murder of two men on Stantonsburg Street, but was acquitted, claiming self-defense. It was common knowledge on the East Side that he killed them because they owed him money, but no one would talk, and he paid an eye witness to support his story. He served some time in a Federal Penitentiary for selling non tax paid liquor. Price knew Dan sold liquor at The Bluenote, and that could be his pass to information, and a weekly pay-off.

"We got off on the wrong foot, but you were a big help and I'll remember that when you need me, and you will, sooner or later," said Price, with a sly grin.

"Yes Sir, but please don't mention my name. I don't want any problems with Big Dan. You know how he is. He don't care if you're a man or woman, he'll hurt you. I'm scared to death of him."

"I told you, your name will never come up." The detectives walked toward the door. "If you hear anything else, let me know." He gave Carol five-dollars; they walked out of the door toward their car, got in and headed toward 301. The wino that identified Carol's house was being supported by a stop sign, when they got to the intersection. His red eyes were half-opened when his attempted wave was shortened by a sudden flop to the ground, but he didn't drop his wine bottle.

"Look at that," said Batts, pointing at the wino; they glanced at each other and smiled.

When the slaves were taken from Africa, they were cut off from their family ties and chained to ships like beasts. Nothing is more tragic than to be divorced from family, language and roots.

-Author unknown

Chapter 6

January 6, 1952
3:00 P.M.

Price looked at his watch and thought for a moment. "It's after three now. Before we go to the station, I need to make a quick stop on Smith Street." They were heading west on Nash Street.

"What's going on around there?"

A cold smile popped on Price's face. "Nothing really, I just need to collect some money. A colored bootlegger ain't paid me in two weeks, but he will today, or else."

Smith Street was a one block street, known for violence and illegal activity. Price was going to collect his weekly payment from bootlegger, Eddie "Bad Feet" Brown. "Turn right at Pender Street, then left at the Stop Light Grill, Smith Street." Batts turned at Pender, then onto Smith. "Some of the white officers go in that grill to eat. They said that they have some good food in there, but I don't eat no colored-cooked food." Batts smiled. Price continued. "This is one of those streets where you have to really be careful who you confront. At the end of this block is Pettigrew, and the next street over is Church. Most of the serious assaults take place on these three streets. Some of these people don't give a damn about the police, and the spook we're going to see can pull a razor and cut your throat before you can blink your eyes, so stay alert. I don't think we'll have a problem, but you never know." Batts swallowed, remembering what Price said about showing fear. "You can park in front of that house with the green chairs on the porch." Price was pointing to a wood-framed, white house near the end of the block. Batts pulled his trench coat open with his .38 in full view, after they parked, and were walking toward the house. The door opened as soon as they walked up the high steps onto the porch.

"How are you doing Sergeant?" Eddie asked. He was a short, chubby, dark complexioned man in his mid fifties. Price gave Eddie a cold look, but didn't respond; he walked by Eddie making slight contact. Eddie managed a half-hearted smile and walked behind him. "I was going to call you today, when I got a chance," said Eddie. "Someone stole my liquor, and some money I had stashed away."

Price looked like he wanted to kill Eddie right there. "Don't give me that shit; you had two weeks to call me." He walked through the small living room into the back room. Several people were sitting at a card table, drinking from paper cups. An intoxicated, fat woman, with a twisted wig on her head and ruby-red lip-stick smeared on her lips, was dancing. Fats Domino's "Blueberry Hill," was blaring from the jukebox in the corner near the small plywood bar. She was stuffed into a dirty, two piece suite that was a size too small. Price smiled at her shaking his head, then walked to the jukebox and pulled the cord, Batts stood at the door. The room fell dead quiet. Price stood there and scanned the room before speaking. "Everybody get out of here, unless you want to go to jail." Price then walked behind the bar, crossed his arms and leaned a hip against it; his gaze was steady around the room. "I mean now, move." He slammed his hand on the bar. The doorway was suddenly overflowing as people spilled out; Batts managed to step aside quickly. The dancing woman fell twice before making it to safety; leaving her wig and the heel of one of her red, high-heel shoes on the dance floor. Moments later, the room was empty, except for Eddie, Batts and Price. Eddie stood near Batts at the door. He was fear stricken, like a man with a gun at his head.

Price gave Eddie an unnerving stare, and smiled. "Come over here Eddie." Eddie walked, or more appropriately, shuffled toward Price;

every step was painful as his bad feet touched the hardwood floor. He walked to the front of the bar facing Price. A distressed frown creased his face. He had once before been the victim of one of Price's prized, ass-kicking. Price stood there a long moment and stared at Eddie. "Detective Batts, this is Eddie Lee Brown, known as Bad Feet Brown. Eddie don't like to pay his bills on time."

"How are you doing Eddie?" Batts asked. Eddie turned toward Batts and nodded. When he turned back, Price leaned over the bar and slapped him. The force of the lick knocked him against the juke-box. Blood fell freely from his nose. When he regained his balance, Price was standing in front of him with his .38 revolver pointed at his head. Eddie raised his hands fear stricken. Price pulled a .32 revolver from his inside coat pocket. "This is your gun Eddie, and you have about ten seconds to get my money. If you don't have it, I'm going to blow your brains out and throw this gun on your dead body. You bad feet Nigger, I should kill you anyway."

Fear gripped Eddie's throat as he spat the words out of his mouth, "I got it, please don't." His eyes grew wide.

"Get it, or I'll kill your monkey-ass right now." Eddie knew Price was violent enough to kill him. He walked behind the bar and pulled out a small cashbox; counted out fifty dollars and gave it to Price. He got a towel from under the bar to catch the blood flowing from his nose. Price counted the money, and looked at Eddie. "You know Monday will be another week you owe me." Eddie counted out twenty-five more. "If you get behind again, the next time I come, you're a dead man. I don't want to hear shit about somebody stole your liquor. That was bullshit anyway. You probably gave it to one of them young whores that hang around here."

Eddie pulled the towel from his mouth and nose long enough to answer, "Yes Sir."

Price walked by Batts and signaled with his head. "Let's go, we need to see the chief." Price gave Batts twenty dollars, when they got to the car. "This is yours."

Batts hesitated as if he wasn't sure if he should take it. Price stared at him, then Batts said, "Thanks Sergeant."

"You're welcome, let's go."

Batts pulled off heading towards Pettigrew Street. He stopped at the corner of Smith and Pettigrew. "What if Eddie didn't have the money?"

Price's answer was explosive and immediate. "I would have killed him," he said, without hesitation. "It wouldn't be nothing but a dead nigger, with a prison record. Who cares? Let's go" He pulled a pack of cigarettes from his coat pocket, shook one out and lit it. "I need to see the Chief."

Batts turned left onto Pettigrew, drove the short block to Nash, and turned right, heading west on Nash. Watson was getting out of his car as they pulled into the parking lot. "Sergeant Price," he yelled, "I'll be in my office."

"All right, Chief. Batts, you can check out, I'll see you Monday morning."

"All right Sergeant."

The desk officer handed Price a note. "This is from Dr. Pitt. She died between three a.m. and seven a.m.," said Price, looking at Batts. He put the note in a trash can near the chief's office and knocked on the door.

Watson responded in a low, hollow voice, not looking of himself. "Come in." Price walked in and took a seat. The chief sat quietly for a moment. He was smoking a cigarette and occasionally flipped ashes into an ashtray overflowing with the remains of others. "This has been a busy day for me; busy and somewhat depressing."

"What's wrong, Chief?"

Watson didn't answer right away; he took a drag on his cigarette. "Do you know Bret Pope?"

Price thought a minute before answering. "I've seen him, but I don't know him personally."

"Anyway, he's one of our new officers I had to swear in today. I know you heard the name, Red Pope."

"Yes, I know him. Some people call him the, President of Wilson." He was smiling.

Watson didn't respond to Price's humor. "Bret is Red's only child, and the only one left in the family, since his wife was killed in a car crash last year. Red made it a point to let me know that, and he also let me know my job was on the line if anything happens to him, anything. Money and power is the name of the game in this town. Some people can make a phone call and you have no future, or no life. I don't know if President Truman can do that, but Red can, in Wilson."

Being the riches of the rich, Red Pope pushed his power around and usually got his way. He owned several tobacco warehouses and most of the rental property on the East Side. Whatever Red said was the law. He handpicked Watson for the chief's job and with one phone call, he could take it away, and Watson knew it. Watson stood and looked out his office window. Moments later he turned his attention to Price. "Did you get any more information on Carroll Street?"

"Dr. Pitt said she died between three and seven this morning. We looked around the house, but found nothing that would help us. But we did find some money, seven-thousand dollars she had stashed away."

Watson changed expressions. "What did you do with it?"

Price hesitated before answering. "She left a note with the money for the old woman next door, asking her to take care of her children. I had to give it to her; she saw the money and the note. I had no choice."

Watson stared at his detective, then spoke in a crude tone, the volume rising with each word, showing his outrage at Price's decision. "That money was made illegally from prostitution. I don't care who she left it for. The next time you do something stupid like that, you can stay down there with them niggers. What were you thinking?" He lit a fresh cigarette with one still burning in the ashtray. The office went dead silent while Watson collected himself. Moments later he stared at Price again, rolled his eyes and took a deep breath. "The people from the newspaper will want a story for Monday's paper. Just give them the general information and say nothing about white men being involved. Interview a few more people, then let it go. Maybe this thing will just go away. Write the report and go home, and don't ever leave any money down there again."

There was a great deal of bitterness in Watson's voice. Price stood and walked out without saying a word. He knew Watson wanted the money for himself.

Complacency is dangerous, especially in the African American community.   *-Algernon McNeil*

Chapter 7

January 7, 1952
3:05 P.M.

Maggie had just finished serving Sunday's dinner, when there was a knock at the door. She walked slowly from the kitchen, wiping her hands on her apron. "Come in." Maggie looked tired and depressed. Sam and Virginia opened the door and walked in. Sam was six-foot three-inches tall and was still very trim for a man in his mid-forties. His dark complexion and salt and pepper hair complimented his rugged good looks. And his blue, tailored suit looked immaculate on his long muscular frame. He looked much younger than his years. Sam was the basketball coach at Darden High School.

"How are you and the boys?" Virginia asked, dressed in a long, camel coat with a fox-fur collar.

Maggie took a deep breath before she answered with a degree of uncertainty. "We're trying to hold on." Sam and Virginia walked across the room and sat on the couch facing Maggie, who was now seated. Maggie closed her eyes and tried to compose herself. "The boys are in the kitchen eating dinner, but I want to show y'all something before they come in." She walked toward the back room and returned moments later with a brown paper bag. She slowly walked to Virginia and gave it to her. Virginia opened the bag, looked inside, then looked at Maggie. Maggie looked overwhelmed. "I ain't never seen that much money in my life." Virginia took the letter out and began to read to herself; she finished and passed it to Sam. After Sam read the letter, they both had a look of surprise. Maggie sighed, and then spoke slowly. "I don't know what to do; I'll be 82 years old my birthday. I love them boys, but I'm too old to take care of them.

I can't even help them with their school work; I can't read or write. They don't have nobody else. I just don't know what to do."

A long pause followed before Sam spoke. "Mrs. Wade, Virginia and I will help you through this and make the best decisions we can for the boys. The first thing we need to do is get this insurance policy to Washington's Funeral Home, the arrangements have to be made. School is closed tomorrow, so we can take care of some business. Okay?" Maggie nodded, looking somewhat relieved; she rocked back and forth in her chair. Sam continued. "We also need to get this money in the bank. If you don't have an account, we'll get one in your name. Don't worry, things will work out, you're not alone. Virginia and I will help you and the boys through this. Things are always hard at first, but they'll work out. Just remember what I said." Sam's words were like a breath of fresh air. Maggie looked like the world was lifted off of her shoulders.

Ronnie and Butch entered the room. Butch had a milk ring around his mouth, Ronnie was smiling. "Hi Miss Howard, and Mr. Sam."

"Hi yourself," she said with a big smile. "Come over here and give me a big hug," extending her arms. "You to Butch with that milk ring around your mouth."

They both walked across the room into her arms. Butch wiped the milk away with the back of his hand, and smiled.

Sam extended his arms, smiling broadly. "Don't I get a hug?" They turned and hugged him, Butch, reluctantly. "What have you been doing today, other than eating and watching T.V.?"

"Nothing," said Ronnie.

"What about you Butch?"

"Nothing." His head was lowered.

"Butch, you're almost as tall as Ronnie, you must eat a lot?"

Butch then smiled and rubbed his stomach. "I do, I can eat more than Ronnie."

"I bet you can." Sam smiled and rubbed the top of Butch's head.

Sam and Virginia made small talk with the boys for a while, then

Virginia said, "We need to talk with Mrs. Wade some more, so you Boys go in the back and watch television. School is closed tomorrow, so we'll be here early to see you. Okay?"

"Yes Ma'am," said Ronnie, "Come on Butch." He and Butch walked toward the back room. Just before opening the door, Ronnie turned and waved to Virginia, then gave her a smile that melted her heart.

Maggie was looking at the boys trying to hold back the tears. When they closed the door, she said, "My mother was born a slave, so you know she saw some hard times. She told me something a long time ago that I'll never forget. She said, *When you don't know what to do, you know what to do,*" so I called on God and left it in his hands. I know He sent you." Tears were running down her face. "I just know He did."

Virginia took a handkerchief from her handbag, walked over in front of Maggie, and slowly dropped to her knees. "You're right Mrs. Wade, He did." She wiped the tears from Maggie's face. "We understand how you feel, but things will work out. Sam and I will do everything we can to help you."

Maggie nodded and smiled as she said, "Bless your heart."

Let nothing, and no one stand between you and your God given right, freedom.   *-Algernon McNeil*

Chapter 8

January 8, 1952
2:45 A.M.

Price lit a cigarette, and then pulled some papers from his inside coat pocket. "This is the break in report from Gills' Grocery, down on East Nash Street." He stuck the cigarette in the corner of his mouth, while he unfolded the papers. "We'll go to see Dan Williams, after I talk with one of my informants. The Bluenote is just around the corner from where we're going." He took a short puff from his cigarette and threw it out of the window. "Let me tell you something about good detective work." Smoke was coming from his mouth and nostrils as he talked. Batts shot Price a short glance and nodded. "Physical evidence is good, you need it, but if you don't have a good snitch, you don't have nothing. A good detective always has a good snitch, and knows how to use him. You have to pay some of them, but your best information comes from niggers with long arrest records. You take them to the station and threaten to beat their ass with that rubber pipe, or lock them up, and they'll sing like Little Richard. If they don't know anything right then, check with them a few days later, they'll have something for you."

Batts looked shocked. "What if they don't know anything, or can't get any information, then what?"

"Then, you've solved your case, charge him with it. Put his ass in jail; a nigger snitch is a dime a dozen."

Batts couldn't believe what he was hearing. He flashed a short smile. "Are you serious, would you do that?"

Price narrowed his eyes and spoke sharply. "You damn right I'm serious; let me tell you something. This is a jungle down here; I told you it's dangerous. That bullshit they feed you in the training manual ain't worth a shit; you can throw it out the window. When you're dealing with people like this, you do what you have to do, right or wrong." He leaned back and pulled on his earlobe. "Anyway, most of them live better in prison than they do on the street. At least they eat regular and have a roof over their heads." Batts sensed from Price's expression that it would be in his best interest to remain silent.

They crossed the intersection of Nash and Pender Streets. "Gills is about two blocks down on your left. Turn in the parking lot and park behind the two-story building next door. Buddy White lives on the second floor. His apartment was once a trick house for street walking prostitutes. He has an arrest record as long as my arm; everything from public drinking to attempted murder. He did some time for the attempted murder of a prostitute; one of his whores."

Batts slowed down and turned into the parking lot at Gills. His attempt to park behind the building was cut short. The small, dirt parking area was littered with broken wine and beer bottles. "Damn, look at this shit. We'll be changing a tire if I don't stop here." Batts stopped and attempted to get out.

"Wait; let me tell you about this place." Batts pulled the door close and faced Price. Price nodded toward the building as he said, "Down stairs is a club, Ray Jones Inn, they sell white whiskey in there."

"Do you collect money from Ray Jones for selling whiskey?

"Are you joking? It wouldn't be worth the effort. I would have to shoot my way in and out; this is a dangerous place. Scarface Smokey, that hard looking nigger at the dice game hangs in there. On any given night, there are probably ten or fifteen more just like him in there. If you don't have to go in there, don't. If you have to, don't ever go in alone and have your gun in your hand. They don't give a damn about policemen, white or colored. And most of them don't care nothing about going back to jail or prison, that's their second home."

"All right Sergeant, I'll remember that."

"You better, if you want to live."

They got out and cautiously zigzagged their way through a maze of broken glass. A young couple was standing near the back entrance to the club with paper cups in their hands, and immediately stepped inside after seeing the detectives. Price started the steep climb up the steps, which ran up the side of the building, overlooking Gills' Grocery and parking lot. Batts was a few steps behind. When Price reached the top landing, he waited for Batts before knocking on the door. "Buddy White, this is Sergeant Price, open this door right now." He waited a second or two and knocked again. "You got five seconds to open this damn door, or I'll kick it down." Buddy immediately opened the door. He shaded his red-rimmed eyes from the mid-day sun, with the back of his hand. A strong odor of alcohol was present on his breath even before he opened his mouth. Price frowned and covered his nose and mouth. "Damn! If that's your breath, you need to see a doctor. That white liquor you had was poison. Ray better stop selling that shit before it kills somebody." Buddy forced a short smile, and stepped back. "You must have one of them young, hot-ass, colored gals in there," said Price, as he and Batts were walked in.

"No Sir. I had a little too much to drink last night."

Price smiled and immediately walked inside, did a quick inspection of the room, then walked to the back of the four-room apartment, briefly scanning each room. Batts and Buddy waited in the living room. A single floor lamp cast a dim glow around the room as sunlight tried to creep in through the dingy, bedspreads nailed over the windows. An old card table and four folding chairs were the only furniture in there. There was a coal and wood-heater that sat near the entrance of the hall-way leading to the back of the apartment. Price made his way back up the hall into the living room. "I don't see you much now Buddy. What you been doing?" Price was still looking around.

Buddy looked intimidated. He was well aware of Price's reputation. "Nothing much Sir, I work when it ain't raining or too cold."

Price stared at Buddy, and then walked to the window. There was a full view of Gills' Grocery and parking lot. He looked out a few seconds, looked back at Buddy, and looked out again. "What do you know about the break-in at Gills' over there?" He was looking out as he talked. Before Buddy could respond, Price turned around quickly. "I asked you, what you know about the break-in over there." His voice was loud and vicious.

Buddy responded quickly, his voice cracking with fear. "I don't know nothing, Sir. God knows, I would tell you if I did."

"Don't give me that shit. How can someone break that back door down and you not hear it. Do you think I'm stupid?" The fire in his voice came through loud and clear.

"No Sir, I don't think that, I just didn't hear anything; I sleep hard when I drink." Buddy swallowed to get rid of the lump in his throat.

Price stared at Buddy, and looked out the window again. He calmed himself before he turned to faced Buddy with a huge smirk. "You just got out of prison last year. Is that right?" He pulled a cigarette out and lit it.

"Yes Sir."

Price pulled a chair from under the card table and sat down. He was facing Buddy with his back to the table. His muscular, six-foot three-inch frame was taller sitting down, than Buddy's short, small frame was standing up. Buddy was a medium-complexion man of below average size and height. A sly smile tugged at Price's lips. "How many years do you have to stay on parole?"

"About seven Sir, but I ain't been in no trouble since I've been home."

Price smiled. "You hear that Batts? Buddy said that he ain't been in no trouble." Price stood up, dropped the cigarette and crushed it with the toe of his shoe. His face immediately underwent a radical change. "That's good Buddy, but that don't mean shit to me, cause I know you heard something or saw something. Don't try to bullshit me" Buddy attempted to speak, "Shut up! I've got some unsolved cases just waiting for your name, and some eye witnesses to back me up. I don't want to hear that bullshit anymore. Someone could piss in that parking lot down there and you could hear it hit the ground up here, so I know you heard that back door being chopped down." Price's mood went from foul to fouler. Buddy could sense the depth of Price's anger. He tried to speak again, but no words would come out. Price took a step toward him in an attack mode. "I told you to shut up. I'll clean this nasty flood up with your little ass." There was a short silence. "I'd better hear from you soon, or I'll make sure you pull them seven years, plus. You get me a name, or kiss your monkey-ass goodbye." Buddy nodded. He knew Price wouldn't hesitate to frame him and send him back to prison.

Price motioned to Batts with his head, "Let's go." He stared at Buddy again. "Either you get me a name, or I got yours." He walked toward the door, then turned to face Buddy again. "What have you heard about Rose Grant; that whore that got herself killed on Carroll Street? I know that you know all of them prostitutes."

"The only thing I heard was some, white men killed her; I heard it was the Klan."

Price stared at Buddy for a second. "You just remember what I said. I'll see you later; you better have something to tell me."

As the detectives descended the stairs, two men were approaching the bottom step. The detectives stopped, as did the two men. They stared at each other a short moment, then the detectives continued their walk down, the men their climb up. Turning sideways in their attempt to avoid contact, the detectives made their way down the steps. The man walking in front never broke his stride, or tried to avoid contact. His expression was cold and fearless. He rolled his cold, jet black eyes in the direction of the detectives when he reached the top landing. "Y'all want something?" He said smiling, and then crossed his massive arms and nodded slowly toward the detectives. "Here I am, if y'all want me."

"Do you know him? Batts asked, after they were seated in the car.

Price clinched his jaw and narrowed his eyes. "Yes, I know him, they call him Big Larry. He and Smokey are best friends. They grew up on Daniel Hill together; he hangs in the club too. Now you see why I don't try to collect whiskey money out of there, somebody would get killed."

Batts nodded, then said, "I thought Smokey looked hard, but damn, and he looks like he can pick that building up."

Price shot Batts a sideways glance. "You're right, they say that he's as strong as a bull, and I know he's dangerous, very dangerous, got a death wish. You'll have to kill him, or he'll kill you. Don't even think about trying to arrest him; just shoot that nigger as many times as you can, reload and shoot him again, kill'em."

"I knew something was wrong, he's looking for trouble," said Batts.

Price looked uneasy as he lit a cigarette. "Some years ago, his daddy was drunk and disorderly over on Barnes Street. When some officers tried to arrest him, he resisted, and his neck was broken in the struggle; he was paralyzed from the waist down. Big Larry was a child when it happened, but he always said that he will kill a white policeman before he dies. He always carries a gun. Didn't you see the print of the barrel in his pocket?"

"No Sir, but that's carrying a concealed weapon; that's against the law. We should've arrested him."

Price looked at Batts like he was crazy. He rolled his eyes and threw his cigarette out of the window. "I just told you that you have to kill him, or he'll kill you!" Price was fuming. "If I had proper backup, maybe I would have stopped him. Do you want to arrest him? He's still at Buddy's; you go up there and arrest him." Batts didn't respond he lowered his head. "I didn't think so, said Price. Let's go; turn right out of the parking lot.

Injustice can deprive you, but the effects of injustice should never de-fine you, or weaken your resolve.

- Algernon McNeil

Chapter 9

January 8, 1952
3:15 P.M.

Expensive cars lined the fence at the Bluenote, when the detectives pulled in. Big Dan Williams ran a card game for big gamblers from the surrounding areas. Batts parked near the front entrance. The Bluenote, and the Do-Drop-Inn, at the corner of 301 and Nash Street were the most successful clubs in Wilson.

"Watch this. As soon as they see this unmarked police car, the side door will look like a Georgia cotton field, full of nig-gers. They pay someone to watch for the police." Moments later the side door opened. Men and women strolled toward their cars; each making a fashion statement as a testimony to their criminal success. "See that boy getting in that black Cadillac with them three whores," said Price, glancing at Batts. That's Pretty Roddell Cut, a notorious pimp and gambler from Rocky Mount. Don't be fooled by his size. He almost killed a big nigger with his hands for assaulting one of his whores. Hey Rod," Price yelled, his head half way out the window. "You need to keep your whores in Rocky Mount; we have enough over here.

Roddell looked at Price with a mischievous smile. "Ok, Boss." One of his women frowned, rolled her eyes at Price and spat on the ground.

Price swung his attention to a car near the fence. "That ugly nig-ger in the Blue Hudson is Charlie Green; they call him, Big Money Green." He paused for a moment. "I think we have a warrant for him for assault, but I don't have time to check now." Price looked at Batts. "Charlie is a dangerous man. You need to remember that when you get out here on your own. He don't give a damn who you are. If you mess with him, and he get's half a chance, he'll cut your head off. He killed a man on Church Street and stayed in prison for fifteen years. You get help if you have any problem with him, you'll need it. Don't try to be no damn hero. Charlie will kill you. He's one of them niggers that don't care about going back to prison; he'll tell you that. Out of all of them bad niggers I've told you about, Charlie is the most dangerous, and Big Larry is running a close second."

"Yes Sir, Batts nodded understandingly.

Within the next two minutes, the parking lot was empty. They got out and walked toward the red brick building. Batts pulled on the black painted door, but it was locked. Price yelled, then kicked on the door, "Open this door Big Dan, you know we're out here." The door opened instantly; the smooth sound of Charlie "Yardbird" Parker was blaring.

Dan's plastered-on smile faded, when he saw Price; he tried to muster another. "Come in Boss."

"Why did the boys leave so fast?" Price asked suspiciously.

Dan swallowed and tried to maintain his composure. "Boss, you know the boys get nervous when the police come around; won't doing nothing but talking." Dan was now smiling from ear to ear.

Price and Batts walked in. They first walked behind the long bar, their image showing on a mirror that ran the bar's length. They walked down the hall, bypassing Dan's office in favor of a storage room at the end. Price opened the door and peeped in; he looked back at Dan, then pushed it wide open and smiled. Boxes were stacked on the floor in a corner of the room. "What's that Dan? That wouldn't be whisky, would it? If it is, you could go back to prison, you know that." Dan didn't answer; he dropped his head and massaged the back of his neck. Price closed the door and walked back up the hall to Dan's office; Batts and Dan were walking behind him. Price stopped in front of Dan's office door. "I think we need to talk. What do you think Big Dan?" Dan nodded, extending his hand toward the office door; Price opened it and walked in. He walked behind Dan's desk, sat down and propped his feet up. "You Boys grab a chair." Batts was smiling, Dan was sweating. They got a chair and sat in front of the desk. Dan closed his eyes. Price stared at him for a moment and lit a cigarette. "I got a tip, you saw some white men at Rose's house the night she was killed." Smoke was coming from his mouth and nostrils.

Dan shifted in his seat before answering. "I ain't seen nothing," he said scratching his head. "How did you hear some bullshit like that? I ain't never been to Rose's house. Somebody told you a lie. I didn't leave the club that night she was killed."

Price shot from his chair, dropped his cigarette and as fast as Dan could blink, Price was in his face. "Stand up, you fat piece of shit." He stood over Dan with his fist clinched. He then grabbed Dan by his suit coat and pulled him up, in the same motion, pushed him against the wall. Shock registered in Dan's eyes; his body was shaking with fear. He knew Price would do anything to get the information he needed.

"I didn't just hear it, I got a witness, so don't tell me no damn lie." Price's anger was growing fast. "Now, you listen. I can send Batts to get a search warrant and you'll be in Raleigh before the sun comes up." He was now nose-to-nose with Dan. He pushed Dan again, then let go of his coat. Dan knew the liquor in the storage room was enough to send him back to prison. At the very least, the beer permit that he paid five times the going rate for because of his prison record would be taken.

"I was there," said Dan, breathing deeply through his nostrils. "You know I can't do no more time; I'm too old for that."

Price smiled and nodded, agreeing with Dan. "I know you can't. One of them young bucks would turn your old ass into a housewife. So if you don't tell me everything you know, you're as good as gone."

Sweat was running down Dan's face into his eyes. "I'll tell you what I know." He reached in his coat pocket for a handkerchief to wipe his face.

In a flash, Price had his 38 pointed at Dan; Dan froze. "Don't you ever go in your pocket, when I'm talking to you. That's a good way to get your ass killed."

Dan slowly pulled his hand out. "I was just getting my handkerchief out to wipe my face. I didn't mean nothing."

Price nodded and put his pistol away. "Go head, but don't you ever do that again. To be honest, I don't trust none of you coloreds."

Dan wiped his face, his hand was shaking as he said, "Rose called me about two-thirty, wanting some white whisky. I told her I had sold out, but I had some beer. This is the truth."

Price quickly interjected. "It better be, or you'll be in Central Prison shortly, married to one or them lifers. They don't give a damn about how old and ugly you are."

Dan took a deep breath, and exhaled slowly before continuing. "She asked me if I could bring it over, and said, she would tip me good. I didn't want to tell you because I knew I could lose my permit." Price gave Dan a cold look, but didn't respond.

"When I got to the room, there were four or five white men with her. They asked me if I would have a beer with them, but I told them that I had to get back to the club. One of them gave me twenty dollars and I left, that's all I know. I swear to you Boss, that's all I know."

Price eyed Dan suspiciously. "Did she call any names, or did you hear a name?"

"The only name she called was mine."

"Would you know them, if you saw them again?"

Dan took a little time thinking, then said, "I probably would, but if they killed Rose, you know they would kill me. Dan again wiped sweat from his forehead.

"What did they look like?" Price asked. "Batts, take this down." Batts got a notepad from his pocket and pulled the chair up to the desk, he nodded when he was ready. "Go on Dan," said Price.

"I didn't look at them too good, but I know the two of them that were standing was as tall as you. And the one that gave me the money was blonde, and had a big tattoo on his left shoulder, two crossed pistols; he had his shirt off."

"Did you see a car?"

"No Sir, I didn't even see Rose's car."

"They had a car around there somewhere, or someone dropped them off and came back to get them." He hesitated. "I want you to come to the station and look at some pictures. That's a long shot, but it's the only one I have right now."

Dan looked at Price like he was crazy, as he said, "I don't need to be seen going into the police station. They know my face too." Dan was wiping sweat from his face. "They could be riding down the street and see me going in there; then I'll be just as dead as Rose."

Price ignored Dan's plea. "You get someone to drop you off in the alley off of Douglas Street; it will be good and dark by seven. I'll be waiting for you tomorrow night. Now, if you don't show up, you close up, and the next time I see you, I'll have some handcuffs and a good ass kicking for you." Price was again nose-to-nose with Dan. "Do you understand?"

Dan slowly nodded. "I'll be there."

"I know you will." Price motioned to Batts and headed toward the door, then stopped, turned around and stared at Dan a short moment. "You got ten cases of liquor back there; six gallons in a case, at twenty-five cents a shot. After I figure out your take, we need to talk. You owe us for not taking you to jail. You can afford it; I know you're making a lot of money down here." He turned and walked out before Dan could respond. "I'll see you at seven tomorrow night," he said in a loud voice from the hall.

Dan knew several people on the East Side who paid Price weekly to operate. There were also people on the East Side that worked for Price and he would pay them once a week.

Dreams of success without self-motivation, a tireless work ethic and a strong resolve, are dreams only. When you wake up, it will be too late.
-Algernon McNeil

Chapter 10

June 8, 1952
4:05 P.M.

Light rain covered the windshield, when the detectives drove out of the parking lot onto East Street. They drove three blocks to the intersection of East and Nash Streets and turned right, heading west on Nash. When they got to the corner of Nash and Pettigrew, a black police officer was walking across Pettigrew Street heading west on Nash. Batts looked at Price. "It's raining like hell now; he's going to the station for the shift change. Want to give him a ride?"

Price looked at Batts like he was crazy. "You know better than that. If the Chief wanted them to ride he would give them a car." He rolled his eyes at Batts and quickly changed subjects. "If you put some fear in them, you get as much information as you need." He glanced at Batts. "I don't care if they do kill that ugly spook, as long as I get that white trash off the street. A nigger loving white man and a nigger is the same to me."

A hard driving rain had replaced the sprinkle by the time they reached the Police Station. They got out and ran a short sprint to the side door. Chief Watson and some officers were standing at the front desk, when they walked in. "Sergeant Price," said Watson, motioning for Price to walk over. "These are our new officers; Davis, Pope, Johnson and Farmer." Price exchanged handshakes with each officer, as his name was called. "This is Detective, Sergeant Price and Detective Batts."

Batts exchanged handshakes with the officers. "Please to meet you."

"They start today, on the second and third shift. I think we have a good group here," said Watson smiling.

"They're tall and big enough," said Price.

Watson smiled and nodded. "I agree."

"I need to talk to you, when you get a chance," said Price.

"I'll only be a minute. You and Batts can wait in my office."

"Good luck men," said Price, with a short wave. He and Batts walked toward the chief's office.

A few minutes later Watson walked in. "You must have something new on the case," he said as he sat down behind his desk.

"I have an eye witness, not to the murder, but he saw the men in the room; they were white men."

"From the reports we had, I really thought they were. Who is the witness?"

"Big Dan Williams, he owns the Bluenote on East Street."

Watson smiled widely. "I know Dan, I sent him to prison, and he should be there now; Dan is a dangerous man. Before you came on the force, he killed two men on Stantonsburg Street and got away with it; people were afraid to testify. So don't be fooled by that Uncle Tom grin."

Price nodded in agreement, "I know Dan is dangerous, and he almost got his ass killed today. When we were talking, he went in his pocket to get a handkerchief. I didn't know what he was going to pull out, so I pulled my pistol out. He didn't know it, but he was a gnat's ass away from death."

Watson smiled, "You should have done the world a favor and killed that S.O.B."

Price smiled as he nodded. "Anyway, he said he was in the room between two-thirty and three, and he could identify them if he saw them again. You know, I had to put some fear in him. I told him to come up here to look at some mugshots tomorrow night. We might get lucky."

"We might, but remember what I told you. If he picks out a suspect, I need to know who he is, and who his family is before we move. Understand?" Price nodded. Watson leaned forward in his chair. "C.L. Washington called me again. He said rumors were still going around about white men killing that gal. Some even said it was the Klan, and colored people will protect their families. I don't give a damn about them killing each other, but I don't want them shooting at every white man that cross the tracks, thinking that he's down there to kill them, and that could happen. They're paranoid, that's dangerous."

"To be honest Chief, I don't think there's much of a chance that he'll pick out a mugshot, but it's the only chance we have. I'll let you know if he does," said Price.

"I think we did enough. After Dan looks at the mugshots, we'll let it go, we did our job. Things should get back to normal in a few days."

"Ok Chief."

The chief stood up and got his hat. "I'll be glad when this shit blows over." They walked out together.

Chapter 11

January 8, 1952
11:30 P.M.

Smooth jazz was blaring as usual at the Bluenote. Patrons lined the long bar from end-to-end and most of the booths and tables were filled. When the front door opened, a tall, well-built man stepped inside and said in a loud voice, overriding the music. "Big Dan, someone outside wants to see you."

"You tell that nigga to come in here. I ain't going out there in the rain."

"It not raining and it looks like a white man," the man said, walking toward the bar.

Dan stood there for a moment. His big dark face showing signs of surprise and fright. He was thinking it was one of the white men that were at Rose's house. He reached under the bar, pulled out his .38 special and put it in his right front pocket. He got his suit coat off the coat rack and reluctantly walked toward the front door, putting his coat on as he walked. He pushed the door open and walked outside. A street light provided the only light for the parking lot that was full of rain-filled potholes. Car lights flashed near the fence to his right. Dan turned his suit coat collar up and walked toward the car, ignoring the pot holes, but trying desperately to see the occupant. The street light didn't provide enough help, so he lowered his head.

"You don't need to see nothing, Nigger," a voice said from inside the car.

Dan stood straight up. He didn't see a face, but he saw a large, nickel-plated pistol held by a white hand, pointing at his stomach. "Yes Sir." He was now looking up into the cold, black sky. His heart was threatening to jump out of his chest and his knees began to shake; he fought the urge to flee.

"I know, you've been talking to the police."

"Yes Sir, Boss, but I didn't tell them a damn thing." Dan's voice was trembling, forcing out the words.

"How did they know you were at Rose's house?"

"Somebody saw my car and told the police I was there. I told them I went there to take her some beer, but she paid me at the door. I swear to you Boss, that's all I told them." Dan was still looking up. "Then, they asked me if I saw a car near the house. I told them I didn't remember."

All was quiet for a moment, for the exception of a car pulling into the parking lot, and the thumping of Dan's heart. After the car parked near the front door of the club, the voice said, "Now you listen good. If I find that you lied to me, I will personally burn that monkey-club down, with your dead body in it. You got that?"

"Yes Sir. You ain't got to worry about that Boss. I ain't telling them a damn thing, nothing." He tried to smile. The car pulled off, spinning tires through the muddy parking lot onto East Street, heading toward Nash Street.

In the silence that followed, Dan stood still and took a deep breath of relief, allowing the fear of death to vanish from his thoughts; making it possible for him to simply put one foot before the other. He walked toward the door, sweat was running down his face; his hands and knees were shaking violently. Sugar Ray Reed, Dan's right hand man was working behind the bar, when Dan returned. Dan motioned for him to come to his office, moments later, Ray walked in. Dan was sitting down behind the desk, still visibly shaken. "Something has come up, serve one more round on me and close up."

"What's wrong?"

"I'll tell you after you close up. Just get them out of here." After Ray left, Dan tried to light a cigarette with little success; his hands were still shaking violently.

About a half an hour later, Ray knocked once and walked in. "Everyone is gone." He paused, looking at Dan. "What in the hell is wrong with you? You look like you just saw a ghost."

Dan's throat became painfully tight with emotion. He glanced at Ray, cleared his throat and responded slowly. "Do you remember when I told you about them white boys at Rose's house the night she was killed? That was one of them outside. They ain't playing around. I thought that white boy was gonna kill me. The whole time we talked, his gun was pointed at my belly. I ain't never felt that scared and helpless in my life."

"What did he say?"

"He wanted to know if I had talked to the police, and what I told them." Dan paused. "Get me a drink, make it a double; I need it." Ray walked out of the office. Dan got up and walked to the window. He stared into the black of night, still not of his usual calm. Ray returned with the drinks. Dan's hand was unsteady as he reached for his drink. "You know that dirty cop, Sergeant Price, don't you?" He sipped on his drink.

Ray frowned before speaking with a degree of anger. "Everybody knows that crook; I'm surprised he ain't dead by now, but sooner or later, somebody will get him. That young nigger that kicked his ass on Nash Street should have killed him then. From what I heard, he damn near did."

Dan nodded agreeing. "He came here today to ask me about Rose. He looked around and saw that liquor in the storage room. He told me if I didn't talk to him, I was going back to jail. After I told him what I saw, he wants me to look at some mugshots at the police station; I'll have to think about that. "

While Dan talked, Ray sipped on his whiskey, appearing attentive. Although he speaks his mind freely, his greatest gift is listening. "I know you don't want too, but you got to meet him. You deal with first things first, just try not to be seen. Then, maybe the other things will fall in place."

Big Dan leaned forward to place his elbows on the desk. "One thing you didn't think about. After Price gets all the information he can, he don't give a damn if they kill me or not. I don't understand why he wants them white boys so bad. He don't give a damn about Rose being dead."

"You're right, but you still have to go, or get out of town. Price would hound you like a dog. You know if they take your beer permit, you'll have to close the club."

Dan leaned back in his chair and thought for a moment before saying, "You're right." He paused to sip on his drink. "If I see all of them white boy's pictures, I ain't telling him shit. As long as he needs me, he'll try to keep me alive. I'm the only one who saw them crackers, so he needs me too." Dan removed the gun from his pocket and put it on the desk. "I'm gonna sleep with this. Them crackers might get me, but it won't be easy."

Now in a more confident mood, Dan contemplated the next day. His problem now was getting in and out of the police station without being seen. "I want you to take me up there about six-thirty; it will be dark by then. I don't want my car to be seen, so we'll go in off Douglas Street, through the alley; I'll walk from there. I'll probably be in there about a half an hour, so you wait for me. As black as I am, nobody can see me dressed in all black." They both grinned and sipped their whiskey. "I think that white boy in the parking lot was the one who gave me the money at Rose's house, the one with the blonde hair and them big pistols tattooed on his shoulder. He didn't kill me, that was his mistake. If I get a chance, I'll blow his brains out."

Ray sipped his drink before speaking. "I know you're angry, but you have to think about the best way to deal with this. Killing a white man is different from killing a Negro, even in self-defense."

Dan interrupted. "What am I supposed to do, just let them kill me?"

"No, I'm not saying that. What I'm saying is, you lead with your brain, not your gun. You got to protect yourself, but you think before you act."

Dan sipped his drink, lowered his head and looked at Ray under-eyed. "You're half-ass right, Sugar, but I had rather face a judge for killing one of them crackers, than to be laid face up at Edwards Funeral Home". Ray slowly shook his head and smiled.

Chapter 12

January 9, 1952
12:20 A.M.

Rose's funeral was set for Thursday. Maggie talked with C.L., and they agreed not to open the coffin because of the boys. She asked him to talk with the Howards about buying Rose's car, house and furniture.

Ronnie and Butch were sitting on the floor beside Maggie's bed watching television, when she walked in and playfully rubbed the top of Butch's head. He responded by putting his hands on top of hers, followed by a short giggle. Maggie smiled warmly and sat down on her bed. "I want y'all to sit up here beside me, so we can talk a minute. Ronnie, you turn the TV off. After we talk, I'll fix dinner and y'all can look at TV again."

After they were seated on each side of Maggie, she put her arms around them and kissed Butch, then Ronnie softly on their foreheads. She then closed her eyes in a short, silent prayer. After a moment or so, she turned her attention to Ronnie. "Ronnie, what is the first thing we do in the morning when we get up, and the last thing we do at night before we go to sleep?"

Ronnie thought for a moment, and smiled. "We pray Miss Maggie."

Maggie smiled and nodded. "That's right. We pray because we love God and He loves us, and we thank Him for everything. Is that right?" She looked from one to the other as they nodded. "Now, we know that God loves us, but He sometimes do things that hurt us, but God don't make mistakes." She hesitated and took a deep breath. "God took your mama because He wanted her to be with Him. I can't tell you why, but I can tell you this. Y'all be good like Rose always said, and y'all will see her again one day." Her eyes were slowly watering, but she fought for control. Butch looked at Maggie through tear filled eyes, and laid his head on her lap. He didn't understand, but he knew his mother was gone. Ronnie stared straight ahead; tears were slowly making their way down his face. "I know it hurts because she ain't here, but remember what I said; God don't make mistakes. We'll keep praying just like we always do, and God will make things alright. He always do."

Butch lifted his head and looked at Maggie. He began wiping his eyes with the back of his hand. "Miss Maggie, how long will it be before we see mama again?"

Maggie smiled and pulled him close to her. "I can't answer that Butch, but you will, and I'll be right there with y'all." Maggie held them as they sat in silence for a moment. "Now, I don't want y'all to worry about nothing, cause you know I love you, and you know I'll take care of you. Mr. and Mrs. Howard are going to help us, cause they love y'all too." Maggie stood up and faced the boys. "All right," she said playfully. "We're gonna eat our food, then go to Mr. Kirby's store and get some ice cream, but y'all got to eat all the vegetables. Now remember what I said, don't worry about nothing. With God's help and Mr. and Mrs. Howard helping us, everything is going to be all right. Now let's eat so we can go and get some ice cream." Butch and Ronnie managed a slow smile through their teary eyes. They both nodded.

Chapter 13

January 9, 1952
1:46 P.M.

Maggie was sitting in her living room recuperating from her walk to the store, when there was a knock at the door. "Come in," she said after a deep breath.

Virginia opened the door and walked in; forty plus but looking not a day over thirty. "Surprise, I took a personal day off. The basketball team is playing Durham-Hillside tonight, in Durham. Sam asked me to tell you and the boys' hello and he'll see you tomorrow. How are the boys?"

Maggie took a deep breath and lowered her head. "They're full of pain and very confused. I told them that their mother was with God and one day they will see her again. It hurts me to see them hurt so bad. They don't understand, especially Butch; he cries for his mother a lot. I heard him crying last night, so I went in their room to check on him. Ronnie was holding Butch and was crying himself." Maggie took a handkerchief from her apron pocket and wiped the tears running down her face. "Bless their little hearts."

Virginia's eyes were now drenched. "I know it's hard on you and the boys, but God will make a way, he always does."

"Come and sit down," said Maggie, trying to compose herself. They both sat on the couch, Virginia held Maggie's hand. "Mr. Washington called this morning. He wanted us to view the body tomorrow, but I told him since the coffin will be closed we didn't need to do that. He also said he would give a fair price for the car, furniture and house. I told him to talk to you and your husband about that."

"That's fine; Sam and I will see him tomorrow."

"I don't know what I would do without you and your husband. Everything has worked out so far. The only thing that bothers me now is what to do about Ronnie and Butch."

Virginia patted her hand. "Don't worry Mrs. Wade, Sam and I have discussed that, but we'll talk with you and the boys after the funeral." She smiled and put Maggie's hand between hers, gently rubbing the top. "Just don't worry, it will be alright." They were both quiet for a moment, then Virginia said, "What are the boys doing?"

Maggie snapped out of a short daze. "After I talked with them, we had dinner, and walked to the store to get some ice cream. After they ate their ice cream, they went out like a light. I'm still trying to catch my breath after that walk." She smiled.

"Tell them I came by and we'll see them tomorrow. If you need anything before then, you have our number." Virginia was walking toward the door.

Maggie stood and walked behind her. "I thank you and your husband for everything y'all are doing to help us; bless your heart."

Virginia patted Maggie's hand. "You are very welcome, now don't worry. I told you everything was going to work out, and they will."

"I hope so. All I want is for them boys to be all right."

"They will." Virginia opened the door. "We'll see you and the boys tomorrow. Don't forget to tell them I said hello."

Chapter 14

January 9, 1952
3:15 P.M.

"Lawyer Washington, the Chief can see you now." The desk officer stood up and pointed toward the Chief's office. "It's at the end of the hall."

"I know where it is, thank you." Washington walked toward the Chief's office, carrying a brown leather briefcase. He wore a wool, camel coat over a brown suit, white shirt and brown silk tie. In the early 40's, while attending N.C. A&T, Washington was twice crowned the heavyweight boxing champion of the CIAA, and still looked to be in boxing condition. He boxed as a pro briefly while attending law school at Georgetown University.

The Chief's office door was open, so he knocked on the door frame. Watson stood up and attempted to tuck his shirt tail in over his bare-belly. "Lawyer Washington, come in." Watson extended his hand. "How are you?"

Washington shook Watson's hand as he said, "I'm fine, and you?"

"I'm all right, but I don't have any more information about Rose Grant's murder. I wish I did, but nothing has come up yet. Have a seat."

Washington sank into one of two straight-backed chairs in front of Watson's desk, and placed his briefcase in the other. He looked over the black rim of his glasses. "That's not why I'm here Chief. I want to talk with you about the murder at the Sinclair Station on Highway 301. And from what I've learned, that's exactly what it was, murder, manslaughter at best."

Watson sat up in his chair, took a pack of Camel cigarettes from his shirt pocket and shook one out. "I have the report and the gun used in the robbery. Do you want to see it?" He lit his cigarette.

Washington took his horn-rimmed glasses off before he spoke. "I read the article in the newspaper, so the report probably wouldn't tell me anything different. But let me tell you something I know." Washington shifted in his chair and crossed his legs. "I knew Earl Cooper for twenty years or more. He worked two jobs and was a Deacon in his church. He was a family man and has never been in any trouble. He wasn't well off by any means, but he worked hard and managed to save some money. Now, does that sound like a man that would try to rob someone?"

Watson shook his head in agreement, then took a long pull on his cigarette before answering, "No, it don't sound that way, but I didn't know him personally; I can only go by the report. Detective Price was the investigator. Do you want to talk with him?"

Washington blew out a long, frustrated breath and put his glasses back on. I'll talk with him, but I know about his reputation."

Watson didn't respond to Washington's statement, but said, "I think he's in the station, I'll get him." Watson called the front desk and a few minutes later, Price knocked on the office door. "Come on in Sergeant Price. Lawyer Washington wants to talk to you about the Sinclair Station case. Have a seat."

Price nodded, as Washington was moving his briefcase out of the chair. Washington didn't respond to Prices nod, but spoke quickly. "I told the Chief about what I personally knew about Earl Cooper, and it's not adding up with what was reported." Price started to respond, but Washington stopped him with a wave of his hand. "Wait, let me finish. I did some investigating myself and I know that Billy Roy Bass is the brother of Judge Bud Bass."

"The report I gave was what was told to me. I don't care who Billy Roy's brother is." He pulled out a cigarette and lit it. "I did my job and reported the best I could, that's it."

Washington detected a bit of nervousness in Price's voice. He gazed deeply into his eyes as he leaned forward. "Let me tell you something, Sergeant Price. I talked to Jimmy Cooper and he tells a very different story. The story he tells is more like the Earl Cooper

I knew for twenty years or more, but you probably don't remember him. Am I right?"

Price looked uncomfortable as he answered, "No, I don't know him."

Washington smiled. "I didn't think you did, but I'm not going to argue that point. I know what happened, and you know I know."

Watson's eyes drifted between Washington and Price. "Who in the hell is Jimmy Cooper?"

Washington responded quickly, still smiling, "Since Price, I'm sorry about that. Since Detective Price doesn't remember Jimmy, I'll answer that Chief." He glanced at Price. "Jimmy was with Earl when he was killed; he's Earl's cousin. They went in the Sinclair Station to buy a can of brake fluid. After Earl bought the fluid, Billy Roy refused to put it in his car, like he would if a white person was buying it. Earl asked for his money back; that's when Billy Roy got angry and shot him. During the investigation, Detective Price learned that Billy Roy was the brother of Judge Bass, so he told Jimmy to get out of town, and he would shoot him on sight if he saw him again. Jimmy left Wilson the same day and called me a few days later."

Price held still as long as he could, then pushed his chair back and stood up, he was fuming. "That's a damn lie!"

"Sit down Sergeant," shouted Watson. Price was slow in responding. "I said sit down." Price slowly sat back in his chair, but kept his eyes on Washington.

"First of all, Detective Price, you standing up, trying to look tough, doesn't scare me. Don't let this suit and tie fools you; I know how to take care of myself." He smiled and nodded once as a show of confidence. "Secondly, it's the truth and I'm going to do everything I can to prove it. I know about your reputation. A Negro's life doesn't mean anything to you. The old saying goes, "Ain't nothing but a dead nigger." And that's the way you think." Washington hesitated for short moment, then said, "If I have to go to Raleigh for help, I will." Price didn't move a muscle; he just sat there looking straight ahead.

The room fell dead silent before Watson said, "Lawyer Washington, you're saying, Jimmy Cooper is the man that got away. Is that right?"

"That's half-right Chief. He didn't get away, Detective Price ran him away, out of town."

Price broke his silence, "If you know where Jimmy Cooper is, you need to tell us. He was involved in an attempted armed robbery. You could get in trouble for that."

Washington shot right back, as he said, "Detective Price, you're supposed to be enforcing the law and you don't even know the law. I'm licensed by the North Carolina Bar Association, and Jimmy Cooper is my client. You figure out the rest." Washington stood up and grabbed his briefcase. "I'll get to the bottom of this, one way or the other. You gentlemen have a good day." He started to walk out, then said, "Chief Watson, Jimmy said that your officers found Earl's money. Detective Price put the money in his pocket and said that he would get the money to Earl's wife. I checked with her; she never got it. He also said that it was over two-hundred dollars." He stared at Price. "You gentlemen have a good day." He smiled, did a phony bow toward Price and left.

Heat rose in Watson's face. His complexion turned crimson with anger. He got up and turned his back to Price, looking out of the big window behind his desk. Price looked very uncomfortable, bracing himself for the worst. After a minute or so Watson sat back down; his eyes widened and his anger flared. "That Mississippi, bull-shit you got in your head that all colored people are stupid, is a myth. If you had half the brain that Washington has, we wouldn't be in here now, and I believe everything he said." He hesitated and gave Price a stern look. His thick gray eyebrows came together above the rim of his wire-frame glasses. "Running Jimmy Cooper out of town was stupid. You knew if the case went to court, Billy Roy would walk out a free man. Now, I don't give a damn about that nigger being killed, but you lied to me when I asked you about it. I'll ask you again, and if you stick to your story, I'll call Billy Roy. If he tells me something different, you put your gun and badge on my desk and get your stupid ass out of this building, and don't come back."

Price couldn't say anything for a moment or so, He just shook his head. "Lawyer Washington was right, Chief."

Watson stared at him for a long moment, and said, "If you're thinking about getting a warrant for Jimmy Cooper, your best bet is to forget it. Washington would chew you up and spit you out in court. You screwed-up enough, so let it go, I mean, let it go."

Price got up and attempted to speak. "Chief I'm......"

Watson cut him off. "I don't want to hear shit, just get your dumb-ass out of my office. And pay-day, you take that money to Washington's office. I'll check with him to make sure you did. If you don't pay it back, don't you come back. And I see you didn't learn anything from that ass-kicking you took from that nigger on Nash Street. Some of them niggers don't give a damn about you or your gun. Washington looks like he can take care of himself. So you keep jumping at them niggers, you'll learn, after one of them breaks your damn neck. Now get out." Price dropped his head and walked toward the door. Watson walked behind him and slammed the door after he walked out.

Chapter 15

January 9, 1952
6:30 P.M.

The night had turned damp and cold. Sugar Ray pulled into the driveway at Big Dan's house; a single family, three bedroom house on Cemetery Street. Ray was called Sugar Ray because of his Hollywood good looks; tall, thin, with smooth, dark brown skin. Dan made no serious business or personal decisions without Ray's approval. Ray blew the horn, and Dan was out in a matter of seconds. "It's cold out here," said Dan as he got into the car, dressed in all black.

Ray broke into a huge smile and jokingly said, "If you close your eyes and mouth, they couldn't find you with a searchlight."

"This is one time in my life I'm happy to be coal black." They shared a brief glance and smile, as Ray backed onto the street. They drove the short block to South Pender Street. At the stop sign they turned left, heading north on Pender toward downtown. Dan turned his coat collar up around his thick neck and the brim of his black hat down over his dark face, as they turned into the alley off of Douglas Street. "You can wait for me here Ray; this won't take but a few minutes." Dan reached in his coat pocket and pulled out his gun. "I don't want to take this in there," handing the gun to Ray.

"Wait one second." Ray switched the interior lights out.

Dan got out and walked toward the police station. He looked rattled as he walked through the side door. The officer at the desk stared at Dan, then asked, "What you want, Boy? Who you looking for?"

Dan glared at the officer before answering. "I'm here to see Sergeant Price."

"Sergeant Price, a colored boy is out here to see you."

The door to the file room swung open. Price walked out and motioned to Dan. "Down here." He looked at his watch. "I knew I could count on you." His crimson face was smiling at Dan as he escorted him to another room beyond his office. Case files and mugshot books lined the walls. This room doubled as an interview room, where a black man was shot to death, after he reportedly attacked an officer with a knife. He had been under arrest for assault on an officer. There was little or no investigation into the incident, and no outside investigation. The case was quickly closed.

"Come in and sit down." Price pulled out a chair.

"Thank you." Dan flopped his near three-hundred pounds down.

Price placed some books in front of him. "Scan through these, see what you can find." Dan and Price sat across from each other.

Dan took the book off the top and pushed the others aside. The book was marked, white photos. He began to turn the pages, pretending his focus on each photo. After he looked through most of the book, he said, "I don't see anything yet."

"I knew it would be a long shot, but keep looking, we might get lucky."

Dan looked through the books another fifteen minutes. When he finished the last book, he said, "One of them white men came to my club last night. I'm not sure, but I think it was the same one that gave me the money; the one with the blond hair and tattoo. I thought he was going to kill me."

Dan's words got Price's full attention. "What happened?"

"I was told a white man wanted to see me in the parking lot. You know how dark East Street is. I couldn't see his face that good, but I saw the blond hair, and he made sure I saw that gun pointed at me. He told me, if I gave any information to the police, he was going to burn my club down, with my dead body inside."

"What kind of car was he on?"

Dan shot Price a crazy look. "You heard me say I thought he was gonna kill me. I didn't see nothing but that big gun and a white hand. They ain't playing around. I took a hell of a chance coming up here. If one of them sees me, I'm a dead man."

Dan leaned forward and pushed the books back. He put his elbows on the table and dropped his head in the palms of his hands. Price got up and walked to the door. "Officer Anderson, would you come down here for a minute?" He yelled to the officer at the desk.

A few seconds later the officer walked in. "Can I help you Sergeant?"

"Who's working the Eastside tonight?"

Anderson thought a moment before answering, "Officer Roberts and one of the new officers." He paused. "I think his name is Johnson."

"Tell them to come in. I want them to ride by the club on East Street every now and then. If they see any white men in that area, I want them to stop that car and get some ID; make sure they record their name and address. Pass this on to the midnight shift."

"Yes Sir," said Anderson. He turned and walked out.

"Oh Anderson," said Price.

Anderson reappeared. "Yes Sir."

"Tell the officers not to go in the parking lot, just circle the block."

"Yes Sir, I will."

Dan was reluctant to speak, but thinking about the threat on his life hit a nerve. "I know if I get caught with a gun, I'm going to jail. But I'd rather the police catch me with it, than them white men to catch me without it."

There was an uneasy silence in the room, then Price said, "You do what you need to do."

Dan looked relieved and somewhat surprised. "Can I go now?"

Price hesitated and stared at Dan before speaking, "Yes, but one more thing. I did some adding and you're making a lot of money off of that liquor. I think about fifty dollars a week would be fair, to you and me." He paused. "I'll see you on Monday, every Monday."

Dan looked stone-faced, then nodded. "Ok."

The air was filled with thick cigarette smoke, when Dan got back to the car. "How did it go?" Ray asked.

Ray's words, though delivered kindly, stung. "I told that cracker

I was gonna keep my gun on me," said Dan with a degree of anger.

Ray reached across Dan and got his gun from the glove compartment. "What did he say?"

"What could he say? If I can't protect myself, then I need to do like you said, get out of town. Now, I got to pay that cracker fifty-dollar a week to keep selling liquor. Somebody needs to kill him."

Chapter 16

January 9, 1952
7:35 P.M.

Ray drove back through the alley to Douglas Street, turned left, then a right onto Green Street. Mercy Hospital was in the next block near the intersection of Green and North Pender. East Green Street was where the affluent blacks lived. The street was lined with large, two story houses. Expensive cars occupied the driveways and were parked along the tree-lined street. Booker T. Washington made several trips to Wilson after the turn of the century as a house guest of educator, Sam Vick, a Green Street resident. "If we had half of the money on this street, we wouldn't need no club and could live damn good," said Ray. A cigarette was hanging from the corner of his mouth.

Dan looked at Ray and grinned. "If we had some of this money, I would go to New York and hire a professional hit man to kill that cracker Price. But like you said Sugar Ray, somebody will, sooner or later."

They drove the two, long blocks heading east on Green Street, then made the first right turn onto North Vick Street. Two more right turns and they were in the parking lot at the club. There were a few cars waiting for the club to open. Dan glanced around the parking lot as the head lights made the parked cars visible. They parked at the front entrance; Ray got out first to unlock the door. When Ray opened the door, Dan got out and quickly walked in, gun in hand. "Man, I can't live like this, wondering if one of them cracker will try to kill me." He looked agitated.

"We'll talk about this later; go in the office and relax," said Ray.

The smell of stale beer and cigarette smoke filled the air. When Ray turned the lights on patrons walked in and began to line the long bar. Dan sat at his desk emotionally spent, when the telephone rang. "Hello." He listened, then said, "I'll send Sugar Ray to get you, he should be there in about twenty minutes. Ray," he yelled. "I need to see you for a second."

"What do you need?" Ray asked, walking in the office.

"Ruth's car won't start and she needs a ride. You know what cold weather does to old men and old cars."

"All right, when I get back, I want to talk to you about something that might help you."

Dan was working the bar, when Ruth and Ray returned, about thirty-five minutes later. Ruth Richardson was a tall, half- white, attractive woman from Spring Hope, about fifteen miles west of Wilson. She worked as a secretary in a doctor's office during the week, and part-time at the Bluenote on Tuesday and Thursday nights, and weekends. "Redbone, I told you Ray would buy you a car, if you act right," said Dan smiling.

Ruth responded quickly. "They don't call him Sugar Ray for nothing." She hung her coat on the rack. "He has too many women for me." She looked back at Ray and smiled. Ray smiled, his pearl white teeth highlighting his smooth dark skin. "Lady Day" Billie Holiday was blaring as Dan and Ray walked toward the office.

"I touched those pretty legs when we were coming back," said Ray smiling.

"What did she say?"

"You know just about what she said; she don't want no part of me. I've been trying to get with her since she started working here. She ain't gonna let me near her." He unfolded a chair and sat down in front of Dan's desk, his expression immediately changed. "You know Dan, this city don't give a damn about nothing on this side of the track." Ray's tone of voice and expression got Dan's attention.

"What are you talking about Man?"

"There was a house about three of four houses down from Ruth's that had burned down to the ground." Ray spoke with a degree of sadness.

"How did it start?"

"I don't know, but they said a freight train had stopped on the tracks and the fire truck couldn't get across. There are two or three Fire Stations across town and not a damn one over here." Ray paused and shook his head. "This isn't the first time this has happened, and until they put a fire station down here, it won't be the last. There were five people in that family standing out in the cold, no place to go. Right now, incidents like this are the norm, rather than the exception for Negroes in Wilson and the south; this has to change."

Dan had a look of disgust. "They were lucky tonight, nobody got killed, but sooner or later it will happen." He paused and shook his head. "When you go back out, ask Ruth who the family is, so I can donate some money; maybe that will help them."

"All right, I'll donate some myself, but here's what I wanted to talk with you about. You know it's better to be safe than sorry. Those white boys are not playing, and that ass-kicking cop doesn't give a damn if you live or die. You need someone to watch your back, and I know the right person that could do it, if he would."

Dan sat up in his chair and leaned forward. "Who are you talking about?"

"Do you remember that tall, big dude that told you about the white boy outside?"

"I remember, but I don't know him. I've seen him in here a few times before, but I've never talked with him."

"His name is John Blue and he lives in Elm City. I don't know if this is true or not, but they say he works on a farm all day, then walks to Wilson to have a few beers. After that, he walks back to Elm City."

Dan smiled broadly. "That's a walking man; Elm City is seven miles from here."

"The newspaper said that he was the only Negro in a special combat unit in Korea. He received the Silver Star and a bunch of other medals. The way they talk, he is one big bad brother. He comes in here and has a few beers; shoot pool and leaves." Ray smiled. "I was talking to a guy from Elm City one night; he knows Blue. He said that he worked on the farm with him for a while. I don't know if this nigger was drunk or just plain lying, but he said that Blue got pissed-off about something one day and hit a mule, right between his eyes with his fist. He said the poor mule fell to his knees and rolled over like he was brain dead, he didn't move; knocked out cold."

Tears began rolling out of Dan's eyes; his big bellie was shaking in laughter. "That nigger won't during nothing but lying; can't no nigger knock no mule out." Dan was still laughing and barely got the words out.

Ray was laughing too as he said, "I said the same thing, but Frank, the guy that told me, called another guy from Elm City to the bar, and he said the same thing. He said that Blue damn near killed that mule; the mule was brain damaged."

Dan's laughter had calmed down, but kicked back up again as he said, "If I ever meet Blue, I will damn sure ask him about it." He wiped the tears away with the back of his hand. They both calmed as Dan said, "Do you ever talk with him?"

"No, but he seems friendly enough. You said you wanted a bouncer on the weekends, and I'm sure that his white boss don't pay him no more than twenty or twenty-five dollars a week. We can pay him a little more than that. I'm sure; he had rather look at these pretty women around here, than smell cow shit all day. I can watch your back, but I'm no killer. From what I heard, John Blue will kill you, no question about it."

Dan got up and walked around his office thinking about what Ray said. He walked back behind his desk and sat down. "I know you're right Sugar, but I need to think about this." He hesitated. "The next time he comes in here, we'll talk with him. But I don't know if I want a crazy man like that around me with a gun." Dan's solid gold tooth sparkled as he smile.

"I'm around a crazy man, with a gun every day," said Ray, playful ly. They were both smiling as Ray walked out.

Later that evening, Ray and Ruth were busy working the bar; every seat was occupied from end-to-end. The front door opened, John Blue walked in and lowered his head to avoid a collision with the door frame; dressed in dark grey pants, a blue sweater, and a navy pea coat. He stopped, casually swinging his eyes around the club, then walked toward the end of the bar near Dan's office. Ruth walked over, removed the empty beer bottles and began wiping the counter in front of him. She smiled at the tall, good looking man, then said, "May I help you?"

"Yes, I would like a beer, it doesn't matter what kind," Blue said in a low strong voice, his dark eyes were showing mutual attraction to Ruth.

Ray saw John Blue and immediately walked from behind the bar toward Dan's office. He knocked once, then opened the door. Dan was sitting behind the desk; his chair pushed against the wall. There was a woman sitting on his lap. "I told you to lock that damn door," said Dan, to the woman. "Ray, just give me five minutes." Sweat was running down his face.

Ray smiled, backed out and closed the door; he walked behind the bar and stood directly in front of Blue. After he emptied the ashtray and wiped the counter, he asked, "Would You like another beer?"

Blue took a short sip from his beer. "Yes, thank you; after I finish this one."

Ray extended his hand and smiled. "My name is Ray Reed; my friends call me Sugar Ray. What's yours?"

"John Blue," he said, shaking Ray's hand.

Ray pretended to be totally ignorant of Blue's existence, when he asked, "Where are you from?"

Blue chugged his beer before answering, "Elm City. I'll have that beer now."

Ray took the empty bottle off the counter and replaced it. "This one is on me."

Blue stared at Ray for a second, then said in a cold strong voice,

"Look man, I don't know who you think you're talking too, but if you're a faggot trying to pick me up, you're talking to the wrong man. I'll pull you over that bar and break these fifteens off in your little, boney ass."

Ray stepped back from the bar, arms extended, palms facing Blue. "I didn't mean any harm man, just trying to be friendly. I've bought a lot of people beers before. I'm sorry you took it that way." He was looking up at the six-foot five strong man. "Big Dan, my boss, wants to talk with you about a possible job."

Blue looked around the club, and then said, "I have a job." He was still not sure of Ray's intentions.

Ray was quick to respond. "Well, it sure wouldn't hurt to talk with him."

Blue looked away, hesitated for a moment. "Where is he?"

Ray took a deep breath, showing a sign of relief. "He's in his office, but he'll be out in about five or ten minutes." Blue nodded and walked to the front of the bar where there was now an empty stool.

A short time later, the door to Dan's office opened; a short, chubby woman walked out ahead of Dan and headed toward the lady's room; Dan to the men's room. When Dan emerged from the men's room he yelled, "Sugar Ray," then motioned with his hand.

Ray promptly walked from behind the bar to Dan's office. "First of all, you need to air this place out; it smells like leftover love in here." Big Dan smiled; Ray smiled. "Secondly, I should tell your old lady on you. You dirty old man."

"I didn't do nothing," said Dan, still smiling.

"The truth will set you free," said Ray.

"You're right Sugar, but a lie can sometimes save your ass."

Ray smiled and shook his head as he said, "The demolition man is out there."

"Bring him back here."

"You know, that big nigger went off on me; thought I was trying to pick him up."

"You do look sweet Ray, and they call you Sugar. What is a man suppose to think?" Dan was smiling. They both smiled as Ray walked out, giving Dan the middle finger before closing the door. A few minutes later, Ray knocked once and walked in. Blue walked in behind him, again ducking his head under the door frame. Ray got two folding chairs and placed them in front of Dan's desk. Dan stood up, extending his arm across the desk. "My name is Dan Williams; my friends call me, Big Dan. What's yours?"

"John Blue. My friends call me, Big Blue," he said, shaking Dan's hand.

"Have a seat. I want to talk with you about working here as my security. I need a good man to work here and double as my bodyguard. Whatever you make on your job now, I'll beat that by twenty dollars a week."

Blue looked at Ray, then looked back at Dan. "Why do you need a bodyguard?"

"Did you hear about the woman that was killed last week on Carroll Street?"

"Yes, I heard about it."

"Well, I saw the crackers that killed her. When you called me to the door, that was one of them in the parking lot; they mean business. Now, if you're afraid of white people."

Blue interrupted, his eyes narrowed. "I ain't afraid of nothing and no one."

"Calm down, I just wanted to know. It don't make no sense to get you and me killed." There was a short moment of silence; Blue gave Dan a cold look.

"Are you married? Dan asked.

"No. Why do you want to know?"

"If you take the job, you can live in the trailer behind my house. How much do you make a week?"

"About twenty-five dollars."

"Well, how does fifty sound to you?"

Blue looked at Ray, and then back at Dan, "I'll take it."

"Welcome to the Bluenote," said Ray smiling. Blue nodded and smiled.

Dan reached down and pulled out the bottom left, desk drawer. He then pulled out a long barrel, .44 Magnum in a shoulder holster. "If you have to shoot one of them crackers, I want him to be gone. This…," he said, pulling the gun out of the holster, "will send him where he needs to go." Dan then reached to his right and pulled a cashbox from the desk drawer. He opened it, counted out two-hundred dollars and gave it to Blue. "Tomorrow, I want you to go uptown and buy two or three nice suits, white shirts and ties. Make sure the coat is big enough so the gun can't be seen."

"Where in the hell can you find a coat that big?" said Ray. They all laughed.

Dan looked straight at Blue and spoke in a serious tone. "Look Blue, them white boys ain't playing around. They will kill me, you and anyone else to stay out of jail. Unless you're willing to do the same, you need to walk out of here, right now, and I'll understand."

"I'll do what I have to do. It won't be the first time I killed a man."

Dan didn't show any reaction. He tipped his chair back and put his feet on the desk. He was impressed, but remained expressionless. Dan got a pen and a piece of paper off his desk and began to write. "This is the numbers to my house and the club. When you finish shopping tomorrow, you call me." Blue nodded, got up and walked toward the door. "Let me ask you something before you leave." Big Dan started smiling. Ray started to smile; he knew what the question was.

Blue looked at Dan, and then said, "What is it?"

"Somebody told me that, you knocked a mule out cold, with your fist. Is that true?"

Blue smiled for a long moment, but didn't respond. He waved his hand and walked out.

Dan slowly shook his head, smiling. "Just as sure as my name is

Daniel Williams Jr., that big nigger knocked that mule out. It was all over his face." Ray nodded in agreement. Dan turned his attention to Sugar Ray. "What do you think Ray?" Do you think he'll be alright?"

"If I had a problem, that's who I'd want with me. John Blue will kill, right now, and wouldn't blink an eye." Ray sat up in his chair and cleared his throat. "Look Dan, I don't think you're being realistic."

"What do you mean?"

"I'm convinced, when that white boy came to see you last night, he came to kill you. The only reason he didn't was because he didn't know if Blue could identify him or his car, or not. You got to understand, you're the only one that can send them to prison, and they don't know what you told the police." Dan's face stiffened as Ray talked with a degree of certainty. Ray continued. "You got a little money and a prison record. They know if they kill you the case will be closed the next day. The police ain't gonna investigate jack-shit." Dan sat back in his chair; his expression was blank, nothing in his eyes. Ray continued. "Whatever he said to you outside, the number here is in the phone book; he could have called to tell you that. And I'm sure, they know where you live by now. You need to be real careful."

Dan nodded and now seemed a little jittery. "I guess I was thinking that way, but I didn't want to face the facts. I don't need to take no chances. I know now, these people will do anything, they're dangerous." He sat there, his mind lingering between anger and fright. He now realized everything Ray said was true, and Blue was his lifeline. Even with Blue watching his every move, his life still hung in the balance.

Chapter 17

January 11, 1952
4:30 P.M.

The driver from Washington Funeral Home got out of the black limo and opened the back door, extended his hand to help Maggie out; Ronnie and Butch, then Sam and Virginia followed. Maggie walked in the house and flopped down in the chair near the picture window; out of breath from her walk up the steps. "Ronnie, go in the back and change your clothes and help your little brother. Ok?" She was speaking in between short breaths. Butch and Ronnie walked out without saying a word. Their little faces showing obvious pain from attending their mothers' funeral.

Virginia watched the boys leave the room before speaking.

"I asked Reverend Powell to make the service short, so the boys wouldn't have to go through any unnecessary pain; I thought he did a good job. Everything went as planned and the good news is, it's over. Now, we can concentrate on getting the boys settled."

Maggie had to swallow to get rid of the lump in her throat. "I can't tell you much of what Reverend Powell was saying because I was thinking about the boys. I love them boys and if I was younger, I would keep them right here with me."

Virginia smiled. "Remember when I told you, Sam and I would talk to you after the funeral."

"Yes, I remember."

Virginia was about to say something, then stopped. "You tell her Sam."

Sam put his arm around Virginia, pushing himself closer to her. "Mrs. Wade, Virginia and I would like to adopt the boys, if it's alright with you, and they want to live with us. We have always wanted children, but we never questioned God as to why we didn't have any." He took his arm from around Virginia and took her hand. "You said before that God sent us to you, but you didn't know why. Well, we know why, and why He picked this time for us to have children, and those boys to have a mother and father. God don't make mistakes. He knew this day was coming."

Maggie broke down in a loud display of happiness. "God is good, He is real. He is so good." Her face was in her hands, tears running through her fingers. With her eyes now closed, rocking back and forth, she threw her head back and started to pray, just above a whisper.

Sam gave her a moment or so before speaking. "We went to Washington's law office yesterday. He said he didn't think there would be any problems, since you are their legal guardian. Our house should be finished by the time the papers are ready to be signed. When we move in, we want you to come over and spend some time with us. The boys would like that."

Maggie was smiling. "I talked with them last night. As soon as I told them I was too old to keep them, Ronnie said, "*What about Miss Howard and Mr. Sam.*" So I know they want to live with y'all."

Virginia looked at Maggie seriously, "Now, there is only one problem."

"What's wrong?" Maggie was looking even more serious.

"You'll still have to baby-sit. We're not going to let you off that easy, no way." They all laughed.

Chapter 18

January 12, 1952
11:40 P.M.

Friday nights are usually good at the Bluenote, this one was no different. Dan had the pot holes filled and lights spaced around the parking lot. A trio played smooth jazz as a parade of beautiful women walked to and from the bar area, trying to attract the attention of a potential trick.

Dan walked out of his office and motioned to Sugar Ray and Blue. Dan was sitting behind his desk; his look expressing legitimate danger when they walked in. "I just got a call."

Ray and Blue glanced at each other. "From who and what did they say?" Ray asked.

Dan took a deep breath to calm himself. "It was one of them white boys. He said he knew I had talked to the police at the station, and that was my last chance."

Ray interjected. "Dammit, he didn't need to call now, we already knew that."

Dan thought for a second, and spoke with a sense of urgency. "Blue, the police don't come in this parking lot at night, so if you see a white face out there, I want you to light his ass up; dead men don't talk, so make sure you kill that cracker." He was now bubbling with anger. "Sugar Ray, keep your eyes open in the club. If you see a strange face, keep your eyes on him and let Blue know. They can hire a nigga just like they can a cracker."

Blue nodded, his eyes were cold and intimidating, with his six-foot five, two-hundred and fifty pound frame. "I'll walk outside every half-hour or so. I know what to do."

"All right," said Dan. "Now, get to work." Dan knew the white men were now in an attack mode, and there would be an altercation, probably sooner than later. "Ray, I want you to leave about two or two-thirty, so you can be here to open about mid-day; the boys want to gamble. Me and Blue will take Ruth home."

"Ok Dan, but be careful man, and you need to put some lights around your house too. I'm sure they know where you live by now."

"I've already ordered some for the front and the back. You know how dark Cemetery Street is."

"Now you're thinking," said Ray.

"Ray, one more thing; tell Ruth to tell her half-white cousins from Spring Hope to be careful how they come in the parking lot. I don't want Blue to kill one of them by mistake.

Ray nodded. "Ok."

Chapter 19

January 13, 1952
3:35 A.M.

Ray left the club about two-thirty. Dan and Blue closed up about three and took Ruth home on Moore Street. Blue got out first, when they arrived at Dan's house on Cemetery Street. He walked around the back, his .44 Magnum in his hand. "It's all right." He motion for Dan to get out of the car.

Dan got out quickly and walked toward the house, his gun was in his hand. "Let's have a few drinks before we go to bed."

"All right, let me change my clothes first."

Dan was sitting at his kitchen table with a jar of white lightning, when Blue came from his bedroom. Dan took a sip from his drink and smiled.

"That must be some good liquor to make you smile like that," said Blue.

Dan smiled again before speaking, "It is good, but I was thinking about that dog-ass Price, wanting me to pay him fifty-dollars a week to sell liquor."

Blue looked confused. "That ain't nothing to smile about."

"No, but I was also thinking about how he got his ass kicked one time."

"That probably was funny. Who kicked his ass?"

Dan took another sip from his drink. "I can't think of his name, but he was young, strong and fast, and damn near as big as you. Price is a big, strong cracker, but that young nigger was bigger and stronger than him. It was downtown on Nash Street, in front of Yancy's Drug Store. Price slapped him for some stupid reason, and called him a nigger. The first time he hit Price it sounded like a gunshot. He kicked Price's ass all the way to Pender Street. Every time Price tried to get his gun, that young nigger would hit him. The last time he hit Price, he knocked him down; damn near knocked him out. Price was crawling on all fours trying to get up. He was bleeding from his nose and mouth, and one of his eyes was damn near closed. He looked like he didn't know where he was; he didn't even try to get his gun again. That nigger stood in front of Price and told him to get up. Price couldn't, so he got behind Price and kicked him dead in his ass. He took his gun and left a smoke trail down South Pender Street. I can't say for sure, but I think he was off of Daniel Hill; you know them niggers over there don't play. Anyway, about two weeks later, he mailed the gun back from New York; that was the talk of the town. But if he ever comes back to Wilson, they'll kill him. There are some niggers over here that will turn him in for ten dollars, or to keep Price off of their ass. As soon as he hits town, Price will know."

"You're right, said Blue. I hope he never comes back. If he beat Price's ass that bad, I know they'll kill him. They have killed a Negro before for a lot less than that. They would shoot him down like a dog."

"Yeah, and the funny thing is, Price said it was two men. That nigga kicked his ass so bad, he probably thought it was two of them, but I know, because I was standing right there looking."

They laughed a bunch, while Blue poured himself a drink. "This will help me sleep; I still have dreams about Korea."

"I was too old to go, but I didn't miss a damn thing. I knew several people who got killed over there. "What unit were you in?"

Blue made a pained face and propped against his chair. "I was in the 24th Inf. Reg.; an all Negro unit. Did you ever hear the name, Buffalo Soldier?"

"Yeah, everybody heard about them. They was some bad niggers."

Blue took a sip from his glass before speaking, "That was a damn good unit. For the first two years of the war, we had more Silver Star winners than any white unit in Korea. We had a white commander that made sure we got credit for what we did, but after he got killed, the white people didn't want to give us credit for anything we did.

They said we ran in combat and later disbanded the unit. Most of the men were sent home; I was sent to train with a special unit; I was the only Negro there.

"Why did they put you in that unit with all them white boys?"

Blue shrugged. "Need, they wanted men with proven combat experience; I won the Silver Star. About the same time they were disbanding the 24th, they were putting that new unit together, so they threw me in. We were called the "Death Squad," because we carried out assassinations behind enemy lines. Sometimes we would be out a week, or as long as it took to carry out our mission. Whoever we were sent to kill was dead before we came back. It didn't matter how long it took, he or she had to die."

Dan looked at Blue stunned, eyes wide open. "What! Are you serious?" He was shaking his head smiling. "Ray told me you were dangerous, but he didn't know how dangerous. He had no idea you were a trained killer." He sipped his drink. "If you did that shit, and lived to talk about it, you're a bad nigger." He shook his head. "And y'all killed women too?"

"Yes, some of their best snipers were women."

"Damn, you're a cold blooded nigger."

Blue smiled and continued. "I was sent home after I got hurt. Thinking about how they did us still bothers me today. That's why I got upset when you asked me if I was afraid of white people."

Dan shook his head apologetically. "I'm sorry, I didn't know. I sure as hell don't want no problem with you. You're a damn killer," he said smiling.

A slow smile spread across Blue's face. "That's all right, I'm better now, but when I first came home, I couldn't stand to be around white people. You and Ray probably thought I worked on a white man's farm. Am I right?"

Dan smiled, nodding his head. "Yeah, we did."

Blue beamed a quick smile and shook his head. "No, I worked for a real nice negro family near Elm City; my mother and father lives near their farm." He hesitated and took a deep breath. "I was so full of rage when I came home; my father insisted that I didn't leave the house for a while, and I didn't, for over two months. My father is a minister, a good man, but a stern man." Blue took a sip from his drink. "My sisters and I were brought up under real strict rules. It seems like all we did was go to school, to church, and work on the farm. Our social time was basically spent together as a family. I had a girlfriend when I was in school, but the only time I saw her was at school, or in church. We didn't have a car, so that was it."

Dan smiled. "I pity the first girl you get too. You're going to jail for assault. If I was you, I would get me a good lawyer before I get near a woman, you'll need one."

Blue smiled, shaking his head and continue. "That was hard, but I appreciate it now." He sipped his drink. "My twin sisters were one year older than me. Get this; they finished at St. Aug. in three years, smart as hell." He smiled with pride. "We had a family plan to send the girls to college, then they would help me after I got out of the military. The whole time I was in the military, I took only ten dollars a month for my pay; the other money went to help my sisters. I joined the Airborne, so I'd get extra money.

Dan smiled, giving a brief look of disbelief. "You've got more nerve than I got. My porch is too high for me to jump off of; I know damn well I ain't jumping out of no airplane."

Blue smiled and continued. "When I came home, I knew I couldn't go to college then; my head wasn't ready for that. People don't realize that when you leave a war zone, it takes time for the war zone to leave you, and sometimes it never does. You have to understand, that one day your parents are telling you not to steal or kill, and to respect everyone. The next day, you're surrounded by death and the only way to survive is to kill. You can't turn it on and off, just like that. The unit I was in made it even harder for me to adjust. I can remember the face of every man I killed. That will never go away." Dan looked on attentively and shook his head. "But I think I've done well, considering what I went through in Korea. I'm pretty much in control of my emotions now." He lowered his head and closed his eyes.

Dan nodded "You'll be all right. But there's one thing I want to ask you." He tried to hide his smiled, but couldn't. He sipped his drink and sat back in his chair.

Blue ignored Dan's request at first, then held his head up as a slow smile covered his face. "What is it, Big Dan?" I know it's some bull-shit, but go on, what it is?"

Dan sipped his drink again. "Somebody told me that you walked to Wilson after work, and back to Elm City at night. If that's true, you're a walking nigger."

Blue's handsome face lit up with a huge smile. "Yeah, that's true, but I ride a taxi back now. I had a problem with some white boys."

The laugh that rolled out of Dan was spontaneous. "Who in the hell is dumb enough to give you a problem? They must have been blind. As big as you are, they had to be blind, drunk, or crazy as hell."

Blue clenched his jaw for a second, then forced out a short smile. He laid his massive forearms on the table and leaned forward. "Several times, when I was walking home at night, white people would ride by and throw bottles or anything at me and call me all kinds of names; nigger, ape, spook, you name it. Let me correct that, some white people, because there were times when some good white people would offer me a ride." Anger stabbed him like a knife in the chest as he relived the incident. He took a deep breath and slowly exhaled to calm himself. "One night, two white boys passed me, and the driver threw a bottle at me while rounding a curve. He lost control of the car and ended up in a ditch; two wheels were in the ditch and the other two were off of the ground, still spinning. I ran toward the car in a kill mode, but I thought about my family before I got there." He narrowed his dark eyes that glared with burning anger. "When I got there, one of them was half-way out of the car. I pulled him out and twisted his arm until I heard it snap. He screamed in pain until I hit him and knocked him out. By that time, the other one jumped out and tried to hit me. The head lights were still on and provided enough light for me to see the punch coming. I caught his fist in my hand and hit him. I didn't get a solid lick in, but he fell. I twisted his arm until it broke, then I knocked him out."

Dan was shaking his head, laughing and spilling tears that were quickly wiped away with the back of his hand; he nearly fell out of his chair. "I know them crackers screamed like somebody had a hot iron to their ass when them bones broke." He broke out laughing again, slapping his hand against the table; tears were still spilling from his eyes. "You should have broken their damn necks." This time he slapped his upper thigh, still laughing.

Blue shook his head, waiting for Dan to calm down. "Mr. Winsted, the old man I worked for, said the same thing. But if I had killed them, the police would have found an innocent Negro man and beat him until he confessed, then executed him. I'm glad I didn't."

Dan was still laughing when he said, "You're probably right."

Blue flashed a grin that was just short of being cold. "Now here's the funny part. It came out in the newspaper that the white boys gave a colored man a ride and he tried to rob them with a gun."

Dan's jaw dropped before he had a chance to catch it. "What!"

Blue nodded. "They said the car ran into the ditch when they tried to take the gun from him. That's how their arms were broken, and one of them had a broken jaw, but they were lucky. If that had happened when I first came home from Korea, I would've killed them without hesitation, no question about it."

They sat in silence briefly, then Dan gave one of his ice breaking chuckles. "You said, if you had killed them, they would've executed an innocent Negro man." He tried to hold a straight face as he said, "Hold your hands up."

Blue looked confused. He placed his glass on the table and held his baseball-glove size hands up.

Dan could no longer hold his laughter. "If them white people knew you knocked a mule out, and hit them white boys with them…" He pointed at Blue's hands. "They would execute your ass two times. I had rather you shoot me, than for you to hit me; either way I'll probably die. "

They laughed out loud and had a few more drinks as Blue talked about some of his experiences in Korea. They went to bed about an hour later.

Chapter 20

January 13, 1952
10:55 A.M.

Dan got up about eleven o'clock to start cooking breakfast. "Hey Boy, its damn near eleven-thirty, get your funky ass up so we can eat breakfast," he said jokingly.

A few minutes later, Blue walked in the kitchen from his bedroom. The alluring aroma of country sausage and eggs filled the kitchen air. "Give me about ten minutes to shower."

Dan looked at Blue for a second, then broke out into a big laugh. "It will take you that long to wash them big-ass feet of yours." Blue walked through the kitchen and across the hall into the bathroom. A short time later, there was a knock at the door. Dan walked to the door and looked through the peep-hole. "What you want Boy?" He asked the young boy that lived next door.

"Mr. Dan, a white lady is going around to every house giving away free soap. Can I get them bottles on your back porch and sell them?"

"I knew it was something else you wanted; go on and get them. I'll see her when she gets here."

"Thank you, Mr. Dan."

Dan went back in the kitchen and sat down to eat. A few minutes later Blue came out of the bathroom. "Save me some, I'll be right back."

A few minutes passed and there was another knock at the door. "This little black-ass boy is going to worry me to death about them two cent bottles," said Dan, as he was walking to the door. He looked through the peep-hole again and saw a tall, red-head, white woman standing on the porch. There was a black Ford parked on the street in front of his house with the trunk up, filled with boxes of soap powder.

When she saw an image through the peep-hole, she held a large box up. "This is a promotion; my company is giving this soap powder away for you to try. May I speak with you?"

"One minute, let me get my robe." Dan went to his bedroom, got his robe and walked back to the door. "Come in. How are you?" The lady walked in and gave Dan the box of soap powder. She was a tall, thin woman with shoulder length red hair; dressed in a black leather coat with a matching bag and black low heeled shoes. "Thank you," said Dan, as he turned to lead her to the living room. As soon as he turned his back, she pulled a black revolver from her handbag and shot Dan in the back of his head. He fell forward and was dead before his body hit the floor; blood and brain matter were visible on the walls and ceiling. Blue heard the shot and grabbed his .44 Magnum. He ran from his bedroom through the kitchen, as she aimed for a second shot at Dan. She heard Blue's footsteps, and in an instance the gun was pointed at him. Before he could react, she shot him once, hitting him in his left shoulder. The roar of gunfire echoed through the house. Blue fell back against the wall, as she turned and ran out the door onto the porch. She then jumped to the ground, twisting her ankle and landing in a sitting position, facing the porch; her gun fell to the ground. Blue staggered out on the porch and shot her once in the upper chest. The bullet went through her, leaving a fist-size exit wound in her back. She fell back and made a gurgling sound; blood ran from her nose and mouth as her head tilted to the side. She was dead.

Blue slowly walked down the steps, his .44 Magnum still pointed at her dead body. Blood was running from his shoulder down his long arm and body onto the ground. He stopped and focused on his wound, carefully balancing himself as he turned around and sat on the step. He knew from his experience in Korea, that he would bleed to death if he didn't get help soon.

Within the next two or three minutes, a middle age man, with a bald head carefully walked up to Blue. "I called the police and ambulance, they should be here soon. How do you feel?"

Blue took a deep breath in obvious pain. "It burns like hell and I'm losing a lot of blood; I'm starting to feel a little weak. My friend is lying in the hall, shot. Would you check on him?"

The man nodded and jumped from the ground onto the porch. He opened the door slowly and looked in, then closed the door and jumped back to the ground. He shook his head first. "He has a bad head wound and is not moving; I think he's dead."

Blue had no reaction or couldn't react. There was bright red blood everywhere. His white undershirt was drenched; blood was dripping onto the cement step and formed a large pool beneath him.

The crowd that had formed on the street cleared a path, when a car flashing emergency top light and siren turned off South Pender onto Cemetery Street. The police car pulled behind the dead woman's car and two uniformed officers got out, guns in hand, pointing at Blue. "Drop that gun Boy, or I'll blow your black-ass away," said one cop.

Blue dropped his .44 Mangum in the pool of blood on the step. The cop walked over and kicked the gun to the ground. The other cop knelt beside the dead woman, checking for any signs of life. "Sergeant Dew, this one is dead."

Blue raised his right hand, pointing backwards towards the front door. "My friend is shot," he said in a weak voice.

"Officer Morgan, check in the house," said Sergeant Dew, his gun still pointed at Blue. "What's your name Boy?"

"John Blue." His voice came out in barely a whisper.

Morgan walked up the steps, trying to avoid the blood pool, as Blue leaned over. He walked on the porch and cautiously opened the door, holding his gun shoulder high. He opened the door and walked in; moments later he reappeared. "This one is dead too; most of his head is gone."

The crowd again made a path for an ambulance from Edwards Funeral Home. The driver turned off of the street in front of the dead woman's car, onto the grassy section in Dan's front yard. The two attendants got out, went to the back and pulled the stretcher out; immediately pushing it toward Blue. Sergeant Dew shot the attendants a crazy look. "How you Boys know that woman is already dead?"

"Don't matter, we from a colored funeral home. You know we ain't allowed to carry white people…especially a white woman."

They put the stretcher down in front of Blue and carefully helped him up, and onto it. His long legs were dangling off the end. Dew walked behind the stretcher as Blue was being pushed to the ambulance. "That Boy killed that white woman and…"

The attendant interrupted. "If you need to talk to him, he'll be at Mercy Hospital. We need to get him there as soon as possible; he's losing a lot of blood." The two cops exchanged glance as Blue was being loaded in… His eyes were aimless.

The driving attendant said in a low voice, "This man has lost a lot of blood, he might not make it."

They took off in the emergency mode, lights flashing and siren blaring, heading toward South Pender Street. Sergeant Dew called the police department and Detectives Price and Batts arrived within the next ten minutes. The crowd was again forced back onto the curb. Price got out and viewed the body, then ordered Batts to get a blanket from the car to cover it. "One more in the house and the boy that killed that white woman is on his way to Mercy Hospital," said Dew. "His name is John Blue."

"Okay," said Price. "You call the station and get the ID boys down here to get pictures and prints. I'll go to the hospital after I leave here." Price knew it was probably Dan in the house, and his chances of catching the killers of Rose could be gone. He also knew the dead woman was probably a paid killer, after he saw the gun next to her body. Now, she was the only link to the nigger loving killer he wanted so desperately to catch. "Detective Batts, after the boys get pictures and prints; I want you to get her handbag and lock it inside the car. You keep the keys and have the car towed to the station. I want to get from around this crowd as soon as possible. We can search the car better at the station. I'm going inside to look around." Price walked toward the house and started up the steps when he saw Blue's gun on the ground. "Batts, make sure the ID Boys sees this gun."

"That's the gun that killed the woman," said Officer Morgan.

"Officer," Price hesitated and looked at his name-tag. "Morgan, you cover every inch of this yard and make sure they get a picture of everything you find. We don't want to miss nothing." Price then navigated up the blood-drenched steps onto the porch. When he entered the house he saw Dan's body, face-down on the floor. Half of his head was blown away by what look to be a large caliber bullet. He stopped and looked at the blood-stained ceiling and walls, then walked around the body; skull fragments were cracking against the hardwood floor with each step. He carefully looked in every room and left through the back door, as not to disturb the crime scene before pictures and prints could be taken. The whole complexion of the case had changed. Price knew whoever paid to have Dan killed had to have good contacts out of state, and a lot of money. The dead woman's car had Kentucky tags.

Chapter 21

January 13, 1952
1:15 P.M.

Blue was taken to Mercy Hospital and immediately given a blood transfusion. His chances of survival were forty-percent less than that of a white person with the same injuries at the white, Woodard Herrings Hospital. Although not in grave condition, death was still a possibility at the poorly equipped and understaffed Mercy Hospital. But the doctors and staff did the best job possible, considering the poor working conditions.

Price went to interview Blue, but his condition, although not yet grave, wouldn't allow it. Later that afternoon the bleeding stopped, and after the transfusion, Blue began to regain his strength. His greatest enemy was now infection. He was placed in the overcrowded, Ward C, with twenty other patients, many of them near death. He was now able to talk and feed himself.

Attorney C. L. Washington was his first visitor. Tall, good looking and dressed in a blue suit and red bow-tie, he looked the part. "How do you feel?" He said, standing beside Blue's bed.

Blue responded in a weak, but clear voice. "I'm in a little pain, but better."

"My name is C. L. Washington, I'm a lawyer, and I'm sure you'll need one."

Blue looked up at him innocently. "But it was self defense, she shot me first."

Washington nodded sympathetically and drew in a long, patient breath. "Son, you need to understand that self-defense is when a Negro kills another Negro, defending himself. When a Negro kills a white person its murder, no matter what the circumstances are. I don't know the details yet, but you killed a white woman, that's even worst. This is the Jim Crow south; you don't have any rights when it involves white people. To them, your life is worthless." Blue grimaced and groaned as his shoulder throbbed; Washington hesitated a second or two. "I don't want to upset you, but I want you to understand where you stand. Let me tell you a few things you probably don't know. A white woman slapped a Negro woman twice at the Carolina Theater; she slapped the white woman back and got two years in prison. Two white men attacked a Negro man with baseball bats; he shot one of them in the leg and went to prison for seven years. Now you killed a white woman, so you tell me if you think you need a lawyer or not."

Blue's expression changed. He now realized that he was in deep trouble and could go to prison, or even worst, get a death sentence. "I understand."

"Don't worry about any fee. You just get well and I'll be back to talk with you on Monday."

"Thank you Sir. If you will, I need you to do something for me. My family lives in Elm City, and I don't think they know I'm in the hospital. Will you call them for me, please Sir?"

"I'll do that." Washington pulled a notepad and pen from his inside coat pocket. "Give me the name and number."

Rev. Donald Blue. The number is 6463.

"All right, I'll make sure they know. You get some rest, see you Monday." He turned to walk out. "Oh, one more thing," now facing Blue again. "The police will come here to talk with you. Don't make any statements or sign anything. Tell them who your lawyer is, and you want me present before you can answer any questions. Okay?"

"Yes Sir," said Blue. Washington walked out.

Half-awake, Blue tried his best to catalog the day's events. Medication soon overpowered his attempt to focus. "Blue, Blue," a voice said, moments after he fell asleep. "How do you feel?"

Blue was still half-asleep when he said, "A little better." He turned his head toward the voice. Ray's handsome face then appeared through the fog of medication.

"I got up here as soon as I could. I feel better, now that I know you're alright. Dan didn't have any family close to him, so he left the club to me. I was his right hand man, now; you're my right hand man." Blue looked at Ray through watering eyes and smiled. "I'll let you get some rest now, but hurry and get well. I need you at the club." Blue nodded, then closed his eyes. Ray rubbed the top of Blue's hand. "Now, if you die on me, I'll break these tens off in your big ass. Do you remember telling me that?"

Blue smiled. "I remember." Ray rubbed his hand and left.

Chapter 22

January 15, 1952
9:50 A.M.

The dead woman's car was towed to the parking lot behind the police station. Price and Batts searched the car and found her identification. She was thirty-one year old Kitty Tuck, and was a resident of Louisville, KY. Price contacted the police in Louisville and the state police in Ohio. She had been under investigation for several murders in the Kentucky and Ohio areas, but was never charged. They also found a key to Room 223 at the Briggs Hotel. After they finished searching the car, they walked two blocks from the police station to the Briggs.

The Briggs was an old, five-story hotel that was built in the 1800s. Time had taken its toll on the old building, but it was still the center piece of uptown Wilson. The detectives walked in the eloquent hotel lobby; their shoe heels clicking against the white marble floor. A large crystal chandelier hung from the ceiling between the dining room and the elevator. Over the double wooden-doors to the spacious dining room was a gold-painted, framed portrait of Confederate General, Robert E. Lee.

There was a short, middle-aged, white woman at the front desk. "Can I help you Sir? I know you're a policeman, but I can't think of your name."

"Sergeant Price and this is Detective Batts." Batts nodded. Price pulled out the room key. "We need to look inside this room. We found it in the car that belonged to the woman who was killed over the weekend."

The lady behind the desk put her hand over her mouth in disbelief. "What happened?"

"She was killed in the colored section, but I can't go into details now. But we really do need to look inside the room."

"One of them damn niggers probably killed her after they robbed her. I talked to her when she first checked in; she was a very nice person. She didn't look like she would hurt a fly. She worked for a soap company." She slowly shook her head. "Take the elevator to the second floor. When you get off, the room will be down the hall on your left."

"Thank you, but one more question. What name did she use to check in?"

"One second." She looked in her register and then said, "Here it is, Martha Tucker. She gave an address in Nashville, Tennessee."

"Thanks again," said Price. He and Batts walked toward the elevator.

An old, black man took his uniform cap off and bowed as Price and Batts approached the elevator. He was dressed in a burgundy and gray doorman's uniform, and black shining shoes that were slit to accommodate the bulging corns and bunions on his wide, flat feet. "What floor Sir?"

The detectives walked in and the old man closed the gate behind them. "Second," said Batts.

"Yessir."

The elevator at the Briggs was a chrome box about the size of a triple-wide phone booth.

Price stared at the old man before asking, "What's your name, Boy?"

"Fred Taylor, Sir." His face was creased in what could be mistaken for a slight smile.

"How long have you been working here?"

Fred grinned, "About thirty years, Sir; only job I ever had, other than working in the tobacco fields.

When they got to the second floor, Fred opened the gate, took his cap off again and bowed. Price and Batts walked out and to their right, toward Room 223. They first knocked on the door, waited a few seconds, then used the key to enter. There was a suitcase on the bed, open but already packed. Batts looked in the bathroom, while Price looked in the suitcase. The room's carpet, drapes and bedspread were all different colors of green. A tall, gold tone lamp sat in the corner of the room, behind a black leather chair. Price found an envelope in the suitcase. "What in the hell," he said, holding an envelope full of money. His reaction was in part to the address on the business envelope. It read: Pope's Tobacco Warehouse, Hwy. 301 South, Wilson, North Carolina. He then counted the money. "Three-thousand," he said looking at Batts. Price knew he had to think this thing through. He frantically searched his mind for an answer, then said, "Batts, get that boy on the elevator and bring him here."

Batts walked out and was back with Fred within two or three minutes. Fred walked in, pulled his cap off and held it to his chest "You wanna see me Sir?" He said in a trembling voice looking down at the floor.

"Yes. I want to know if you saw anyone visit the woman in this room, Friday night or Saturday morning."

"I didn't work Friday night, Jack Forbes worked, but I let two white men off on this floor, Saturday morning. I didn't see them come in this room, but they walked this way."

"How long did they stay up here?" Price asked.

"Not long, Sir. When I got back to the lobby and opened the gate, the second floor light came on, that was the white men. About nine-thirty or ten, the white woman from this room left, but she never came back."

"Do you remember what the white men looked like?"

"Yessir. They was both tall, and one of them had blonde hair. That's all I remember, Sir."

"Okay, you can go now." Fred backed up holding his cap to his chest, and bowed his head as he was backing out. "I understand Red Pope has red hair and freckles, so he wasn't one of the men up here," said Price. "But someone who works in or around one of his warehouses used this envelope; if so, Red needs to know about it." He hesitated. "Put everything back in the suitcase, we can go through it later. We'll go to Red's office, maybe he can help us." They left the hotel and walked back to the police station. When they got to the rear door Price said, "Put the suitcase in our office, I'll get the car and pick you up here." After Batts got in the car, Price drove out of the parking lot and turned left onto Goldsboro Street, heading south. Several warehouses lined both sides of the street from Barnes to Hines Streets. They turned right onto Hines Street, drove two blocks and turned left onto Tarboro Street, heading south. Red's office was at the corner of Tarboro and Garner Streets. Price was going to make Red aware of someone using his business envelopes, not to question him; Price didn't think that would be a problem with the chief. They turned right at Garner Street and made a quick left into the parking lot at Red's office. They got out and walked toward the modern, two-story brick building. Price looked around the elaborately, decorated lobby when they walked in. "Now I know Red has a lot of money, cause he put at least a half million in this place."

A beautiful, young woman was sitting behind the desk using the typewriter. "Can I help you?"

"I'm Sergeant Price and this is Detective Batts. We would like to see Mr. Pope, if he's in."

"Mr. Pope has someone with him, but you can wait. He should be out in ten or fifteen minutes. Just have a seat."

"Thank you," said Price. He was still looking around the lobby when he saw a picture of Red and his family at the beach. He got up to take a closer look and noticed Bret with his shirt off; a tattoo on his left shoulder. He stood there for a minute dumbfounded. He called Batts and said in a low voice, "Look at Bret on that picture. Do you see what I see?"

Batts looked at the picture, then looked back at Price. "Crossed pistols, I can't believe it."

Price walked to the desk. "We'll be back." He motioned to Batts and they walked out.

Chapter 23

January 15, 1952
10:05 A.M.

They exited the parking lot and headed north on Tarboro Street. Price glanced at Batts. "You know, a blind man can see this. Bret gave that money to the woman at the Briggs. Dan said, the man that gave him the money at Rose's house was tall, blonde and had a tattoo on his left shoulder. Fred, at the Briggs said that the men he took to the second floor were tall, and one of them was blonde." The detectives were passing one of Red's warehouses on Tarboro Street. "Bret is tall, blonde, and you saw the tattoo. Dan also said the other men at Rose's house were tall. The officers that started on the force with Bret are all tall. This is too much to be a coincidence." He accelerated up Tarboro Street. "I don't know what the chief will say about this, but it's as clear as day; the nigger loving killers are right here on the police force with us." Price knew the respect Chief Watson had for Red Pope and his tobacco money, but it was his job to tell him, and he wanted them caught. When they pulled into the parking lot at the police station, Chief Watson was at the side door. "Hey Chief, I need to see you," said Price.

"I'll be in my office."

When detectives parked the car and walked inside the station, the desk officer asked, "Sergeant Price, are you working the case on Cemetery Street?"

"Yes."

"The boy that killed that white women died about an hour ago, I think his name was…" He paused and looked down at his desk. "John Blue."

"Thank you," said Price as he walked past the desk, never breaking his stride, heading to the chief's office. He knocked on the chief's door.

"Come in, you men have a seat. This has been a busy day, trying to get ready to leave for a few days. I'm going to Winston Salem to the Police Chief's Convention. This will be my first one, kinda excited you know."

Price took the envelope from his coat pocket and put it on the chief's desk. "What do we have here?" Asked Watson.

"This was found in the dead woman's room at the Briggs," said Price. Watson sat straight up in his chair, leaned forward putting his elbows on the desk. "Three-thousand dollars in there, and that's not all, said Price. Dan Williams, Rose Grant's son, and the old elevator man at the Briggs described Bret Pope to a tee. I saw the tattoo on Bret's shoulder myself."

Watson interrupted. "Have you talked with anyone else about this?"

"Just Officer Batts. But there are too many signs to be a coincidence." He looked straight into Watson's eyes. "I didn't put things together until I saw a picture of Bret with the tattoo on his arm at Red's office."

Watson slammed his hand on the desk. "What! Are you out of your mind? Didn't I tell you to check with me first if something came up?" His eyes were wide open. "Red Pope can make one phone call and tomorrow we'll be looking for a job. The only thing you have is an envelope, what a dead man and an eight year old boy said. And the old man at the Briggs, who's blind in one eye and can't see out of the other. You'll need a lot more than that if you go messing with Bret Pope. I don't know who put this money in this envelope and you don't either." He was pointing his finger at Price.

"But Chief, I didn't go there to question him. I wanted him to know that someone was using his business envelops and could be involved in a murder. "

Watson interrupted. "Shut up." He got up and walked around his office, stopped and rolled his eyes at Price, then sat back down. "The officer at the desk told me, the boy that killed that woman died at

Mercy Hospital." He paused. "Let me tell you something you probably don't know. We have three coloreds and a hired killer dead. It will be impossible to find twelve people in this county that would convict the son of the riches man in the county of killing a nigger. You need to forget about this. I'm sure Red didn't like you coming to his office. You know not to discuss this with anyone, not even your wife. I'll talk with Red before I leave and let you know what he said when I get back. A man with that much power and influence don't want his family's name connected to nothing like this. Don't say a word to anyone about this. Now, get the hell out of my office."

"Chief, we didn't talk to Mr. Pope, he was busy."

"I don't care. I told you not to do anything unless you check with me first. Now get out of my office."

Price and Batts walked out in total silence. They looked at each other quizzically. Price knew Red would do anything to protect his son, and would not hesitate to have them killed. Watson's attitude was to save his job, so whatever came with that was collateral damage. They walked out into the parking lot and toward their unmarked car; Price gave Batts the keys. "Here, you drive. I need to think about this thing." He looked at Batts seriously, and lit a cigarette. "We could be in danger you know." Smoke was coming out of his nostrils as he spoke.

When they got in the car Batts asked, "Where do you want to go?"

Price didn't respond to Batts' question. He hesitated. "Just drives anywhere, so I can think; just don't go anywhere near Red, or Bret Pope."

They glanced at each other and smiled. They drove out of the parking lot, and then turned right onto Goldsboro Street, heading north. "Do you really think that, Red would have police officers killed?"

Price looked at him like he was crazy. "Of course; he would have his mother killed to protect that nigger loving son of his." They crossed the tracks off of Goldsboro Street onto Herring Avenue, heading north. "A lot depends on what the chief tells him. If he thinks you and I will be a problem," said Price, looking at Batts, "then you and I have a problem."

A look of concern invaded Batts' face. "Maybe we could talk to someone who could help us."

"Who, who in the hell is going to challenge Red in this town? The only thing we can do now is be careful and keep quiet."

"What about your Klan brothers; you said they carry a lot of weight around here. Will they help us?"

Price shook his head. "If Red wants us dead, no one can help us. Red has enough money to have the Klan killed. In this town, anything Red does is right; even if he's wrong, he's still right." There was dead silence in the car as Batts turned off of Herring Avenue and headed east on Ward Boulevard. "Three-thousand dollars got Dan killed. Red has millions of dollars, so if the chief says the wrong thing, he'll pay ten times that much to have us killed."

Price now appeared troubled. He knew their lives were now in Watson's hands. He also knew Watson would do or say anything to keep his job. Whatever Red wanted, Watson would do.

Chapter 24

January 19, 1952
9:15 A.M.

Chief Watson walked out of his office and called for the detectives. He was making a fresh pot of coffee when they walked in. "Have a seat. Want a cup of fresh coffee?"

"No thank you, we just had some," said Price. "How was your trip?"

"Fine, I had a good time and met people from all over the state. That was my first convention, and hopefully the first of many to come. I just wish I could have stayed the weekend." He lit a cigarette and sipped his coffee. "I talked with Red before I left. You know he wasn't pleased about y'all going to his office, but he said he understood you Boys were just doing your job. But don't ever do that again without checking with me first."

A sign of relief flashed across Price and Batts faces. They looked at each other.

"Now, you Men didn't discuss this with anyone, did you?"

Price smiled and said, "No Sir, we didn't."

A smile crossed Watson's face. "Good, now all we have to do is slowly close the murder cases. Dan and the woman that killed him are dead, and the money won't be mentioned in the report. So what do we have?"

Batts smiled and said an ass-kissing, "Nothing, Sir, not a damn thing."

Watson cleared his throat before speaking. "You might not be satisfied with the end result, I know I'm not," he explained. "But sometimes we're put in a situation where we have no choice." He looked in the eyes of Price, then Batts. "This is one of those situations. Money and power rule this city and everywhere else. We're in a winless situation, so we have to let it go. Do we agree?" Again he looked at Price and Batts.

"Yes, Sir," said Price.

"One more thing; now I need a favor from you Men. I have an old friend that lives on Black Creek Road. He called me this morning about seven-thirty; you know how old people are when they know the chief of police. Someone tried to break into his house last night and he wants to talk to an officer. I told him to call the sheriff, but he said he didn't know the new sheriff. His house is about two miles out of the city, but don't worry about that. It's a brick, two-story house right beside a pond. There should be an old Ford truck in the yard. Just talk to him, get a report and tear it up when you leave. I would really appreciate that, Men. His name is Mr. Lamm."

Price nodded, and then had his ass-kissing moment. "No problem Chief, we'll get right out there on it. And Chief, thanks for helping us. We had no idea what Mr. Pope would say, but you don't have to worry about that again."

"You're welcome; but one more thing, don't mention this on your way out. It's out of the city, you know."

"All right," said Price. They left the station headed to Black Creek Road. They pulled out of the parking lot, turned left on Goldsboro Street, then left at Nash, heading east, Batts was driving.

"Watson had to save our asses, to save his," said Price.

Batts glanced at Price and smiled. "I don't give a damn why he did it, as long as he did."

They drove through the business districts and turned right at South Pender Street, heading south. At the corner of Suggs and South Pender, Price pulled his gun. "Slow down; pull over there behind that nigger."

The black man turned around and looked at Price, who had opened the car door. "Wrong man," he said. He closed the door and Batts pulled off.

Batts looked confused. "What was that all about?"

Price put his gun back in the holster before answering. "I thought that was somebody else."

"Somebody we got a warrant for?"

"No." He hesitated. "A few years back, I was downtown on Nash Street and got jumped by two niggers. I fought then tooth and nail until they overpowered me and took my gun. They mailed it back to the station about two weeks later. I thought he was one of them." He looked at Batts, his anger was rising. "The first one I see, I'm gonna blow his damn head off. If I have to shoot him in the back and put a gun in his hand, I will."

Batts had heard the true story around the station of how Price got his ass kicked, but didn't comment. He waited for Price to calm. "Let's go out there and talk with the old man for a few minutes, then get some breakfast."

They drove south on South Pender Street and turned left onto Stantonburg Street. When they crossed 301, they were then on Black Creek Road. They drove a little over two miles before they saw the house beside the pond. "I know this is the right place, but it don't look like anyone lives here," said Batts. They pulled off the road and parked behind the old truck in the driveway; they got out and walked onto the cement porch. Batts looked to his right, and walked over to a large picture-window. His attempt to look inside was blocked by thick, black drapes. He then joined Price at the front door. Price pulled the screen door open and knocked.

"Come in, the door is unlocked," a voice said from inside the house.

Price hesitated, then pushed the door open. "Mr. Lamm," he said as he walked in.

"In the back, too old to move fast, come back here," the voice said.

Price had an eerie feeling and thought about it for a moment, then started a cautious walk down the long, half-lit hall; there were two closed doors on both sides of the hall. The door at the end of the hall was half-opened and fully lit. When they got about half-way up the hall, a door from both sides opened. Before Price could react, a shotgun blast struck him in his face. His head exploded into a mass of red matter, death was instant.

Batts froze in terror. "No, please," he said as he turned to escape. Before he reached the front door he was hit by two shotgun blasts in his back. A loud scream tore from his throat; his body slammed against the door. He fell to his knees and rolled over to the floor. His eyes were flooded with fear as he screamed out again, pleading for his life. He struggled to get up. "Please don't." Another blast hit him in his chest, then another in his face, which instantly disappeared; he was dead.

They couldn't be reached later that day, the Chief ordered all off duty officers to report in. They searched the city and the county the next week or so, with no success. Three weeks later their unmarked car was found, burned in a wooded area near Dillon, South Carolina. Their bodies were not recovered. The case was never closed, but there was no long investigation ordered by Watson, and he refused any help from the S.B.I. or any state agencies.

Chapter 25

January 21, 1952
1:10 P.M.

Maggie, Ronnie and Butch attended Saint John Church on North Pender Street, with Sam and Virginia Howard. Saint John was the largest church in the black community. They had planned to talk with the boys about being adopted when they got home from church. Sam had suggested they wait a few days after the funeral to talk with them.

"I ain't never been in a church that big and beautiful," said Maggie. "I felt right bad putting my twenty-five cents in the plate."

"You gave what you had, that's all that matters to God," said Virginia with a smile.

It was a beautiful, sunny Sunday. Sam drove the short block to Nash Street and turned left at the light, heading east. "Mr. Howard, how much did you pay for this car?" Asked Ronnie, his eyes focused on the soft, black seats.

"A lot, but you'll have one if you study hard and be a good person," answered Sam, looking at Ronnie through his rearview mirror. They turned off Nash Street onto South Carroll Street and parked in front of Maggie's house. Ronnie got out of the back seat on the passenger side and ran around the back of the car to open the door for Maggie. "That's what I'm talking about," said Sam. "Only good people do things like that." He rubbed Ronnie on the top of his head, Ronnie smiled.

"That's my Big Boy," said Maggie, slowly making her way out of the back seat. When they got in the house, Maggie sat down and took off her shoes. "Ronnie, look in my room and get my bedroom shoes, these corns is smoking," she said smiling. Sam and Virginia took a seat on the long chair. They were nervous, not knowing how the boys would feel about leaving Maggie.

"Here are your shoes, Miss Maggie," said Ronnie, placing them on the floor in front of her.

"Thank you, Sweetheart. Go and get Butch, we want to tell y'all something." Ronnie walked in the back and was back with Butch in a matter of seconds. Maggie and the Howards exchanged glances and smiles. "Ronnie," said Maggie, her voice low and clear. "Do you remember when I told you that I loved you and Butch very much, but I was too old to keep y'all?"

Ronnie thought for a moment before speaking. "I think so, Miss Maggie."

Maggie took his hand and pulled him close to her. "You told me you'd like to stay with Mr. and Mrs. Howard, if you couldn't stay with me." Ronnie looked at Maggie as if he knew what she was about to say. "Well, Mr. Sam and Miss Virginia is your new Mama and Daddy. They love you and Butch very much and want y'all to come and live with them. Don't worry; y'all will see me almost every day." Ronnie turned and looked at the Howards. He smiled slowly, but sincerely.

"Both of you come over here and give me a hug," said Virginia. They both walked over and hugged her. "What do you think?"

Ronnie and Butch both smiled and nodded in agreement. The adoption was finalized a week before they moved into their new house on Fikewood Street. The adjustment went smoothly. Maggie spent a lot of time with the family before she got sick and died four years later, at the age of 85. One of her last requests was to see Ronnie and Butch.

1968

Justice for Rose

"I was willing to give my life for my country, but now, my country won't give me anything, not even justice for my mother."
Ronald Grant-Howard

Chapter 26

June 27, 1968
9:05 A.M.

Ronnie was asleep on his stomach, his head buried in his pillow and his long legs were dangling off of the foot of the bed, when Virginia knocked on his bedroom door. "Time to get up, Ronnie." She knocked again.

Ronnie then responded in a half-sleep haze. "All right Mom; I'll get a quick shower. Would you please cook me two eggs and three strips of bacon?"

I'm cooking now; you just get your lazy butt up. The train arrives at ten-forty-five, so you need to get up now. You know how slow you are about getting up."

"First Lieutenant Ronald Grant-Howard was home after serving two years in the U.S. Army. He graduated from North Carolina College in 1966, and entered the Army as a second Lieutenant. He served with the 1st Inf. Division in Viet Nam and was awarded the Silver Star for his actions in combat and the Purple Heart after being injured.

They were going to meet Butch, who was coming home from college. Sam and Virginia went to his graduation in May, but he stayed in Indiana for a month with his girlfriend and her family, recuperating from a knee operation.

After Ronnie ate breakfast, they left their house on Fikewood Street heading to the train station. They drove on Fikewood and turned right at Queen Street, then a left at North Carroll Street. When they got to the intersection of Nash and North Carroll, Ronnie could see the house where his mother was killed, and the front porch of Maggie's house next door. His emotions started to swell as he said with a degree of sadness, looking at Sam, "Dad, I can't help from thinking about my mother and Miss Maggie when I come this way, but I also think about where Butch and I would be, today, if you and mom didn't adopt us. I know Miss Maggie loved us, but she was too old to take care of two young children." He looked in the rearview mirror at Virginia who was seated in the back. "Mom, I've never said this before, but I want to thank You and Dad for giving Butch and me a good home. I don't know what we would have done without you. Miss Maggie died four years after mom; after that, I hate to think about what would have happened to us; we could have been separated."

Virginia's eyes began to water. "Like Mrs. Wade said all the time, *"Bless your heart."* She leaned forward and rubbed Ronnie's shoulder. "I know you don't remember this, but Mrs. Wade would always say that God sent us, and I believe it. You and Butch grew up together and we love you very much; that's all that matters." Ronnie nodded and turned right heading west on Nash Street.

"When I was in Viet Nam, I thought about them a lot; Miss Maggie as much as my mother, because I remember her more. Butch probably doesn't remember mama at all; he was just six when she died." He hesitated, then said, "I saw Butch play several times on television and I can't tell you how proud I was to tell the guys he was my younger brother; that really made me feel good after what we went through as kids; I guess we have a special bond. You probably don't know this, but I held him a lot of nights when he was crying for mama." He looked at Sam, "That made me grow up fast. I knew that we had you and mom, but I still felt responsible for him."

Ronnie blew the horn and waved at several people he knew from high school as he drove through downtown. They parked at the train station across from Terminal Drug Store. The Atlantic Coastline Station was a one-story, brick building that sat in the shadow of the old, seven-story Cherry Hotel. The building had been renovated to combine the separate waiting areas after the Civil Rights Bill was passed. Ronnie got out and opened the back door for Virginia. When they got in the waiting room, Ronnie walked to the ticket office to check the train's arrival time.

A pale-white, fat man was sitting in the screened-in ticket office. He released a loud belch before speaking. "What do you want Boy?" He then took a soiled handkerchief from his pocket and blew his nostrils.

Ronnie's eyes narrowed as he glared for a moment. "Do you see a Boy?" He asked. The muscles were bulging from his six-foot four frame.

The man stared at Ronnie for a second. "Are you looking for trouble Boy?"

"No, but it sounds like you are, and if you come out of that office, you found it." He looked back at Virginia, then leaned over and smiled, as he whispered, "I'll kick your nasty, white ass, you fat bastard, and then you'll know who the boy is." The man quickly stood up and locked the office door.

Sam walked over and pulled Ronnie by his arm. "Forget it, people like that aren't worth your time."

Ronnie walked away still looking at the ticket agent; his facial expression showing anger. "I know Dad, but that really bothers me. I went to Viet Nam and nearly got killed, and as soon as I get home," he raised his voice so the ticket agent could hear him, "a nasty cracker calls me a Boy. He's lucky you and mom are here. I'm not going to take that anymore" He walked over to Virginia. "Sorry you had to see that Mom."

Virginia nodded and grabbed his hand. "That's alright Son. You have to realize, you're back in the south now." They sat there for about twenty minutes before they heard the train's arrival being announced. They walked out of the door toward the train tracks; the train pulled in about five minutes later. Butch was the first one to exit. After seeing his family, his muscular frame stiffened; Virginia's eyes lit up. "There he is," she said, as she walked toward him. Butch saw his family and waved, smiling broadly. He first hugged Virginia, then Sam; he shook Ronnie's hand, then hugged him.

Ronnie looked at Butch from head to toe, shaking his head in disbelief. "You've gotten taller since I saw you last. How tall are you now?"

"A little over six-six,"

"How much do you weigh?"

"About two-sixty or two-sixty-five."

"You're big," said Ronnie. "I had no idea you would grow like this." He slowly shook his head and smiled.

They got Butch's bags from the baggage car and headed home. It was spring, and flowers were blooming everywhere. Emotions swept over Ronnie as memories of their childhood spilled through his mind. For a passing moment he felt great sadness. Stumbling over his words he said, "This is the first time in three years we've been together. The older I get, the more I've learned to appreciate being with the people I love the most in this world. This is a special day in my life." He reached over and playfully rubbed the top of Butch's head.

Butch looked at Ronnie and smiled, "That made me think about Miss Maggie. She rubbed my head all the time. I'll never forget that and I'll never forget her. The few times in my life when I explained her relationship to me, I always said she was my grandmother."

Virginia and Sam were riding in the back seat. He took her hand and they exchanged smiles.

Chapter 27

June 27, 1968
11:15 A.M.

Sam asked the family to gather in the dining room when they got home. After they were all seated he said, "Ronnie said this was a special day, and it is. Your mother and I are very proud of you. Except for a few spankings," he smiled, "you have never given us any problems. Now both of you have graduated from college; we couldn't ask for more as parents." Sam reached in his pocket and pulled out two checks. "Ronnie, this is yours, and this is yours Butch." Butch and Ronnie looked at the checks, then looked at each other and smiled.

"Thanks Dad," said Butch. Ronnie nodded.

"You know Virginia and I have never talked to you about your mother, for the simple reason we didn't really know her. Virginia met her at some P.T.A. meetings when you were in her class. But one thing we do know, she loved you very much and wanted you to have a good life. That money you have was money from the sale of your mother's house and car, and money she was saving for your education. She left Mrs. Wade a letter, telling her what to do with it if anything happened to her." Ronnie gave Butch a curious look, then looked back at Sam. "What's wrong Son?" Sam asked.

Ronnie looked distant, but spoke in a calm tone. "Nothing is wrong; I was just wondering why someone as young as she was would write a letter like that. He paused. "It's almost like she knew something was going to happen to her. I never knew about a letter."

"Sam looked like he was at a loss of words. "I don't know anything about the case. There was not a lot of investigation. You know how the police are in this city when a black person is killed. But anyway, we put the money in the bank and added to it every month. With the interest, you have a good start at whatever you want to do, but don't spend it all in one place," he said smiling.

Butch got up and hugged Virginia and Sam, Ronnie followed. "Thanks again." He winked his eye at Sam and said, "But You and mom took care of us, and as much as Butch eats; some of this money should be yours." He looked at Butch and smiled; Butch lightly punched him on the shoulder and smiled.

"You and Butch are our son's. It was our job to take care of you." Sam smiled, then said, "But when I was writing the checks, I did think about all of that food, and those size fifteen shoes I had to buy." They all laughed as Sam hugged the brothers. Ronnie and Butch walked out, and toward Ronnie's room.

When they closed the door, Sam said in a low voice, "Ronnie was old enough to remember a little about his mother, and I don't think he ever got over it. Remember what he said today when we got to Nash Street?" Virginia nodded. A few minutes later Ronnie and Butch came out.

"Dad," "Butch and I are going out for a while."

"Here are the keys," said Sam. "Remember what your mother said, you're in Wilson now."

"Be careful," said Virginia.

"We won't be gone very long," said Ronnie. He and Butch hugged Virginia. "And we'll be careful." They left with Ronnie driving. They drove to Hwy. 301 and made a right turn, heading south.

"Where are we going?" Butch asked.

"To our house, on Stantonsburg Road. I think I'll probably get out of the military, so I'm having it renovated. Dad had some work done on it about five years ago, but I wanted a soundproof room put in; you know how I like Jazz. If I get married, I don't want to hear about the music being too loud. I put in an application for a teaching job at Darden. Louise said she had a job offer in D.C., but I can change all of that with a ring," looking at Butch smiling.

"Don't be so sure about that, you know how women are." They drove on 301 to Black Creek Road, turned left, then drove three blocks and turned left onto Stantonsburg Road. "How do you feel being home again? It's been a few years since you've been here."

Ronnie glanced at Butch, then said, "I don't know, I guess you could called that having mixed emotions. I'm overjoyed at seeing you, mom and dad again, but when I come home I think about how mama died. I probably thought about that every day when I was in Viet Nam. Now that I'm home, I think about it even more." He pulled in the yard at the old bricked, well kept house. Sam and Virginia lived there before they moved to Fikewood Street. Ronnie looked puzzle, like he was trying to figure out how to say, what he wanted to say. "I don't know if you heard it or not, but I was told some years ago that mama was killed by some white men. When dad said what he said about the money, I just thought about that." He was looking straight ahead, showing no emotion. Before Butch could respond, Ronnie started backing the car out of the driveway.

"Hold up." Ronnie stopped. "I thought you wanted to see the house," said Butch.

"I was out here a few days ago, I wanted you to see it, but I forgot the key. We'll come out here again when they start working. You remember Mr. Williams, don't you?"

"Mr. Williams, that renovates houses?"

"Yeah. He said he was going to start next week. Let's go home, I'm hungry."

"Wait, let me ask you something," said Butch. "Why did you say what you did about white men killing mama?"

"I don't know, but it crossed my mind when dad told us about the letter she wrote to Miss Maggie, and the fact that the police comes down here to kick black people's asses, and collect money from bootleggers. They don't investigate much. So I know back in fifty-two, when mama died, they didn't look too hard. But they almost had something to investigate today, at the train station."

"What happened?"

"I went to the ticket booth to check on your arrival time. Before I could ask, that fat, nasty looking, white ticket agent said to me,

"What do you want Boy?" I just looked at him for a second, trying to digest what he said. It took all of my strength to keep me off of his ass. If mom and dad weren't there, I would have pulled him out of that booth and kicked his ass." He looked at Butch and smiled. "He didn't know that I just came out of the killing zone in Viet Nam, and I'm still on go."

"I don't know if that would have stopped me," said Butch. He paused in thought, then said, "You did the right thing. Mom and dad would have really been disappointed in you."

"I know, that was the first thing I thought about. But I will never live in fear of a white man again, or let him just disrespect me, or treat me like I'm less than a man, never."

Butch slowly nodded. "That reminds me of something. We had a football coach from Georgia. When he addressed the white players it was, you Guys, you Fellows or you Men. But when he addressed the black players, it was, you Boys. You know me; I didn't have shit to say to him. I was in my room one night and I wrote a poem about that word Boy, and how it demeans a black man, when a white man calls him that. I never forgot it. When I was around him and he called me, or a black player Boy, I would think about that poem to stay off of his ass. I had planned to give it to him after I graduated, but he got fired about that same word, Boy. He had no respect for the black players. They knew what the team would have been like without us, so they got rid of him. They sent his tobacco- chewing, red-neck-ass back to the Georgia Pines."

"Let me hear it," said Ronnie.

"It's not that good, but it was how I felt when I wrote it. I named it. *"I know who I am."*
You called me your Boy, and I smiled to survive.
I knew who I was, I smiled to stay alive.
You worked me like an animal, from sun-up to the end of day.
At night, when you came for my wife, I smiled, I had no say.
I ask God, why me? I don't understand.

You were the first man here, God said. You're a part of my plan.
After two-hundred years of slavery and all the blood I've shed.
I'm still a part of God's plan, and I'll be here when you're dead.
You still called me Boy, and I watched the years pass.
But now, I don't smile to survive, I smile to stay off of your ass.

"Damn that's good, that's all right," said Ronnie smiling.

"Thanks; that was the way I felt. That poem kept me off of his ass and out of jail."

Ronnie went into a short thought mode, then said, "You know, I think about this race shit a lot, probably because of mama. I don't know for sure, yet, but she probably died because of her race; they knew nothing would be done about it. But I do know, if she had been white, we would know what happened, and probably who killed her." Ronnie slowly shook his head as he said, "It won't happen in our life time, but one day this race shit will be over. America is getting darker, not lighter. Blacks and whites are beginning to mix. As you know, that's the white man's greatest fear; a black man and a white woman. You said it in your poem; that's a part of God's plan for everyone to be equal; I truly believe that; until then," he shook his head. "I don't know."

Butch nodded as he said, "Let me tell you something that I learned several years ago. When I was in High School, my friend, James Blackston and I were walking uptown in front of Blackwell's Donut Shop. There was a beautiful, little white girl, probably about three or four year's old, standing up in the front seat of a car. With the friendliest smile and wave you could ever see, she said, *Hey Nigger.* She didn't know any better; just trying to be friendly. At that age, where did she get it from? White people are not born to hate, they're taught. I've seen pictures of little white children dressed up in Klan sheets. That was the beginning of their education to hate. That was hard for me to understand. Mom and dad never used the word hate. Dad would have whipped our asses good, if he knew that we disliked someone because of their race."

Ronnie nodded as he said, "What did you say to her?"

"Nothing, I just waved back and smiled; she waved again and even threw me a kiss. She was a beautiful little girl."

"That's good. Now let's go home; I'm ready for some of mom's home cooking." They rode in silence the rest of the way home. The Four Tops blared from the radio; WLLY, a local station.

Chapter 28

June 27, 1968
1:05 P.M.

Virginia opened the refrigerator and pulled out the orange juice. "I heard the car pull up, and I know you're ready to eat. Your lunch is ready."

"Yes we are, and thank you Mom," said Butch, as he leaned down and gave her a peck on the cheek. He and Ronnie then sat at the kitchen table, while Virginia prepared their food. "Most of the guys on the football team were from the north and had never tasted southern fried chicken," said Butch. "I told them, my mom cooks the best in the world."

Virginia walked around the table and gave Butch a hug, and then playfully pinched his cheek. "Thank you, that was so sweet of you to say."

Ronnie broke out into a huge laugh. "Did you tell them, you could eat a whole chicken by yourself when you were ten years old?"

Butch looked away trying to hide his smile, but moments later he broke out into laughter, Ronnie and Virginia joined in. After lunch Ronnie and Butch joined Sam in the den. They sat on the couch facing Sam, who was seated in one of twin recliners.

"How does it feel being home again?" Sam asked, looking at Butch. When I was in college, I came home almost every week-end, after basketball season was over."

Butch shot Sam a prolonged smile. "Different, but I feel good. I'll take a few days off, and then start a two-a-day workout to rehab my knee. It feels good, but I know it's not a hundred percent ready for football. I know I'll have to sit out this season. I've talked to the people in Pittsburg several times."

"When you're ready to start, let me know, I'll workout with you." said Ronnie. He looked at Butch and smiled. "Now, when you get that first check from the Steelers, don't forget me."

"Thanks Bro and I won't forget you."

Sam cleared his throat to get the boys attention. "Ronnie, I couldn't help but notice your reaction to the letter your mother left Miss Maggie. I wish I could tell you more, but I don't know anything."

Ronnie nodded with a slight frown. "Dad, my reaction was to the fact that most people in their twenties think about living, not dying."

Sam nodded, but was at a loss for words. He looked like he wanted to make a point, but wasn't really sure how to start. "There're a lot of things you Boys can't remember about that time period, because you were so young when your mother was killed." His statement got Butch and Ronnie's attention. "During that time blacks had two major problems; the first was racism and the other was tobacco money, and plenty of it." Ronnie and Butch looked confused at Sam's statements. "You know, Wilson County was per-capita, the riches county on the east coast and one of the riches in the nation. The more money they made, the more they wanted, and the worse conditions got in the black community.

Ronnie responded quickly. "It seems like it would have been the opposite, since black people were doing all the hard work."

"You're right, but they didn't think that way," said Sam. "I was raised over on Vance Street, so I saw it firsthand; streets flooding after heavy rains, outdoor toilets that sometimes spilled into the streets and the schools were in bad shape. Their thinking was, keep them dumb, and keep them in the fields, and it worked for a while." Ronnie and Butch looked at each other shaking their heads. Sam continued. "And the police department was really bad. A lot of the officers were members of the Klan, and they didn't try to hide it. They had a cell up there where they took colored men and beat them with a rubber pipe. Policemen took money from bootleggers and prostitutes to let them stay in business. There were several black women raped, and knew their attackers, and the police did nothing. But, if a white woman was raped, they would turn this town upside down. Several black men went to prison for raping white women. They would beat them until they confessed; one man was even put to death. So if you think it's bad now, when your mother was killed in the fifties, it was a lot worse." Sam paused like he didn't want to continue.

"Go on, we're grown now," said Ronnie.

After a moment or so Sam continued. "I don't know if you heard it or not, but it was said that white men killed your mother."

Ronnie nodded like he knew. "Yes, we heard that."

"During that time, some rich whites could do anything, even murder, and wouldn't be questioned. If the police know who killed your mother, and they probably do, nothing would be done about it, especially if they had money. It would just be covered up. They look at it as, "*Just another dead nigger.*" You have to understand, that in the mid-to-late eighteen-hundreds, it was estimated that a colored man or woman was lynched every three to four days in the south; it was like a recreation event. They had more respect for a dog's life, than they had for a colored person's life. If a colored man did something the white man didn't like, he could hang him, or do whatever he wanted to. In nineteen-forty-four, they executed a fourteen year old boy in South Carolina for killing two white girls. The trial lasted three hours and the jury was out ten minutes. Under threats of being hung, the boys family was ran out of town. There was no law against it; they were the law. They didn't have a lot of proof; they just wanted to execute a colored for the murder. That kid was in the wrong place, at the wrong time. When your mother was killed in the early fifties, we were just a few years removed from the south's lynching fervor, but their disrespect for a colored person's life never changed, even today. The men that killed your mother were the sons of that generation of men that were lynching colored people for whatever reason; so don't you ever think that attitude wasn't passed down, it was. I could sit here all night and tell you about things that would be hard for you to believe, not only in the deep south, but right here in Wilson."

Ronnie shifted in his chair and looked down at his hands that were clutched together. He looked like he was trying to hold his thoughts, but his words were out before he could stop them. "If I knew who killed my mama, something would be done. I don't care how much money they have, who they are, or what color they are." Before Sam could respond, Ronnie got up and moments later was in the bathroom, where he washed his hands and face and tried to collect himself.

Sam and Butch looked at each other, but remained silent for a moment or so. "Butch," said Sam in a low voice, "you were too young to remember your mother, but Ronnie does and he never got over it, and probably never will. I just hope he never finds out who was responsible for her death. I don't want him to get in any trouble." Butch nodded, but didn't respond. Sam continued. "Maybe I shouldn't have said that much. I thought our talk would help him get over it, but now I don't think he ever will, especially now. Viet Nam has surely changed him. I noticed something different about him when he first came home; your mother said the same thing. When we were waiting for you at the train station, a white man called him a boy. At one point in their conversation, Ronnie smiled at him, but his eyes were as cold as ice. I've never seen him look like that." Sam shook his head. "I knew a lot of men that came home from World War Two and Korea that had some problems. Back then, they called it being, "Shell Shocked." Now they call it, "Post Traumatic Stress Disorder", but it's the same thing. I don't know for sure if that's his problem, but it could be. If it is, we'll just have to pray for him and hope he gets better." Sam slowly shook his head and cast his eyes downward.

Chapter 29

June 28, 1968
12:30 P.M.

After lunch, Ronnie and Butch headed for the Reid Street Community Center. Growing up, they spent countless hours playing on recreation league teams, and Butch's dreams of playing college and professional football started there. They parked at the corner of Academy and North Reid Street. Butch started to get out when Ronnie grabbed his arm. "Wait, let's talk a minute."

"What's up?"

"I didn't sleep much last night. Mama's death still bothers me, and talking to dad last night didn't help any. I just can't understand how these rich white people can be so cold and uncaring about the very people that made them rich."

Butch quickly interjected. "Come on Bro; don't let that get you down. Even if the police know who killed mama, and they probably do, nothing would be done about it. Dad said that last night, and it's true."

"They probably wouldn't do anything, but let me tell you something before we get out. I don't know if you remember this or not, but when I was about twelve or thirteen, I was uptown in front of the courthouse and decided for one reason or another that I was going to drink some water out of the "white only" fountain. There was a white man sitting on the bench near the fountain, and as soon as I took a swallow of water, he jumped up and grabbed me."

Butch looked surprised and smiled. "Damn, what did he say, what happened?"

"He pushed me down and told me, if I ever did that again he was going to kick my nigger ass. I got up and walked toward downtown. When I got to the corner of Douglas and Nash, I saw Dad. As soon as I got in the car, I told him what had happened. That's the first and the last time I've ever seen him angry; veins popped up in his neck."

"Damn," said Butch smiling, "I wish I could've seen that."

Ronnie interrupted. "Let me finish. Dad turned the car around and headed back up Nash Street. He parked in front of the courthouse and we got out. The man was still sitting there. Dad asked me if he was the one, and I nodded. He walked over to that man, grabbed him by the coat collar and picked him up."

"Man, if I could've seen that," said Butch.

"He told that man, if he ever put his hands on me again that he would kill him. I've never seen dad look like that; I knew he meant it. When we were on our way home, I told him it was a lot of white people uptown, and I thought they might try to hurt us." Dad looked at me in a strange sort of way, and said, *"If a man don't have something that he would die for, then he don't have anything to live for."* I never forgot that."

Butch nodded before speaking. "I've heard him say that too, but we were just talking and he wasn't angry."

"So if I knew who killed mama, I would kill them or die trying. Right now, that would be the only way to get justice," said Ronnie.

Butch weighed his brother's words before speaking. "No, they would have to kill both of us." They sat quiet for a moment or two. Butch looked at Ronnie and punched him on the shoulder. "Let's go in."

Ronnie looked at Butch and smiled as he said, "One more thing. If I was uptown and saw that cracker that pushed me down, I would kick him in his ass. I don't care how old he is now." He and Butch smiled.

"All right Bro, let's go in."

Children were running to and from the gym and game room, when Ronnie and Butch walked in. Two, very skilled high school aged boys were playing ping pong on a table near the gym door. There was a large trophy case on the wall near the game room. Ronnie stopped and pointed at a picture in the trophy case of Butch playing midget football.

"We should never forget people like Boot Bell, Milt Bynum and Gene Cox. I remember those trick plays Boot taught us playing midget football," said Ronnie, "and they worked. He's not a big man, about a hundred and fifty pounds at best, but dad said that he could hit as hard as anyone on the team, and was probably the fastest player on the team when he played at Darden. Any success we enjoyed at Darden was due to their efforts when we were kids, playing midget football and basketball, and I don't think Boot and Milt were getting paid. They did it from their heart, because they wanted to help us. Their names are on both of those State Championship trophies, they're invisible, but they're up there." He looked at Butch and smiled. "I don't know why they let you play midget football. Look how big you are over those other boys."

"We were the same age," said Butch, smiling. "That wasn't my fault."

A young man stepped out from an office dressed in shorts, tee-shirt and sneakers. "Butch," he said in a friendly voice.

Butch and Ronnie walked toward him, they were both smiling broadly. "What's up Mac," said Butch. "Are you over here playing some ball?"

"No, I'm working here this summer. I have one more year in school." Ronald McCrimmon was a team mate of Butch's on the 64 State Championship team, and was now an all conference player at North Carolina College, in Durham. Mac exchanged handshakes with Butch, then with Ronnie. "What have you guys been doing? Someone told me they saw you last week," looking at Ronnie. "How long have you been home?"

"I've been home about two weeks," said Ronnie, "Butch came yesterday."

"Oh, before I forget, for the last two summers, we played the police department in a benefit basketball game. I always try to get as many of our teammates as I can. I'm asking you now," looking at Butch.

"Who else is playing?"

Mac thought for a second. "I've talked to a few of our teammates; Tank, Rick, Bernard Barnes and Sonny Mac, but I have about five high school players that wants to play with us."

"That's good enough for me," said Butch. "When is it.?"

"Tomorrow night."

Butch looked at Mac and shook his head. "Damn man, that's short notice, but I'll play."

"Great, be over here about six, the game starts at seven." "How is your knee? I saw the game on TV when you got hurt."

"Not good enough to play football yet, but I've been doing a lot of running."

"What about you Ronnie, why don't you play? We can always use another big man."

"No, you guys have enough."

Mac looked at his watch. "I need to run across town and get some recreation equipment. We don't get a lot over here, so I need to go and get that." Mac paused for a second. "If you guys don't have any plans tonight, I'm going down to Diggs Grill about eight-thirty or nine. Why don't you guys come down, so we can sit and talk some? I'm sure there will be a few people there you'll know."

Butch looked at Ronnie. "We'll be there," said Ronnie. "See you tonight."

Chapter 30

June 29, 1968
6:15 P.M.

When Ronnie and Butch arrived, the gym was already half-full. "Things have changed a little," said Butch. "Look at all the white people in here. I remember when they wouldn't dare come down here, and we couldn't go up there."

Ronnie looked around nodding in agreement. "I'll sit over here; you need to go in the locker room where the other players are."

"See you after the game," said Butch.

Ronnie walked to his right, then up on the bleachers; dressed in off-white linen pants, brown sanders and a dark brown silk shirt. He sat there thinking about the good times he and Butch had playing there as kids. Just before the game started, a white couple walked up the bleachers and sat down in front of him. Having long legs at six-feet four, he moved to his left where his right knee was outside of the man's left shoulder. When he shifted to a better position, his right knee touched the man's shoulder. "Sorry about that."

"That's alright Buddy," the man said looking around at him. "It's hot in here now, so I know, when they start playing it's going to get really hot," he said in a friendly voice. Ronnie nodded in agreement.

The man and woman stood and applauded when the Police Department Team came on the floor. "I played with them until I left the police department," he said, looking around at Ronnie.

"That's great, you look tall enough."

Minutes later, the Reid Street team came on the floor; Ronnie stood up and applauded. "That's my brother, the big kid with the knee brace on."

The man turned around to face Ronnie. "How tall is he?"

"He says that he is six-six, but he's more like six-seven. He was drafted by the Steelers, but he had a knee operation in January. He got hurt in his last college game."

"Where did he go to college?"

"Indiana, he played football and basketball," said Ronnie proudly.

"That's great, I wish him luck. "What's his name, so I'll know him when I watch the Steelers next year?"

"Butch Howard, he plays tight end."

"I'll remember that," the man said, as he stood up and pulled his shirt off. "If I don't pull it off now, it'll be wet before half time."

"You're right; it's really hot in here." Ronnie noticed a tattoo on his shoulder that got his attention, after the man sat down. He looked away several times, but his eyes crept back to the tattoo. His thoughts tumbled over themselves as he struggled to figure out why. His discomfort was growing; he touched the man on the shoulder.

"By the way, my name is Ronnie Howard," extending his hand. "What's yours?"

"I'm Bret Pope." He turned and shook Ronnie's hand.

"Please to meet you."

"The same here," said Bret, "and this is my wife, Sally." She briefly turned her head toward Ronnie and nodded, then looked at him again with a prolonged smiled. His Hollywood, good looks and tall muscular frame captured her attention, he was almost too handsome.

Ronnie sat there, his discomfort now growing in leaps and bounds. His eyes kept going back to the tattoo. He sat there as long as he could, and then finally said. "Excuse me Bret; I need to go to the men's room. I'll be back in a minute."

"All right Buddy, watch your step, and hurry back so you don't miss the tip off."

"I'll be right back." Sweat was rolling down his face into his eyes. When he got outside he took a handkerchief from his pocket as he walked toward the car, still not understanding his emotions relating to the tattoo. Suddenly, a fuzzy image of a man with blonde hair and a tattoo on his shoulder began to come clear. He was with his mother the last night he saw her alive. He struggled to maintain his composure; sitting there in an emotionally spent state until Butch came to the car. Butch's shirt and shorts were soaked with perspiration.

"Did you see any of the game?" Butch asked, Ronnie didn't respond. Butch looked over at him. "What's wrong with you man? I didn't see you in the gym. What's wrong?"

Ronnie looked like he was in a daze. "I'll tell you about it." He started the car and drove off heading south on Reid Street. The image of the tattoo stamped in his mind.

"Where are we going Bro? Home is that way," Butch said, pointing at Queen Street.

Ronnie responded just above a whisper. "We'll be there in a minute, just hold on." When they got to Nash Street, Ronnie stopped, then turned left. He drove one block and made a right onto South Carroll Street. He pulled over to the left and parked directly in front of the garage and room where their mother was killed. He turned the lights out and looked straight ahead.

"Why did you come here?" said Butch. "This damn place gives me the creeps. What's wrong, what's wrong with you man?" He touched Ronnie's shoulder.

Ronnie hesitated, trying not to get emotional. "I'm ninety-nine percent sure I met the man that killed mama tonight at the game."

Butch sat up, speechless for a moment or two. "Are you sure?"

Ronnie shot Butch a strange look. "You know me better than anyone, so you know I wouldn't say that unless I was sure."

"What happened, how did you meet him?"

Ronnie hesitated, then said, "This man." He hesitated again. "This white man and woman sat down in front of me. You know how hot the gym gets, so he took his shirt off." He hesitated and thought for a second. "When I saw the tattoo on his shoulder I couldn't keep my eyes off of it. I tried, but I couldn't. Before he took his shirt off, he told me he worked at the police department before. After I saw the tattoo, I asked him his name. He said he was Bret Pope. I sat there for a while, but felt so uncomfortable I had to leave. When I got to the car, it all came back to me. I remembered the tall, blonde white man and the tattoo like it was yesterday. This man was tall and blonde." Ronnie's voice was cracking with each word. "He was there, I know he was."

Butch grabbed his hand. "I believe you, just be cool." They sat there for a minute in the quiet of the night. "How can we be sure, and what can we do?"

Ronnie didn't respond right away. He was looking straight ahead. "I don't know; I'll have to think about it. But if I find it to be true, he will not walk away free, I'm sure about that." his voice was now cold and serious. "But, whatever you do, don't tell mom and dad about this."

"I wouldn't do that," said Butch. They sat quietly for a few minutes, and then Ronnie turned the car around and headed home. When they got home, Sam and Virginia were watching television.

"Who won the game?" Virginia asked, walking from the den to the living room.

Butch shook his head and smiled. "We did, but it wasn't much of a game."

"I left some food out on top of the stove," said Virginia, looking at her sons proudly.

"I'm not really hungry Mom, maybe Butch wants some." He walked toward his bedroom.

"I do, but let me get a shower." He kissed Virginia on the forehead and walked toward his bedroom.

Sam walked in from the den. "How did your knee feel Son?"

"Good," said Butch, "the more I run, the stronger it gets. But I know I have a lot of work ahead of me before I can play football again."

"Ronnie," yelled Sam. "Mr. Williams called. He said that he was going to start on the house Monday morning."

"Thanks Dad." Ronnie was standing in the door of his bedroom. "After Butch gets a shower, I'll get one and go to bed. I'm a little tired."

Sam walked from the kitchen towards Ronnie's room. "Don't wait for Butch, use the shower in our bedroom."

They both showered and after Butch ate, they went to bed. Later that night, Ronnie went to Butch's room. "Butch," he said, pulling on his shoulder. "Wake up, I just thought about something."

Butch half-asleep rolled over. "What man?"

"Remember Rodney Barnes, my friend in high school. He came here to see me a lot" He was still pulling on Butch.

"You know I remember Rodney, but stop pulling on me, I hear you."

"I think I know how to get the information we need, I'm almost sure I can."

Butch sat up in the bed, still half-asleep, but trying to be attentive. "How?"

"Rodney is on the police force, I talked with him last week when I first came home. He usually rides a police car, but he hurt his ankle playing basketball, so he's working inside until his ankle gets better. Tomorrow, we'll try to find him. I'm going to ask him to look in the old case file on mama's murder and let me know what he finds; I think he'll do it. The way he talks, they still treat the black officers like dirt… no promotions, no nothing. If he can get us a name or two, who knows? And I'll be sure to ask him about Bret Pope."

"Ok, we'll find him tomorrow, now get your ass out of my room and let me rest; I'm tired."

Ronnie smiled and lightly punched him on the shoulder. "You wouldn't have said that ten years ago. I'm still your big brother, and I can still whip your ass, I don't care how big you are." Butch smiled and shook his head slowly, like Ronnie was crazy, then pulled the sheet over his head.

Chapter 31

June 30, 1968
9:30 A.M.

Ronnie had awakened with a renewed resolve, and after breakfast, he and Butch discussed their plans for the day. Ronnie was confident, Rodney Barnes; his friend from high school would help him. "First thing we should do is call the police station to see if Rodney is working," said Butch. He got up from the kitchen table, walked to the telephone in the hall, and was back within the minute. "Rodney had a doctor's appointment, he hurt his ankle. The officer I talked to said I should call back about twelve and Rodney should answer the phone."

"Okay," said Ronnie. He thought for a minute then said, "If the appointment is about his ankle, I know where he is, let's go." They got up from the kitchen table, Ronnie yelled, "Mom and Dad, we're going out, shouldn't be too long."

"Okay," said Virginia, walking in from the dining room, "be careful."

They both kissed her on the forehead and left. When they got to the intersection of Nash and Carroll, Ronnie looked toward their old house. "Nothing we can do will bring mama back, but I want some justice, that's all I want, justice for her." He turned right onto Nash Street, heading west; Butch never looked toward the house.

"Where do you think he is?"

"Probably at the doctor's office, at the corner of Nash and Pender, let's hope he's there." Just before the intersection at Nash and Pender, Ronnie turned right into the parking lot at the doctor's office. He pulled in and parked, and minutes later a dark green car pulled in and parked beside them.

"Look," said Butch. "That looks like Rodney; you were right."

They got out, as did Rodney. "How are you doing Man?" Ronnie asked.

"I twisted my ankle playing basketball. Other than that, I'm all right. What are you guys doing down here?"

"Running you down; Butch called the station and they said you had a doctor's appointment, so I guessed it was here," said Ronnie, extending his hand. Rodney shook hands with Ronnie, then with Butch. Ronnie looked at Butch then back at Rodney. "What time is your appointment?"

"I have another twenty minutes before I have to go in." Rodney looked at Butch. "Damn you're big! This is the first time I've seen you since you graduated." He looked at Butch again from his head down. "Damn you're big!" Butch smiled.

"Let's sit in the car," said Ronnie. They got in the Cadillac; Ronnie and Rodney sat in front, Butch in back. Ronnie turned toward Rodney; his back was against the door. "I'll tell you the story later, but we need you to get some information for us."

"What kind of information?"

Ronnie looked at Rodney as if he were searching for words.

"I'm sure you heard about it some time ago; I mean about my mother's murder. Butch and I need some information."

"Yeah, I heard about it, but go on, just tell me what you need."

"We need for you to look at the case file and get what information you can about the murder. I don't expect a lot to be in there; there was not a lot of investigation."

Silence followed as Rodney wrestled with what Ronnie was asking. He looked straight ahead and after a moment or two he looked at Ronnie. "I'll do it man, but you'll have to promise me that you and Butch will never mention it."

"You have my word," said Ronnie.

Rodney looked in the back at Butch. Butch nodded. "That's all I need. I'll call you after I get off."

"Thanks a lot," said Ronnie, "I'll never forget this."

"Glad I can help you man. I'll need her full name, and the year it happened."

"Rose Ann Grant and it was in nineteen-fifty-two, January nineteen-fifty-two, on South Carroll Street."

"Okay, I'll call you at your house. The number is in the book, right? Oh, what am I saying? As many times as I have called there, when we were in high school, I could never forget that number."

Rodney got out and limped toward the doctor's office. Butch got in the front seat. "Take care of that ankle," he said. Rodney waved and nodded without turning around.

Chapter 32

June 30, 1968
10:05 A.M.

Ronnie drove out of the parking lot onto Nash, heading west. "Where do you want to go?"

"Don't matter," said Butch, "but you need to see your girl, or at least call her."

"I know," said Ronnie, "but this thing has been pressing on my mind. I didn't get a lot of sleep last night thinking about it. Maybe after we talk to Rodney, we'll have some answers." He drove west on Nash as the beautiful summer day asserted itself.

Large, plantation styled mansions were shaded by tall oak trees on both sides of the streets, from Park Avenue west on Nash. There were several African-Americans working on the manicured lawns and flowerbeds, which were a part of the nation's attraction to West Nash Street; named one of the most beautiful streets in America.

"Up here is like being in another world, but if you think about it, most of these houses were bought and paid for from the blood and sweat of blacks, working in the fields and factories for little or nothing," said Butch.

Ronnie nodded. They rode several more blocks west on Nash Street. "I'll turn at the next street, circle the block, and head back." He turned left on North Carolina Avenue, then left onto Anderson Street, after stopping at the stop sign. There were no mansions on North Carolina Avenue or Anderson Street, but they were both tree-lined streets that featured large, expensive homes and beautiful manicured lawns.

Midway the block, a police car pulled behind their car with the red light on. Ronnie pulled to the right side of the street and parked. "What did I do?" He glanced at Butch.

Butch looked back at the police car. "I don't know, but be cool.

Some of these crackers are looking for any excuse to kill you; just be cool."

The officer got out, put his dark glasses on, and did a poor- man version of John Wayne's walk to Ronnie's car. "Give me your license and registration." He pulled his hat off and slicked his hand back over his greasy, black hair. Ronnie got his license and the car's ID from his wallet and gave it to the officer.

The officer looked at both documents, then asked, "Who is Samuel Howell?"

"He's my father." He looked at the officer's name tag. "Officer Spivey, would you tell me why I was stopped?"

Dismissing Ronnie's question, the officer pulled his sun glasses off and stared at him a second or two. "I'll ask the questions here, you answer, Boy." he said, raising his voice.

Before Ronnie could respond, Butch grabbed his arm and shook his head. "Be cool Ronnie."

Spivey leaned forward and placed his hands on the door. "What are you Boys doing riding around up here? I know you don't live up here."

Ronnie clinched his jaw for a second to calm his temper. "Officer Spivey, this is a public street, and we haven't broken any laws. And we're Men, not Boys."

Butch again grabbed Ronnie's arm. "Ronnie, I told you to be cool."

Spivey then looked at Butch. "You got some identification, Boy?"

"He doesn't have to show you anything, he wasn't driving. Now, you need to write me a ticket, take me to jail, or I'm leaving," said Ronnie. His eyes widened as anger flared in them.

Spivey put his hand on his gun. "If you start that car, I'll blow your damn head off, Nigger Boy. Get out, both of you Niggers." He pulled his gun out and pulled the door open. Butch started to open the door on his side. "Don't open that door, slide out on this side." Spivey's boney frame stiffened as the tall, well built brothers exited the car. He backed up two or three steps and pulled his walkie-talkie from the case attached to his belt. "Headquarters, headquarters! This is car 10, over."

"This is headquarters, go head car 10."

"I need back up. I'm on Anderson." He hesitated. "I'm near North Carolina Avenue, on Anderson Street, over."

"10-4 Car 10, you all right? Over."

"10-4 headquarters, I'm all right. Just send some back-up. Over and out."

Spivey dropped his walkie-talkie in a nervous attempt to put it back in the case. "You Niggers turn around and put your hands up, and give me a reason to blow your black ass away." He backed up a few more steps. Ronnie glared at him, considered his situation and put his hands up, slowly turning around.

Sirens echoed from the direction of West Nash Street, and seconds later two police cars pulled up, stopping just short of where Spivey was standing. He stood there looking visibly shaken. The commotion outside was clearly audible to the residents in the area. A crowd began to form on the lawns and sidewalks along Anderson Street.

The first officer to approach Spivey was a tall, middle-aged man with lieutenant bars on his shirt collars, and a hearing-aid in his right ear. A thin wire connected the hearing-aid to a battery in his shirt pocket. "What's going on here?" He asked. Spivey now looked confused and a bit angry. "Put that gun away. You men turn around and put your hands down," the lieutenant said, before Spivey could respond. Ronnie and Butch turned and faced the officers.

"Lieutenant, them boys were riding around up here in a suspicious manner, so I stopped them. They were probably looking for a house to break into."

The lieutenant caught the trembling in Spivey's voice. He didn't respond to Spivey, but stared at Ronnie and Butch a second or two. "Did you get a license?" He asked, still staring at the brothers.

"Yes Sir." Spivey handed the lieutenant the ID's.

"All right, I'll handle it, you can go." He looked back at the other officer that arrived with him. "You too." He walked toward Butch and gave him the documents without reading them. "You're Sam Howard's Sons."

"Yes Sir, but how do you know that?" Butch asked.

The lieutenant smiled, then said jokingly, "I guessed." He extended his hand to Butch. "I'm Lieutenant George Capano. I was one of the white faces at some of the basketball games when your father was coaching, and I saw you play in 64, on the championship team. That was a damn good team."

Butch smiled and nodded. "This is my brother, Ronnie."

After shaking hands, Ronnie said, "Let me explain what happened here."

Lieutenant Capano held his hand up and slowly shook his head. "You really don't have to. The fact that you're black men, driving a new Cadillac, and was stopped by Spivey is explanation enough for me. One day, somebody is going to take that gun from him, stick it up his ass, and shake him until it goes off." They all laughed. "Tell Coach Howard I said hello, he knows me." He walked back to his car and opened the door. Just before he sat down, he said, "Howard, good luck with the Steelers." He then winked his eye.

Silently, Butch and Ronnie watched Lieutenant Capano get in his car and drive away. They stood there for a short period, dumbfounded. "He's not from this area, that's for sure," said Butch.

"How do you know?"

"His last name and the northern accent, no doubt."

They drove to the next block to Woodland Dr., and turned left, heading back to West Nash Street. They then turned right and headed east on Nash. Ronnie's mind was locked on what had occurred. He was so absorbed in his thoughts that he nearly drove onto the sidewalk. "Do you want me to drive?" Butch asked.

"I'm all right; I was just thinking about what happened." He looked at Butch stone-faced. "Now, do you understand why I have mixed emotions about being home? We could have been killed for just being black, and nothing would've been done about it. Just covered-up; like mama's murder was. I'm now convinced about that." They rode a few blocks in silence. "A man with a problem like Spivey's is dangerous. I can't understand why they would let him work in the public."

"They don't care," responded Butch quickly. "And I would bet that Lieutenant Capano had no say-so in the matter. He knows Spivey has a problem. I would like to catch his little ass in an alley one night, then he would have a problem."

Ronnie nodded in agreement. "Here's what people like Spivey don't understand or simply don't care about. Right now, this very minute; there is a young eighteen or nineteen year old black man in the jungle, in Viet Nam scared to death. At night, it's so dark you can't even see your hand a foot away from your face, and every small sound could mean death. The same people that sent him over there to protect this so called democracy, allows a fool like Spivey to ride around with a gun. When, or if that black man comes home from Viet Nam, he is again put in fear for his life, simply because he's black." All the pent-up anger came rolling out of Ronnie. He narrowed his eyes and gritted his teeth. "I'll tell you this. If I ever have a reason to pull a gun on one of them racist crackers, he's a dead man." He glanced at Butch. "I mean it, I'm sick of this shit, being pushed around like I'm less than a man, nothing."

Butch reached over and patted him on the shoulder trying to calm him down. "I understand, I'm sick of it too, just calm down."

They rode in silence until they crossed Tarboro Street, on Nash. "Don't tell mom and dad about this. You know how they worry," said Ronnie.

"All right, just get our asses across the tracks," said Butch smiling.

The remainder of their ride home they talked about what they remembered about the old neighborhood. "What do you remember about the old neighborhood, other than ice cream at Mr. Kirby's store?"

Butch thought for a moment. "I remember playing with Charlie

Jr. Ward and Randolph Williams in our back yard. All of us were in the same class."

"Randolph's nick-name was Huley-B, because of his father. But why did you call Charlie Jr., Charlie Cheese?" Ronnie asked.

Butch smiled. "Look at him. What do you think?"

Chapter 33

June 30, 1968
4:35 P.M.

Ronnie did a good job of keeping the anxiety out of his voice. He and Butch were in the den with Sam, waiting for Rodney to call; Virginia was preparing dinner. "Dad, tell us about Wilson when you were growing up. I mean, what did you do, other than go to school and work?"

Sam tilted his head to one side and narrowed his eyes in serious thought, then came back to the task of answering the question. "It was hard Son, really hard. At a young age, I remember asking God to bless my family with a better life. Now, I just thank Him for blessing your mother and me with a good education, so you and Butch could have a better life than we did." Before the brothers could respond, a big smile suddenly invaded Sam's face, "Now, about the second part to your question." He leaned forward and placed his elbows on his knees. "Fun, it was big fun."

Butch and Ronnie flashed a big smile. "All right Dad, let's hear it, come on with it." said Butch.

Still smiling, Sam said, "Let me tell you, on the weekends, downtown on Nash Street was like 42nd Street in New York. Both sides of the street were crowded, from Pender to the tracks. There were several clubs, dance halls, and restaurants; anything you wanted to do. And we had two movie theaters. Everyone came to have a good time; there was almost never a fight in that area, it was big fun. The only time there was a problem was when a white cop came down there."

"Two theaters, I only know about one, The Ritz," said Ronnie.

"The other one, The Global, was closed in the late 40s or early 50s. It was in the same building as Carroll's Pool Room, upstairs. Anyway, downtown was big fun and everybody dressed up; suits, ties, and hats, the works. If you didn't have but one outfit, you had it on every

Friday and Saturday night. And the ladies put on a fashion show, they had to, because." He held one finger up. "Wait a second." He went to the door, peeped down the hall, then pushed the door nearly shut. Reducing his voice to an undertone, he said, "They had to because, during tobacco season, tobacco buyers came to Wilson from all over the world. They bought tobacco and everything else. Prostitutes, colored and white also came to Wilson to make their share of the big money the buyers were spending. Looking good was just part of their job, and they looked good, but the Wilson girls looked just as good. There was a lot of money in this town." Sam paused briefly and looked toward the door. "The white women lived and worked in the hotels, but the colored women lived in two rooming houses on Jones Street, near Lodge Street. When that sorry, police chief, Watson, was a uniformed officer, he and some other white officers were regulars on Jones Street. The women had to service and pay them to stay in business. Now, Watson is masquerading as a nigger hater, so he says." Sam shook his head in disgust; footsteps in the hall got his attention. Moments later Virginia stuck her head through the crack in the door.

"What's this, men talk?" She asked smiling. "We can eat in about ten or fifteen minutes." She smiled and closed the door completely.

"I think we need to change subjects. I know you're grown men, but your mother would kill me if she knew what we were talking about."

Butch and Ronnie nodded in agreement. "All right Dad, let's talk about sports," said Ronnie. "Give me three names; the best football and basketball players, and the best coach you ever saw at Darden. Now, you have to exclude yourself, your son, and Booker T. Briggs, your favorite player."

Sam thought for a moment. "I'll start with Coach Gray. He won a State 4-A title in three years, at one of the smallest 4-A schools in the state. That's amazing, when you think about having to play against schools in Raleigh, Charlotte and other big cities. He didn't just beat those big schools, he killed them. They probably had more students in the school system, than we had colored people in Wilson. Football, Ike Lassiter for obvious reasons; he played in the NFL for several years, but I had to consider some others; the McNeil brothers, Herman and Joseph, Jerry Williams, Charlie Floyd, Robert Shaw and a few others. Now, basketball made me think a little. I had to consider players like Reggie Henderson, Raymond Atkinson, Bernard Barnes and several more, but I'll have to say, Donald Ray Jones; the best shooter I ever saw in high school. I saw him step across half-court and let it go; nothing but net; I think we were in Wilmington. He still holds the school record." Sam started smiling. "I asked Jones one day about his defense. He said, *"Coach, my man might get 8 or 10 on me, but I'll get a bunch on him."* And he would." The telephone rang in the hall.

"I'll get it Mom," said Ronnie. Seconds later he walked back in, looking at Butch. "That was Rodney, Butch. I told him you were home and he wants to see you. He said he hadn't seen you since you graduated from high school."

"How long will you be gone?" Virginia asked. "I don't want your food to get cold."

"Not long, I'm hungry," said Butch.

Butch and Ronnie met at the front door. "Where is he?" Butch asked.

"He's on his way to Lane Street Park," said Ronnie. They left Fikewood heading toward Hwy. 301, and made a right onto 301, heading south.

"He must have something for us," said Butch.

"Probably, he said he didn't want to talk on the phone."

They drove the four blocks south on 301, then took a left onto Lane Street. The park was about five blocks down on the right. When they got to the park Ronnie said, "This is supposed to be a park; a softball diamond and two picnic tables. Now go across town and look at their park. I don't know how they can live with themselves," shaking his head in disgust. "I couldn't treat an animal the way they treat black people, but that's what some of them think we are, animals."

"There he is," said Butch, pointing at the green Pontiac parked on the street near the softball diamond.

When Ronnie parked behind Rodney, Rodney got out, walked back to the car, and sat in the back seat. "I didn't want to talk on the phone, you never know. They don't trust me and I damn sure don't trust them." He then looked around out of the rear window. "Here is what I have. You got something you can write on? I didn't want to take a chance on writing it down."

Ronnie got paper and pen. "Go on."

Rodney looked at him for a moment. "Do you want it all?" Ronnie nodded slowly. "Okay. First of all, she died from strangulation and was sexually assaulted by three or more men."

Ronnie felt paralyzed. The information was overwhelming to him. He looked at Butch and took a deep breath; his heart sunk like the Titanic. Butch turned his head and stared out of the window as his eyes began to water. Ronnie turned back to Rodney. "Go on."

Rodney hesitated. "Are you all right?"

"I'll be all right, go on Man."

Rodney gave the brothers a short moment to calm, then said, "They had three names on the report and two of them are dead. Dan Williams and John Blue are dead; the other one is Carol Spells. Dan was the owner of The Bluenote on East Street. Blue was shot when Dan was killed, but died a few days later. They had Dan as a witness, but no description of suspects. Carol Spells was your mother's best friend. Now here is what I know. The two detectives that were assigned to the case disappeared, and were never found. Their police car was found in South Carolina. I got this from talk around the station. I looked, but I couldn't find a case file on their disappearance. Here's what you need to do. The Bluenote is not what it was back in the day, but they still have a good business. From what I heard, the owner now has been there a long time. I don't know his name, but

I've seen him a few times. He's a cool dressing, smooth looking old dude. He might be able to help you. I'm sure he knew Dan Williams." Ronnie and Butch looked at each other. "I didn't write Carol Spells address down, but I know she lives on Carolina Street, across 301. She might be able to tell you something."

The image of his mother being gang raped by those perverted cops, and fighting for her life suddenly invaded Ronnie's thoughts. No amount of inner strength he could muster could hold back the tears. Butch looked straight ahead; his eyes were teary. "That's all I know," said Rodney. "But if I come across anything else, I'll call you."

"Thank you Man," said Ronnie, his voice was trembling.

Rodney nodded, and got out of the car. Ronnie and Butch sat silently for the next few moments. "What do we do now?" Butch asked.

Ronnie didn't answer right away; he started the car and turned around. "The Bluenote, we're going to The Bluenote." He looked at Butch, "I'm now on a mission, and I won't stop until I find those animals that raped and killed mama." He lifted his chin and narrowed his eyes. For a long moment there was complete silence, then Ronnie said, "If it takes the rest of my life, I'll find them, I'm telling you, I'll find them."

Chapter 34

January 30, 1968
5:18 P.M.

When the brothers drove into the parking lot, Sugar Ray's white Rivera was the only car there. The club had changed in appearance over the past fifteen years. The pothole filled parking lot was now pavement, and night lights were spaced around the club. The side door was facing a three-room shot-gun house that had burned down early that morning. They got out and attempted to open the front door, it was locked, but moments later it swung open. Sugar Ray looked at the tall, clean cut, young men a moment. "Can I help you?"

"Yes Sir, we would like to talk with the owner," said Ronnie.

Sugar Ray extended his hand. "I'm the owner, Ray Reed is my name."

Ronnie shook Ray's hand. "My name is Ronnie Howard, and this is my brother, Butch. If you have a few minutes to spare, we would like to talk with you, Sir."

"I guess I can spare a few, and duck your heads." He smiled. They followed Ray into the office. Ray sat behind the desk and invited them to have a seat. "What can I do for you?"

Ronnie and Butch glanced at each other. Butch nodded for Ronnie to speak. "I really don't know where to start....but do you remember Rose Grant, who was killed back in the fifties, on Carroll Street?"

Ray sat up and leaned forward. "Yeah. What about her?"

The brothers again exchange glances. "We're her Sons," said Butch.

Ray sat there for a moment, speechless, then a broad smile appeared on his older, but still handsome face. "I don't know what to say; I knew your mother well. I remember you Boys, but that was years ago. How in the hell did you get so tall?" Ronnie and Butch smiled, and now felt relaxed about asking Ray about Dan. "When you said Howard....that threw me off, but I wouldn't have known anyway, but now that you've said it, the eyes, the color of your eyes. Rose had the most beautiful eyes I've ever seen. You're her sons for sure, I see it now."

"Our name is actually Grant-Howard, but we always say Howard," said Butch. We were adopted by Sam and Virginia Howard a few months after our mother was killed."

Ray was still looking from one to the other and smiling like he couldn't believe his eyes. "I liked your mother a lot; she was a good person, and a good friend of mine; I met her through my girlfriend. Sometimes they would come around here when the club was closed and we would talk, have a few drinks and listen to some good jazz; your mother loved jazz."

Butch looked at Ronnie and smiled. "Now I know why you love jazz so much; you got it from mama."

Ronnie smiled as he nodded, then turned to Sugar Ray. "Someone suggested that you might have known the previous owner of this club. We were told that he was a witness to something that had to do with mama's murder."

"You're talking about Dan Williams, and yes, I knew him very well, we were best of friends; I took over the club after he was killed. He was like a brother to me."

"What we want to know is, if he talked to you about what he saw or how he became a witness?" Ronnie asked.

Ray stood up and walked around his desk. "I need to get me a drink before we talk. Do you want one, or maybe a beer?"

Butch shook his head before speaking. "We don't drink, but thank you anyway." Butch and Ronnie looked on with anticipation, while Ray went to get his drink.

"Before we start, let me ask you one question," Sugar Ray said walking in. "I'm a big sports fan and I watch games on television whenever I get the chance, and I read the sports page every day." He looked at Butch. "You play for Indiana, right?"

"Right, and maybe next year I'll be in Pittsburg with the "Steelers."

"That's great; you're getting ready to make some serious money. I've seen you play on TV; they called your name and said you were from Wilson, but I had no idea you were Rose's son. I know Rose would be so proud of you, and I know your parents now are very proud." He then looked at Ronnie. "What are you doing?"

"I'm a First Lieutenant in the Army. I did my thing in Viet Nam, but I think I'm getting out. If I decide to stay in, I'll be promoted to Captain. I have three months to decide if I want to re-enlist or not. I graduated from North Carolina College in Durham; I'll probably end up teaching. My mother and father were teachers. That's what I want to do."

"You know what they say. Do what you love and you'll never work a day in your life." Ray looked from one to the other like he couldn't believe his eyes. "Both of you young men have done well. Now, I'm proud of you. Both of you have a good education; Rose would really be proud of that." Ronnie and Butch smiled, and after a short moment Ray said, "Now, let me get right to the point. Dan was killed because he saw the white men at Rose's house. They hired a white woman from out of town to do the job. She also shot my friend, John Blue. He killed her, but he died later at Mercy Hospital."

"Do you remember what Mr. Williams said they looked like?" Ronnie asked.

"I remember him saying that all of them were tall, but the one he remembered most had blonde hair and had a tattoo on his left shoulder." Ray paused in thought. "Two pistols, I remember him saying that for sure."

Emotions swept over Ronnie. His jaws clinched from the impact of Ray's words. He looked away for a moment, and then turned to Butch. "What did I tell you?" His face was Arctic cold. There was a brief period of silence, then Ronnie turned to Ray and said, in a low and serious voice. "Do you know a white man named Bret Pope?"

Ray put his elbow on the desk before answering. "I know the

name, but I've never met him. I heard his daddy died and left him a lot of money. He owns half of these run down shacks on this side of town. The one next door that burned down last night was one of his. He has a big office building on the corner of Tarboro and Garner Street. How do you know him?"

"I met him at a game at the Reid Street Center. When I saw the tattoo on his arm, it all came back to me. He was one of the men in the room the night she was killed, he probably killed her. I remember the tall, blonde man with the tattoo like it was yesterday."

"According to what Dan said, he fits the description, and there were three others with him, or maybe four. I can't remember, that was a long time ago, but I know he said that there were at least three of them."

"I don't remember how many, but I know there were others in the room," said Ronnie. "I didn't remember his face, but the blonde hair and the tattoo came right back to me. He didn't have a shirt on and he was real tall. I also remember him giving me some money. That was a long time ago, but I remember. "

Ray lit a cigarette and thought for a moment before speaking. "I don't know what your intentions are, but I can image how you must feel. Now, there were five people killed, including two policemen in connection with your mother's death. There was a cover-up, and it took a lot of money to do that, especially with the two policemen, so whatever you do, be careful...real careful. There is still a lot of money over there. Money can buy anything in this town."

Ronnie nodded, not so much in agreement, but as a signal that he understood. He smiled and said, "Thank you." He didn't underestimate the task ahead, but his Viet Nam experience had prepared him for what he was about to do, to get justice for Rose. He leaned back against the chair and stared a hole through the wall before speaking. "It took us two days to find what the police couldn't in sixteen years. That goes to show, there is no justice for a black person in this city, but I'll get justice for my mother, one way or another." He got up and motioned to Butch. "Mr. Reed, my brother and I thank you for your help; please let our talk stay among the three of us."

Ray immediately responded. "My two best friends were killed, so you won't have to worry about that. If I can do anything to help you please let me know, anything, money, whatever."

"Thank you Sir," said Ronnie, "you've helped us enough already." Ronnie and Butch stood up, extending their hands.

"Don't let this be the last time I see you," said Ray as he stood to shake their hands. "I've really enjoyed seeing you again; it's been a long time."

"We'll be sure to stop by again," said Butch, "and thanks again for your help."

"Don't forget to duck your heads," said Ray smiling. "And Ronnie, I got some smoking jazz that will knock your socks off, you name it, I got it; check me out."

"I'll do that," said Ronnie smiling.

Chapter 35

June 30, 1968
6:07 P.M.

Ronnie and Butch left The Bluenote heading south on East Street. "We need to talk to Rodney again," said Ronnie.

"What about?"

"I forgot to ask him about Bret Pope. Bret told me he was once a policeman. The crossed pistols tell me that he was probably a policeman the night of the murder. If he was, then the others were probably policemen too. Policemen don't have a lot of outside friends because of their job. Maybe Rodney can find the date he started, and who his best friends were. The other could have tattoos; maybe I just didn't see them."

"You're right," said Butch.

"I'll call Rodney tomorrow and see if he can meet us on his lunch break. There were others, and I want all of them," he glanced at Butch.

They stopped at the corner of East and Nash Street, Butch was driving. "Do you remember what Carol's last name was? Ronnie asked.

Butch responded immediately. "Spells."

"She probably doesn't know a lot about the case, but I'd like to talk with her about mama."

"What about mama?"

Ronnie didn't respond to Butch's question, but said, "Turn left, we'll see if we can find her."

Butch turned left heading east on Nash Street, then asked Ronnie again. "What do you need to talk to her about?"

Just as they were passing South Carroll Street, he said, "I don't know if you heard it or not, but when I first went to Darden in the seventh grade, some older boys teased me about mama being a prostitute." Butch looked shocked, like he had never heard that before.

"Some of the teasing was because my parents were teachers, you know how that was. I never asked dad anything about that, because if he knew, he wouldn't say anything, if he thought it would hurt me, but I want to know. Miss Spells was mama's best friend, so if anyone knows, it would be her."

Butch thought for a second. "It's up to you, whatever you want to do." He turned off of Highway 301 onto Carolina Street Extension. "She shouldn't be too hard to find. The first person we see, we'll ask."

"No, stop here, this is it," said Ronnie, pointing to a freshly paint-ed, gray house on the right side of the street. A mail box with Carol Spells name and house number was in front of the house.

"This is it, let's go in," said Butch. They got out and walked up the cement walkway. Flowers in bloom were spaced on both sides of the walkway, and in the flower bed around the front porch. Beautiful, neatly trimmed grass covered the front yard and around both sides of the house to the back.

Ronnie knocked on the glass storm-door, and moments later Car-ol opened the inside door. She was now a forty year old, very attrac-tive woman. She stared at the brothers for a second, then asked, "Can I help you? Before Ronnie or Butch could respond, she said joyfully with a big smile, "Ronnie, Butch," then opened the storm-door, smil-ing.

"You're Miss Spells," said Ronnie. "I can remember your face now."

"Yes I am. As soon as I saw those eyes I knew who you were, please come in." Carol led them into her small, well-kept living room. A small table with two chairs sat in the middle of the kitchen that was across the hall from the living room. "Both of you give me a hug. I've thought about you so much over the years." Butch, then Ronnie hugged Carol. "Please sit down, this is such a surprise."

Butch and Ronnie sat down on the couch. A picture of Rose and Carol was on the end table next to Butch. He picked the gold framed picture up and smiled, showing it to Ronnie. "This is beautiful, both of you," said Ronnie looking at Carol. As a child, he often wondered how different his life would have been if his mother had lived.

Carol smiled. "Thank you; now tell me who is who." She sat down facing them.

"I'm Ronnie, he's Butch."

Carol looked at the tall handsome men for a long moment before speaking. "Both of you are tall, very handsome, young men."

"Thank you. You're beautiful yourself," said Butch.

Carol was still smiling. "The last time I saw you'all was at your mother's funeral, that seems so long ago," she said with a degree of sadness.

"That was a long time ago, but we're fine now and we hope you are," said Butch.

"I'm all right; working hard like everybody else, but I'm fine," said Carol. "Now tell me what you've been doing."

"I just finished college; Ronnie has been out about two years."

Carol looked overjoyed after Butch's statements. "That's great, Rose would be proud of you. She always said that she wanted both of you to get a good education. She talked to me about saving money for your education. Before she paid her bills, she would put some money up for you."

They made small talk for a while, then Carol said, "I often think about Rose, we were best friends." Butch and Ronnie nodded. Carol looked away, breaking eye contact. She looked like she was thinking about what to say. She cleared her throat, and turned her attention back to Ronnie and Butch. "I owe my life to your mother," she said in a very serious tone. "The night before she died, we had a long talk. If not for the promise I made to Rose, to get my life together, I would probably be dead now." Carol hesitated for a moment. "I took a drink before I went to her funeral, and that was the last drink I ever had." Carol looked away again.

Butch and Ronnie nodded their understanding of Carol's state-ment. They sat quiet for a moment, then Ronnie said, "We're happy to know you've turned your life around." He looked around the room and smiled. "From what I see, you've done a good job." The brothers were both charming and mannerly.

Carol then turned her attention back to Ronnie and Butch smiling. "Thank you."

Ronnie spoke quickly in a very serious tone. "Miss Spells, I want to ask you a question about mama." He hesitated for a second. "Whatever the answer is, I need to know the truth."

Carol looked at Ronnie as if she knew what the question was. "I'll tell you the truth, but I already know what your question is."

Ronnie looked surprised, but didn't respond. "Go on," she said. Ronnie still didn't respond. "Okay, then I'll tell you, but I want to tell you the whole story, then you'll understand."

Ronnie nodded and spoke softly. "All right."

Carol lit a cigarette. "I want you to know what was going on at the time." She pulled on her cigarette, and said, "I'd been in the streets since I was eighteen years old; no education, no job, nothing. I worked in the tobacco fields and factories off and on. I met Rose at the factory on Mercer Street. Those white men were behind black women like dogs. Being young and dumb, I allowed them to take advantage of me. By the time I was in my mid-twenties, I was a used up alcoholic. I had convinced myself that I had no other choice, I was wrong. When Rose started working there, they were after her too, but she made them respect her. That's the choice I had. Rose was so beautiful, and carried herself in such a way, that men just wanted to be seen with her. Her hair, eyes and skin color allowed her to go anywhere she wanted to go. When she left Wilson, people didn't know what race she was." Butch and Ronnie smiled at Carol's statement. Carol smiled, and continued. "In the late forties and early fifties, very few black people owned cars or lived in nice houses; times were hard." Carol shifted in her seat and crossed her legs. "During tobacco season there were people coming to Wilson from everywhere. Most of them were looking for honest work in the fields and factories, but some came to make money in prostitution, and the police allowed it to happen, on indirect orders from the tobacco industry; they simply turned their heads. There were a few black women, but mostly white. The police would arrest a black woman every now and then to mislead the general public, but people knew what was happening. Rose had a nice car, a beautiful home and took good care of you. She was not from Wilson, so they thought she was a prostitute. She went out with some of the rich tobacco men and they gave her a lot of money, but that was it. She told them from the start that she was not a prostitute. They just wanted to be seen with a beautiful, young woman." Carol took a deep breath and looked away. She pulled on her cigarette again. "I was a prostitute, not Rose. I'm not proud of it, but it's the truth. Does that answer your question?" Ronnie nodded, Carol continued. "The police thought she was a prostitute; that was the reason why they never looked too hard for the killers, after the two detectives that were investigating the case were killed, and the fact that it was white men who killed her. I'm sure you heard something about that." Ronnie and Butch nodded. Carol sucked the last of her smoke, then continued. "I told the police what I knew about Dan Williams seeing the white men with Rose the night she was killed. Money, big money covered it up, enough money to have the detectives and Dan Williams killed."

"Did you know mama's friend, Bret Pope?" Ronnie asked.

Carol looked surprised at Ronnie's question. "No, Rose never called anyone's name. Where did you get that from?"

"That was a name that came up," said Ronnie.

Carol again looked away; a small tear ran slowly down her face. "Please excuse me." She got up quickly and made her way to the bathroom. Ronnie and Butch sat quietly while she was gone. When she returned she sat down and wiped her eyes.

Ronnie and Butch gave her time to compose herself. "Are you all right, Miss Spells?" said Ronnie.

Carol nodded slightly. "I'll be all right; I get emotional when I think about Rose. I loved her like a sister."

The three of them sat quietly for a minute or so, then Ronnie said, "Miss Spells, thank you very much. If anyone knew our mother it was you. You were her best friend and we believe you. I feel better after what you said. I'm sure Butch does too."

Butch nodded in agreement, he stood up and walked over to Carol, Ronnie followed. When Carol stood, they both hugged her. "We'll be back to see you", said Butch.

Carol was now smiling. "I hope so, and don't let it be too long."

Ronnie reached in his pocket, pulled out a roll of money and attempted to give some of it to Carol. "This is yours."

Carol smiled, then said, "That's very generous of you, but I can't take it. I stopped taking money from tall, handsome men a long time ago." She winked her eye. "Just kidding. You just come back to see me. That would mean more to me than money. I'm doing all right; just come back to see me."

"I'm sure mama would want us to do something for you, but we'll come back," said Butch.

Carol escorted them to the door and waved as they walked off of the porch. When Ronnie got to the mailbox, he opened it and put some money inside, as did Butch. They waved, got in the car and drove off smiling. Carol stood on the porch shaking her head and smiling. "I'll get you when you come back," she yelled, pointing her finger, and still smiling as tears rolled down her face.

Chapter 36

July 1, 1968
4:15 P.M.

The overcast morning had turned into a beautiful, sunny day. Ronnie met Rodney for lunch and asked him to get some information about Bret Pope. Butch and Sam were in the den; Butch was reading the newspaper. "Someone got shot in the School Yard," said Butch.

"That's a bad area over there; something is always going on," said Sam.

"I know, it was like that when I was in school, but I never knew why they called it the school yard. Elvie Street School is about two blocks over."

Sam looked surprised. "I thought I told you about the school that was on that site, but I remember now, it was Ronnie I told."

"Now that I think about it, I remember one of my teachers at Sam Vick telling us something about it. That was so long ago I forgot what she said. Go on, tell me about it."

Sam took a sip from his cup. "Before they built those apartments there, it was a school on that property. I can't say for sure, but I think it was the first school built by the city for colored children. This was around the turn of the century."

"Do you remember when it was built?" Butch asked, smiling.

Sam laughed, and continued. "It was called the Graded School or Sallie Barbour School. Grades went from the first to the eighth and after that, if your family could afford it, you went to a boarding school in Raleigh, or some other large city."

"That was bad", said Butch, "children having to leave home that young."

Sam nodded in agreement. "They said a young teacher from Washington, DC came to Wilson to teach there. She was highly educated, very bright, Mrs. Nowell was her name. She brought some new teaching methods to Wilson, and her students were learning really fast, as fast as the white children, so you know the white people didn't like that. The principal and the superintendent of city schools, Charles L. Coon called her to the office. She was told; she had to change her teaching methods. When she protested, Charles L. Coon slapped her."

"Are you serious?"

"Yes, that was a story."

"And they named Charles L. Coon High School after him," said Butch. He shook his head in disgust.

"That's right, and that was the first time the colored community had ever protested anything that whites did. There was outrage in the community," said Sam. "The colored residence took their children out of the Graded School and built their own school about two blocks from where I was born, on Vance Street."

"I'm surprised to hear that, especially during that time in the early 1900s," said Butch.

"That's right Son, it took some brave people to do that. They successfully, operated the school for several years."

"What was the name of the school?"

"It was called the Independent School and children did very well there," said Sam. "The school board asked the colored community to send their children back to public school, and the colored community did, after a while, on the condition that the city builds a high school. In 1923, Wilson Colored High School was completed and later named Darden High School. So you see Son, there is history in that area.

"I didn't know that," said Butch. "But they need to clean that area up."

The telephone rings. "I got it." Butch walked in the hall to answer it. "Ronnie that was Rodney; he wants to meet us at the park again," he said in a low voice, walking into Ronnie's room.

"Let's go, so we can be back before dinner," said Ronnie.

"Mom, Ronnie and I are going out, but we'll be back before dinner," said Butch.

"Okay, hurry back," yelled Virginia from the kitchen. "Just be careful."

Chapter 37

July 1, 1968
5:01 P.M.

Butch spotted Rodney's car when he turned off of 301 onto Lane Street. He parked behind Rodney near the corner of Snowden Drive. Rodney got out and walked back to their car. "What's up?" Ronnie asked. "What did you find?"

"You were right," said Rodney. "Your mother died January six, and Bret started his shift the next week, but here's what's most interesting. His three best friends started with him; Sergeant Davis and Detectives Farmer and Johnson. The four of them did their training together. From what I heard, when you saw one, you saw the others."

Ronnie looked at Butch. "That's what I was thinking," he said.

"If you ever see a brown, unmarked, police car on the East Side, that's Farmer and Johnson. When they are not working together, Farmer drives a black car. Sergeant Davis is in the uniform division," said Rodney.

"Do you know if any of them has a tattoo?" Ronnie asked.

"I know Farmer and Johnson does, I've seen them, because we have played basketball together. But I can't tell you about Davis. He's too damn ugly to play anything." They all smiled.

"What are the tattoo's?"

"Crossed pistols," said Rodney. "A lot of white officers have them. You know the old, one shot pistols."

Ronnie looked straight ahead, a flurry of images pulling his emotions in every direction. "Thanks Buddy."

"Thanks," said Butch.

"All right, see you later," said Rodney. He opened the door to get out.

"Hold up, there's a police car coming down the street," said Ronnie.

Rodney closed the door, and then looked out of the rear window. "Oh, that's the Captain and Big Len Dixon.

"I didn't know they had a black Captain up there," said Ronnie.

Rodney smiled. "We don't; his name is Floyd Dickerson, we just call him that. He and Big Lin Dixon are new officers. They're all right." He quickly changed subjects. "You need to know, Farmer and Johnson are supposed to be ass-kickers, so be careful." He looked at Butch and smiled. "But I don't think they're dumb enough to try that ass-kicking shit with you."

Ronnie nodded and smiled. Rodney got out and walked toward his car. Ronnie and Butch sat quietly for a moment or so, then Ronnie positioned his back to the door and faced Butch. "Look, I want you to look at me and try to understand what I'm about to say, and why." Butch faced Ronnie. Ronnie took a deep breath and said, "First of all, you're my brother, and I love you more than anything on this earth, more than I love myself. The same day mama died, I started feeling responsible for you, and that will never change. I can remember silently crying in bed at night, when we were at Miss Maggie's house, and when we first moved into our house. When I heard you crying, I dried my eyes and held you. When you came to Darden in the seventh grade, I was in the ninth. The boys in the upper grades were bigger and stronger than me, but they knew if they bothered you, I would fight them until they killed me." Butch was absorbing the information as he slowly nodded. "I'm sure you've heard me scream in my sleep, since you've been home, right?"

"Yes, I've heard you."

Ronnie hesitated, his eyes narrowed and hardened. "Some of the things I saw, and had to do in Viet Nam will never leave me. Any way that you can think of to kill a man, I saw or did. I'm not proud of it, but it's true; and there is not a day that goes by when I don't think about it. You can kill a man in a second, but you'll have to live with it the rest of your life; I don't want you to have to live with that." He glanced out of the window, and said, "Because of the way we were raised, you know, church and all; the thought of having to kill a man, or the sight of blood would have turned my stomach. Now, after Viet Nam, nothing bothers me. What I am trying to say is, you probably don't have the stomach for what I'm about to do, and if you think hard about what I said, you don't want that." Butch sat there speechless. He looked like he wanted to say something but remained silent. "The way I look at it," said Ronnie, "three things could happen and two of them are bad." He explained. "I could be killed, go to jail, or get away with it. Now, if any one of the first two happens, you need to be here for mom and dad. They're getting old, and will need you, so I don't want you to be involved. That's the way it has to be.

Ronnie started the car and headed to Fikewood. Just as they passed the corner of Lane Street and Snowden Drive, Butch said, "Pull over." Ronnie pulled over and stopped the car near the cemetery. Butch turned, facing Ronnie. "I have something to say. You don't know what I have the stomach for, and you didn't bother to ask me how I felt. I'm not a child and I make my own decisions. They didn't take your mother, they took our mother, and there's not a day that goes by when I don't think about it." He paused and glared at his sibling. "We work together or we work apart." He looked off to the north, across the cemetery, toward the trailer park.

Ronnie looked agitated, but after a moment or so he calmed, and grabbed Butch's arm to get his attention. "All right, Mr. Grant-Howard, let's do it, but you remember what I said. Whatever has to be done, I'll do it. I don't want you to have to live with anything that might affect you." Butch nodded in agreement, then said, "All right, you'll need me to watch your back."

"I could take half of Wilson out and not be seen." They smiled and hugged. Ronnie looked at his watch. "You drive; I need to think about something."

Chapter 38

July 1, 1968
5:35 P.M.

Butch headed toward 301. "When are you going to see Louise?"

Ronnie glanced at Butch and folded his arms across his chest. "That's what I was thinking about, ride with me over there; I'm not going to be in there very long. Mom is waiting for us."

"I'll go with you, but you need to spend some time with her. You know, she has called several times, but you never call her back. What's going on?"

Ronnie didn't respond he didn't even blink his eyes, looking straight ahead. After a minute or so he said, "You're right Bro, but my head is not there now. I don't need any distractions from what we have to do. I'll talk with her, I think she'll understand."

"What if she doesn't?"

Ronnie immediately responded. "Nothing, or no one is going to interfere with what we have to do."

Butch watched Ronnie's eyes drift shut and his head fall back. "Look, I'm with you, but you can't allow this to totally consume you. If it does, you'll lose your focus, we can't afford that."

Ronnie slightly nodded in agreement. "You're right, but you worry too much."

"Maybe, but you don't worry enough."

Butch turned off of 301 and headed west on Nash Street. Off of West Nash, he took Park Avenue heading south toward Walnut Street. Walnut ran through the heart of Daniel Hill; a low income, African-American community, surrounded by a large white community on the West Side of the city. Three room shot-gun houses, built around the turn of the century occupied the landscape in the small, close-knit community. "The Hill" was laced with talent; both academically, and athletically, but very few managed to escape the jaws of poverty. Being isolated in the middle of a white community instilled a true sense of unity; any act of aggression against any resident, was answered by the community. That's the way it was on, "The Hill".

"Back in the day, you couldn't come over here to see a girl unless you were tight with one of the hill boys. If they caught you, they would kick your ass back across the tracks," said Ronnie.

Butch chuckled. "So that's it; that's why you wanted me to come over here with you. You thought the hill boys might kick you in the ass."

Ronnie was smiling, looking at Butch like he was crazy. "Oh, hell no; I wouldn't worry about no shit like that. I survived combat in what is now considered the most dangerous place on earth; the jungles of Viet Nam. The hill boys don't want any part of me." He punched Butch on the shoulder, nodded once and smiled. Butch looked at Ronnie and smiled as he turned off of Park Avenue, onto Walnut Street.

"What was that football players name that lived over here; the one dad talked about all the time?" Butch asked.

"Booker T. Briggs, you should never forget that as much as Dad talked about him."

"Yeah, that's it, that's him," said Butch. "I remember playing midget football and basketball against the boys over here. They could be ahead by twenty, or behind by twenty, but they never quit. You had to kill them. It must be in the water."

Ronnie nodded in agreement, then said, "I didn't know it, but someone told me that Booker T. was married to Bernice. She lived across the street from us when we lived on Carroll Street, beside Mr. Kirby. She would baby-sit us, when Miss Maggie had something to do. Do you remember her?"

Butch went into a short thought mode, and said, "I think I do, but I'm not sure."

"I bet you remember her parents, Mr. Fletcher and Miss Lossie;

they give us candy and cookies when we were playing in our front yard. Remember?"

"I remember them," said Butch smiling.

Ronnie spotted Louise on the porch about a half-block on the right; a broad smile illuminated his face. After Butch parked, Ronnie got out and slowly walked toward the house. He paused at the bottom of the steps, and looked up at her. A hint of nervousness now covered his face.

Louise smiled, he was even more handsome than she remembered, and well dressed as always. Her warm smile eased his nervousness. "You can come up," she said in a warm voice. Her hair was perfectly done, her make-up flawless and her expression as natural as a sunrise.

Ronnie then flashed a relaxing smile. He walked up the steps onto the wooden porch and stopped directly in front of her. "I'm sorry it took so long for me to see you, but I'm here now, and you know I love you." They looked at each other passionately before she stood and pressed her face against his muscular chest. He softly tilted her head, face up, and wrapped his arms around her waist. The sweetness of her smile and the feel of her body close to his made him realize how very much he had missed her.

"I love you too, and I've missed you so much. I'm just happy you made it home alive," said Louise. They stood in silence, holding each other, until she took his hand to lead him inside.

"My girl, talking bout my girl," said Ronnie, singing along with The Temptations from a stereo in the small, but tastefully decorated living room. Louise smiled as they sat on the couch facing each other. They attempted to speak simultaneously. "Go on," said Ronnie.

Louise hesitated and stared at him for a moment. "I was going to say that there is something different about you." She slowly shook her head like she was confused. "I can't put my finger on it, but you're different."

"Being in a war and having to kill or be killed will change anyone;

I'm blessed to be alive." He moved close to her. After a long passionate kiss he said, "I didn't stay away because I didn't want to see you, I want you to know that."

"I never thought that. I knew you would come; I didn't know when, but I knew you would."

Ronnie sat back, cleared his throat and took a deep breath. "I've learned a lot about mama's murder since I've been home, and the strange thing about it is, I wasn't looking." The words came out barely above a whisper, tight with anger and pain.

Louise had a look of disbelief. "Are you sure?"

"Yes, I'm sure. I was at a basketball game at the Center and met one of the men that were at our house the night she was killed." He lowered his head, looking down at the floor in an attempt to calm himself. Louise looked overwhelmed, Ronnie continued. "I remembered the tattoo on his arm, and I've talked to a few people since I met him. I wasn't sure at first, but I am now."

"You need to talk with the police."

"Why?" He said raising his voice. He then took her hand. "I'm sorry." After a short pause he said, "I want to tell you something, but don't you ever repeat it, never. I mean to no one, your mom, dad, no one."

"I promise, never."

Ronnie spoke slow and deliberate. "The man I met at the Center was a policeman when Mama was killed. I'm almost sure that the other men there were policemen too. If I go to the police department, how do I know I wouldn't be talking to one of them?"

"I didn't know that, but you're right."

"So whatever is done, I'll have to do it myself."

"You can't," Louise pleaded. "Revenge is never the answer. You'll either get killed or end up in jail."

"Revenge and justice are different, all I want is justice. Sometimes desperate times call for desperate measures, and these are desperate times. If I don't do it, who will? Those white officers are just as bad now as they were when mama was killed."

Louise stared at Ronnie through tear filled eyes; her heart aching for him. There was a short period of silence as tears were slowly making their way down her face. "I'm afraid that something will happen to you."

Ronnie shifted in his seat, and looked directly at her. "When I was injured in Viet Nam, I was sent to a hospital in Japan. I was there for a little over two months, so I had a lot of time to think. I thought about my family and you, but most of all, about my mother and the senseless way that she died. I promised myself that if I ever found the people responsible, I would get justice for her, or die trying. I don't care who they are, what they are, or what color they are." He narrowed his eyes. "So, if I'm killed in the process, so be it." Determination burned in his face. "I almost got killed defending a country that doesn't give a damn about justice for me, my mother, or any black person. If I didn't do something, knowing who is responsible, I couldn't live with myself. To me, that's worse than death." He tried to steady himself against the onslaught of painful memories.

Louise nodded, not in agreement with what Ronnie said, but for her understanding that the Ronald Grant-Howard she once knew, no longer exist.

They sat in silence as Ronnie's battered, emotions calmed. After a minute or so, Louise stood up. "I'll be right back." She walked out and was back within the minute, smiling.

Ronnie looked at her puzzled. "What's up, where did you go?"

Louise hesitated still smiling, then said, "I told Butch, you said that I would take you home later."

"You lied."

"I did." She sat down on his lap and wrapped her arms around his neck. "I've missed you so much." After a long, wet kiss, she slowly and seductively, traced his lips with the tip of her finger, as she said, "My parents went to D.C. for a few days." She smiled and winked her eye.

Ronnie smiled. "You haven't change a bit."

"For you, I'll never change."

Chapter 39

August 15, 1968
4:05 P.M.

The house on Stantonsburg Road had been renovated. The living room contained a sectional sofa and an arm chair, surrounding a round, glass, cocktail table. The family room was littered with barbells for Ronnie's and Butch's daily workouts. Smooth Jazz filled their newly renovated, sound proof room; where Ronnie spent most of his time. "It feels kind of funny without mom and dad," said Butch.

"I thought about that, but here we are."

"What time do you want to leave?" Butch asked.

"He's usually there until about five-thirty; we can leave here about five. I told him about you being drafted, so I knew he wants to meet you. And after what we've seen, I knew he wouldn't turn down an invitation to meet some young, black women."

For the past month, the brothers had followed Bret Pope several times, from the time he left his office on Tarboro Street, until late at night, when he went home on West End Avenue. They knew he was a regular at the motels on Hwy. 301, and was usually with a black woman. "His secretary leaves about five-fifteen, so after she leaves, we can go in," said Ronnie.

They left home on Stantonsburg Road and headed toward Black Creek Road. They turned left onto 301 off of Black Creek Road, heading south. "Are you nervous?" said Ronnie.

"No, are you?"

"No. I've thought about this a long time, so I'm not going to blow it now. We both know what to say, we'll be all right."

They made a right off of Hwy. 301 onto Ward Boulevard southwest, and headed west, then drove another twelve blocks and turned right onto South Tarboro Street. "Look, his secretary is leaving now," said Butch.

They passed Garner Street, drove one block and turned left onto Forest Road, then took the first left onto First Street. "I'll park down near Garner Street," said Ronnie. They parked near the corner of First and Garner, got out and walked one block to Bret's office. His white Corvette was the only car in the parking lot. Ronnie knocked on the glass, double doors and moments later Bret appeared.

"Can I help you?" He looked at Ronnie and said, "Ron," with a huge smile. "The only reason I unlocked the door was because I recognized your face, but I couldn't remember your name right away. Come in." Bret was wearing an expensive off-white summer suit and brown and white wingtip shoes. After the brothers were in, he locked the door behind them.

"Damn, you're clean," said Ronnie; admiring Bret's attire.

Bret smiled. "Thank you."

"This is my brother Butch. Butch, this is Bret."

Butch nodded and extended his hand, "Pleased to meet you Bret."

"The pleasure is mine. Come on back to my office so we can talk." Bret walked into his office and sat behind his desk in a high back leather chair. Ronnie and Butch sat in two, black leather, arm chairs in front of his desk. "You look even bigger up close. How tall are you?"

"A little over six-six," said Butch.

"Damn, you're a big guy, and I can't wait to see you play, so I can brag about knowing you. What position do you play?"

"Tight end."

"All right," said Bret smiling.

Ronnie then changed the subject. "I have a friend that lives on First Street. We were going to her house last week when I saw you in the parking lot. I told Butch I met you at Reid Street, so when I saw your car today, we decided to walk around here."

"That's great, I'm glad you did."

"Look," said Ronnie. "Butch and I are having some friends over tomorrow night. Would you like to come?" He hesitated. "Damn, I forgot you're married; these are lady friends."

Bret looked around the walls of his office, leaned forward and whispered. "If you don't tell, I won't." They all laughed.

"That's fine, it's kind of a house warming," said Ronnie. "We just moved in."

"Where do you live?

"On Stantonsburg Road; when you go around the curve on Stantonsburg Road, our house is the only house on the right; we're almost in the county. You'll see a new Chrysler in the yard; I just bought it a few days ago. You need to pull around the back. It's not hard to spot a white Corvette," said Ronnie.

"What time are we talking about?"

"Seven or seven-thirty would be all right. Now, it's your decision, but if I were you, I wouldn't tell my wife where I was going; you never know. You know how women are."

"No, I wouldn't dare tell her where I'm going, and thanks for inviting me. I need to get out from around the old lady for a while. I get tired of sitting home all the time." Ronnie and Butch stood up; Bret stood and walked around the desk. "I'm glad you guys stopped by," he said as he was leading them out of his office.

Before Bret unlocked the door, Ronnie saw a picture of Bret with his family. Seeing the tattoo again triggered discomfort. When Bret unlocked the door, Butch and Ronnie walked out. "See you tomorrow night," said Butch.

Ronnie smiled with a half-wave. "See you." Emotions swept over him as they walked back to the car. "He's not only a killer, but did you hear him tell that lie about needing to get away from his wife for a while?" When they got back to the car, Ronnie gave Butch the keys. "You drive."

Butch turned left at Garner Street, heading east. He turned right at Tarboro, drove one block and turned left onto Ward Boulevard, heading east. He looked at Ronnie. "What's going on, are you all right?"

Ronnie gave him a half glance. "Every time I think about mama being raped and killed by that cracker, I want to…" He checked himself abruptly; pulled in a deep breath and shook off what he was about to say. A glint of fury had invaded his bluish-gray eyes. They rode in silence the rest of the way home.

Chapter 40

August 16, 1968
5:25 P.M.

Ronnie and Butch spent the day with Sam and Virginia. Ronnie cut grass, while Butch helped Sam and Virginia wash windows. They ate dinner and headed back to Stantonsburg Road. Ronnie had been watching his sibling all day for any signs of tension. He glanced over at Butch, who was listening to Smokey Roberson on the radio. "How do you feel?"

Butch turned the radio down. "First of all, Smokey is bad, and I'm all right," he said smiling.

Ronnie looked at Butch out of the corner of his eye. "You can stay with mom and dad tonight if you want to."

Butch glanced at Ronnie before speaking. "I thought we had discussed that already."

"I just wanted to make sure."

When they got home, Butch went to his room, and Ronnie listened to music; having no second thoughts about Bret Pope. He thought about Sam and Virginia and what their reaction would be if they knew about their plan, but that thought was quickly erased when he thought about Rose, and how she was murdered. Minutes later he fell asleep. After a period of time, he felt Butch pulling his arm. "Ronnie, get up. It's time for you to get up. You need to get a shower."

Ronnie's head snapped around. He blinked his eyes for a short moment, and then said, "What time is it?"

"Almost six, you need to get dressed."

He sat there for a moment; his nap had done him a world of good. He got up and headed to the bathroom. After he showered and dressed, he joined Butch in the living room. His mid-tan, linen pants and brown shirt complimented his mid-brown complexion.

Butch sat on the sofa with a clear view of the driveway. His massive biceps and muscular chest were defined in his red and white, Indiana t-shirt. "Let me ask you a question," he said, shooting Ronnie a quick glance, then looked out of the window.

"What?"

He glanced at Ronnie again and spoke in a serious tone. "Do you hate white people?"

Ronnie first shook his head. "No, I don't now, but there was a time when I did. I was very young when I heard that white men murdered mama; that would make anyone hate. My best friend in Viet Nam was white. A matter of fact, I got a letter from him last week. He told me he was going to be stationed at Fort Bragg as an instructor, at the Sapper School. As I got a little older, I realized that there were some good white people in the world, even in Wilson. Anyway, mom and dad didn't raise us to hate people, no matter what color they are. If Bret was black, I would do the same thing. I could never hate anyone because of their color." He thought for a short moment, then said, "Preston Young, my friend at Bragg, saved my life. He's white, but risked his life to save me; I think about that every day. I never talk about it, but I think about it."

"What happened? Now, if you don't want to talk about it, I'll understand." Butch glanced out of the window again.

Ronnie thought about it for a long moment, then said, "We were in the Iron Triangle, on operation Cedar Falls. I got hit in my thigh. It was a flesh wound, but it left a big hole and I was losing a lot of blood. Under heavy fire, he exposed himself to get to me and pull me back to safety. I think about him every day." He hesitated, and then a smile popped up on his face. "Our company commander was a short, white boy from New York, Captain McGriff; he had nerves of steel. The Viet Cong had us in a horseshoe ambush; in other words, we were cut off on three sides. We were out numbered about five to one. Before I got hit, I was about five yards from Captain McGriff; bullets were flying everywhere. I didn't think we were going to get out of there. I heard him yell, *"Lieutenant Howard, We got them just where we want them."* I couldn't believe what he said. They were kicking our asses good. It's funny now, but it wasn't funny then. That was the time when I wet my pants."

Butch smiled. "I probably would have wet mine's too, if I was wounded that badly."

Ronnie chuckled. "No, I wet my pants just before I was wounded. When they first ambushed us, I was so scared, I pissed all over myself. That was the first time I had been in an ambush." Ronnie's smile disappeared quickly. "We had about eight, maybe ten dead, and about fifteen wounded, including me. We called in for air support; that was the only way we got out of there."

"Damn, I know that was tough. What unit were you in?"

"The First Infantry Division, "The Big Red One." I don't know if you remember Thomas Purdie, we called him Tuck; he was two years ahead of me in school. He was also in The Big Red One. I didn't see him over there because we were in different units. I was in the Second of the Sixteenth; Tuck was in the First of the Twenty-sixth. But he won the Silver Star for bravery in combat. I heard he did some unbelievable things, under fire, damn! That was so hard for me to believe, because he was so easy-going when we were in school, but it's true. Dad's cousin, Alton Smith was also in the Red One. I didn't see him over there."

Butch stood up. "There he is; that's Bret."

Ronnie got up from the arm chair and walked to the door. He opened it and motioned Bret to drive around the back. Bret parked his white Corvette and walked back around to the front door where Ronnie was standing. "Come in," said Ronnie in a friendly voice.

Bret extended his hand, shaking Ronnie's hand, then Butch's. "Am I early?"

"You're all right," said Ronnie, escorting him to the sound proof room; Butch was walking behind Bret.

The room contained a sofa, matching recliners and a cocktail table. A color television was in a build-in wall cabinet; a reel to reel tape system and speakers were also contained inside the cabinet. "Have a seat," said Ronnie.

Bret was looking around smiling. "This is a nice room. I see you like music," he said as he sat in one of the recliners.

Ronnie sat in the other recliner facing him. "Yep, jazz is my passion, I love it." He nodded toward Butch, Butch then walked out of the room. "I want to show you something before our guest arrives."

Moments later Butch reappeared, handing Bret a gold-framed picture of Rose, Ronnie and himself. "That's me, Ronnie and our mother, Rose. Do you remember her?"

Bret didn't answer, but an alarm surged through him; he made an attempted to stand. Butch pushed him back in his seat. "If I were you, I would stay there."

Ronnie pulled a silver plated, .38 Magnum from his pocket. "Before you answer Butch's question, we need to reintroduce ourselves."

Bret attempted to speak, "I …"

Ronnie pointed the gun at this face and stared at him coldly. "Shut up killer." Bret closed his eyes, paralyzed with fear.

"We're Ronnie and Butch Grant-Howard. Our mother's name was Rose Ann Grant; I'm sure you remember her, South Carroll Street, January, fifty-two, remember?"

"No. Why do you think I remember her?"

Ronnie managed a weak laugh, "Because, I remember you. When I went in the room, you were standing up with your shirt off; that's how I remember the tattoo. You rubbed the top of my head and gave me some money. Remember now?"

Bret shook his head. "No, I swear to you, I don't."

"Hey, come on man, let's stop playing games; we know what happened." Ronnie paused and smiled. "Now you don't have much of a chance to walk out of this room, so the little chance you have depends on how much you tell me, and if I believe it or not."

Bret attempted to stand again. Butch was still standing over him and pushed him back down. His temper snapped. The cool demeanor that he was known for shattered like broken glass. "I don't want to hear shit. Kill that killer right now. Give me the gun, I'll do it. Give me the gun Ronnie."

"No, please don't," pleaded Bret.

"Be cool Butch. Remember what I said about this; come over here." Butch walked toward Ronnie, never taking his eyes off of Bret. Bret was now showing signs of panic. Ronnie's eyes narrowed as he stared at Bret. "Here's how we do it. I'll ask the questions, and the first time I think you've lied to me, I won't hesitate, I'm going to blow your ass away. Do you understand?"

Bret sat there; his hands and knees were shaking. Unable to speak, he nodded. Unable to control his fear, a mixture of sweat and tears ran down his face. "Please don't kill me. I'll tell you anything you want to know, just don't kill me, please don't."

Ronnie stared at Bret with a cold expression. Butch stood there, his muscular frame as tight as a drum. "Remember the rules," said Ronnie, "one lie and you die, now." Bret nodded.

"Who were the other men with you at our house?"

"Ronald Farmer, Kent Davis and Will Johnson," said Bret without hesitation. He wiped the sweat from his forehead with the back of his hand.

"Who paid to have Dan Williams killed?"

"I did." His voice was still trembling.

"What about the two detectives, why were they killed?"

"I gave the money, three thousand dollars to the woman that killed Dan Williams. Detectives, Price and Batts found it in her room at the Briggs Hotel; in our business envelope. They pieced things together and went to Chief Watson. Chief Watson told my father and my father gave him the money to set Price and Batts up; they knew everything." He wiped the sweat and tears from his face again.

"How did he set them up, and what happened to the bodies?"

"Watson told Price and Batts to check on a friend of his, Mr.

Lamm, who lived on Black Creek Road. He told them that his friend was an old man and someone tried to break into his house. When they went out there, Farmer, Davis and Johnson were waiting and killed them."

"Where is the house on Black Creek Road, and what did they do with the bodies? And I want specifics."

It's an old, two-story, brick house beside a pond, about two miles out. They buried the bodies behind the house, just inside the tree-line, near the back porch. They drove the car to South Carolina and burned it."

Ronnie looked up at Butch, then looked at Bret. "Why was our mother killed, and who killed her? And I want a straight answer. This answer is for your life."

Bret hesitated, and swallowed deep to digest the lump in his throat, then tried to gather his thoughts before speaking.

"You need to answer now," said Butch.

Bret threw his hands up. "All right, I'll tell you." He hesitated a short moment, then said, "I was in love with Rose; I never meant for her to get hurt. We went there to have some drinks and have a good time. I had too much to drink and passed out. The next thing I remember was waking up in my bed; I didn't even know she was dead."

Heat rose into Ronnie's face and his eyes widened as he said, "So you're telling me, you don't know who killed her. You were there, but you don't know. Is that right?"

"I don't know. I swear to you, I don't know. If I knew I would tell you. I was in love with Rose, I didn't kill her." Bret then came out of the chair and fell to his knees; his hands together in a praying position, then a helpless scream jumped from his throat, "Please, I swear, I don't know. I didn't kill her, I loved her. "

Ronnie got up and stood in front of him. "Get up! Get up now! Do you think I'm going for that bullshit? Your friends had no reason to kill my mother. All of you raped her, but you killed her; now get up." He pointed the gun at Bret's face.

Bret got up slowly, like a man going to his doom. He was shaking all over; urine darkened his light summer pants. "Please don't, my children need me, I beg you, please."

Ronnie challenged Bret belligerently, raising his voice. "My brother and I needed our mother. You knew she had children, but that didn't mean a damn to you, so it don't mean a damn to me." Ronnie took one step toward Bret; his eyes were narrowed and cold, almost nothing. He put the barrel of the gun to Bret's chest and said, "Damn you!" and pulled the trigger. Bret fell back in the chair; the bullet to his heart killed him instantly; his eyes were open. Butch and Ronnie stood there for a moment, looking at Bret's dead body. Ronnie looked at Butch, then back at Bret. "I never talk about Viet Nam much; because I never felt what we did over there was right. The people in Viet Nam were victims of money and power just like mama was. The Viet Cong would put signs and leaflets in the jungle addressed to black GIs. They said things like, *"The white man is killing your people in America, while you're over here killing us."* Another one I remember said, *"You're fighting a war for a country that won't give you justice,"* and they were right. So, if I can kill those people over there, who were only trying to protect and unite their country; I can kill an animal like that," he said, pointing at Bret, "who raped and killed my mother, just because she didn't love him." Ronnie looked at Butch.

Butch nodded understandingly. "One down, three to go."

"No," said Ronnie. "One down, four to go, Watson. Now let's get to work."

There was very little blood since Bret died instantly. They folded the body and tied it up with a rope; making it small enough to fit in the trunk of Bret's Corvette. Later that night, Ronnie drove the Corvette to a deep pond near Elm City, Butch followed. "Roll the windows down, so this thing will sink," said Butch. Ronnie rolled the windows down and got out; they pushed the car into the pond and headed back to Wilson. "Who's next?" Butch asked.

"Farmer and Johnson; they're ass-kickers who like black women; probably the same ones we saw with Bret at the motels on 301. They ride the East Side a lot, so they should be easy to track. We have to figure out a way to get both of them at the same time. Let this thing with Bret cool down first."

Butch nodded, turned the car around and headed back to Wilson. Ronnie sat quietly in a thought mode. "Are you having second thoughts now?" Butch asked.

Ronnie's jaw instantly tightened. "No, hell no! If I could bring him back and kill him again, I would. He and his gang- raping, murdering, cop-friends killed mama for nothing. And even if I had second thoughts, they would quickly vanish when I think about how they raped and killed her, and had Watson cover it up. To them, her life meant nothing." That thought alone angered him beyond words. He slowly shook his head in disgust, then said, "Mama, is on a long list of blacks, murdered by whites, and nothing was done about it. That cop that stopped us across town wanted to kill us, simply because we were black; he made that clear. To him, like Bret and his gang, a black person's life don't mean nothing." His eyes narrowed to slits and anger bubbled in his gut. "It's time for someone to stand up. I want justice for mama, but now it's deeper than that; I'm fighting for my life too. And if those cop that killed mama, and any other cracker that threatens me, don't kill me first, I'll kill them all, that includes Watson." He clinched his jaw for a second, then relaxed for several moments. "If I could go through the justice system to get justice for her, I would. I don't want to go through this shit, or take you through it, but right now, I don't have any other choice." He hesitated for a short moment, and said, "I took an oath in the military to defend this country with my life if necessary, and I was willing. Now, my country won't give me anything, not even justice for my mother." He slowly shook his head. "No, I don't have any second thoughts, not a damn one."

Chapter 41

August 17, 1968
8:10 A.M.

After numerous, unsuccessful attempts to contact Bret, Sally's mind was crowded with negative thoughts; she sensed something was wrong. It was totally out of character for him not to come home or call. She was now forced to see Chief Watson at the station. "Is the Chief in?"

"Yes," answered Officer Rodney Barnes. "Mrs. Pope, how are you?"

"Not too good, Bret is missing. I need to see the Chief."

Rodney got up and walked down the long hall to Watson's office. Moments later he called Sally. "Mrs. Pope, you can come back here."

Sally walked toward the Chief's office. "Thank you," she said. Rodney held the door for her.

Watson got up from his desk to greet her. He was fat and aging badly. He walked like an old man with bad feet. "How are you Sally? Have a seat."

A tear trickled down her face. She reached into her purse for a handkerchief, and wiped the tear away; trying not to smear her makeup. "Not too good, I can't find Bret. He never stays out without letting me know where he is. I think something has happened to him."

Watson interrupted. "Wait, let's not think the worse. I'm sure he's all right; he probably had too much to drink and fell asleep. Let me call Farmer and Johnson, maybe they saw him last night, or know where he is."

Watson got up and walked to the door. "Officer Barnes," he yelled. "Will you come back here?"

Moments later Rodney walked in. "Yes Sir."

"First of all, what time is the phone company supposed to fix the intercom? I'm tired of yelling and I know you're tired of walking."

"It should be anytime now, Chief."

"Call Farmer and Johnson in, I need to see them, ASAP."

"Yes Sir."

Watson turned his attention back to Sally. "When was the last time you saw him?"

Sally wiped her eyes again and gave a light sniff before responding. "He came home yesterday after work. We had dinner, and then he told me he was going out to meet some friends. He never said who the friends were, or where they were going to meet. He changed clothes and left; that was the last time I saw him."

"I'm almost sure he's alright, but after I talk with Farmer and Johnson, I'll have our patrol cars start looking for his car. Was he driving the Corvette?"

"Yes Sir."

"That shouldn't be hard to find; everyone in this city knows Bret and that car".

After a period of time Johnson and Farmer came to the Chief's officer. They walked in, and were surprised to see Sally.

"Hi Ron, Will."

They both nodded, Farmer hugged Sally. "What's wrong?"

"I can't find Bret. After we had dinner last night, he left to meet some friends. I haven't seen him since. I don't know where he went, or who he went to meet."

Farmer smiled and took Sally's hand. "If I know Bret, and I do know Bret, he probably had too much to drink and fell asleep. I don't think you have anything to worry about."

Watson nodded in agreement. "That's the same thing I said."

Sally's face brightened after Farmer's statement. He put his arm around her. "Go on home, we'll find him. I'm sure he's all right."

"Thank you. If anyone can find him, I know you can. Thank you Chief." She smiled and said, "When he gets home, something will happen to him, for not calling me." They all smiled.

Watson walked from behind the desk and took her hand. "Don't worry; before this day is over he'll be home."

Now with a ray of hope she said, "I hope so," as she was walking out.

Watson walked back behind his desk, still standing; he placed his hands on the desk and leaned forward. "I want you Boys to get on different cars; you can cover more ground that way. Stay on different cars until you find him. I don't care how long it takes, you find that boy."

Farmer and Johnson were convinced, Bret was in a motel on 301, where the three of them had met prostitutes in the past. They left the station in different cars, heading for 301. They went to every motel and questioned every manager, but there was no sign of Bret. They then concentrated on the East Side, where they sometimes made contact with prostitutes, but Bret, nor his car were nowhere to be found. Later that afternoon, they met at Wheeler's Amoco station at the corners of Nash and 301. "I believe he was robbed and killed by one of them niggers, so one of them will pay, guilty or not. I'll get a confession if I have to beat one of them to death," said Farmer.

Johnson looked at Farmer and smiled. "Damn, I was just thinking the same thing. Bret didn't have any enemies; he got along with everyone, so that's probably what happened. One of them niggers robbed him and killed him. It could have been one of them nasty, nigger whores, you never know. If something doesn't come up within the next month, we'll get one."

"Headquarters to car 3, over."

"Car 3 go head," said Johnson.

"Car 3, what's your 10-20? Over"

"Nash and three 301, over."

"Car 3, meet cars 10 and 14 on Powell Street, near Finch. A colored male, Wiley Ricks Jr. has threatened several people with an axe. Subject has a history of mental problems; you need to approach with caution, over"

"10-4 headquarters, over and out.

Farmer, that crazy-ass Wiley Jr. has flipped again. He's over on Powell Street with an axe, threatening people. We'll meet cars 10 and 14 over there."

"Lead the way," said Farmer.

Johnson pulled out into traffic with his emergency light on top of his car; Farmer was close behind. They crossed 301 on Nash and made the first left onto Powell Street. Cars 10 and 14 were nearing Powell, on Finch, when the detectives arrived at that intersection. The detectives exited their cars, as did the four uniformed officers; two of which were armed with high powered, 30 caliber rifles.

Cement-block, single family and duplex houses lined both sides of Powell, from Finch to Lane Streets. The three-block, dirt street was lined with tall, oak trees, and grassless front yards.

A short, medium complexion man was standing in the middle of Powell Street with a long-handle axe at his side. There was a long scar on the left side of his head that ran from his hair-line to the base of his ear; he looked disoriented.

"Wiley Jr., you better drop that damn axe," said Johnson.

Wiley Jr., dressed in boxer shorts only, raised the axe to a striking position. "I ain't never going back to that place, ain't nothing but crazy people over there; I ain't going back."

Wiley Jr. suffered brain damage after being struck by a car when he was ten years old. He was now twenty-seven and has been hospitalized several times in the state hospital in Goldsboro, North Carolina.

"I told you to drop that damn axe Boy, and I ain't gonna keep telling you," Johnson repeated.

"Officer," said an elderly woman, standing just a few feet behind the military style firing line, and directly behind Johnson. "Wiley Jr. is my grandson. Please don't hurt him, he's all I got. He ain't gonna hurt nobody. He's been like this since he was a little boy. A car hit him and he got hurt real bad." She stepped forward, between Johnson and Farmer, pulled a handkerchief from her apron pocket and began wiping her watering eyes. "Wiley Jr., ain't nobody gonna bother you Son, just put that axe down; it will be alright. Please Son, put that axe down."

Johnson stared at the old woman, then asked, "What's your name Gal?"

"Annie Mae King, Sir," she answered in a low, cracking voice. "I've had him since he was a little boy. His mama died when he was just two years old; she was my daughter. He's all I got left, Sir. Please don't hurt him."

Wiley Jr's eyes were red and aimless, and were constantly blinking. "I ain't going back Grandma, I ain't going back."

"You don't have to go back Son, just put that axe down, and we'll go home."

"We don't have all day to mess around with him. He needs to put that axe down," said a uniformed officer, his rifle beamed on Wiley Jr.

"Please don't hurt him, he don't know what he's doing," said Annie Mae. "He's on medication, and he gets like this when he don't take his medicine right."

"All right Boy, this is your last chance, I told you to drop that damn axe," said the gray-haired, fat-faced officer. He was ignoring Annie Mae's plea.

"I ain't going back," said Wiley Jr., as he raised the axe and threw it toward the officers; landing ten feet short of their position. The officers opened up with a wall of gunfire. Wiley's body lifted up as hollow-point bullets and 30 caliber rounds ripped through him; his left arm was severed, landed five feet away from his body. He was dead before his body hit the ground. A thick fog of smoke from the high powered rifles, and pistols drifted into the hot and humid, summer air.

Annie Mae turned her head and screamed out, "No!" Two young ladies held her; she knew he was dead. She screamed again, "No."

The crowd turned their heads, stunned at the bloody scene before them. "That ain't nothing but cold-blooded murder. He was unarmed when you shot him," said an old man who stepped out from the crowd. "You could have taken him without killing him. I've seen Hank Williams and Rudolph Best, walk up and take that same axe right out of his hand. But I know the way you think." He hesitated and shook his head. "I've known him since he was a little boy; I knew his mother. He had problems, but he never hurt anyone."

Farmer stared at the old, well dressed man. "We ain't Hank and Rudolph, and we ain't colored. He hesitated, then said, "You want to get locked up Boy? You better move your black-ass back and shut up. I ain't gonna tell you twice." He then put his hand on his holstered pistol.

An expensively dressed, young man who looked enough like the old man to be his son pulled his arm. "This is not going to help anything, let's go. We'll help Miss Annie Mae file a complaint; this is plain murder." He stared at Farmer for a second or two. "And you were talking to a man, not a boy. And Miss Annie May is an old lady, old enough to be your grandmother; so she's not a gal." They both shot Farmer a hard glared and walked away. Farmer didn't respond to the clean-cut, young man.

Annie Mae had fallen to her knees. "Please help me God. They didn't have to kill my baby, he was all I had. God please help me."

Johnson nodded toward a uniformed officer to check the bullet-ridden, body. After checking, he slowly shook his head.

Farmer, standing next to Johnson, said in a low voice, "That crazy nigger could have been the one that killed Bret; who knows? If we don't find the one that killed Bret, we killed us a nigger."

Chapter 42

September 20, 1968
9:35 P.M.

A month had passed, and despite the extensive and well-organized search, neither Bret's body, nor his car had been found. Chief Watson had detectives working around the clock trying to get a lead on the case. They followed every possible lead with no success, and a ten-thousand dollar reward for information brought in calls from all over the state and as far away as Texas. Since there was no ransom demand, they were almost sure he was dead; robbed and killed by someone on the East Side. Johnson and Farmer knew he carried large amounts of cash, so they were now looking for a body, and a suspect. They were convinced, Bret's death was connected to his association with prostitutes, but that theory alone was not enough to discourage them. Their sexual appetite for black women overpowered their sense of rational thinking. They continued their regular visits to motels on Highway 301; sometimes together, sometimes alone. Ronnie and Butch were watching their every move. "The Chevy," said Butch "that must be Johnson. He's getting out, so Farmer is probably not coming tonight."

"You would think policemen would be smart enough to change their routine," said Ronnie.

"If they were smart, we wouldn't be watching them, because they wouldn't be killers," said Butch.

Johnson parked his unmarked police car on a used car lot across Highway 301 from the Southside Motel. Ronnie and Butch were on the same side at the Kenwood Motel. From their vantage point, they had a bird's-eye view of the used car lot and the Southside. They had followed Johnson and Farmer enough to know their every move, even the room they would rent.

Johnson sprinted across 301 and into Room 11. A short time later the manager left his office and walked to the room. After collecting the rental fee, he went back to his office. Like clockwork, a Redbird cab pulled off of 301 into the motel's parking lot, in front of Room 11. A young, attractive, black woman got out and walked to the room's door. Using the room's outside light, she pulled a small mirror from her purse to check her makeup and fluffed her hair before knocking on the door.

The night was cool with overcast skies. Traffic on 301 was heavy as usual, with travelers heading north and south. "He usually keeps them about forty-five minutes," said Ronnie. "You know what you have to do."

"I know," said Butch, "I just wonder what lies we'll hear tonight."

Ronnie's jaw involuntarily clenched as his eyes narrowed and hardened. "I don't know what he'll say, and I don't care. He'll say anything to save his ass. As far as I'm concerned, they all raped and killed her. He was there, so the end result will be the same as Bret's."

The car lapsed into silence as they watched a convoy of out-of-state vehicles traveling north and south on 301. Ronnie pressed his lips into a line, as he contemplated speaking his mind. He turned the radio down as he said, "You were on my ass about calling Louise, and now your friend in Indiana has called you. Have you called her back?"

Butch squeezed his eyes shut. The words brought to him a clear image of Bella. After a long moment, he said, "No, our relationship is different."

"Why is that, because she's white? Is she the reason you asked me if I hated white people?" Butch glanced at Ronnie but didn't respond. Ronnie continued. "Indiana is a big school; you could have dated a black girl. Don't get me wrong, there's nothing wrong with you dating her, or marrying her if she's who you love. I just wanted to know."

Butch couldn't say anything for a moment. His heart was sinking deeper and deeper as he thought about what Ronnie said. He gathered himself, and said, "Indiana is a big white school. You can probably put all of the black girls on campus into a school bus; I didn't have much of a choice. A week after I got there, I was ready to go home. I called home two or three times a day." He took a deep breath.

"I didn't know that," said Ronnie sympathetically.

"You know how mom is, she told me to come home if I wanted too. Dad said, I should at least stay the first semester, give it a chance. All freshmen athletes are assigned a tutor; Bella was mine, the rest is history." He turned away and blew out a long breath. "After I met her family, they treated me like I was one of the family, a car and anything I wanted. Her father owns two car dealerships in Bloomington." He glanced at Ronnie with a short smile. "That helped." He then stared out at the passing traffic for a long moment. "When mom and dad came to my graduation, her family insisted that they stay at their house. Mom invited Bella and her family to visit Wilson. Bella wants to come, but I really wouldn't feel comfortable with her here."

"Why?"

"You remember what that cracker cop said, *"Give me a reason to kill you niggers."* If Bella had been with us, that would have been reason enough for him. He probably would have killed all of us, and nothing would have been done about it. To people like him, a nigger loving white person is the same as a nigger. I couldn't put her life in danger like that, I just couldn't."

Ronnie's eyebrows shot up as he said, "Look, I'm not dismissing the seriousness of what you said, but you can't let anyone control your life; mom, dad, me or anyone, especially them crackers. I would ride around with two guns if I had too. They would have to kill me before I let them control my life."

A long pause followed, a span of time in which Ronnie calmed. "I'll be right back," said Butch. He got out to relieve himself and was back moments later.

Ronnie touched Butch's arm. "Look Man, if you love her, you'll do the right thing. I don't have to tell you what that is; just follow your heart." Butch nodded.

They talked about Butch's future in football. About an hour later Ronnie grabbed Butch's arm to get his attention. "Look, the cab just pulled up; you know what to do." Ronnie got out of his car and ran to the car lot. He positioned himself behind the car next to the unmarked police car. Johnson walked out of the motel room and sprinted across 301, when there was a break in traffic. His keys were in his hand when he got to his car. Before he could open the door, Ronnie put the barrel of the gun to his right ear, he flinched. "Don't try anything, and you won't get hurt. Put your hands up."

"Do you know who I am? I'm a police detective, and if you're trying to rob me, you got a big problem, Nigger Boy."

Ronnie hit him on his upper jaw with the butt of the gun; Johnson fell to the ground, blood was gushing from a gash in his face. "That's the last Nigger Boy I'll be tonight, and I don't give a damn about who you are. One more word and I'll blow your ass away. Go on, Bad-ass, say something." He pressed his lips together and tamped down the urge to do just that. "Now get up."

Johnson got up; Ronnie turned him around and searched him. "Where is your gun? And I'm only going to ask you once."

Johnson was barely able to open his mouth, and he felt his knees going weak. "It's under the seat."

Ronnie pushed him back, got the keys from the ground and opened the door, never taking his eyes off of Johnson for a moment. He got the gun from under the seat and pointed it at Johnson's head. "Now where is the other one?" Johnson pointed to his inside coat pocket. Ronnie pushed him against the car and got the gun out. "How did I miss that?"

Johnson's white shirt was drenched with blood. "Get in the car," said Ronnie. He pulled the back door latch up and got in, seated behind Johnson. The barrel of the gun was touching Johnson's head. "Here's what you do, and if you make a mistake, you're a dead man." Johnson nodded. His head bumped the barrel of the gun, he flinched. "Get on your car radio. Have the officer to call Farmer, and tell him to meet you in front of Wainwright Warehouse. Tell him you have someone with you who knows something about Bret Pope's disappearance, and tell him to hurry. I know your jaw is probably broken, but you better make it sound good. One mistake and your ass is gone, Cracker Boy."

Johnson got the car radio, "Car 3 to headquarters."

"Go head," said the dispatcher.

"Call Detective Farmer, tell him I have someone with me who knows something about Bret Pope. I'm at Wainwright Warehouse on 301, tell him to hurry. "

"10 – 4, I'll call you back with his reply."

"10 – 4," said Johnson.

"That was good," said Ronnie.

Moments later the dispatcher called back, "Headquarters to Car 3."

"Car 3…go head," said Johnson.

"That's a positive, over."

"Thank you, over and out."

"Now drive to the warehouse. It shouldn't take him long, since he doesn't live that far from here."

When there was a brake in the heavy traffic, Johnson pulled out onto 301 and headed north. They passed Parker's Barbecue on the left and the Fair Grounds on the right. At the light, he crossed the intersection and made a right turn into the warehouse parking lot. A large, brick framed sign gave plenty of cover from the headlights of cars heading north on 301. "Pull your coat collar up around your neck, so Farmer can't see the blood on your shirt when he pulls up; do it now." Johnson took his right hand away from his face and pulled his coat collar up. Blood was still running from the cut on his jaw. They sat there quietly, for the exception of an occasional moan from Johnson; his face was swollen to a pulp.

Farmer's dark-brown, Ford was at the light; his right turn signal was on. When the light changed, he pulled into the parking lot on the passenger's side of Johnson's car; he got out and walked around the back of his car. Butch tipped up behind him, as quiet as a cat. He picked him up and slammed him to the ground. Farmer landed on his right side and attempted to get his gun. Butch stepped on his arm, pinning him to the ground. "If you move, I'll break your damn neck." Farmer lay motionless under the weight of the two-hundred and sixty pound strong man. Butch got his gun and pulled him up, pointing the gun at his chest.

"What the hell is going on?" Farmer asked.

"Be quiet and get in the car," said Butch.

"Wait, he probably has another gun," said Ronnie.

Butch pushed him against the car and pressed the barrel of the gun against the back of his head; Farmer put his hands up. "Here it is," he said, pointing down to his inside coat pocket. Butch got the gun and pushed him in the front seat.

"Put both of your hands behind your head and lock your fingers together. If you move one of them, I'll kill you," said Ronnie. He put the gun to Farmer's head.

"What's going on?" Farmer asked again.

"Be quiet, you'll know soon enough. Johnson, go north," said Ronnie.

Butch jogged across 301, got his car and followed. When they got to Black Creek Road Ronnie said, "Turn right, then turn left at Stantonsburg Road."

"Can I smoke?" Farmer asked.

"Yes, if you can light a cigarette with your hands locked behind your head," said Ronnie. "I told you not to move your hands, and shut up!"

Johnson turned left at Stantonsburg Road, Butch was close behind. When they rounded the curve, Ronnie said, "The house on the right, pull in the back yard."

Johnson pulled around the back; Butch parked behind them, got out and ran to the passenger's side. "Get out", he said, pointing the gun at Farmer. Farmer got out and Butch motioned him to walk around the car. Ronnie and Johnson were waiting. Butch then ordered them to stand against the wall, while Ronnie opened the back door. He opened the door and walked in first.

"Follow me, and keep your hands behind your head." Ronnie was walking backward to the sound proof room.

"Somebody tell me what's going on?" Farmer asked.

"We ask the questions," said Ronnie. He motioned for them to sit on the floor. Johnson and Farmer sat down side- by-side. Ronnie pulled the leather chair in front of them and sat down. His gaze slid from Farmer to Johnson. "My name is Ronnie Grant, and this is my brother, Butch. Does the name Grant mean anything to you?" He looked at Farmer, then at Johnson; neither one responded. "I'll cut the bull...I'll tell you. Rose Grant was my mother, you know, the woman you raped and killed in fifty-two, on Carroll Street. How can you forget that?"

Farmer raised his hands, palms up, and hunched his shoulders. "Not me, I don't know what you're talking about."

"Well, let me tell you this. We know what happened, even about you killing Price and Batts. Now, cut the bull, I want to know who killed my mother, and the first one that tells me a lie, I'll kill him. Now, one of you needs to start talking, and fast."

Farmer and Johnson looked at each other. "Bret," said Johnson. "Bret killed her. I swear to you, and he also raped her. We didn't touch your mother."

Ronnie knew that was a lie; he had heard enough from Johnson. He got up, stood in front of Johnson and shot him in the head, Johnson fell back. The head shot tore away most of his skull. Blood and brain matter sprayed Farmer's face. Ronnie fired another shot into Johnson's chest. Farmer looked at Johnson, then at Ronnie and threw his hands up, terrified. "This ain't no damn game, man; he's dead, said Ronnie. Now, are you going to talk, or what?" Ronnie stared at him a short moment, and said, "That shouldn't bother you; you should be use to seeing blood. I heard about how you, Johnson, and some other officers shot Wiley Jr. down like an animal on Powell Street. Everyone in the community knew he was harmless. I know this doesn't mean anything to you, but three days after you and your killer-cop friends killed Wiley Jr., Miss Annie Mae, his grandmother, took her own life. So in reality, you killed two people." Ronnie narrowed his eyes and stared at Farmer, then shook his head. "Some of you crackers don't have any regard for a black person's life." He pointed at Johnson. "That should tell you, I don't have any for yours."

Farmer knew his life could end at any second. "Don't kill me, please....I'll tell you what you want to know." His face was laced with fear.

Ronnie put the gun to Farmer's head and smiled. "Ok, killer, tell me." He backed up and sat back down. Farmer's body shook involuntarily; his first words were barely audible. Ronnie stared at him coldly and shook his head. Wishing he could shake off the memory of that terrible night his mother died.

"Speak up killer, I can't hear you," said Butch.

"Bret was in love with Rose, but she didn't love him and wanted to date other men." Farmer voice was trembling. "He gave her a lot of money and bought her a car, so he felt like she had used him. We didn't go over there to hurt your mother, but after Bret got drunk, he got violent. He wanted to get back at her anyway he could, so he told all of us to rape her. She resisted, so we held her down. When we finished, we left the room and sat in the car. Bret stayed in the room about five or ten minutes. When he came out his knuckles were scraped and bruised, and his face was bleeding from being scratched. We didn't know he had killed her until the next day. That's the truth." He looked up at Ronnie and begged for mercy. "Don't hurt me, please. I didn't want anything to happen to your mother, please don't," he cried out. Sweat was rolling down his face into his eyes. "I won't say anything about this, just let me go, I won't say a word. Please let me go."

Ronnie stood and looked at Farmer, then almost managed a cold chuckle; showing no concern for Farmer's plea. "That's the problem; you white bastards think you can kill, rape or do anything to black people and get away with it. You could have walked away that night. You didn't have to rape her, but you did. Well, your raping days are over, Buddy." He pointed the gun at Farmer. "If you think you can rape my mother, say you're sorry and I'll let you walk away, you're wrong, dead wrong." Without hesitation he fired; the bullet hit Farmer in the center of his chest. He fell back easy and never moved.

Ronnie looked at Butch then at Farmer. "Three down, two to go." He paused for a moment then said, "Okay, you know what the plan is, let's go."

They wrapped the bodies in bed sheets and put them in the trunk of Johnson's car. Ronnie wiped the car clean and drove toward Stantonsburg; Butch followed close behind. They left the car in a wooded area near Stantonsburg, and returned home to clean up.

Chapter 43

September 21, 1968
8:15 A.M.

Farmer's, unmarked car was found in the parking lot at Wainwright's Warehouse. His wife reported him missing, so the police suspected foul play. The ID officers were getting prints off the car when Chief Watson pulled up; Sergeant Davis was already at the scene. Watson walked over and looked in Farmer's car before turning to Davis. "What do you think?"

"I don't know, but it doesn't look good. We still haven't found Johnson's car. The only thing we know is, Johnson called the station at ten-fifteen last night and asked the officer on the desk to call Farmer. Johnson had someone with him who knew something about Bret's murder. He said he'd wait for Farmer here, that's it, that's all we have right now."

Watson motioned for Davis to follow him to his car. When Davis got in, Watson asked. "Are you thinking the same thing I am?"

Davis nodded looking at Watson. "What else could it be? The only question is, who and how many." They sat there in deep thought.

"Headquarters, to Car 1."

"Go head," said Watson.

"Detective Johnson's car was just found in a wooded area off Stantonsburg Road, about two miles from Stantonsburg. The man who found the car will wait on Statonsburg Road to show you where it is. His name is Jeb Dawkins, over."

"Was anyone in it? Over."

"He didn't say, so probably not, over."

"Sergeant Davis and I are on the way, over and out." Watson put his portable red light on top of the car and headed north on 301, siren blaring.

"This doesn't look good at all," said Davis. The heavy traffic on

301 moved over as the white, unmarked Ford approached the intersection of Black Creek Road. Watson turned right onto Black Creek Road, heading east, then left onto Stantonsburg Road. Traffic was light, so he was there within five minutes or so. Dawkins was standing on the right side of the road waving his arms. "There he is," said Davis.

Watson pulled to the right side of the road. The old man pointed down a path as he walked toward the car. "The car is about fifty yards down that path."

"Get in," said Watson.

Dawkins got in; Watson turned right off Stantonsburg Road down the path. Tobacco fields lined both sides of the path from the road to the tree line. Johnson's car was parked at the end of the path near a foot trail that ran into the woods. Dawkins rolled the back window down before speaking. "I was checking my rabbit traps when I saw the car. When I walked by I saw a red light in the front seat and a shotgun rack; I knowed it was a police car. I yelled out, but nobody answered." He stopped and spat out of the window. "I went back home and called the police in Wilson. I live right over yonder, across the road" He was pointing to a white, wood-framed house. He rolled the window back up.

Watson pulled in behind Johnson's car; he and Davis got out. Watson then walked to the driver's side, Davis to the passenger side. Watson got the keys by reaching through the downed window. He looked around the wooded area as he walked back to the trunk, unlocked it and pulled it up. The stench of death forced him to step back. The blood-stained sheets sent shivers down his spine. "Damn," he said, looking at the blood soaked sheets. "Both of them are in there. Davis, call the station and get some ID Boys out here." He covered his nose with a handkerchief and pulled enough of the sheet back to see Johnson's face. Half of his head was blown away. He looked back at Davis and slowly shook his head. He closed the trunk and walked back to his car.

"They're on the way," said Davis, when Watson sat down in the car.

"All right," said Watson. He was shocked at the scene in front of him.

Davis turned to look at the old man in the back seat. "You're Mr. Dawkins?"

Dawkins rolled the window down again and spat. He wiped his mouth with the back of his hand. "Jeb Dawkins. How many bodies in that trunk? Look like two or three from here."

Davis ignored the question. "Mr. Dawkins, did you see anything or anyone over here last night?"

"I saw a car over here at eleven-thirty. I knowed it was eleven-thir-ty, cause the news was just going off. I just thought it was somebody over there making-out. But it was another car parked on the high-way, right in front of the path."

"Did you see anyone?"

Dawkins spat out of the window again. "Hell no, just can see my television; don't know if they were white or negra."

Davis turned to Watson. "That means we can't get a tire print pho-to, the other car waited on the highway." Davis then turned his atten-tion back to Dawkins, "Is that all you saw?"

"That's it, ain't nothing but a nigger would do something like that. Them niggers always talking about going back to Africa; I wish they'd get the hell on back, every damn one of them."

Davis smiled. "Okay Mr. Dawkins you can go, but if you think of anything else, call me at the police station. My name is Sergeant Da-vis, this is Chief Watson; we thank you for your help."

"I'll call if I do, see you later," said Dawkins. "And you too Buddy." He tapped Watson on the shoulder. "I sure hope you catch them." Watson responded by nodding.

"What do you think?" Davis asked.

Watson was not sure how to describe his thoughts. He continued to sit in silence, gazing at the sky. After a moment or so he responded slowly. "I don't know for sure, but I believe they're going after you next, or you and me. Our only hope is to find them before they can get to us, and that won't be easy. They cover their tracks very good. I don't think we're dealing with your everyday crook." Watson looked at Davis. "These are smart people; smart enough to trap Farmer and Johnson together."

Davis glanced at Watson. "What can we do?"

"Be careful and hope they make a mistake. The ID officers might help us out. But I think the same people killed Bret and hid the body. They could have done the same with Johnson and Farmer, but they wanted us to see, give us something to think about. This is personal to them. That's what I think."

Davis nodded in agreement. "I'm sure they were smart enough to wipe the car clean, so we'll have nothing to go on, except maybe a foot print. Who will you assign to the case?"

"I was just thinking about that. Do you have anyone in mind?"

Davis thought for a moment. "Ray Smith and Don Best would probably do a good job, and I'm sure they wouldn't be intimidated on the East Side, where I believe our killers are. You see," he explained, "the way it looks now, this started when Bret killed that whore on Carroll Street." He paused. "Eight people have died because of one nigger whore, and it won't stop until you and I are dead, or we kill them."

Watson didn't respond right away. "If I had to guess who I think it is, I would say a family member of that nigger gal or Dan Williams."

"That's a good place to start," said Davis.

Watson picked up the car radio, "Car 1, to headquarters."

"Headquarters, over."

"Have Ray Smith and Don Best sent out here, ASAP, over."

"10-4, over and out."

Watson wanted to talk with Smith and Best. He needed their best effort in finding the killers. The homicides were unusual because the victims were police officers, which would make it a more difficult case. Smith and Best did not have a lot of experience on the East

Side, but they were hardnosed cops. Watson didn't want any outside help in the investigation. Johnson and Farmer were the second team of detectives killed since he was named Chief. An extensive investigation might lead back to him and Davis, and the murders of Price and Batts. Ten minutes later the ID team arrived. Watson and Davis got out of their car. "Morning Boys," said Watson.

"Good morning Chief," said the officer walking toward Johnson's car.

"I don't know if you were told at the station, but Detectives Johnson and Farmers bodies are in the trunk," said Watson, with a degree of sadness.

"The dispatcher didn't say, but we knew they were miss-ing, so it's no surprise," said the officer. "Maybe we can find something that could give you a lead. We'll do our best."

"I appreciate that, we need all the help we can get on this one," said Davis.

The officer nodded. Smith and Best pulled up and parked, behind the ID officer's car. Watson and Davis met them. "Get in my car, I need to talk with you," said Watson walking back to his car. Smith and Best got in the back seat; Watson cleared his throat before speaking. "Johnson's and Farmer's bodies are in the trunk of that car. I didn't see Farmer's body, but Johnson's head is half-gone. So you know these people are not messing around; you need to be careful." Smith and Best looked at each other in total shock, speechless. "We have no leads as of now, but we hope the identification officers can get some prints we can use. If not, it will be up to you Boys," said Watson. "We need to find these people before they kill again, and they will, if we don't find them."

"We'll do our best, Chief," said Smith.

"I have some old case files I want you to look at. Maybe they can give you a start. After you finish here, come to the station. Davis and I need to see the families of Johnson and Farmer," said Watson, shaking his head. "This is the worse part of my job, but I have to it.

Chapter 44

September 21, 1968
12:40 P.M.

Smith and Best searched the area around the car for evidence. The ID officers finished, and the remains of Johnson and Farmer were taken to the morgue at Wilson Memorial Hospital. Chief Watson had informed the families and was waiting for Smith and Best at the Police Department. The image of Farmer's face was still fresh in his mind. He was now thinking that whoever committed the murders probably knew about his involvement in the cover-up. His life, as well as Davis' was in danger. There was a knock at his office door. "Come in." Smith and Best walked in and sat down. "Did you find anything?"

"Not a thing," said Best. "And the car was wiped clean. Whoever it is, knows what they are doing."

"That's what I thought," said Watson. "Hold on a minute." "Sergeant Davis, would you come to my office. Smith and Best are here," he said on the intercom. Moments later, Davis walked in with a case file in his hand and gave it to Watson. "They didn't find anything and the car was clean," said Watson. "We're dealing with smart people." Davis nodded. The chief then turned his attention to Smith and Best. "Sergeant Davis and I talked a little about this case and came up with something we think is worth looking at." He opened the case file and looked at it for a minute. "Back in nineteen-fifty-two, which was, what, fifteen, sixteen years ago? Anyway, a nigger prostitute was killed by what was said to be white men, but that was never proven. Bret Pope's name came up, why I don't know, but it did. Now Bret is missing and probably dead. Johnson and Farmer were his best friends along with Davis." He paused. "It was said that four white men raped and killed her, so I think Bret, Johnson and Farmer were killed because of that." Davis nodded. "The only witness in the case was Dan Williams. He was killed about two weeks after the murder, so we think that some family members or close friends of Dan's could be responsible for the murders. It's a long shot, but very possible, and one other thing. The dead woman had two sons, and one of them said he saw some white men with his mother the night she was killed. I think he was about seven or eight then, so he's good and grown now. Dan Williams owned that club on East Street, the Bluenote, so you need to check there too."

"Where are her sons' now?" Best asked.

"I don't know, but I was told that they were adopted by a family here in Wilson," said Watson.

"Write this name and address down." said Davis. "I'll bet you, this nigger knows something about them."

Smith got his notepad. "Go on."

"Frank Ellis, 906 Manchester Street; I should never forget that, as many times as I have been there when he was selling whiskey. I bet he knows who adopted them and where they are now. Give him ten dollars and he'll tell on his mama. That's the way he makes his wine money now. The dead woman's name was Rose Grant, and she was killed on South Carroll Street, back in fifty-two."

"One more thing," said Watson. "Be careful, but find them nigger killers. Whatever you find, you need to come to me or Sergeant Davis before anyone sees the report, that's an order. Find them before they kill again!"

"Okay Chief," said Smith, Best nodded.

Watson stood up and with a firm voice said, "All right, go to work." Smith and Best got up and walked out.

"For a minute you had me believing it," said Davis, after the door was closed.

"That's the only way I knew how to do it."

Chapter 45

September 21, 1968
2:35 P.M.

Detectives Smith and Best left the station eager to start their first homicide investigation. Det. Smith, at twenty-five was the youngest detective on the force. He had the face of a bulldog to go along with his six-foot three inch, two-hundred and twenty pound frame. He looked tough and intimidating and at the same time, easy and approachable.

Detective Best came over from the identification division. Born in Newark, New Jersey, his family moved to Wilson County when he was in high school. He graduated from Charles L. Coon High School and Atlantic Christian College. He joined the Police Department the next year. They were good, honest cops and their work ethic enabled them to rise to the ranks of detectives.

"I think Manchester Street is the next street to the right," said Best. They crossed South Pender, heading east on Nash, then turned right at the first block, Manchester Street, and headed south

"There it is," said Smith. He pulled in front of 906 Manchester Street. The wood-framed, white house had two straight-back chairs on the front porch, occupied by two very drunk, middle-age men. Smith and Best got out and walked onto the porch. "Where is Mr. Ellis?" Smith asked.

The man to his right lifted his bloodshot eyes and pointed to the door. Saliva was running from his mouth at record speed. Smith looked at him, smiled and knocked on the door.

"Come in," a voice said.

Smith, then Best walked in what looked to be a living room. Steam was coming from a cooking pot on a wood stove near the back of the room. "Are you Mr. Frank Ellis?" Smith asked, talking to the man lying on a couch of undetermined color.

"Yeah, who wants to know?"

"My name is Detective Smith and this is Detective Best. We need to talk with you, Sir, if you have time."

Frank sat up and looked from Smith to Best. "I ain't sold no liquor in ten years. So if that's what you want to talk to me about, you're a few years too late."

"That's not why we're here. We need some information, but it's been so long ago you might not be able to help us," said Smith, as he pulled a money clip from his front pocket.

Frank looked at the money and giggled. "Try me. The sight of money, always do someum to my brain. If the price is right, I can look up a cow's ass and tell you the price of butter."

Smith and Best glanced at each other and smiled. "Do you remember a woman that was killed on South Carroll Street back in the early fifties?" Smith said.

"Rose Grant, hell yeah, I remember her. One of the prettiest women ever been in this town. I kept her yard clean and did all the painting around her house until she got killed. She was so pretty, I stole her draws off her clothesline, cause I know'd I won't never gonna get close to her; that was a pretty gal." said Frank with a big smile.

"You dirty old man," said Smith smiling.

"You got that right, and I'll be a dirty old man, till I'm a dead old man…. What you want to know?"

"She had two sons that were adopted. Do you know where they are now or who adopted them?"

"Hell yeah I know, Sam Howard, live over there behind Darden High School. I don't know where them boys is now, but somebody showed me one of them playing football on television; said that was one of Rose boys. He was a biggon; looked like he could pick up a shot gun house. I wouldn't mess with him if I had two guns."

"Do you know what street Mr. Howard lives on?

"No, but it might be in the phone book."

"Can I see yours for a minute?" Best asked.

Frank looked around the room before answering. "Do you see a telephone?" He asked, his smile showing all three of his gold teeth.

Smith and Best both smiled. "I think we have one in the car," said Smith.

"All right Mr. Ellis," said Best, "we appreciate your help." They turned to walk out.

"Hey Buddy, did you forget someum?" Frank looked at Smith.

Smith looked confused for a moment, then said, "Sorry about that." He gave Frank ten dollars, and said, "Before we leave, let me ask you another question."

Frank held his hand out and grinned. Smith gave him ten more dollars, shook his head and smiled.

"Thank you, shoot," said Frank.

"Do you remember Detective Price? He was investigating Rose Grant's murder, when he and a rookie Detective, Batts disappeared. I'm almost sure they're dead."

"Yeah, I remember him, and if you find the man that killed him, give him a bus ticket and ten dollars, then come to see me, I'll pay you back." Frank shook his head and narrowed his eyes. "That damn crook was taking money from every bootlegger on this side of town. If you didn't pay him, he'd kick the skin off your black ass; didn't matter if you was man or woman. I won't making but twenty or twenty-five dollars a week, and he was taking most of that. When he disappeared, it was like Christmas around here, people gave parties. But, there is one good thing I can say about him. Some of them other white officers would take your money, kick your ass and try to take your woman too; not Price, he didn't play that shit. He didn't want no part of no colored woman. He was a bad man, but there was a few bad niggers down here that he didn't mess with, he didn't even try that shit."

Best and Smith exchanged curious glances. "Did you hear anything about his disappearance?" Best asked.

"Not a damn thang. Everybody was just glad he was gone. I don't know nothing, except he's gone." Frank smiled.

"All right Mr. Ellis, but don't you think you owe me some change? You didn't give me any information."

Frank tilted his head with a mischievous smile. "Hell no, I answered your questions."

Smith and Best smiled broadly. "All right old man, see you later. But what in the hell is that you're cooking?" Best said, waving his hand in front of his face, the smell assaulting his nostrils. "Damn, it stinks."

"Catfish heads and onion. You want some?"

"No," answered Best, laughing out loud. "How can anyone eat that and live?"

Frank smiled. "Seventy-six years old and ain't dead yet; I eat this two days a week. An old root-doctor out of South Carolina told me about it and sold me some roots to put in it. Now, when I told you I ain't dead, I ain't dead. My old lady is thirty-six years old." He sucked his gut in and pushed his chest out. "Ask her if I'm dead." He then winked his eye and walked with the detectives to the door. "That old root-doctor also sold me two rabbit feets; told me to put them on the table when I was gambling and I would win all the money. I went to a card game that same night and put them on the table. Them niggers won all my money and the rabbit feets." Frank shook his head and smiled.

They all laughed as Smith and Best were walking out of the door. The two men on the porch waved as the Detectives got into their car. They were still smiling about Frank. "That's a funny old man," said Smith. Best nodded in agreement. "Look in the glove compartment, should be a phone book in there." said Smith.

Best got the phone book. "Here it is, Samuel Howard, 114 Fikewood.

"That should be it. Let's go to see Mr. Howard," said Smith.

Chapter 46

September 21, 1968
3:05 P.M.

Smith made a U-turn and headed north on Manchester Street, toward Nash. They turned right onto Nash Street, drove four blocks east and made a left onto North Carroll Street. "Mr. Ellis said it was behind Darden High School, so when you get to Queen Street, turn right," said Best. Smith turned right onto Queen Street, then turned left onto Blake-wood. "There's Fikewood," said Smith. "These are some really nice houses over here." He was looking around at the well-kept lawns and beautiful brick homes. "I was told at a young age, that all black people lived like animals, and I believed it. When I was in high school, I came to this area for some reason and it blew me away." He slowly shook his head. "Damn; I really believed that bullshit for a long time."

By the mid-sixties, the Fikewood, Bel-Air and Imperial Estate areas had replaced East Green Street as the showcase of the African American Community.

Smith turned right onto Fikewood, followed the numbers and stopped at 114. They got out and walked to the front door. Smith knocked twice and moments later, Sam Howard opened the door. "Can I help you?"

"Yes Sir. Are you Mr. Samuel Howard?" Smith asked.

"Yes, what can I do for you?"

"My name is Detective Smith and this is Detective Best. We would like to talk with you for a minute or so, if it's alright, Sir."

"Come in." Sam led them into the living room. "Have a seat." Smith and Best sat down; Smith was looking at pictures of Ronnie and Butch on the fireplace mantel. "What can I help you with?"

"Your two sons, are they here?" Smith asked.

"No, they're not, but why do you need to see them?" Virginia asked, before Sam could respond, as she walked in.

"These are detectives, Smith and Best," said Sam. "This is my wife, Virginia." Smith and Best stood up and nodded.

"Pleased to meet you," said Virginia, sitting down beside Sam.

"They asked me about Ronnie and Butch,"

"What about them?" Virginia asked.

"We would like to talk with them," said Smith.

"They're not here now, but I'll have them contact you, or we could have them here around five, if you'd like to come back," said Virginia.

"We'll come back," said Smith. They got up and walked toward the front door, Sam and Virginia walked behind them.

"Thank you Mr. and Mrs. Howard," said Best. "We'll be back around five."

Virginia and Sam looked at each other. "What could that be about?" Virginia asked.

"I have no idea, but I don't think Ronnie or Butch would get in any trouble; they're not that kind. I'll call them."

Moments later, Sam walked to the hall and called, Ronnie answered. "Ronnie, where's your brother?"

"He's asleep."

"Wake him up, and both of you come over here."

"What's wrong, has anything happened?"

"Nothing bad has happened, just be here before five."

"We'll be there."

"Ok, see you then," said Sam.

Chapter 47

September 21, 1968
4:50 P.M.

The detectives arrived on Fikewood about the same time as the brothers. They parked on the street and walked toward the front door. Ronnie and Butch parked in the driveway and walked in through the kitchen. They were in the living room when Sam opened the door for the detectives. "Come in, my sons are here."

Ronnie and Butch stood up when the detectives walked in. Smith extended his hand to Butch. "Someone told me you were big…. but damn. How tall are you?"

"Six-six," answered Butch, in a not so friendly voice, as he shook Smith's hand.

Smith then shook Ronnie's hand. "You're a big man too. This is Detective Best. My name is Detective Smith." He looked up at Butch again and shook his head.

Ronnie and Butch had no expression and remained cool. They knew they had covered their tracks, but had expected to be questioned, especially after Johnson and Farmer were found.

Virginia walked in. "Sit here Mom," said Butch.

"You're the Sons of Rose Grant, is that right?" Smith asked.

Sam interrupted. "Look, my sons were so young when that happened, they don't know anything about it. So you…"

Ronnie was becoming agitated, he interrupted. "Wait Dad. Are you reopening her case?" He was directing his question to Smith. The tension in the room was almost unbearable.

"No, we're not. Did you hear about the two detectives that were killed last night?"

Ronnie shot Smith a crazy look. "Yes, but you asked me if we were Rose Grant's son's first. What does that have to do with her case, and my brother and me? The only thing we know is what someone told us."

"We don't know, but it could be a connection, and it's our job to look at any and every possible lead," said Smith. "Nothing personal, just doing our job."

"My brother and I don't remember anything about our mother's death, and we sure don't know anything about the policemen that were killed, so we can't help you. Now, if you have papers for our arrest, we're willing to go. If you don't, then you need to go, now!"

"Wait," said Smith.

Ronnie stood up, his anger was growing. "Wait for what? I understand there was nothing done about my mother's death. They didn't even look at it after the two detectives that were investigating the case disappeared. Now, on the same day two of your people get killed, you're down here trying to intimidate us. The only thing I have to say is, you leave this house, now, and I won't say it again. If you don't leave, you'll need your guns."

Smith looked at Butch, and again at Ronnie, he motioned to Best. Ronnie and Butch escorted them to the door without saying a word. They walked out on the porch behind the detectives. Smith and Best got in the car and looked at the huge brothers for a moment, then drove off.

"One thing is for sure," said Ronnie.

"What's that?"

"They don't have anything, or our asses would be in the back of their car."

"They don't even know where we live, so I know they don't know anything," said Butch.

"Let's go back inside and talk to mom and dad, so they won't worry. I just thought about something; I'll tell you about it when we get home. Oh! One more thing; they saw our car, so we need to park in the back of our house. I don't want them to know where we live," said Ronnie.

Sam and Virginia were still in the living room when they got inside. "What was that all about?" Sam asked.

"I don't know, but someone at the police department sent them here. They're too young to know about mama's case," said Ronnie. "So it's probably about the officers that were killed last night. They were just fishing, trying to connect something."

"Maybe you need to talk with C.L. Washington," said Sam. "He's getting old, but still does a good job."

"Dad, I don't think we need a lawyer yet, and I know Mr. Washington is a good lawyer; but a black man, with a black lawyer wouldn't stand a chance in a southern court for killing a white man, guilty or not. If it was a black man killed, he could help, but two white cops, no way. That would be suicide," said Butch.

"You're probably right, so if there is a problem, I'll call Robert Farris, he knows me. His son, Robert Jr., and nephew, Allen Thomas are with his law firm now. They're young, but they're smart and tenacious. They'll fight just as hard for a colored as they will for a white, just like Robert would. I met them a few months ago; they're really nice young men."

Ronnie and Butch nodded. "I don't care who they are, if they're good lawyers and white," said Ronnie smiling. And if we ever have to go to court, I hope they have blond hair and blue eyes, so there will be no mistake. They all smiled.

Virginia spoke softly with a concerned look. "I just want you to be careful. You know how mean and nasty they can be."

"Don't worry Mom, we will," said Ronnie, putting his arm around her.

"I cooked enough for you'all, stay and eat with us," said Virginia.

Chapter 48

September 22, 1968
3:10 P.M.

Detectives Smith and Best pulled into the parking lot at the Blue-note. Sugar Ray's, Riviera was the only car there. They got out and before they could knock, Sugar Ray opened the door. "Can I help you?"

Smith extended his hand. "I'm Detective Ray Smith. This is Detective Don Best. Are you the owner?"

Shaking Smith's hand, Ray answered, "Yes, I'm the owner, Ray Reed is my name."

"Mr. Reed, is there some place where we can talk?" Smith asked.

"Come in, we can go to my office." The Jazz Crusaders were blaring from speakers mounted around the club.

"That's good Jazz, I like that. What group is that?" said Best. "You don't hear anything but country music on the radio around here."

"They're the Crusaders, Street Life." They walked toward Ray's office. Smith and Best were looking around like kids at Disney World. When they walked in the office, Ray sat behind his desk.

"This is a nice place you have here," said Smith.

"Have a seat, and thank you."

"Let me get right to the point," said Smith. "First of all, this is an unofficial visit. We would just like to ask you a few questions, if it's alright with you, Sir."

"I know I haven't done anything, but you never know. How can I help you?"

"I'm sure you heard about the policemen that were killed last night," said Smith.

Ray nodded. "Yes, I heard."

"Well, we think it could be a connection between the murders last night, and the murders in fifty-two of Rose Grant and Dan Williams;

so we want to know how well you knew Mr. Williams, and Miss Grant, or if they had family or friends that…."

Ray interrupted. "Look, I don't know what you know about the case of Rose and Dan, but it was a lot more to it than most people think. First of all, the two detectives that were investigating the case just disappeared. Four white men killed Rose because Dan saw them, that's why he was killed. She had two sons and one of them saw some white men in her room. It's was clear that the detectives knew who it was, so they were killed. One more thing; the woman that killed Dan was a paid killer. In nineteen-fifty-two, black people didn't have the money, or the connection to have anyone killed, especially policemen. Now, I don't know if you men are honest or crooks and personally, I don't give a damn, but there was a big cover-up." Ray looked down, but only briefly as his nostrils flared and he drew in a deep breath through his pearl, white teeth.

Best and Smith looked at each other and gave Ray time to cool down. "We went to talk with Rose Grant's sons, and I thought for a minute we would have to shoot our way out of there," said Best smiling. "They're big men; and now I understand why they're bitter, I would be, under similar circumstances."

"I've seen them, and they are big," said Ray smiling.

"I guess we need to start from square one; that will be the only way to find what we need to know," said Best.

"The man that disappeared, Bret Pope, was named in Rose's murder," said Ray. "Dan told me that one of the men, or maybe all of them had tattoos of crossed pistols on their shoulders. I was told Bret Pope had one. When I say named, I don't mean officially, I mean his name came up years later. Bret's family had a lot of money." Ray leaned forward, put his elbows on his desk and lit a cigarette. "You know what that means in this town. Bret and the two officers that were killed last night were best friends. That was what I was told. That's all I know. It doesn't take Sherlock Holmes to figure this one out."

Best stood up and smiled, extending his hand. "Mr. Reed, you've helped us a lot and we thank you, Sir."

"I don't need any problems with anyone, so if you don't mind," said Ray.

Smith interrupted. "We know, and again we thank you, Sir." He shook Sugar Ray's hand.

The Detectives left the Bluenote, now with more questions than answers. "Either Mr. Reed is the best liar in the world or Watson and Davis are crooks," said Best. "Mr. Reed said, Bret, Farmer, Davis and Johnson were best friends. Watson said the same thing, and did you notice, Watson never let us see the case file. That means there was something in there that he didn't want us to see. Like Mr. Reed said, it doesn't take Sherlock Holmes to figure out why." They stopped at the intersection of East and Nash Streets.

"Where do you want to go?" Smith asked.

"Pull over there, let's think for a minute," said Best, pointing to a gas station.

Smith turned right onto Nash Street, then a quick left into the parking lot at Little Bobbie's Store. Edwards Funeral Home was across the street at the corner of Nash and East. "I would like to see the case file on Rose Grant, Dan Williams and the two detectives," said Best. "That should tell us a lot.

"It's a little after four now and the Chief usually leaves around this time, so let's see what's in the files," said Smith. "We need to talk with Ronnie and Butch again, but with a different approach."

"You're right," said Best. "They're too big to fight."

"We'll see them tomorrow, and I want to see the bodies of Johnson and Farmer. The autopsy was probably this morning, so we can get the report while we're out there." said Smith. "But I'm more interested in the tattoos. If they have tattoos, we'll know the story."

"Let me ask you something. If we find that Watson and Davis did take part in a cover up, and the murders of Detectives, Price and Batts, what can we do?" Best asked.

Smith looked at Best, but didn't answer right away. After a moment of thought, he said, "We do the right thing. What and how, I can't answer right now."

"Let's go," said Best. "I can't wait to see the files."

Chapter 49

September 22, 1968
3:58 P.M.

It was warm and humid…. but not uncomfortable after an overcast morning. Nash Street was crowded. "Davis should be gone, I think he's working first shift, unless the Chief just called him in," said Best.

Smith and Best got to the station and went straight to the file room. They searched for the files, but kept their eyes open.

"Damn, I don't see anything," said Best.

"I don't either," said Smith, "but keep looking. They could be out of place."

"Out of place my ass, they are not here," said Best.

They continued their search until Best said, "There's something wrong with this picture. Let's get out of here and go to our office."

Smith and Best were now very interested. They knew the missing files were simply no mistake. They also knew they had to be very careful. This police department now has a history of detective teams being killed, or missing. They went to their office and closed the door. "After we see the bodies and talk with Ronnie and Butch, we'll probably know more about the case than what would be in the files. A cover up usually means, the recorded paper evidence has been destroyed or altered," said Best.

Their desks were facing, pushed together. "You asked me what we could or should do if we uncover something," said Smith. "I still don't know all the answers, but I know we can't go to the Chief or Davis. The other option is to get outside help, but we need to have all the facts before we even think about that."

They were silent for a minute, then Smith said, "I don't know if you thought about this, but the first thing Watson said about Rose Grant was, she was a nigger prostitute. Now, my father used that word as much as anyone I've ever heard, but he believed that all people should have protection under the law, and insisted my sister go to an integrated college. That's a strange combination, but it's true. I learned a lot from my father, not all good, but he taught us to be fair. I don't care what she was or what color she was, she didn't deserve to be killed and have it covered-up." He looked at Best.

Best nodded in agreement, "That's true. I don't know if she was a prostitute or not, but if she was, she might not have had any other choice. She had to take care of her children, one way or another. I know this happened in fifty-two, but things shouldn't have been that way, just because she was black." He paused for a short moment. "That church bombing in Alabama that killed those four little girls, is proof that hate is still alive; not only in Alabama, but right here in Wilson. Black people are not going to take this anymore, and I don't blame them. Sometimes you have to fight fire, with fire. I don't know who killed Johnson and Farmer, but if they turn out to be black people, I..." He stopped. "Let's go home and get a fresh start tomorrow."

"Go on, what were you about to say?"

"Nothing really, forget it."

Before they could leave, the phone rang. "Detective Smith, may I help you?" Smith listened for a minute. "I'll be right out."

"What's up?" Best asked.

"The desk officer said, someone was out there and wanted to talk to a detective."

When they got to the front desk, there was a short, dark complexion man standing near the side glass door. He was covered in dried mud from the waist down and his blue, long-sleeved shirt was torn to threads.

Smith and Best approached him. "How can we help you, Sir?" Smith asked.

The man was looking out into the parking lot, as if he was expecting someone, and flinched at the sound of Smith's voice. He turned toward Smith, then looked back outside before answering. "I need to talk to a Detective."

"We're Detectives, come back to our office," said Smith.

The man nodded and looked out again before following Smith and Best. When they got to the office, Best got a folding chair out of the closet. "Have a seat."

The man sat down, but looked uncomfortable, now looking toward the office door.

"How can we help you?" Smith asked.

"I ran away from a work farm."

"What's your name?" Best asked.

"Leroy Brooks."

"Mr. Brooks, let's start over again," said Best. "What do you mean, you ran away?"

"I was working on Mr. Jack Green's farm on Highway 117. Mr. Jack had a nigger, named Black guarding us in the field."

Best interrupted, "Was Mr. Black a black man?"

"Yes Sir, that's what I said."

"No, that's not what you said."

Leroy started to speak, but hesitated. "You right."

"Okay, go on," said Best.

"Black had a dog and a shotgun to guard us. If we try to run, he turn the dog loose. If the dog don't stop us, he shoot."

Best and Smith were alarmed at what they were hearing. "How did you get away," Asked Smith.

"I told Black I need to dump, so he let me go in the woods. I ran through the woods till I saw the highway. I end up on 301. A nigg…. He paused. "I is sorry, Sir. A black man and he wife gave me a ride to Wilson, on the back of their pickup truck. I know Black is looking for me now and if he catch me, he gonna kill me for sure." His facial expression and the trembling in his voice showed signs of fright.

Best and Smith looked at each other. Smith nodded like he believed what Leroy was saying. He gave Leroy a moment or two to calm. "Where are you from?" Smith asked.

"Florida, that where I meet Black. Bout twenty of us come up here to work in the tobacco field, and round the farm."

"Do you get paid?" Best asked.

Leroy shook his head in disgust, before answering. "Yes, but we had to pay for our food, and at the end of the week, Black tell us we owe him money," again he was shaking his head.

"Damn! How can you eat that much food?" Best asked.

"Easy, a twenty-five cent drink cost you a dollar and a half, that how. If you eat breakfast in the morning, that was five dollars. We won't making but a dollar a hour working, and we had to eat dinner and supper."

Smith and Best both shook their head in disgust. "Did you eat today?" asked Best.

"No Sir, ain't got no money."

Smith looked at Leroy's feet. "Where are your shoes?"

"Ain't got none. Black take our shoes so we don't run, but that ain't stop me." Leroy's feet were covered with blood-stained cloth. "I tore my undershirt up to cover my feet after I got in the woods."

Smith shook his head. He couldn't believe what he was seeing. Best stood up, "I'll get him something from the vending machine."

"I'll go with you," said Smith as he stood up. "Mr. Brooks, we'll be right back." Leroy looked uneasy and stood up.

"No one is going to hurt you here," said Best, "just relax."

Leroy sat back down, but still looked uneasy. Smith and Best walked up the hall through the lobby to the vending machine. Best propped his arm on the machine. "What do you think?

"I think he's telling the truth; that's modern day slavery." said Smith, "but there's nothing we can do. Highway 117 is in the county, and anyway; this is a case for the Justice Department. We need to get the FBI; they should investigate this."

"We can call the agent in Rocky Mount. This is a violation of Federal Labor Laws," said Best.

When Smith and Best returned to their office from the vending machine, Leroy stood up as they walked in. "Mr. Brooks, you're safe here, just relax," said Best.

Leroy sat down and Smith gave him two packs of nabs and a drink. "Eat this, then we'll talk about what we need to do," said Smith. "Before we leave, I'll give you a few dollars to get you something later."

"Thank you Sir." Leroy asked to use the restroom, after he finished eating. He looked a little more relaxed when he returned.

"Mr. Brooks, I talked to Detective Best, and here's what we have to do," said Smith. "First of all, the farm is out of the city limits, so we can't touch it. We decided to call the FBI in Rocky Mount, since this involves Federal Labor Laws and kidnapping." Leroy nodded. "We know the agent over there; he's a real nice guy, he'll help you."

"I'll try to get him now," said Best. "Hopefully he can get over here before long." Best looked up the phone number and called.

"F.B.I. Field Office, how may I help you?"

"I'm Detective Best, Wilson, P.D. Is Agent Young in?"

"Yes Sir, would you hold please."

"He's in," said Best, looking at Smith.

"This is Agent Young. Detective Best, haven't heard from you in a while. How in the hell are you?"

"I'm all right, and you?"

"I'm fine, what can I help you with?"

"We have a man here that said he and several others were held at gun point on a farm in Wilson County. They were brought here from Florida to work in the tobacco fields. He ran away and came up here," said Best.

"I've heard something about that farm before, but we never had enough proof to get a search warrant. This could do it; I'll be over there within the hour."

"That's great," said Best. "His name is Leroy Brooks. We'll be gone, but the officer at the desk will help you when you get here."

"All right, thank you."

"Thank you." Best turned his attention to Leroy. "Mr. Brooks, the agent will be over here within the hour. His name is Special Agent Young."

Leroy nodded and looked somewhat relieved. "Thank you, Sir. I want to go back to Florida."

"They need to get on this before someone gets killed," said Smith.

Best pulled out his wallet and gave Leroy five dollars. "Mr. Brooks, you can wait back here, or sit in the lobby. You'll be safe either place."

"Thank you, Sir, I stay back here."

"The machine will give you change, if you want something else to eat," said Smith. "Good luck."

Smith and Best walked out. "Some of these people in this county will do anything to make a dollar," said Best glancing at Smith.

"Damn right they will," said Smith." I hope the Feds put them under the jail. Let's go home, I'm tired as hell."

Chapter 50

September 23, 1968
10:45 A.M.

The Detectives got to view the bodies of Johnson and Farmer. They also got an autopsy report, along with three .38 Magnum bullet. "Were you surprised to see the tattoo?" Smith asked.

"No, there was something about Mr. Reed that convinced me he was telling the truth. Davis probably has one too, which means..." He stopped and looked at Smith.

"Go on," said Smith. "What?"

"I was just thinking, that means Davis could be next." They drove north on Tarboro Street.

"I hope the brothers are home," said Smith. He turned off of Tarboro Street onto Hines heading east.

"I'm sure they know something that would help us," said Best.

"Probably so, but will they talk," Smith said. They turned left onto Lodge Street off of Hines, heading north.

"It don't take a super-cop to figure out what happened to Price and Batts, and who was behind it, but without their bodies, it will be hard to prove," said Best.

Smith thought for a second before responding, "You're right and it was so long ago." They turned off of Lodge Street onto Nash Street heading east.

"When I was a kid, I can remember my father and his friends talking about Watson and the Police Department," said Smith, "and nothing was good. This was when he was a street-cop." He paused and looked at Best. "He's even worse now, because he has more power."

Sam was in the front yard, when the detectives pulled up. "Mr. Howard, can we talk with you, please Sir?" Best asked.

Sam stared at them before speaking. "What about?"

Best quickly interjected, "I can understand how your sons must feel, so we're going to reopen their mother's case, but we'll need their help."

Sam shot Best a suspicious look. "How can they help you? Ronnie was only eight when she was killed, he can't help you. Butch was six, I know he can't."

"I know that," said Best, "but they knew about the two detectives who were investigating the case, so they might know something else, and we think we know who killed their mother. We need all the help we can get in order to prove it. Any little thing they might be able to tell us might help."

Sam didn't respond, but stood there for a moment, then said, "You wait here." Sam went into the house. "Virginia," he yelled. "Where are you?"

"In the bathroom, I'll be right out." Moments later Virginia appeared. "What's wrong?"

Sam was sitting on the arm of the chair in the den. "The two detectives that were here looking for the boys are back. They said they're going to reopen the case because they think they know who killed Rose."

Virginia walked over and put her hand on his shoulder. "What do you think?"

"I don't know what to think. You know how they are, saying one thing and doing another. But there is something different about these two, I can't tell you what it is, I just don't know."

"The best thing is to let the boys decide what to do," said Virginia.

Sam nodded. "You're right." He got up and walked to the door and onto the porch. "They're not here now, but you come back in about an hour or so."

Best nodded and smiled. "Thank you Mr. Howard, we'll be back and thank you for your time, Sir."

They left and Sam went back into the house. "Virginia, I know what's different about those cops. As old as I am, I have never heard a white policeman call a colored man Sir, or Mister. That shows a certain amount of respect. Respect for colored people has never, ever, existed in this city." Virginia nodded in agreement.

Sam called Ronnie and Butch, who reluctantly agreed to meet with Smith and Best.

"Come in, my sons are here," said Sam, when the detectives arrived about an hour later. They followed Sam into the den. "We'll let you talk," he said closing the door.

"How are you today? Smith asked, extending his hand to Ronnie.

Ronnie looked at Smith with a cold stare. "I'm alright," he said. He didn't shake Smith's hand. "Have a seat."

Smith and Best sat down facing Ronnie and Butch. They looked at each other as if they were trying to decide who would talk first. "We understand how you must feel about losing your mother, then finding out nothing was done about it; even worse, it was covered-up," said Best. Ronnie was nodding with a blank expression. "We've learned a lot about her case since we left here, but we need your help."

Ronnie and Butch looked at each other. "First of all, let me correct you. You have no idea how we feel. What have you learned?" Butch asked.

Best stood, "First of all, you'll have to trust us. I'm…"

Ronnie interrupted, looking at Best like he was crazy, smiling. "You must be out of you mind!" He raised his voice. "After all these years of corruption, murder, rape and God knows what else, committed by your police department. Do you really think you can come down here and say, trust me, and we do it? I don't know anyone that dumb. I know we're not. We must look really dumb to you." He rolled his eyes at Best.

Best stood there not knowing what to say, but the urgency of the situation didn't escape him, so he took the only other option, he tried again. "I said at the beginning, I understand how you feel, you were right, I didn't lose my mother, but just listen to me, then draw your own conclusion." He was swinging his eyes from Ronnie to Butch.

"Go on," said Butch. He was not yet impressed.

Best looked at Smith, Smith nodded. "Detective Smith and I think we know who was responsible for the murder of your mother, Dan Williams, and Detectives, Price and Batts, but we have to prove it, and that won't be easy." He paused and looked at Smith again. Smith nodded in agreement. Best continued, "We think Chief Watson and Sergeant Davis are involved; and what I'm saying could get me fired, or even worse, killed." The room fell quiet for a moment. "We don't know how, but we're almost sure they're involved in some way. If Davis was involved, so were his best friends; Pope, Johnson and Farmer, the people who we think killed your mother, and they could also be involved in other murders." Ronnie couldn't believe a white policeman in Wilson was saying this. Best continued. "We can't get any help from the department; we can't even find the case files," said Best. "If you don't help us, all the information we have will mean nothing. If you know something, I don't need to know how you know it, just tell us.

Ronnie looked at Butch and motioned for him to go out of the room. "We'll be back," said Ronnie.

"Wait," said Best, "here is one more thing for you to think about. Dan Williams said, one of the men he saw in your mother's room had a tattoo, it was crossed pistols. We saw Johnson and Farmer's bodies this morning, they have them. That's why Dan Williams was killed; he saw them with your mother." Ronnie again motioned to Butch. They walked out without saying a word.

"Are you all right?" Virginia asked, as she walked out of the kitchen.

"Yes," said Butch, "we need to talk about something for a minute, but we're all right."

They walked in Ronnie's room and closed the door. They were both puzzled by Detective Best's statements. "What do you think?" Ronnie asked.

Butch hesitated before answering. "I don't trust them; they could be working with Watson and Davis. If they are, and we talk too much, we could go to prison and probably get the death sentence."

Ronnie was slowly nodding while Butch was talking. "I thought about the same thing, but here's how we can find out. They know we were too young to kill Price and Batts, so if we tell them where the bodies are, they can't touch us. But, before we tell them anything, we need to know what they can do, or better still, who would help if they had more information."

"I guess we can do it that way," said Butch. "But that's all we tell them. If we find the remains and they call Raleigh for help, I'll feel better."

"Okay, let's go," said Ronnie.

When they walked in, Best was staring out the window. He walked back and sat down. Ronnie stared at the detectives for a moment or two before speaking. "You said you couldn't get any help from the police department. Where could you get help from if you had more information?"

"If we had information, I mean good solid information; we could call the State Bureau of Investigation or the Attorney General; they would be glad to help us," said Smith.

Ronnie and Butch looked at each other. "And your names will never come up, so help me God," said Best.

"Ok," said Ronnie. "We were told where the two detective's remains are."

"Are you sure?" Best asked.

"We've never been there, but we think we know where it is," said Ronnie. "We're almost sure the remains are there."

Smith and Best looked at each other. "If we can find the remains, that might be enough to get outside help," said Smith. "Is there anything else you can tell us?"

"That's all, right now," said Butch, putting emphasis on, right now.

Smith and Best got the message, so they didn't want to push them. "Tomorrow morning, we need to get an early start, so if we have some luck, we can get someone from Raleigh down here," said Smith. He got his notepad and pen. "Where are the remains suppose to be?"

Ronnie looked at Butch and took a deep breath before speaking, "On Black Creek Road, behind a two-story, brick house. It's an old house beside a pond. The bodies are buried just inside the tree-line, behind the back porch."

"I know where that is," said Best. "I passed that house a million times, going to see my wife before we got married. It's a little over two miles out. I don't remember seeing anyone living there, but whoever owns the house keeps the weeds cut down. Let's say we meet at the Boat Company on Black Creek Road about nine-thirty. Do you know where it is?"

Ronnie didn't answer, but said, "We'll be there."

Smith and Best got up. "If we find the remains and get some outside help, I think we may be able to put Watson and Davis where they belong, under the jail," said Smith smiling.

Ronnie and Butch got up, they all shook hands; Best and Smith left. In their minds, Pope, Johnson and Farmer were no longer victims; they were killers, along with Davis and Watson.

Chapter 51

September 24, 1968
9:20 A.M.

The clouds parted and the sun suddenly spilled out on this late September day. Ronnie and Butch were waiting for the detectives in the parking lot at the Wilson Boat Company on Black Creek Road. "I hope the snakes are gone," said Butch. "I know you saw a lot of them in Viet Nam."

Ronnie nodded and smiled. "I did, but I sure don't want to see one today."

"Here they come," said Butch.

The detectives pulled beside them in their unmarked police car, Best was driving. "Why don't you ride with us, so we don't attract much attention," said Smith from the passenger side of the car.

"All right," said Butch. They got in the police car and headed south on Black Creek Road. Traffic was always light on country roads, so they were there in a matter of minutes.

"This is it," said Best.

"Go around the back," said Smith.

Best pulled around the back and parked under an old car port. The screen-door was hanging on one hinge, and the door looked as if it had been forced open. They all got out with a degree of caution. Smith opened the trunk of the car and got four shovels out, along with rubber boots. "Where's the best place to start?"

"Just inside the tree line, behind the back porch," answered Ronnie.

The woods were littered with tall, pine trees that prevented any sunlight from sneaking through. They used their shovels to knock down the tall weeds between the back porch and the tree line. "This is probably a good spot to start," said Best. "If the remains are here, they shouldn't be buried too deep. I know they were in a hurry, and probably did it at night."

They started digging about five feet inside the tree line, but kept a watchful eye on the back door. They dug about three feet deep before deciding to try another spot. "Let's move about four or five feet back," said Smith.

They moved a few feet back, trying to stay aligned with the back porch. A carpet of pine straw blanketed the ground, keeping it moist. The dirt was firm, but soft. They marked off an area about six square feet and began to dig. After digging about three and a half feet, Ronnie said, "I think we're in the right area, but it doesn't look good. This is the general area where we were told the bodies were buried."

Moments later, Smith hit a hard object. "We might have something." He dropped the shovel, got on his knees and began to rake the dirt away with his hands. "This is it." The skeletal remains of a human hand appeared. They all looked relieved at the sight of what looked to be the remains of Price and Batts. Smith started to dig again.

"Hold up a minute, let's think about this," said Best. "I think the best thing to do is get some people from Raleigh down here. They know what to do and how to do it. I don't want us to destroy any evidence."

"Ok," said Smith. "We'll cover everything up and put the pine straw back in place. We'll discuss our next move on our way to Wilson."

After they covered the dig-areas up, they walked back to the car. They were overjoyed at finding the remains, as they grasped the situation. "We need to look inside the house when we come back with help," said Best. "There still might be something in there we could use. We need all the evidence we can get to nail their asses."

They got in the car; Best was driving, and headed toward Wilson. "The Attorney General has what they call the Special Homicide Investigation Team, known as the SHIT squard." said Smith. "That might be our best chance. I see a lot of SBI agents at the station; I really don't want to go to them. I'm not saying they're dishonest, but they know Watson well, so let's not take a chance."

"Ok," said Best, "we'll call the Attorney General's office. I think I saw a pay phone in front of the store next to the boat company; we can call from there."

They crossed the railroad tracks on Black Creek Road separating the boat company from the store and drove into the parking lot. Best parked the car and got out. He picked up the pay phone and dialed the operator.

"Operator, may I help you?"

"Yes," said Best. "I want the Attorney General's Office and there might be a listing for a Special Homicide Investigation Team, please.

Moments later, "This is Special Agent Dial, how may I help you?" He said in a Northern accent.

"My name is Detective Donald Best, Wilson Police. My partner and I just found the remains of who we think are two Wilson Detectives, killed in fifty-two. I'm calling you because we think the Chief of Police in Wilson, and a Sergeant on the Police Force are responsible."

"Where are the remains?" Dial asked.

"About two miles out of the city," said Best. "We got a tip on where they were, and we went out there. We dug up the skeletal remains of a human hand. We covered it back up so we wouldn't disturb any evidence."

"Good; it's about eleven now and Wilson is about an hour away. I should be there about twelve-thirty, no later than one. Our mobile crime lab will follow. Where can I meet you?"

"Do you know where Highway 301 is in Wilson?" Best asked.

"Yes."

"You take Black Creek Road east, off of 301. There is a boat company about three blocks down on your right, we'll be there."

"All right, we'll see you there," said Dial.

Best hung up and walked back to the car, his smile was increasing with every step.

"I talked to Special Agent Dial. He said he'll be here about twelve-thirty or one with a mobile crime lab."

"That's good," said Smith. "Now we have some help."

"We have about an hour and a half to kill, why don't we get something to eat," suggested Best.

"Let me tell you something before we leave," said Ronnie. He looked at Butch, Butch nodded. That got the detectives attention. "I had to wait until I was sure," said Ronnie.

"We understand," said Best.

"Here's what I was told. Price and Batts found out Bret Pope, Johnson, Farmer and Davis were at our house the night our mother was killed. They went to Chief Watson; Watson turned on them and told Bret's father. He paid Watson three thousand dollars to have Price and Batts killed. Watson sent them out to the old house to see his friend, Mr. Lamm. Johnson, Farmer and Davis were waiting and killed them. After they buried the bodies that night, they drove the car to South Carolina. The three-thousand dollars that Watson was paid, was the money paid to have Dan Williams killed. It was found in the hit-woman's hotel room, by Price and Batts. Dan Williams was killed because he saw Bret Pope and the others at our house the night she was killed. That's all we know."

"Damn, Watson and Davis are snakes," said Smith as he frowned. He paused, "You still have our word, no one will ever know where this came from." Both Ronnie and Butch nodded.

"What you said didn't surprise me at all," said Best. "I thought they were involved, but I just didn't know how. I hope we find some evidence to connect them, or find a way to make them connect themselves," he said with a degree of hope.

"Look," said Ronnie. "Butch and I are going home to eat."

"Where are you going, on Fikewood or Stantonsburg Road?" Smith asked. He smiled. Butch and Ronnie looked at each other, they all laughed. The brothers got in their car and left. "Let's go to Parkers and eat," said Smith.

"All right with me," said Best.

Smith looked at Best and smiled. "I'm glad we didn't have to fight them. Did you see the size of Butch's arms? And his hands look like baseball gloves; and Ronnie is damn near as big as Butch."

"Let's go, I can smell Parker's chicken from here," said Best smiling and rubbing his stomach.

Chapter 52

September 24, 1968
12:40 P.M.

Detectives Smith and Best were enthusiastically discussing their successful day, when Best spotted the mobile crime lab. They immediately exited their car and sprinted toward Black Creek Road. "Over here," Best yelled, directing the lead car into the boat company parking lot.

"You must be Agent Dial," Best said, approaching the 1968 white Chevy.

"Yes, and you're Detective Best."

Best nodded, "This is my partner, Detective Smith."

They all exchanged handshakes when Dial got out of his car; dressed like a Harvard Lawyer, bow-tie and all. "You guys sit in my car and tell me what you have," said Dial, in his thick Brooklyn accent.

"I think it would be better if we move to the crime scene," said Smith. "Police cars are assigned to ride this area; the crime lab would attract attention. I don't need to be seen with you, not yet anyway."

"Okay," said Dial, "lead the way."

Best pulled out of the parking lot heading south on Black Creek Road, Dial and the crime lab followed. When they pulled in the driveway at the house, Smith got out and motioned for Dial and the van to drive around. After they were parked, Best and Smith parked behind them, they knew they would be leaving first. They got out and met Dial near the crime lab.

"Agent Dial," said Best. "Here's what we have. In nineteen-fifty-two, a black woman was killed on Carroll Street in Wilson. Four white men were with her the night she was murdered; they were police officers. The Detectives, Price and Batts, whose remains we think are back here, found three-thousand dollars that one of the suspects paid for a hit on the only witness. The money was in the suspect's father's business envelops. They went to see Chief Watson. Watson, who is controlled by tobacco money, went to the suspect's father. He paid Watson the three-thousand dollars to set the detectives up. Watson told Detectives Price and Batts to come out here and check on his friend, Mr. Lamm. Officers Johnson, Davis and Farmer were waiting and killed them."

Dial nodded slowly, and thought a second before speaking, "You said Chief Watson and Davis are suspects. Where are the others?"

"Farmer and Johnson were killed a few days ago, and the other one, Bret Pope has been missing for a while and is probably dead," said Best. "Bret Pope's father had a lot of money and power around the city. Dan Williams, the only witness who saw the officers in the dead woman's room was killed by the hired killer, who was paid by Bret Pope. That's what we know as of now."

"Do you think Watson had Farmer and Johnson killed?" asked Dial.

"We don't know, but you never know about Watson," answered Smith, "he'll do anything."

"Okay," said Dial. "What we need now are the remains and their identities. Let's just hope we find some physical evidence with the remains, or in the house; something to connect Davis, since he was supposed to be one of the killers. After you show us where to dig, I want you to get the hell away from here. After we dig them up, I want the Chief out here to give him and Davis something to think about. I'll tell him we were acting on a tip. I'll be at the Holiday Inn on 301. We'll get together and discuss how we want to continue."

"Okay," said Best, "but time is not on our side."

"From what I know now, you're right," said Dial. He knocked on the van and motioned for the lab men to follow.

"It's only about ten feet inside the tree line," said Smith, "and the ground is not hard at all. You need to check inside the house too. It's been a long time, but you never know what you might find."

The lab men got their shovels out of the van and followed the detectives into the woods.

"Right here," said Smith, as he raked the pine straw back with his foot.

"Okay," said Dial. "If the remains are here we'll find them. Now you guys need to get out of here before you're seen."

"All right," said Smith, "we're gone." Smith and Best got in their car and raced toward Wilson.

"The conspiracy, and the veil of silence surrounding the murders has held for more than fifteen years," said Best. "But, if they find the remains and some ID, Watson and Davis will surely push the panic button, and probably enough to hang themselves."

Chapter 53

September 24, 1968
1:35 P.M.

"I'm calling your car and you're walking in," said Officer Barnes. "The Chief wants to see you."

"Thank you," said Smith. "Is he in his office?"

"Yes, go on back there."

"What in the hell does he want?" Asked Best his voice just above a whisper.

Smith looked at Best with a hint of concern. "I don't know, I hope no one saw our car out there." They knocked on Watson's office door.

"Come in and have a seat. How's the investigation going?" Watson asked.

"Slow, but I think we'll have something in a couple of days. We have a lead we need to follow up on," said Smith.

"That's good. Who have you talked to?" Watson asked.

Smith had to think of a lie, and fast. "Well, we found Rose Grant's sons. They cooperated and talked freely about what they knew, which is nothing, but we'll keep pressing. They are both college educated, clean cut young men, and very smart. We'll interview them again tomorrow, if they know something, we'll get it."

Watson interjected. "Don't be fooled by that clean-cut bull-shit. An educated nigger can kill just like a dumb nigger can, and use his smarts to fool your dumb-ass. Some of them niggers will smile at you and cut your damn head off." He was loud and nasty. "I sent you Boys down there to do a job. If you can't do it, I'll find somebody who can. That was a heinous crime committed by one of them nig-gers down there, and I want his ass to hang, so do your job and find him. Now get out of my office and go to work." His voice was heard all over the station.

"Yes Sir Chief," said Smith. They got up and walked out of Watson's office. A few officers had gathered in the hall, trying to see whose ass Watson was chewing out. Smith and Best walked into their office and closed the door; they looked at each other and smiled. "Two or three days from now, he might be trying to kiss our asses to help him," said Best, in a low tone.

"His days are numbered. Let's get out of here. They should know something soon."

Chapter 54

September 24, 1968
3:40 P.M.

Smith and Best had stopped at The Stop Light Grill for a takeout, afternoon snack. Best was still thinking about Watson's attitude and chewing on a hamburger when he heard the sound of emergency vehicles. They were at the intersection of Pender and Nash Streets when two Sheriff's cars turned off of Nash, heading south on South Pender. When the light changed, they headed south on Pender. Moments later, Smith, who was driving saw Watson's car in his rearview mirror. Watson pulled around their car and motioned for them to follow. "This is it," said Smith.

"If it is, I know Watson's ass is shaking now. If not now, it will be." said Best.

Smith put the portable light on top of the unmarked car and accelerated across 301, heading south on Black Creek Road. Smith raced past the boat company at nearly 70 mph. and was at the house two minutes later. Watson had parked on the highway and was walking toward the house when they arrived. There were a number of Sheriff's cars parked along the highway. Smith and Best parked behind Watson's car and walked toward the house. When they got to the back yard, several officers were standing around the remains that had been placed on a white sheet. The skeletal remains were still intact with the exception of the shotgun blast Price and Batts took in the face.

Dial saw the detectives and gave them a short glance and smiled. His identification was hanging from his neck by a silver, linked chain. Watson approached him and flashed his ID, then extended his hand. "I'm Chief Watson, Wilson PD," he said in a friendly voice.

"I'm Special Agent Dial; The Attorneys General Special Homicide Team. We think these are the remains of two of your men. Their badges and identification were buried with them, along with what we think are the murder weapons." He pointed at two mud-covered shotguns.

"It's been sixteen years since they were missing," said Watson, shaking his head, trying to fake some emotion. "At least their families will have some closure."

"That's true," said Dial. "And we might have enough evidence to find the killers. There are some serial numbers on the shotguns. We might be able to trace them back to the owners, who are probably the killers."

Sweat began to run down Watson's face. "How did you find this?"

"A tip; they didn't leave any name of course, but they told us how to get here, and the names of a few people that could be involved in the murder." Watson's brain came alive. He started thinking about what the information could be. Dial continued, "We still didn't check the house yet; there could be more evidence in there."

Watson motioned to Dial. "I wonder if I can talk to you for a minute," he said as he walked away from the crowd, Dial followed. "This is Wilson County; the Sheriff's Department has an excellent lab and staff over there. We work together on things like this, so we can take this off your hands, since these are two of our officers. Whoever killed the officers is probably still living in this area."

"I have orders to take everything to Raleigh, so they can examine the remains and immediately start the investigation, these orders came from the Attorney General, Charles Ellis. I'm sure you do a good job here, but our staff in Raleigh are better trained and equipped."

Watson shifted uncomfortably. "I understand, but keep me informed and maybe I can be of some help. They were good men, and as a service to them and their families, we need to do everything possible to find their killers."

"I will, believe me, I will, and thanks for the offer." Dial looked at Watson as he walked away. He shook his head, knowing Watson was trying to feed him a truck load of southern bullshit.

The crime lab team took pictures of the area around the dig site. They also looked inside the house, but were unable to find any additional evidence. They took the remains and evidence back to Raleigh to be analyzed.

Chapter 55

September 24, 1968
4:40 P.M.

Watson left the area at a high rate of speed, heading toward Wilson. A terrible despair settled in his mind. He was helpless to stop the investigation, an investigation that could put him in prison for the rest of his life. "Car one to the station."

"Go ahead Chief."

"Locate Sergeant Davis and have him meet me at the station, ASAP, over."

"10-4. Over and out."

Watson was in his office, chain smoking cigarettes and drinking coffee when Davis arrived. Davis was unaware of Price and Batts remains being found. He knocked on the door twice and walked in. Watson was seated behind his desk, elbows up, his face in his hands; a cigarette was clamped between his fingers.

"What's wrong Chief?" Davis asked.

Watson bit his lip and stared at Davis. "They found Price and Batts remains." He paused, shaking his head. "After all these years, they found them." Davis raised his eyebrows in shock, speechless, unable to muster a sound as he sat down in a chair. Watson didn't give him time to respond. "How could you be so dumb as to bury the murder weapons and their ID's with them?" Watson stood up, glared at Davis and nervously walked around his office, perspiration began to flow. "Who did the shotguns belong too?"

"One was mine and the other one belonged to Johnson."

"You know that fire arms can be traced back to the original owners," said Watson, "and if it is, you have a problem."

Davis immediately stood up. A flood of hot emotion ran through him. "What do you mean, I have a problem?" He glared at Watson with intensity. "You sent us out there to kill them, now you say, I have a problem. If I go, you go."

Watson's eyes grew wide. "Don't you use that tone of voice at me. I'm still the Chief."

Davis snapped back angrily. "You might be the Chief, but you're as deep in this shit as I am, and don't you ever forget it."

Davis rolled his eyes at Watson and sat down. They both glared at each other. After a long moment Watson said, "I talked with the special agent from the Attorney General's Office. He told me someone called in a tip on where to find the remains, along with some other information, but he didn't tell me what the other information was. The tip the agent got probably came from the killer of Bret, Johnson and Farmer. I'm almost sure that they were tortured before they were killed, and told everything they knew."

"That means the killer probably knows about us," said Davis. He looked up toward the ceiling and took a deep breath. "What can we do?"

"First of all, we need to be careful," said Watson, as he sat down. "Special Agent Dial made it clear to me that he was going to investigate the case, so all we can do now is wait. If we keep quiet, he can't prove anything."

"All right, but let me know what's going on, and you remember, I'm not going down by myself." Davis got up and walked out, leaving the door open behind him.

Watson knew the only way he could be connected to the murders was through Davis. He was never in the house and the shotguns were not his. He now began to think about his one problem, Davis.

Smith and Best left the house on Black Creek Road a few minutes after Watson. They were in their office when Davis left. "What did I tell you?" said Best. "Davis was off today, but I knew Watson would call him in. The panic button is just about to be pushed."

Chapter 56

September 24, 1968
8:10 P.M.

It was a little after eight when Smith and Best arrived at the Holiday Inn. Smith got Dial's room number from the desk clerk. He was in room 218, upstairs, facing the main parking lot; Best knocked on the door. "Come in, I was just wondering what happened to you guys. I went to Parkers and got a combination dinner. That barbecue was the best I've ever had; I need to take some back to my wife." he said smiling.

"We both went home to have dinner with the families," said Best. "You know how that goes."

"I know; I'm married too," said Dial. "My wife would kill me if I was in Raleigh, and didn't come home for dinner. You guys have a seat."

Smith and Best sat on one of the twin beds, Dial on the other. "Did you notice how Watson was acting?" Smith asked.

Dial nodded, agreeing. "Ray Charles could see that. He even tried to get me to let the Sheriff's Department investigate the case. His reasoning was, since the officers were his men. He said the Police Department would help. That only showed me how desperate he is, and how guilty. I must have looked really dumb to him, if he thought that I was going for that bullshit."

"We went back to the station to see if he would call Davis in on his off day, and he did," said Best. "My guess is, they don't know what to do, but Watson will try something."

"So what do you think we should do now?" Smith asked.

Dial thought for a minute, then answered. "It will probably be at least two or three days before we get any information from Raleigh, but Watson and Davis don't know that. I plan to put a little pressure on them, starting with Davis."

"You're right," said Best. "Davis will flip a hell of a lot faster, because Watson will do anything to stay out of jail and keep that job. After all he's done the past twenty years or more, which includes framing people; he wouldn't last a week in prison, and he knows it. Some of the same people he framed and sent to prison are still there, and would love to put their foot in his ass."

"I think I'll go to the Police Department and have a little talk with Sergeant Davis," said Dial. "I told Watson I had some information, and I'm sure he told Davis. My visit should be enough to shake Watson up. I want him to think that Davis might cooperate with me. He knows the court would come down a lot harder on him, since he's the Chief of Police."

Smith was nodding slowly, agreeing with what Dial said. "That might work, but we need to keep an eye on Watson. I'm telling you, he'll do anything to save his ass."

"That's where you guys come in," said Dial. "From what I know about him now, he might make a move to take Davis out, since Davis is the only one that can connect him with the murders."

"That's very possible; he took Price and Batts out for three- thousand dollars and job security; so you know he'll take Davis out to save his ass," said Best.

"We need to work fast because everything we talked about tonight, Watson has already thought about. If he gets to Davis first, there's no way we can get him," said Smith. "Watson's plan is in full motion right now, and we better get ours in motion."

"Okay, I'm convinced. Tomorrow I'll call Raleigh and get three or four of our agents down here. We'll put a twenty-four hour tail on Watson. We'll see what happens in the next two or three days."

"All right, but I think we need that tail on Davis, to keep him alive. Right now, he's Watson's only ticket to jail," said Best.

Dial nodded in agreement. "You're right, that's probably the best way. I'll get some agents here as soon as possible, but it will probably be tomorrow. Get me their addresses, Davis' and Watson's."

Chapter 57

September 24, 1968
11:20 P.M.

Sergeant Davis and his wife Brenda had dinner at the Silver Lake Seafood Restaurant earlier in the evening. It had been a stressful day for Davis learning about Price and Batts remains being found. "What time are you coming to bed?" asked Brenda. "You know tomorrow is another workday, you can't sleep late."

Barrel-bellied, and Halloween-faced, Davis was staring straight ahead, as if he was in a trance. "I'll be there in a few minutes. You go on to bed." Davis knew Watson was all for himself and would throw him under the bus if it became necessary. His only hope now was that the shotgun couldn't be traced back to him. He thought bitterly about Watson, his stomach was churning. Moments later the door-bell rang.

"Who could that be this late?" Brenda yelled from the bedroom.

"I don't know, but I'll get it." Davis walked to the door and switched the porch light on. Two shots were fired as soon as he opened the door; one striking him in his face, the other in his neck. The explosive round nearly ripped his head from his body. Like a punctured balloon, his body collapsed. The right side of his face was torn away. A thin string of skin connected his neck to his body. Brenda ran from the bedroom to the living room, after hearing the shots. Terror froze her reflexes, her color deepened after seeing her husband's dead body.

Fifteen minutes later, Fleming Street was littered with police cars. Smith and Best were called because the lead detective on the West Side was on vacation. They knew who was responsible as soon as they got the call. When they arrived, Watson was already there. "My wife and I were asleep when I got the call," said Watson. "This is the third officer I've lost in the past week, and something has to be done.

Go around the back to enter the house. Brenda can tell you what she knows. I didn't ask her any questions; I wanted to give her a little time."

Smith and Best entered the kitchen through the back door. Brenda and a middle-aged woman, who looked enough like her to be a sister, were sitting at the kitchen table. Smith walked behind Brenda and gave her a comforting rub on the shoulder. She reached back and put her hand on top of his.

"Try to get yourself together," said Smith, "we can talk later." Brenda nodded, but didn't turn around.

Smith and Best then walked through the den into the living room. Davis' body was covered by a light blue blanket. Best pulled the blanket up just enough to view the wounds to his head and neck. "That was a large caliber bullet," said Best. "This was a professional hit; they made sure he was dead."

Smith picked up the telephone and call Agent Dial.

"Hello," said Dial.

"Agent Dial, this is Detective Smith. We're too late, Davis is dead," he said, just above a whisper.

"Did you find out what happened?"

"Not yet, but Watson made sure we knew he was in bed with his wife when it happened. I'll call you first thing in the morning to let you know what we have, which will probably be nothing; this was a professional hit." said Smith.

"Okay, but this puts us back to square one. Watson might just get away now," said Dial. "We'll talk tomorrow."

Smith and Best finished the interview with Brenda. They looked around outside and talked to neighbors on both sides of the street. The ID officers collected what little evidence they could, took pictures of the crime scene, and had the body moved to the morgue at Wilson Memorial Hospital.

Chapter 58

September 25, 1968
9:30 A.M.

Davis being killed was Smith and Best worst nightmare; Watson might now go free. They went on Stantonsburg Road to break the news to Butch and Ronnie. Best rang the door bell and Butch answered. "Nice place," said Best, with a smile, standing in the doorway. Despite the fact they were white cops, Ronnie and Butch liked the detectives.

"Come in, we just started breakfast. Will you join us?"

"No, we just stopped by to tell you the news. Davis was killed in his home last night," said Smith.

"Ronnie, come and listen to this," said Butch, "Watson did his thing again."

"What?" said Ronnie, walking in from the kitchen with a half-full glass of milk in his hand. "What's going on?"

"Someone shot Davis last night, when he answered the door at his house."

"Damn, Watson could get away free now," said Ronnie.

"We'll see." said Smith. "We're on our way to the Holiday Inn to talk with Special Agent Dial. He's in charge of the case. I'm sure you know by now what they found at the dig site."

"Yes, we saw it on the news," said Ronnie. "But without Davis, Dial has nothing."

"You're probably right, but we still have to try something. What, I don't know." He paused. "Write your phone number down. I'll let you know something as soon as we decide on what to do," said Best.

Ronnie went to the kitchen to write his phone number down. "I wrote my parents number down too. If we're not here, try that number."

"Ok," said Best. "You'll hear from us soon." Smith and Best left.

"I thought they had that snake, but once again he might get away," said Butch. He looked at Ronnie. Ronnie looked at him, but didn't respond. "I know that look, what are you thinking about?"

Ronnie didn't respond right away, a deep frown creased his face. "I don't know what to think, but I'm not going to let him just walk away. A lot of black people in this city have suffered because of him. He didn't kill mama, but if he had done his job, it would have made our lives a lot better. At least there would have been an effort to get justice for her, but one way or another, he'll pay."

Chapter 59

September 25, 1968
10:30 A.M.

Smith and Best went to the Holiday Inn to see Agent Dial.

"Come in. I just finished my breakfast in the dining room."

"We don't have much time; we're supposed to see Watson at the station," said Smith.

"I talked to Watson just before I had my breakfast," said Dial. "I asked him to meet with me; he wasn't interested, until I said the name Bret Pope. That got his attention fast. I don't know where to go with that, but I need to keep him thinking."

"When will you meet him?" Best asked.

"I told him I was going to Raleigh to meet with the ID officers about this case, but I would be back here around eight tonight. He said he'd be here about eight-thirty. Hopefully, I would have thought of something by then." He paused. "Didn't you tell me that Bret's body was never found?"

"Right," said Smith.

"Ok, Watson doesn't know if he's dead or not, unless he killed him. That could give us a little play-room. Let me think about it. You call me here about nine-thirty or ten tonight."

"Will do," said Best.

When they left the Holiday Inn heading north on 301, a downpour was falling on the highway. A lightning bolt struck nearby, sending a flash through the low, gray clouds. "Maybe Dial is thinking about calling Watson's bluff about Bret Pope," said Smith.

"That's good thinking, because that might be the only option he has," said Best. "Do you think Watson might go for that?"

"He might, you never know about him, but we'll see."

Smith and Best pulled into the parking lot at the station. The down-pour was now a monsoon.

"Damn, look at that rain," said Smith. "We need to wait here a minute; we'll drown before we get in the station." They glanced at each other and smiled.

"What do you think Watson wants?" Best asked.

"I don't know, he could say anything," answered Smith. "But one thing I do know. He has no feelings for anyone but himself, and he needs to be stopped."

"You're right, but the way things look now, he might get away."

The rain started to slow. "Let's go," said Smith.

When they arrived at Watson's office the door was open. Smith knocked on the doorframe to get Watson's attention. "Come in," he said, with a broad smile, not even trying to hide his feelings about Davis' murder. Smith and Best walked in and took a seat. "I don't have much time, because I have to meet the Mayor about Sergeant Davis. I don't know what you have on the Johnson and Farmer case, but I think the same person killed Davis. You Boys need to go down to nigger town and crack some heads until you find the killer. The Mayor is on my ass, so I need some results."

"We'll do our best," said Smith.

"Your best ain't good enough, I need some results. That's all, you can go, but I want a daily report."

"Ok, Chief," said Smith. They got up and walked out of Watson's office into their office.

Best's eyes narrowed and hardened, "Did you see that smile on his face when we walked in? Jail ain't good enough for him, he needs to be dead. "If Agent Dial can't put him in jail, I've got to leave this job; I can't work under a man like that."

"If you leave, I will too," said Smith. "But right now, let's get the hell out of here."

When they left the station the rain had stopped. The brief monsoon had turned into a beautiful sunny day. "Stop at the first phone booth you see. We need to let Butch and Ronnie know what's going on."

They were heading east on Nash Street. "There is one at the train station," said Smith. "Pull over there."

Best pulled across traffic into the parking lot at the Atlantic Coastline Railroad Station; Smith got out to call Butch and Ronnie.

"Hello," said Butch.

"This is Detective Smith. I just want to let you know that Watson has a meeting with Agent Dial tonight at the Holiday Inn. We hope he can get Watson to talk, but it's a long shot. Now that Davis is dead, there's not much of a chance to get him to talk."

"He has to try something," said Butch. "What time is the meeting?"

"About eight-thirty," said Smith. "We'll call you when we know something."

"Ronnie's taking a shower; I'll tell him what you said when he gets out."

"Ok, good enough."

"We'll be here, talk to you later," said Butch. Butch was in his room when Ronnie got out of the shower. "Detective Smith called a few minutes ago."

Ronnie walked in and sat on the corner of the desk, near the head of the bed. He had a tower wrapped around him and was drying his hair. "What's up?"

"Watson is supposed to meet with the agent from the Attorney General's office, tonight at the Holiday Inn. Smith said Watson will probably get away, now that Davis is dead. Damn!"

Ronnie didn't respond. He sat there thinking for a minute, then said, "This is too much for me. I think I'll ride down to Fort Bragg to see my friend. I just need to get away and think about this. What time is the meeting?"

"Smith said, about eight-thirty."

"I should be back in Wilson around five. He might get away from the agent, but he won't get away from us. We'll talk about it when I get back."

The long, solitary drive to Fayetteville and back would give him plenty of time to think.

Chapter 60

September 25, 1968
8:15 P.M.

Chief Watson stood at the door of room 218. He drew in a long breath, looked around several times and put his ear to the door before knocking. "It's unlocked, come in," said Dial.

"How are you tonight?" said Watson, scanning the room as he walked in.

"I'm alright, Chief. Please have a seat."

Watson pulled the chair from under the room's desk. "What's on your mind?"

Dial and Watson stared at each other for a short moment. "I think we need to talk about the two dead detectives," said Dial.

"Which ones are you talking about? We've had so many killed."

"Price and Batts, the two I'm investigating."

Watson hesitated for a moment before speaking. "I don't know what to tell you; you should be telling me, you're the investigator. I offered my help, but you turned me down."

Dial quickly interjected. "Look, let's cut the crap man. I was told where the remains were and a lot more. I know what happened, and I'm here to make you an offer."

Watson didn't respond. He got up, looked around the room and walked to the bathroom. He looked in, then walked back and sat down.

Dial smiled, and opened his shirt. "We're alone, and I don't have a recorder, nothing." Watson looked very uneasy as he looked around the room again. "I'll tell you what happened, so you'll know this is no bull. I know the whole story, everything."

"Tell me, because I don't know a damn thing, except they were killed and their car was found in South Carolina."

"All right, I'll tell you. Your officers, Pope, Johnson, Farmer and

Davis killed that black woman back in fifty-two. Now you let me know when I mess up." He paused. "Price and Batts found out who killed her and went to you with the three-thousand dollars they found in the hotel room; Bret Pope paid a hit-woman to kill the witness, Dan Williams." Watson shot Dial a nasty look and sat straight up in his chair. "You went to Pope's father, who had a lot of money, and told him about it. You then took the three-thousand dollars to have Price and Batts killed. You sent them on Black Creek Road to see Mr. Lamm. Davis, Johnson and Farmer were waiting and kill them. Is that right?" He said as he smiled.

Watson's tone immediately changed as he stood. "That's a damn lie; I don't know what you're talking about."

"You know it's true, and I'll prove it."

Watson got quiet, sweat started to roll down his face. He sat back down in his chair and folded his arms. "It's my word against four dead men. How in the hell can you prove it?"

"Did you say four dead men? I only know about three dead men; Johnson, Farmer and Davis."

They stared at each other for a moment. Watson's mind was now flooded with thoughts; he cleared his throat. "Bret Pope is dead too," he said, with a degree of confidence.

"Would you bet your life on that? They never found the body. How do you know he wasn't kidnapped and held all of these years? It has happened before." Watson didn't respond. "Now, if you want to talk to me, maybe, just maybe, I can help you. From what I heard, you don't need to go to a state prison; you wouldn't last a day. There are men still in prison that you framed and sent there. If you choose to walk out of this room, you're on your own. You'll probably be walking to your death."

Watson sat there without moving a muscle; his face was as white as a sheet. He started squirming in his seat.

"I don't have all night," said Dial.

Watson looked at him, but didn't respond at first. He sat there for a minute. "So you think you've got it all figured out, all right, prove it. I'll take my chances." He got up and walked to the door. He hesitated for a long moment, thinking about his options, then walked out. Dial could hear him feet pounding down the steps.

Chapter 61

September 15, 1958
9:15 P.M.

Ronnie was relaxing on the recliner. The telephone ringing made him jump. He jumped up and raced to answer it. "I got it Butch." He picked the receiver up and said a slightly, breathless, "Hello."

"Is this Ronnie?" The voice said in a thick Jamaican accent.

"Yes."

"This is Coco. I'm ready.

"All right, we'll be there in about twenty or twenty-five minutes."

Butch looked at Ronnie quizzically. "Who was that?

Ronnie untied his sneakers, stripped his gym shorts off and walked toward his room. "Let me put my clothes on; I'll tell you on the way there." They left home about ten minutes later. Ronnie was driving.

"What's going on?" Butch asked. Ronnie didn't answer right away. Butch looked at him." Stop playing around man."

Ronnie stopped at the corner of Stantonsburg and Black Creek Roads, turned right and headed toward 301. "There's someone I want you to meet." He caught the green light at 301, turned left and headed south.

"Where are we going?"

"To the Holiday Inn, room one-thirty-six, that's on the first floor, in the back."

There were a few cars in the Motel's main parking lot, and only two in the back; a white Ford and a blue Caddy. They got out and scanned the area before knocking.

"Who is it?"

"Ronnie," he said in a low tone; his mouth just inches from the door.

Ever so gently the door opened slightly and Coco peeped through the crack with the chain-lock still on. After seeing Ronnie, she took the chain-lock off and opened it. "Hurry."

Watson lay belly up like a fat red pig, on the king sized bed, when they walked in. He was covered up to his waist with a green and yellow bedspread. A small, white face cloth was stuffed into his mouth. His arms and legs were spread and tied to the legs on the bed with short ropes. His eyes lit up in terror when he saw the tall, well built brothers walk in. He mumbled as loud as he could, shaking his head and trying desperately to free himself. Ronnie immediately turned the volume on the television up, then quickly changed tactics by balling up his huge fist and punching Watson in the face. "Do that again and I'll break your jaw." He stared at Watson a second or two, then turned his attention to Coco and Butch. Watson grimaced in pain from the hard blow that landed on his cheek.

"Coco, this is my brother, Butch."

She smiled. "Ronnie, he's as handsome as you, and taller. I'm pleased to meet you Butch."

Butch nodded, "My pleasure; you're a beautiful, black woman." Something shifted inside him as he stared down at her.

Coco was almost six-feet tall, with smooth, dark brown skin and matching eyes. Her long, jet black hair hung half-way down her back. Her ambiguous appearance was somewhere between hot and unrestricted, and cool and reserved. She was great looking. Her figure got Butch's attention right away, and she made no attempt to hide her attraction to the tall, handsome athlete. For a prolonged moment they looked at each other; excitement cracking in the air between them. Ronnie cleared his throat to break their semi-trance. "How did you get him so fast?"

Coco stared at Watson and smiled. "Maybe you should ask him that; I just did as you suggested. The hardest part was walking around the parking lot, not knowing when he was coming out of the room. After I got his attention, and we started talking, he made all the suggestions, all of them, but he first made sure that I didn't live in Wilson."

Ronnie looked at Watson. Watson's face was puffy, and he was looking up at Ronnie with the same terror he had shown when the brothers first entered the room. "Is this what you and your dirty, cop friends did on Jones Street?" Ronnie looked at him in disgust. Watson's eyelids fell like a ton of bricks. The strain of humiliation now covered his swollen face. "Coco, we'll take it from here." He pulled three, one-hundred dollar bills from his pocket.

Coco lifted her brows and smiled. "This is nice, but it was only two-hundred we agreed on."

"I know, keep it."

"Thank you."

"What name did you register under?" Ronnie asked.

Coco opened her purse, dropped the money in, and pulled out several picture IDs; each with a different name, hairstyles and make-up.

The brothers looked at each other impressed. "You can leave the key; it will take us a few minutes to get him out of here," said Ronnie.

Coco took a pen and notepad from her purse and wrote her phone number down. She gave it to Butch, and said, "I went to school in Kingston, Jamaica, then went to Fayetteville to attend college. After I earned my degree from Fayetteville State, I went back to Jamaica, taught school for a year, then went back to Fayetteville. I changed professions once." She shifted from one leg to the other, eliminating any space between their bodies. "I might be willing to teach school again." Her voice was low and sexy. She then tiptoed and seductively kissed him on his cheek. She hugged Ronnie and walked toward the door. "Oh! I almost forgot. His gun is under the bed, and his handcuffs are on his belt." She stared at Butch, gave him a smile that rivaled the sun's brilliance, and left.

Butch stood there dumbfounded. The silence broke when Ronnie said, in a whisper, "You wouldn't."

Butch shrugged and smiled. "No comment."

Ronnie looked at Butch and nodded toward the bathroom. "Let's talk for a minute." He looked at Watson for a short moment. "If you make any noise, I'll break your face in. Just breathe loud, give me a reason to kick your sorry ass. You fat piece of shit."

Fear laced Watson's face instantly. He shook his head and managed a muffled, "All right."

Inside the bathroom, Butch asked, "How did you meet her?"

"Preston, my friend from Viet Nam introduced me to her. We went to a bar on Hay Street, in Fayetteville. The first thing I thought about was what dad told us about Watson and the black prostitutes on Jones Street. I knew if there was a black woman alive that could get Watson in a compromising position, she could. She's a high priced call girl."

Butch looked at Ronnie smiling. "You didn't."

"No; the only thing I thought about was the possibility of getting Watson." He opened the door slightly to check on him, and then closed it. "We need to get him out of here as soon as possible, but here is what we need to do."

Butch leaned back against the bathroom wall. "What?"

"After I came back from Fayetteville, I went to the house where Price and Batts were killed; that's where we'll take him. When we leave here, you ride in the back seat of Watson's car, but be careful. When we get there and get Watson out, ditch his car in the pond. It's deep enough; I checked it out when I was out there. The water is so dark, they'll never find it."

Butch nodded, "Okay."

"One more thing," said Ronnie. "If you see a car coming toward you, or one behind you, don't let him turn in the driveway. Drive by and turn around; the last thing we need to do is attract attention. Just be careful; now let's get him out of here."

They moved quickly out of the bathroom and stood at the foot of the bed. Ronnie stared hard at Watson. He took a long deep breath, never taking his eyes off of him "Let's get to work," he said. Watson was a nervous wreck. He moved his head from side to side and cleared his throat nervously. "Watson, we have to leave here, but if you try anything, you'll die right then. Is that understood?" asked Ronnie. Watson drew a quick breath through his nostrils and nodded.

Butch and Ronnie dropped to their knees on opposite sides of the bed. Watson's snub-nosed, .38 pistol was on the side nearest Butch. After untying the ropes, they pulled the bed spread off of him; he was nude, for the exception of his socks. Butch and Ronnie laughed, pointing at Watson and shaking their heads. "Some men were blessed, you were cursed." said Butch." Watson again closed his eyes and turned his head to the side. "Get up, put your clothes on and don't take all night," Butch ordered, still smiling.

"Butch, after we get him in the car, take the gag out of his mouth; someone could pull beside you and see it. If he makes the wrong move don't hesitate, kill him." Ronnie looked at Watson and narrowed his eyes.

Watson dressed; Ronnie walked out of the room, looked around, then signaled with his hands for them to come out; directing Watson to the driver side. Butch walked behind Watson with the gun touching his back. After Watson was seated, Ronnie broke the inside door-knob off to prevent any escape attempt. "Be careful Butch, and make sure he doesn't speed to draw attention. I'll be there, when you get there." He ran to his car and left.

Butch was seated behind Watson, the barrel of the gun pressed against his head. "Remember, if you make the wrong move, I'll blow your head off."

Butch then pulled the cloth from Watson's mouth. Watson flexed his jaws a few seconds. "I hope you know what you're doing. I'm the chief of police."

Butch hit him on the right side of his forehead with his huge fist. Watson slumped forward over the steering wheel, dazed. Blood ran from the gash, down the side of his face into his right eye. "I know what I'm doing and I know who you are; a crook and a murderer. Say another word and I'll blow your ass away. Go on, say something." His eyes widened as anger flared in them. Watson shook his head and moaned in pain. "Start the car and drive north." Obediently, Watson started the car. He wiped the blood from his face and eye with the sleeve of his coat, then drove out of the parking lot heading north, still in somewhat of a daze. Watson drove under the overhead train tracks and passed Paramour's Oil Company on the left. He could feel the effects of the blow to his head. Occasionally he would wipe the blood from his face and eye. "Turn right at Black Creek Road," said Butch.

Watson turned right heading east on Black Creek Rd. He mustard what nerve he could and said, "I have about two- hundred dollars in my pocket. Take it, but don't hurt me." His voice was cracking. Butch could see the sweat and blood running down his face.

Butch didn't respond to Watson's statement, but said, "Slow down," as they approached the house where Price and Batts were killed. "Turn in and drive around the back." Butch put the gun to Watson's head again. "We're going to visit Mr. Lamm. Remember him?" Watson didn't respond.

Watson parked under the carport, and Ronnie came from the opposite side of the house, where his car was parked. He opened the door and pulled Watson to the ground, glared at him, shaking his head in disgust. "Search him, he might have another gun."

Butch pulled Watson up, slammed him against the brick wall and searched him. He found Watson's handcuffs tucked in his belt. "Put your hands behind your back." He cuffed Watson's hands; Watson shook uncontrollably.

"Take my money and I can get you more, but please don't hurt me."

Ronnie softly said, "We don't want your money, we want you."

Watson's eyes grew wide. "I didn't do anything to you, I don't know you."

"Shut up!" said Ronnie. "Butch, you know what to do. I'll leave you a flashlight on the step. Be careful, when you walk in, there are holes in the floor."

Butch got in Watson's car and backed up. He turned around and headed toward the deep fishing pond a few yards from the house. About ten feet from the pond, he opened the car door and rolled out onto the ground. The car rolled down the embankment into the pond and seconds later, it vanished in the deep, dark water.

Watson was sitting upright on the floor when Butch walked in; Ronnie was shining a light in his face. They were in what looked to be a large dining room. There was a round wood post in the middle of the room that ran from the floor to a support beam in the ceiling. "This place is about to fall in," said Butch, shining his flashlight around the room. There were large holes in the wooden floor, and dry-walls. "Damn, look at that," said Butch. A cat-sized rat ran out of a hole in the floor into the kitchen. At that instance, another large rat dropped from a hole in the ceiling and landed on Watson's leg. He screamed and managed to shake it off. Another large rat snapped at Butch's leg; he stomped it with the heel of his shoe. The rat attack suddenly ceased; and panic had seized Watson. His hands were cuffed behind his back; sweat and blood was running from his face into his eyes. He tried desperately to wipe his face by hunching his shoulder up.

"Chief Watson, my name is Ronnie Grant-Howard and this is my brother, Butch."

Watson's voice was trembling. "I don't know you. Why do you want to hurt me?"

"That's right, you don't know us, but you knew our mother; the woman your officers raped and killed on South Carroll Street, back in fifty-two. Remember, the nigger whore, as you called her," said Ronnie.

Watson quickly responded, declaring his innocence. "I didn't kill her; I didn't have anything to do with it."

Ronnie shrugged and smiled, unconcerned with Watson's plea. "Look, we know you didn't kill her, so that's not why you're here.

You're here because you denied her justice. You had detectives Price and Batts killed to cover it up and protect your raping, murdering officers." Ronnie's phony smile turned to anger. He stared at Watson, barely controlling the urge to kill him. He clenched his jaw for a second to calm himself. "If a white woman was raped and murdered by four black men, four black men would die, guilty or not. Our mother was gang raped, murdered, and denied justice by five white men. Four of them are dead." He raised his eyebrows, nodded at Watson, then smiled sincerely, "You're number five."

Watson screamed out, "Please don't, I've changed, I'm a different man, please don't."

Ronnie shook his head. "You just had Davis killed last night, now you say you've changed. I really don't give a damn if you've changed or not. You denied my mother justice. Her life meant nothing to you."

"I didn't kill Davis," cried Watson.

"No, you didn't, but you paid to have it done, and shut up. I'm tired of hearing your mouth," said Ronnie.

"I have a lot of money saved, you can have it all. Just don't hurt me," pleaded Watson.

"Money, you can't buy your way out of here, we don't want your money, and I told you to shut up," said Ronnie. He reached behind him and got a canvas bag with U.S. Government written on it. He pulled a long rope and a roll of duct tape out.

Watson's eyes looked like they would pop out of his head at any moment. Desperately he screamed out, "I'm sorry... Please, I'm sorry."

Ronnie sat his flashlight down on the floor, upright. Watson screamed again, determined to delay the inevitable. "Please," he screamed just before Ronnie taped his mouth shut.

"I'm tired of hearing how sorry you are," said Ronnie. "The only thing you're sorry about is you got caught."

Watson then started to struggle. Butch put the gun to his head.

"You ready to go now?" Watson stopped struggling and got quiet.

Ronnie tied his legs together and dragged him to the post in the middle of the room, Butch was holding the light. "Help me stand him up." Butch grabbed Watson under one arm, Ronnie the other. Butch held Watson against the post, while Ronnie got the tape. Butch searched Watson again and got his badge and ID. Ronnie first tied him to the post with the rope, then with the tape to render him motionless. Another large rat came out of a hole in the floor and raced toward the kitchen. Watson struggled with all his might, but couldn't budge.

"Damn Ronnie, that sorry man has wet his pants," said Butch.

"I see it. That big bad man that killed an unarmed black man for nothing has wet his pants," said Ronnie.

"Let's go, I can't stand to look at him another minute," said Butch.

"Chief Watson, my brother and I have to go," said Ronnie. "We're not going to kill you; we'll give the rats and wild dogs a meal. You're a big man, so it will probably take a few days for them to eat you, if they can stomach your sorry ass. That's more time than your officers gave our mother, and more time than you gave that man you killed. Now, you're about to pay the ultimate price. Oh, one more thing. We'll leave the back door open, so the wild dogs and snakes don't have any problem getting in. You have a good trip, my friend." Watson was still struggling, but couldn't move. Sweat was pouring down his face.

The brothers got in their car and headed back to Wilson. "What if Watson manages to somehow get away?" asked Butch.

"He won't. He ordered people killed there, now, he'll die there."

Chapter 62

September 26, 1968
9:05 A.M.

"I hope the brothers are up," said Smith; Best rang the doorbell. Seconds later Butch answered; smooth jazz was blaring from speakers mounted in the living room.

"Come in, we just sat down to eat. Why don't you guys join us," said Butch.

"Thanks, but we've already eaten. Ask Ronnie to come out here for a minute," said Best.

"Have a seat, I'll get him."

Smith and Best sat down in the living room, seconds later Ronnie appeared. "How you guys doing? What's going on?"

"We came by to tell you that Watson is missing and we think he's dead." Ronnie and Butch didn't respond. Smith continued. "Mrs. Watson called the station about one-fifteen this morning; she said Watson hadn't called or come home. About two-thirty, there was a big explosion at the house where we found the remains of Detectives Price and Batts." Butch shot Ronnie a short glance. Smith continued. "They found some body parts about a quarter of a mile away, and they know for sure it was a white person. But they don't know if it was Watson or not; they couldn't find any ID. The A.T.F. and the State Bureau of Investigation are still out there."

Butch slowly shook his head. "That must have been a big explosion, if they found body parts that far away. They might not ever know if it was Watson, unless they find his ID."

"They might not, but they know, whoever blew the house up knew what they were doing. One of the agents said that C-four explosives were used. When you handle that, you better know what you're doing." He rubbed his hands over his face and slicked his hair back. "If it was Watson, and I believe it was; I guess you could call it, poetic justice. He had people killed there, and he died there. You guys finish your breakfast before it gets cold. If we hear anything else, we'll call you."

"Thanks for stopping by," said Ronnie.

The detectives got up and walked toward the door. Best stopped and turned around. "Damn, that sounds good. I know that's Jimmy Smith, but what's the name of the album?"

Ronnie looked surprised. "I didn't know you liked jazz. That's Walk on the Wild Side."

"I need to get that…. Oh, one more question. I know you were in Viet Nam, but what did you do over there, what was your job?"

Without thinking Ronnie said "I was second in command of a rifle company, but I was trained as a sapper, demo….," he stopped.

Best put his right index finger vertically over his lips. "You guys have a good day, a good life." Smith nodded.

Walking to their car Smith asked, "Did Ronnie confirm your suspicions?" Best didn't respond; Smith knew his partner well enough to wait. Best would tell him when he was ready.

After they were seated Best said, "First of all, they're good young men; and yes I've known for a while, but proving it would be a different story. And I'm now sure about the answer, to the question I've asked myself several times."

"What was that?"

He faced Smith, then said, "What I would have done under similar circumstances. You know, I don't condone violence, but if I was black, and they had raped and killed my mother, I probably would have done the same thing. Sometimes you're forced to fight fire with fire. Well, they were forced to do just that. There is no justice for a black person in Wilson or the south, when it involves whites. You know that."

Smith didn't appear surprised at his answer and nodded in agreement. Best started the car. "Where do you want to go?"

Ronnie pulled a container of milk from the refrigerator.

"I think they know, but they also know they can't prove it."

Butch was nodding, while digesting a mouth full of eggs. After washing them down with a glass of orange juice, followed by a short belch, he said, "They probably do, but they didn't want us, they wanted Watson. Now it doesn't matter, it's over.

Ronnie thought for a second and smiled briefly, then said, "I'm happy it's over for you, but it will never be over for me. I've been dealing with death since I was eight years old. Mama was first, and then four years later, Miss Maggie. In Viet Nam, I saw a lot of death. I lost several friends that were really close to me, black and white. Throughout my life, I've thought about death a lot more than I thought about life. In some ways it has strengthened me, but in other ways, it has scared me, probably beyond repair. But I have You, mom and dad." He hugged Butch for a long moment. "Let's finish our breakfast, and then we'll go to see mom and dad."

Courage Determination

Success

Thomas Purdie
Silver Star-Vietnam

Thomas "Tuck" Purdie

For gallantry in action against a hostile force: on Oct. 24, 1967, Staff Sergeant, E-6 Thomas Purdie, was awarded the Silver Star. Sgt. Purdie was acting as the platoon sergeant on a search and destroy mission, in a Viet Cong, infested jungle. While preparing to set up security, they came under extremely heavy and accurate sniper fire. Almost immediately their leader and his radio-telephone operator were hit by the intensive enemy fire. The platoon leader, who had moved to check the status of the two wounded men, was hit. Upon receiving this information, Sergeant Purdie immediately took command. He unhesitatingly exposed himself to a hail of automatic weapons fire in order to deploy the men and direct their fire against the Viet Cong. With complete disregard for his personal safety, Sergeant Purdie moved to a forward position, which was dangerously exposed to enemy fire. He then called for mortar and artillery on the insurgents and adjusted it with deadly accuracy. Throughout the battle he moved from position to position to encourage his men. His courage under fire and aggressive leadership contributed to the saving of one man's life and to the rout of the insurgents. Sgt. Purdie's unquestionable valor in close combat reflects great credit upon himself.

The African American Community of Wilson is proud of Thomas "Tuck" Purdie, a native son.

Read the official general orders from the President of the United States, on the next page.

DEPARTMENT OF THE ARMY
HEADQUARTERS 1ST INFANTRY DIVISION
APO San Francisco 96345

11 February 1968

GENERAL ORDERS
NUMBER   1126

AWARD OF THE SILVER STAR

1.   TC 320. The following AWARD is announced.

PURDIE, THOMAS RA14806283 STAFF SERGEANT E6 United States Army
Company A 1st Battalion 26th Infantry
  Awarded: Silver Star
  Date of action: 24 October 1967
  Theater: Republic of Vietnam
  Reason: For gallantry in action against a hostile force: On this date,
                  during Operation Shenandoah II, Sergeant Purdie was acting as the
                  platoon sergeant on a search and destroy mission in Viet Cong
                  infested jungle. At approximately 1145 hours, his platoon moved
                  into a newly constructed base camp. While preparing to set up
                  security, the left flank squad came under extremely heavy and
                  accurate sniper fire. Almost immediately, the leader of that
                  squad and his radio-telephone operator were hit by the intensive
                  enemy fire. The platoon leader, who had moved to check the status
                  of the two wounded men, was also hit. Upon receiving this
                  information, Sergeant Purdie immediately took command of the platoon.
                  He unhesitatingly exposed himself to a hail of automatic weapons fire
                  in order to deploy the men and direct their fire against the insurge
                  With complete disregard for his personal safety, Sergeant Purdie
                  exposed himself to the sniper's line of fire to move to a forward
                  position, which was dangerously exposed to the hostile fire. He
                  then called for mortar and artillery fire on the insurgents and
                  adjusted it with deadly accuracy. From this position
                  he continually exposed himself to the hostile fire as he marked
                  the enemy's positions with smoke for air strikes. Throughout
                  the battle, he moved from position to position to encourage his
                  men, distribute ammunition, and supervise the evacuation of
                  casualties. When a medevac ship landed, it received claymore,
                  heavy automatic and small arms fire. Sergeant Purdie, nevertheless
                  stayed with the wounded until they could by evacuated. His courage
                  under fire and aggressive leadership contributed significantly to
                  the saving of one man's life and to the rout of the insurgents.
                  Sergeant Purdie's unquestionable valor in close combat against
                  numerically superior hostile forces is in keeping with the finest
                  traditions of the military service and reflects great credit
                  upon himself, the 1st Infantry Division, and the United States Army
  Authority: By direction of the President, as established by an Act of Congress
                  9 July 1918, and USARV Message 16695, dated 1 July 1966.

Dr. Joanne Woodard
Education

Dr. Woodard is the Executive Director of the Sally B. Howard School for the Arts & Education in Wilson, North Carolina.

Dr. Woodard is a 1965 graduate of Charles H. Darden High School in Wilson. She did her undergraduate studies at Bennett College in Greensboro, North Carolina and earned her Masters and PhD in psychology from the University of Michigan.

Her early professional career included a stop in New York, as a researcher for The Children's Television Workshop and Sesame Street. After a brief stop in California, she and her three children moved back to Wilson, in 1986.

After her children enrolled in the Wilson school system, she realized and was greatly dishearten at the educational opportunities for disadvantages children. She was determined to do something about it, but had no answers at the time.

Ill-prepared and armed with determination only, she decided to start an educational camp for disadvantaged children in the summer of 1989, at St. John A.M.E Zion Church on Pender St.

Expecting 75 to 100 children, 400 showed up the first day. Local funding and donations eventually allowed her enough staff and supplies to put on a successful camp.

The success of the camps drew state wide attention and Dr. Woodard was approached about applying for a charter to open a school.

In the early years, she had no answers to the question of how she could help disadvantaged children. 800 students at Sally B. Howard now know the answer.

With a heart of gold, a ton of determination and an unshakable resolve, Dr. Woodard has made a difference in the African American community and the city of Wilson.

David McNeil
Entertainment

McNeil was nationally known as the "Sixty Minute Man," for the 1951 hit single, Sixty Minute Man.

Tall, dark, and Hollywood handsome, McNeil, with a voice that mirrored Barry White's, preformed around America and several foreign countries.

During his 40 year career, he performed with Bill Ward and The Dominoes, The Locks, The Drifters and The World Renowned, Ink Spots. (David McNeil's photo, top left)

Born and raised on Hadley St. in Wilson, he attended Charles H. Darden High School in the early to mid 40's. He is the uncle of Author, Algernon McNeil.

Franklin "Frank" Jones
Community Service

Franklin Jones, the first African American promoted to the rank of lieutenant in the Wilson Police department, walked quietly and served the African American community for over 45 years.

A man of character and conviction, he's willing to stand up rather than compromise his principals, and what he knows is right. A kind word, a dollar or his time, whatever it takes to help a person in need, he is always willing to do.

Mr. Jones spearheaded a relentless effort for John McNeil's release from an unjust life sentence he was serving in a Georgia State Prison. He never gave up hope in spite of the likelihood of McNeil's doom, and encouraged him daily, via telephone to do the same.

McNeil's case made national news, but very few people know the leading role Jones played in McNeil's release, even in Wilson. My guess is, that's the way he wants it.

John McNeil and scores of other African Americans, unjustly convicted, would still be incarcerated if not for the NAACP, supported by thousands of silent warriors, black and white, like Frank Jones.

We don't always know their names, but my guess is that's the way they want it.

Annie Robinson Harding
Oxford Scholar

Mrs. Harding, an Oxford scholar and public school teacher for 49 years, earned her Bachelor of Arts Degree from Bennett College in 1962.

Her teaching career began at Charles H. Darden High School, her Alma Mater, where she remained for five years.

She spent the next 38 years teaching English in the District of Columbia Public Schools ---first at McKinley High School for 30 years as a classroom teacher, yearbook advisor and English Department chairperson; then at Theodore Roosevelt High School, where she remained for 8 years. She ended her teaching career in Prince George County Maryland at C. H. Flowers High School.

In additional to the BA Degree from Bennett College and the Master of Arts in Teaching from Trinity College, Mrs. Harding did further study at Exeter College of Oxford University, Howard University, Georgetown University, East Carolina University and The University of the District of Columbia, but she is most proud of the achievements of her students and the benefits that have enriched their lives.

In 2011, Mrs. Harding retired after 49 years of outstanding service, but still burning in her heart is the desire to help youngsters continue to have an appreciation to be life-long learners so that they may improve their lives through cultural, social, educational, and inspirational enrichment.

She had a wonderful journey in teaching and believes and hopes that she helped out a bit. What she knows is that she met many people who taught her a whole lot and she loved all of it—because truly, it helped to make her who she is. "What a joy, what a blessing!"

Howard"Wal" Jones
President/CEO Wilson OIC

For the past 40 years, Wilson OIC, under the strong leadership of President/CEO Howard Jones, has made a real difference for Wilson and the surrounding areas.

Jones, a Sims native moved to Wilson in the early 70s after retiring from AT&T in New York. But his retirement was short-lived, after he recognized the need for jobs, job training and programs to assist the economically disadvantaged. Spurred by his life-long passion to help people in need, Jones filed for, and was granted permission to open Wilson OIC.

In 1974, Wilson OIC opened its doors in the old Mercy Hospital building on East Green Street; without financial assistance from OIC headquarters in Philadelphia, but that only served to strengthen his resolve. With donations from churches, businesses and individuals, and a second mortgage on his home, he was able to hire a small staff and put the wheels in motion.

After several different locations and years of struggling, OIC is now located in the old Sam Vick School building on North Reid

Street, and has implemented several programs to help the economically disadvantaged.

In 2013, OIC placed 303 people in jobs, with an average salary of $20,800 yearly; 18,000 people benefited from food distribution and 1200 clients were serviced through OIC's health service department.

OIC's youth services has offered alternatives to delinquent behaviors that often times leads to jail time or long prison sentences. Over 175 youths are served annually in programs such as, tutoring, academic enhancement and employment skills training, which increases self-esteem and a sense of self-worth.

Aside from his duties as President/CEO of Wilson OIC, Jones was the first African American to serve on the National Board of Directors for Investments at BB&T. He was also the first African American to serve on the Board of Election for Wilson County.

What started as a passion to help the disadvantaged will end as a legacy for Howard Jones, who has given so much in his tireless effort to serve our community.

SALLIE BARBOUR SCHOOL-Early black public sch⏷
in 1898. Located on Stantonsburg St. in Wilson, N.C.

Donald Ray Jones
Athlete

In 1959 and 60, Jones proved to be one of the best high school basketball players in the state of North Carolina, by being named all-state both years. He was the first athlete from Darden High School to earn that honor. Blessed with a natural shooting motion and court savvy beyond his years, Jones lit the hard-wood up at a pace of 23 points per-game. If the three-point goal had been in effect during that period, his per-game average could have easily been in the low-to-mid 30s. Eight or ten steps across half-court and the deep corners were well within his range.

After one year at Tennessee State, he joined the Air Force and was named on an all-Air Force team. In 1966-68 Jones played at Merced Jr. College in California and one year at Fresno Pacific University.

He graduated from Pacific University in Stockton and is now retired, after teaching school for 32 years in Fresno, California.

Before Darden High School closed in 1970, Jones still held the scoring record and was the only player to make the all-state team two years.

Jones is a 1960 graduate of Charles H. Darden High School.

Wilson's Nationally Known

G. K. Butterfield

Butterfield is a U.S. Congressman and former Superior Court Judge. His father, Dr. Butterfield, was an early leader in Wilson's African American community and played a leading role in the improvements of city services to the East Side of the city. Butterfield is a graduate of Charles H. Darden High School and North Carolina College.

Ollie R. Hodges

Hodges is a former Chief Deputy, U.S. Marshall. Hodges is the strong, silent type, with a heart of gold.

Isiah Jenkins

Isiah played with the Philadelphia Eagles. He was a stand-out defensive player at North Carolina State University.

Samuel Latham

Latham is a former drummer for James Brown and the famous Flames. He was a mentor to super drummer, Aaron Purdie.

Ike Lassiter

Lassiter played several years with the Oakland Raiders, and was Wilson's first professional athlete.

John McNeil

McNeil was released after serving six years of his life sentence in a Georgia State Prison. McNeil's unjust conviction made national news, after the NAACP and McNeil supporters started the drive for his release. His wife, Anita, lost her long and courageous fight with breast cancer, ten days before his release.

Miguel Nu'nez Jr.

Nu'nez is an actor, director and producer. He was featured in movies such as "Life "and "Harlem Nights." What a talent!

Aaron Purdie

Aaron played drums for Al Green and Solomon Burk during his long career; one of the all time grates.

Reggie Smith

Reggie played with the Atlanta Falcons after being named all-conference at North Carolina Central University.

Robert Shaw

Robert played with the New Orleans Saints. He was one of the leading defensive players on Darden High School's 1964 State Championship football team, and later made all-conference at Winston Salem State University.

Dwight "Boobie" Taylor

He played in the U.S.F.L., for the Denver Gold and in Portland, with the Breaker. He was a super athlete, but more importantly, a better person. Dwight was an all-conference player at Elizabeth City State University.

Flora Williams

Blessed with a dynamic voice and a natural stage presence, Flora climbed to the top of her profession during the 70s. Her voice could be heard in the background of numerous top ten, recordings with Donna Summers. She also toured with super rocker, Pink Floyd and others.

Joseph "Bobby-Joe" Williams, Jr.

Mr. Williams, a Cartographer (Map Maker), retired from the Defense Mapping Agency, now, The National Geo-Spatial Agency. He assisted in the design and production of the lunar maps use by astronauts to land on the moon. Other types of products he designed and produced were; nautical charts used by the navy; aeronautical charts used by the Air Force and topographic maps used by the Army, for nautical and targeting. He also developed the guidance system for cruise missiles used for tracking and targeting.

He rose to the highest GS Grade before retiring. His philosophy is "Do not forget to reach back and help someone else...That is very, very important.

Mr. Williams graduated from Charles H. Darden High School in 1958. The African American community of Wilson is proud...*this is high powered stuff.*

Wilson's first African American Police Officers

Pictured in 1950, Lee 'Hank' Williams and Rudolph Best.

Afterword

I am a lifelong resident of Wilson, for the exception of the few years I was away in school and the military; I witnessed firsthand the racist climate that existed in this tobacco rich city, growing up during the 50s and 60s.

Wilson County became one of the richest counties in America, per-capita, off the backs of African Americans, working in the tobacco fields and processing factories for below poverty wages.

Police brutality, sub-standard living conditions, inadequate health care, dirt streets and limited public school funding were just a few of the problems that plagued the African American community.

African Americans, by the thousands were forced to migrate, because of a lack of opportunity at home, and a chance to better their lives in the north.

Wilson is now a beautiful city of 50,000 residents. There are still problems, but African Americans are no longer forced to abandon their roots because of a lack of opportunity.

In spite of limited resources and overcrowding, our schools excelled both academically and athletically. Darden High School was one of the smallest, if not the smallest 4-A school in the state of North Carolina. Winning State Championships in football and basketball in 1964 is a record that had never been accomplished before and still stands today; and the marching and concert bands were recognized nationwide.

We should always remember educators; E.M. Barnes, J. W. Jones, Addie Hagans, Marion Lane, Josephine Edwards, Cleveland Flowe, Spencer Satchell, Marian Miller, Henry Davis, Annie R. Hardin, Sam Gray and many others. Because of their dedication, determination and die-hard attitude, the small African American community of Wilson has produced numerous top level professionals.

Below are the names and occupations of just a "few" of the professionals produced by our small community during the 40s, 50s, and 60s.

Dr. Boisey Barnes	Physician
Bernard Barnes	U. S. Olympic Team, Basketball
Eddie Barnes	Engineer
Ronnie Barnes	NFL New York Giants Trainer
Dr. Reggie Bass	Physician
Dr. Donald Blue	Physician
Dr. Grova Bridges	Education
Dr. W. E. Brodie	Education/Professor
Earl Currie	Lawyer
Clyde D. Herring	Department, U. N.
Angela Edwards	Psychologist
David Faison	Law Enforcement
Milton Fitch Jr.	Superior Court Judge
Patricia Fitch	Lawyer, D.A.
Anthony Harris	Lawyer
Viola Harris	Author
Dr. Harold Hines	Dentist/Professor
Brenda Hines	Education
Wendell Hines	Music Jazz Hall of Fame
James Johnson	Education
Dr. Alton Kirk	Education/Author
Algernon McNeil	Author
E.R. Mitchell	Business/Restaurant
Dr. Charles Murphy	Education/Professor
Edgar Parker	Law Enforcement
Dr. Cleveland Parker	NASA - Space and Missel Systems
Carl Parker	Aeronautical Instructor
Harold Simms	NASA /Engineer
Donna Simms	National Educator Award

David J. Speight	Law Enforcement
Robert Smith	Education
Louis Thomas III	Production Artist
Willa J. Turner	Education/Fashion Model
Jamie Watson	N.B.A. Utah Jazz
Dr. Barbara Williams	Education
Leroy Woodard	Global Marketing Manage

Again, let me thank you for purchasing No Justice No Peace. I sincerely hope you enjoyed it.

Thank you,
Algernon McNeil

Poem, *"I know who I am"*
-Algernon McNeil